Praise for
TARA T...

"Tara Taylor Quinn has c[...]
of the highest quality.... [...]
anything written by such a wonderful storyteller."
—Heather Graham

"One of the skills that has served Quinn best...
has been her ability to explore edgier subjects."
—*Publishers Weekly*

Street Smart is filled with "deception, corruption,
betrayal—and love, all coming together in an explosive novel
that will make you think twice."
—*New Mystery Reader Magazine*

"Combining her usual superb sense of characterization
with a realistically gritty plot, Quinn has created
an exceptionally powerful book."
—*Booklist* on *Behind Closed Doors*

"Tara Taylor Quinn's *In Plain Sight* is character-driven
suspense at its best with rapid-fire pacing
that makes you feel as if the pages are turning themselves.
I inhaled it in two sittings."
—Hallie Ephron, Edgar Award-nominated author of *Writing
and Selling Your Mystery Novel* and crime fiction book
reviewer for the *Boston Globe*

"Lisa Jackson fans will fall hard for Quinn's unique ability
to explore edgy subjects with mesmerizing style."
—*BookReporter.com*

"Tara Taylor Quinn delivers deeply emotional tales,
steeped in psychological suspense....
I consider them essential to my bookshelf, and you will, too."
—Maggie Shayne

TARA TAYLOR QUINN

THE **3**RD SECRET

MIRA®

MIRA®

Recycling programs for this product may not exist in your area.

ISBN-13: 978-0-7783-2834-6

THE THIRD SECRET

For questions and comments about the quality of this book please contact us at Customer_eCare@Harlequin.ca.

www.MIRABooks.com

Printed in U.S.A.

For Kim Barney, Trudy Barney and Jane Barney.
Being one of you means the world to me.

Acknowledgment

I'd like to thank Tim Barney and Paula Eykelhof
for generously sharing their creative talents
with me and this project.
This book is much better because of both of you.

Dear Reader,

Expert witness and psychologist Kelly Chapman is opening another of her files for you. Writing Kelly's stories has introduced me to people I'd never in a million years have the chance to know or get close to. And yet they fascinate me, and I hope you'll feel the same way.

Why does it sometimes take circumstances beyond our control to show us who we are and what we need?

Kelly's a shrink. Maybe *she* knows the answer to that. Maybe she's doing this to me (and to us) deliberately—giving us opportunities to experience life outside our own worlds. But if she is, she's in for a surprise. Because in *The Third Secret* Kelly encounters people who force her to take a good long look at herself. She's starting to open her life on a personal level and discovering that it's *hard!*

In this particular case, we meet Kelly's friend and colleague Erin Morgan. She's a defense attorney—and she's just taken on a client with a few too many secrets in his past. If he even *has* a past…

Rick Thomas (is that his real name?) was a covert ops agent. With him, we share the reality of always being at risk and the unsettling fact that a "normal" existence of small-town friendships and backyard barbecues can never quite be achieved. Erin enters his life when he's framed on a murder charge.

I'm hooked on Kelly Chapman and her files. I'm definitely along for the ride—as evidenced by *The Fourth Victim,* coming next month. Kelly and I hope you'll join us!

I love to hear from readers. You can reach me at Box 13584, Mesa, Arizona 85216. Or through my website, www.tarataylorquinn.com.

Tara Taylor

1

Chandler, Ohio
Tuesday, October 12, 2010

I grabbed for the phone. I'd already turned off the lights and was heading out the door when it rang. The office phone. Not my cell. Deb, my receptionist, waited out in the parking lot.

She'd say I should've let the phone ring. And maybe she was right. But I had a thing about phones. If it rang, someone on the other end needed me for something.

I had to find out who. And what.

I had a thing about pencils, too, but at the moment, I wasn't craving one. Deb and I were going to skate the eighteen-mile converted-railroad skate path outside town.

"Kelly Chapman's office." I'd answered Deb's phone.

"Kelly?" I didn't recognize the voice, and because we'd inherited the ancient phone and intercom system with the office suite, I didn't have caller display to help me out.

"Yes."

"This is Erin Morgan from Temple, Michigan." Oh, right. The defense attorney. She'd found me in the expert witness directory the year before—I'd been able to help her with a case.

"Hi, Erin, what's up?" I couldn't take any out-of-town jobs just now. I had a new foster daughter at home, a girl I hoped to adopt.

Fourteen was a tough age for any kid. And even more so for one who'd lost her virginity and her mother all in the same month.

"Have you got a minute?"

As Erin asked the question, Deb came in to see what was keeping me, and I motioned for her to go on without me. "Sure," I said into the phone. I hadn't felt good about going out after work, anyway. "Let me get the door."

Setting the phone down, I went back and locked up behind Deb.

Maggie had said to go ahead and skate, to keep up with my usual routine. She claimed she'd be fine—and that she'd make supper so it would be ready when I got home. And because I was still feeling my way, still trying to find some bridge between being a therapist and being a mother, I'd agreed, thinking Maggie needed some time in the house by herself. Time to explore unobserved. To make the place her own. To bond with Camy—my very spoiled and bossy toy poodle.

But my instincts had been screaming at me all day to go straight home after work. I just couldn't tell if they were shrink instincts or some completely unused maternal ones.

"I'm here," I said, picking up the phone again as I scooted my Lycra-clad backside onto Deb's desk, facing the door. "What do you need?"

"I'm probably not going to convince you that I just called to say hi, am I?"

"Not likely," I said. Not with an opening line like that. "It's been, what, a year?"

"About that."

"So how've you been?" I liked Erin. And prevarication wasn't her style.

Choosing a pen from the box of new ones in Deb's top drawer—put there expressly for me—I flipped to a clean page in my receptionist's open notepad.

"I've been good. Great. Got my AV rating this year."

The Martindale-Hubbel National Peer Review Rating of ethics and legal ability. A national coup in the legal field. She'd met some pretty high standards. "Congratulations."

She's stalling. I jotted it down. Merely an observation, but I thought better when I was writing.

"Listen, I have a favor to ask." As opposed to a job? Interesting.

Asking for favors wasn't something that came easily to independents like Erin. I knew because I was one, too.

"Shoot." As long as it didn't involve leaving town, I'd do it. If I could.

"Well, not a favor, really. I just… Look, I need someone to talk to. Someone not from around here. Someone no one'll ever know I spoke to."

"A therapist, you mean?"

"I guess. Maybe."

"For you or another person?"

"Another person."

Erin just lied to me. The words appeared on the page.

"You want a referral?"

"No. I don't think so. Maybe. I really just wanted to get your opinion. If I could. Not like a session or anything. Though I'd be happy to compensate you…"

For someone who'd appeared to be as organized and methodical as they came, Erin Morgan hadn't thought this through very well.

"Of course you don't need to compensate me. I told you to call me anytime, and I meant it."

That had been a year ago. On the last day of a highly emotional murder trial involving a mentally handicapped defendant who'd been accused of killing her newborn baby. In my opinion, the teenager hadn't even realized she'd given birth. She'd been exonerated on the grounds of mental incompetence and committed to a home where they'd be able to safeguard her.

I'd assumed, in the heat of the moment, that Erin and I would remain in touch.

If not as friends, then as professional peers.

"You having problems with a case?" I asked as silence hung on the line. Could be she didn't have the budget for expert witness fees this time around.

"No, it's nothing like that. I... This friend of mine, he's really struggling and... Oh...come on, I can't believe I'm being so inane. *I'm* struggling, Kelly, and not finding answers and I thought of you."

"I'm glad you did," I told her honestly. "What's the issue?"

"My job."

"You got your AV rating." I reminded her of what I'd just been told.

"Yeah." The sigh on the other end didn't convey the elation I'd expected. "I'm good at what I do," the thirty-one-year-old attorney continued. "Hell, I should be, it's *all* I do."

"And that's a problem?" *Possible relationship.* I circled the sentence.

"No. I love being a lawyer. I love the law."

"And?"

"I'm not sure I love me."

"Why wouldn't you?"

"Because I'm a risk to society."

Whoa. I scribbled it a second time for good measure. *Whoa.*

"How so?" I asked.

"Cops put dangerous people behind bars and I set them free."

Not the woman I knew. Erin was particular about her cases. She took on only the ones she believed in, clients she was convinced were innocent.

Which was why I'd bonded with her to the point of thinking we'd stay in touch.

"I thought you helped innocent victims. That you considered yourself part of the checks and balances to protect against police and prosecutorial mistakes." I repeated what Erin had told me over a glass of wine the night I'd spent in Temple the year before.

"I thought so, too. But I'm full of crap." *Searching. Vulnerable?*

"Are you?"

"I… That's just it," Erin said, the strength in her voice, the conviction, never wavering. "I don't know."

Gotta love it. A person who was confident even in her struggles.

"Are you lying to yourself?" I asked.

She sighed. "I don't know."

"Do you want to be a risk to society?"

"Of course not!"

"Why do you go to work each day?"

"To do my job."

"Why in a bigger sense?" The words rolled off my

tongue. I was working. Always working. Just like Erin Morgan.

"Because I want to help people."

"That's why you started doing what you do. What about now?"

"What other reason would there be?"

"Glory."

"It feels good to win a case," she admitted.

"And the money?"

"I like it, but it's never been my motivation. That hasn't changed."

I believed her.

"And the AV rating, the security it gives you, that felt good, too, I'll bet."

"Not as good as winning a case."

"So it's all about winning."

"That's what I'm afraid of."

"Why?"

"Because if it's all about winning, then I've lost myself. I've lost sight of why I'm in this business. I've lost sight of right and wrong and everything I stand for."

I've lost myself. We were at the crux of the matter. And it had taken less than ten minutes. Erin was a lot more together than she thought.

"Are you sure about that, or afraid of it?" I asked.

"If I knew, I wouldn't be calling you."

"What makes you think you might have changed?"

"My last case, for one thing."

"Tell me about it." I didn't need the old floral chintz couch in my office. Or the new and luscious leather chairs opposite it that I now used with clients. Or office hours or checks in the bank, either.

They weren't what my life was about. Helping people. That's why I got up in the morning.

And I'd bet my shingle—the one I loved because the city council bought it for me as a thank-you for chairing the committee to beautify Main Street—that my reason for getting up in the morning was Erin Morgan's reason, too.

I got writer's cramp taking notes as Erin told me about the young man who'd had his driver's license for barely a year when he'd skidded on wet pavement, losing control of his car—an accident that had ended up involving three other cars and an SUV, killing a thirty-two-year-old man and seventeen-year-old twin girls.

The young man had been driving a brand-new Corvette, purchased for him by his parents, and he'd been drinking and was subsequently slapped with three charges of vehicular homicide with aggravators, meaning he could be facing twenty or more years in prison.

"The police took one look at that Corvette and the kid never had a chance," Erin said.

I heard doubt in her voice.

"I take it his parents called you?"

"Yeah. They were beside themselves with grief and guilt. They blamed themselves for buying him a car that was far too powerful for his limited driving skills. They'd only wanted to reward him for being such a good kid. He was an A student. Worked for his father's company. Played sports. Dated a girl from church, which he attended regularly."

Kid too good to be true, I scribbled sideways in the margin. It wasn't about Erin. It didn't really go on her page.

"So you took the case."

"I met the kid first."

"And did he seem to be everything his parents said he was?"

"He seemed spoiled and egotistical, but I put that down to a case of bravado due to fear."

Lying to self? That went on Erin's page.

"And you took the case."

"Yes."

"Why?"

"I'd done some checking. The arresting officer, the one who administered the only drunk-driving test, wasn't qualified to administer it."

"Uh-huh."

"His parents were right on that one. The kid hadn't had a fair chance."

Sometimes the obvious was just too…obvious.

"And?"

"The case was highly publicized. If he was found guilty, the kid would be getting the maximum sentence. His life was going to be ruined."

As were three other lives. *Permanently* ruined. I kept the words to myself. My personal opinion meant nothing here.

"And?"

"I knew I could win."

"So that's why you took the case?"

"I don't know. It seemed to me it wasn't the kid's fault his parents had given him a false sense of himself. He hadn't meant to hurt anyone. As a matter of fact, he volunteered as a senior youth leader at his church."

"So you believed in him and wanted to help him."

"I guess so. He had his whole life in front of him. His parents' eyes were wide-open and they had the resources to fix the damage they'd done, to get him into counseling or whatever it took."

"The deaths of three innocent people wasn't enough to smarten him up?"

"I thought it was." Erin's voice dropped and I could hardly hear what she'd said.

"Past tense?" I asked, drawing a tiny star on the rubber sole of my tennis shoe.

"He was acquitted of everything except the traffic ticket for failure to yield. The only price he paid was a fine and points on his license."

"Which is what you expected, right?"

"Yeah, well, what I didn't expect was that afterward, when he turned to me, there was no thank-you, nor any sign of relief. He called me a loser bitch under his breath because of the points. And just then I looked up—" Erin's voice broke "—and into the eyes of the young mother who'd lost her husband in the accident. Standing behind her were the parents of the twins who'd also died. Their expressions were the same. Stricken. Shocked. And filled with more questions than I could ever answer. They'd already lost so much and I'd just robbed them of their chance for a small measure of peace."

I took a deep breath. Read over my notes, though I'm not sure I needed them. Or really saw them. Life wasn't always easy. The way wasn't always clear.

Sometimes there were no right and wrong answers. Or even palatable ones.

And that was part of the process of living, too. Living with the untenable, the inexplicable. Living with the fact that sometimes life just didn't make sense.

And the attorney on the other end of the line didn't need to hear any of that.

"So, when you win, what do you like about it?" I asked her.

"Being good enough to win."

"Why?"

"So I know that when people rely on me, their trust

isn't misplaced. In most cases, my clients' lives are at stake. I have to know that if I take their cases, I'm capable of giving them their best chance."

I could relate to that.

"So what about *this* case? Did the win feel good?"

"I felt like I did my job."

Unresolved.

"And if you had it to do over again, would you still take the case?"

"If I knew only what I knew then?"

"Of course. Unless you've got some kind of crystal ball that's going to help you see the future."

"Nope. If I had that, I wouldn't be where I am now."

Out of the mouths of babes. And defense attorneys.

"So would you still take the case?"

"Yes."

"And knowing that doesn't help at all, does it?"

"No."

"What will?"

"I don't know. Do you have some technique for figuring out if I've lost sight of the bigger picture in my quest to do my job well?"

"Yeah." I doodled on my shoe some more.

"What is it?"

"Listen."

Silence fell between us. And then Erin said, "Okay, I'm listening. What is it?"

"That *was* it. Listen. Listen to your instincts. To the things that keep you awake at night. You're on the right track. You're looking at yourself, trying to be honest with yourself. Your conscience is talking to you. Listen to it and you'll have your answers." I could've talked to her in abstract terms—about cognitive dissonance or the gain loss theory of interpersonal attraction.

Instead, I'd gone with my gut.

"So you think, because I'm struggling, it's my conscience telling me that I've lost sight of what matters?"

"No. I think you're struggling because it's time for a self-assessment. For whatever reason. Either you need a change, or a confirmation that you're right where you need and want to be. Either way, if you listen carefully, you'll have your answer."

"And peace again?"

"That's the idea." I slid off the desk. I wasn't going to be home much earlier than I would've been if I'd skated.

Good thing Maggie hadn't been counting on me. Obviously I still had some distance to go with this mothering business.

Hopefully the relevant instincts would be kicking in anytime now.

"Can I ask you something?" Erin's curious tone caught my attention.

"Of course."

"Do you struggle, too?"

Uh-uh. I was the helper. The questioner. The prober. It was my role in life. My purpose.

"I'm human," I said, because Erin expected an answer.

"So you do struggle?"

"Doesn't everybody?"

And if she asked me about what, I was going to have to be honest and tell her I had to get home to Maggie.

"Thanks." Erin sounded better. Less tense. And I smiled again. From the inside out.

"No problem."

"You have a way of making everything seem manageable."

I hoped so. That was my job.

"Everything generally *is* manageable once we can see what's really there. Because then we can figure out what to do about it."

"So…what do I owe you?"

"How about another phone call sometime. Just to stay in touch?"

"Absolutely."

Giving her my cell number, I hung up and made a beeline for the door. If the phone rang again I was absolutely *not* going to answer it.

2

No one answered his knock at the door. Another man might have tried a second time. Rick Thomas spun on the heel of his canvas work boot, casing the yard around him—the back fence, gravel parking areas, the government-issue four-wheeler that hadn't moved, as far as Rick knew, since before he'd rolled into town the year before.

Nothing appeared to be out of place. In Rick's world, that was usually more indicative of a problem than something obviously out of place would've been.

Taking a step backward, flattening himself against the wall of the building, right next to the door, he listened. His nostrils flared as he inhaled, smelling the air around him. No gunpowder residue. No formaldehyde, incense or rotting. Still, his hair stood on end and he wished he had his .357 Magnum strapped beneath his flannel shirt.

Until his mind's eye played out the scene for him— some sane, rational part of him showing him what he was doing.

"Stupid-ass fool," he muttered. He was a construction worker—a handyman, an odd-jobs guy who owned a modest business in a small town on the craggy shores of Lake Michigan. He'd gone to the Emergency Management Agency and Homeland Security office just outside Temple at seven o'clock in the morning to continue his remodeling build-out, converting a closet into a second bathroom and adding two offices and additional storage space. He was there because the bulk of his work came from referrals and, in a town as small as Temple, he'd have raised eyebrows if he'd turned down the offer of a job this size.

He was not there because of any interest, past or present, in national security.

Construction workers didn't need to keep their backs to the wall. Or .357 Magnums strapped to their chests.

Rick had been on the job a week. Had the bathroom nearly finished—assuming there were no floods or spurts when he actually turned on the water.

He rapped on the back door a second time. EMA officer Charles Cook had the six-to-two shift. He'd be on his third cup of coffee by now—cursing because the automatic brew system had a maximum production capacity of four cups—and he'd have half the paper read. In another ten minutes, at exactly seven-fifteen, he'd be pouring his fourth and last cup of coffee for the day and flicking on his computer.

He'd be humming "Oh, What a Beautiful Morning" as he waited for the state-of-the-art machine to boot up. And by eleven, he'd be asking Rick what he wanted for lunch.

Rather than packing his own meal, Charles hired a runner to bring food out from town every weekday at eleven-fifteen.

People were creatures of habit. Routine. Which made them predictable. Vulnerable to manipulation. Easy prey.

All someone had to do was pay attention.

Where was Charles? His vehicle, a midnight-blue Expedition, gleamed in the early-morning sun in its usual spot at the corner of the building.

Reaching for the back door to the building, Rick might have rattled the handle—if he'd come from a different life. Instead, he turned it slowly, quietly, expecting the nearly immediate catch of the lock preventing his entrance. He frowned when the knob continued to turn.

Charles took his Emergency Management Agency and Homeland Security position seriously. Very seriously. Locked doors were as important to him as the air he breathed.

Rick didn't just assume things were okay. Not ever. In his experience, they generally weren't. Not if you looked deeply enough.

Releasing the latch without making a sound, Rick closed the door, leaving it unsecured, and moved silently along the hallway to the front of the building—and the desk Charles and the other agents used when they were on duty.

He knew something was wrong before he made it five feet down the hall. The coffeepot was half-full.

He rounded the corner. Took in the perimeter of the front office. And stopped, staring down at the floor.

Right in the middle, flat on his back, Charles lay in a pool of blood.

The forty-five-year-old's eyes were wide open. With a blank gaze aimed straight at him.

Erin Morgan was in the Ludwig County sheriff's office at seven-thirty Thursday morning, seeking information on the overnight arrest of one of her clients, when a call came in from the local Emergency Management Agency and Office of Homeland Security. Because the modest station consisted of one front room with four desks, including the dispatch desk, Erin couldn't help overhearing.

"I'm at the Ludwig County EMA office and need an ambulance," the voice said, clearly audible over the speaker phone.

Glancing at the list on the wall beside Josie Winthrop, Erin picked up a second phone and dialed Len Majors, the EMT on call, so the other woman wouldn't have to put her caller on hold to do so.

She'd been around the station often enough to know procedure.

"Okay, sir, I'm sending one now." Josie nodded at Erin. "What's going on there?"

"A man is dead."

Standing, Erin counted the rings on her end. There'd only been one other murder since she'd moved to Temple almost five years before.

And that had been a domestic dispute.

"Are you in danger, sir?" Josie was asking.

"No, I've secured the area, I'm here alone."

"Yeah?" Len's gruff voice sounded in Erin's ear, and she moved away to talk in private. Quickly giving the man the information she had, Erin hung up, returning her full attention to Josie's conversation.

The other woman had put the caller on hold while she alerted squad cars to head out to the scene.

"Sir?" she was asking.

"Yeah. I'm here." There was something…unsettling… about the man's calm. He was with a dead man, and there wasn't so much as a tremor in his voice.

"What's your name?"

"Rick Thomas."

"Okay, Rick, what happened?" Josie asked.

"I'm not sure," the voice said. "I'm doing some renovations here and arrived today as I always do, just after seven. The back door was unlocked and I came in and found Charles on the floor."

"Did you touch him?"

"Of course not."

"Are you sure he's dead?"

"His eyes are wide open, sightless and he hasn't blinked. There's a substantial pool of blood. He's not breathing."

As a defense attorney, Erin knew, at least by reputation, pretty near everyone in the area who'd had a run-in with the law.

She'd never heard of Rick Thomas.

She hadn't met Charles Cook, either, but she knew who he was. He'd never been married and, after Noah's death, a couple of people had suggested that Erin get to know him.

"Okay, Rick, officers are on their way. I'd like you to stay on the phone with me until they get there."

Just in case whoever had killed Charles was still in the area, Erin surmised.

Or because Josie wanted to make certain that Rick Thomas didn't flee the scene. A manhunt would take more time than Temple officers had to spare.

"Of course." The man didn't seem any more bothered by Josie's request than he'd been by what had happened that morning.

"Is anything noticeably out of place?" Josie asked, mostly, Erin figured, to keep the guy talking.

"No."

"Any sign of a weapon?"

"No. Whoever did this got him from behind, though. And they didn't use a gun. There's no sign of injury on the front of his body. No exit wound. No bullet holes on the premises. No smell of gunpowder. No sign of a struggle, either. Looks like he stood and then abruptly fell."

"Maybe he passed out and hit his head."

"The blood pool is lower down."

Sirens sounded and Rick Thomas, announcing that help had arrived, rang off.

And although Erin found the arrest report she'd been seeking without a problem, she couldn't get her morning visit to the police station, or the voice of the man who'd called in a crime, out of her mind.

Idle hands weren't good for him. Rick had learned that lesson the hard way—when he was about three.

If he didn't keep busy, he could get into trouble. If he didn't choose his actions deliberately, tragedy could occur.

And so, facing a full day without work, he made the most obvious deliberate choice, climbed into his year-old black pickup truck—the first vehicle he'd ever owned—and headed toward Ludington and the beachside care facility where he spent much of his nonworking time. With a whole day free, opportunity abounded.

And Rick knew just what to do.

October was a bit cold out on the lake but they had coveralls. Boat rentals were cheaper—especially since it was a weekday. And Steve loved to fish. Which was why the fishing gear was always stowed in the locked box in the back of Rick's truck.

He stopped for bait on the way in rather than waiting to get it at the boat dock because Steve had a tendency to get impatient when he got excited. Before ten o'clock that Thursday morning, Rick was walking toward the group of residents on the beach behind Lakeside Family Care.

At six feet and a couple of inches, with dark hair and brown eyes, Steve was a handsome guy.

"Ricky! Ricky!" The childish call in the deep male voice was jarring—even after more than two decades of hearing it. When they were little, Steve's differences hadn't seemed so devastating. It was only later, after they'd gone through puberty and beyond, when Rick found himself caring for the slightly older man as though Steve was still the five-year-old who'd fallen from the roof of his house, that Rick had fully understood the devastating ramifications of a three-year-old's quest for a flying disk made out of cardboard. A homemade attempt to create a Frisbee.

"Ricky!" Steve was upon him. "Hi! We're walking on the beach. You wanna come, too?"

"Hey, sport." Rick pulled Steve in for a hug, letting the man clutch him for as long as he liked. Sometimes it would be five minutes or more.

Today, in his excitement, Steve released him almost immediately, grabbing Rick's hand. "Come on, let's go."

Rick kept a tight hold on Steve's hand. "How about we go fishing instead?" he asked. Redirecting Steve was something that came naturally now. It hadn't always been that way.

"Fishing? Me and you? Right now?"

"Yeah. You want to?"

Glancing back toward the beach, Steve frowned. "Am I allowed?"

"Yep."

"Just me and you?"

"Yep."

"Okay!" Steve tugged at his hand. "Come on! Let's go! Before someone else catches 'em all."

Meeting Jill's eye, Rick waved. Jill, the forty-year-old

social services director at Lakeside, waved back. They
were good to go.

Having already signed Steve out for the day, Rick hurried to the truck. There was nothing like time alone in a
boat with Steve, on waters that were older and wiser and
stronger than any man could ever hope to be, to wipe out
a lifetime's worth of visions. Of dead men. And regrets.

"I swear, Ms. Morgan, I didn't lift a hand to that
woman. I would never do a thing like that."

"She says you smacked her in the head," Erin read
from the report as she sat with her client, Clyde Sanderson, in one of the two holding rooms at the county jail
down the street from her office.

"More like tryin' to catch her," Clyde said, his blue
eyes weary and filled with disillusion. "She come at me
with both arms flailin', accusin' me of havin' a fling with
some woman. I stepped back and she tripped on a corner
of that dad-blamed rug she insisted we had to have."

Erin believed him. "And the smack in the head?"

"I didn't do it! The mantel did. And it would've been a
lot worse if I hadn't caught her. Probably would've busted
her head wide-open at the rate she was comin' at me."

Good. Just what she'd needed to know. A bruise from
a mantel would appear very different from one administered by a hand. Which meant she should have Clyde out
by dinnertime.

"Give me a couple of hours and I'll see what I can do,"
she said, standing. "We might get quicker results if we
agree to a restraining order. Do you have any objection
to that?"

"Against me? What for? I didn't do anythin'."

"I know that, Clyde, but part of the problem is it's her
word versus yours. Even if the other side believes us,

which I suspect they will, they'll still want assurance that Laura Jane is protected."

"It's wrong, Ms. Morgan, just plain wrong that the woman can lie and create all this mess and then I have to pay for it."

"I know. I agree. We can fight this thing and probably win. But that'll take weeks. I want you out of here today so you can look after your mom, and you don't have any trouble at work. And to save you the court costs."

Her services were gratis.

Clyde had once been Noah's Little League coach.

"Yeah, but what happens if I have this restraining order and then she comes after me, just to get me arrested for bein' around her? That's Laura Jane for you. She'd hound me until I was right back in here."

"Not if we ask for an order against her, too."

"Will they do that?"

"I think so. If we ask for it."

"Oh, Ms. Morgan, I'd be so grateful if you could. I didn't think they'd do that, restrain a woman from goin' near a man. I'd sure be glad if they would. I just wanna get on with it, ya know? To have some peace."

"I know you do."

The sixty-year-old man was one of the gentlest souls Erin had ever met. Like Noah had been.

"Do you mind if I ask a question?" Erin said. She should have all the details, just in case. And to be prepared for anything that might come up later, during Clyde and Laura Jane's upcoming trial in divorce court. But she also just wanted to know…

"'Course not. You're my lawyer. Ain't you s'posed to ask?"

"Is there another woman?"

Clyde's wrinkled face was impassive as he looked her in the eye. "No, ma'am, never has been."

Erin sincerely hoped that someday that would change.

"To infinity and beyond!" Sitting upright on the sleeper sofa in Steve's two-room apartment, Rick stared at the large-screen television he'd purchased for Steve the year before.

It was dark out. Past nine. He really should go. But the weight of Steve's head against his shoulder as Steve slept, worn out and happy from their day, was not an unpleasant thing. Somehow that pressure, Steve's presence, put everything else in perspective.

Funny how it had taken him a tough and finished career and thirty-some years of living to figure that out.

"You! Are! A! Toy! You aren't the real Buzz Lightyear! You're—you're an action figure…"

You had to love Woody. He had things in perspective, too. Maybe that was why *A Toy Story* was Steve's favorite movie. They'd watched it so often, Woody's and Buzz's words often played in Rick's mind, obliterating the other messages there. Lord knew he could recite the entire script in his sleep. It was actually kind of…relaxing.

"Oh, sorry, I didn't realize you were still here." Angela Markham, the night caregiver in Steve Miller's nonmedical assisted-living wing, poked her head in. "I saw the TV flashing through the window and thought he'd fallen asleep with it on again."

"I'll get him into bed before I leave," Rick assured her. Angela was only in her twenties, but Rick had confidence in her.

Which was more than he could say about some of Steve's other caregivers over the years.

"I worry more about you than I do about your friend

here," the frizzy-haired young woman said, nodding her head to punctuate the words in a way that reminded him of a teacher he'd had in grade school. "You spend far too much time in this place."

"He might be just my childhood friend, but he's still my responsibility."

"And you're a young man. You need to get a life."

Rick almost chuckled. Almost. If only she knew. He'd already lived more lifetimes than he had a right to. "I'm thirty-seven years old," he told her. "I've been around."

"It's none of my business," Angela said, backing out the door, "but I want you to know that you don't have to worry about him. If you need to take some time for yourself, go on vacation or something, we'll take good of care of him for you."

"I appreciate that."

"He'll still be here, still be…Steve…when you get back."

Because there was never going to be any improvement. Steve was who he was—exactly who he'd been since he'd climbed up on that roof thirty-four years ago, trying to rescue three-year-old Rick, who'd run away from him.

Did Angela—did any of them—think he didn't know that? Did they think he was hoping for some change? Did they think he spent all this time with Steve because he was hoping that someday Steve would come back, whole once again?

"Steve isn't a burden to me, Angela." He felt compelled to speak tonight, where he would normally be silent. "The time I spend with him is all the vacation I could need, or want."

It wasn't hard to read the pity in the other woman's eyes as she pulled the unlocked door shut behind her.

But he didn't take it personally. She didn't get it. Didn't understand him. She was just like everyone else.

And Rick was fine with that.

3

"So what do you think? Should I tell Mom and Dad that I got the scholarship? Or do I just let it go?"

Sitting in her house on a cliff overlooking Lake Michigan, wearing the sweats she'd changed into after work, Erin studied the beautiful young woman on the couch beside her. Caylee Fitzgerald was the youngest of nine children in the close-knit Irish-American Fitzgerald family. Noah had been the firstborn, Caylee's oldest brother.

He'd also been Erin's college sweetheart, her lover for several years and her fiancé for six brief months.

"You've been awarded a full scholarship to *Yale?*" Erin repeated what she'd just been told, smiling at the girl who was the closest thing to a baby sister she had—while she scrambled for the right words to answer Caylee's question.

"I know. I can't believe it, either." Caylee grinned back. Her attempt to contain her excitement was starting to fail. "I mean, I applied, but I didn't think I had a snowball's chance in hell. I'm from Temple, Michigan! Welfare and redneck capital of the world. Who's even heard of this place?"

"Hey, Temple's a great town! With the lake, it's like a resort."

"Like a resort if you could access the lake from here." Caylee snorted. "You have to drive forty-five minutes to Ludington to be able to do that."

Not everyone had to jump right into the middle of something to appreciate it, or be blessed by it. Though she'd never touched a drop of its water, the lake was one of Erin's closest companions. Every single time she woke up in the dark of night, Lake Michigan was there, splashing against the rocks down below, reminding Erin that she had sources of strength outside herself. And when she couldn't fall back to sleep, or couldn't find peace on a lazy afternoon, she'd gaze out at those waters and see boats sailing assuredly in the distance—or maybe just see the lights bobbing out there—and it was as if she and the lake shared a secret.

The lake was filled with life. Many kinds of life. And filled with answers, too. Answers about what was real and what wasn't, about what was permanent and what would prove to be merely ephemeral.

"Besides," she finally added, "they don't give full academic scholarships to Yale based on where you grew up. Those are based on merit."

Caylee's expression, while still sparkling with excitement, had sobered considerably, the girl's amber hair and green eyes an exquisite complement to her creamy, freckle-free complexion. Erin tried to find a resemblance to Noah. His image was fading now. Where once Caylee had reminded Erin of him, now, when she looked at the young woman, all she saw was Caylee. "So what should I do?"

You have to go. The obvious answer sprang to Erin's mind. But she didn't voice it.

"What about Daniel?" Caylee's boyfriend since ninth grade. A boy who, like Erin, had become as full-fledged a member of the Fitzgerald family as was possible without actually being born into it.

"He doesn't even know I applied," Caylee said. "Honestly, Erin, I didn't think anything would come of it. I was just in a mood the day the counselor visited school and I filled out the forms. But that was it. I'd forgotten all about it until they called me up to the guidance office today."

"What do you suppose Daniel would say if he knew?"

"He wouldn't understand. He thinks we're getting married as soon as we graduate. He's going to work for his dad full-time at the farm and wants to build us a place out there. His dad already told him he'd give us the land. Eventually the farm will be ours and Grady's. We were going to tell Mom and Dad on Mother's Day. We thought it would make the day a little easier for Mom."

It had been more than four years since Noah's death, but time had not healed Patricia Fitzgerald's grief. From what everyone said, the woman was a shell of the person she used to be, though Erin hadn't met her long enough before Noah's death to know that for herself.

There was an immeasurable weight adding to Caylee's dilemma. Her leaving town could very well be another nail in her mother's coffin.

"Does Grady know his father's dividing the farm between the two brothers?"

Grady, older than Daniel by two years, had been working full-time at the family dairy business since he'd graduated from high school.

"Yeah. He suggested it."

"Engleman's Dairy is hugely successful," Erin offered. "You could do a lot worse."

"I know." Caylee didn't look happy. "And I love Daniel,

so much. I'm absolutely certain there'll never be anyone else for me but him."

Erin left Caylee with her seventeen-year-old wisdom on that one.

"But?" she had to ask.

"But I…I feel so trapped in this town. Been there, done that. The thought of spending the rest of my life here, never experiencing more out of life than Temple, Michigan, and having to drive forty-five minutes to get to the nearest mall… Knowing only these same people all my life and doing exactly what I've been doing since I was born— It scares me, Erin. Like why am I even alive if this is all there is?"

Erin wanted to remind the girl about having babies, raising a family, loving her soul mate, having him beside her every single day—but couldn't.

"You said you applied on a lark. Do you really want to go to Yale? Or is this just hard because it's a free ride out of town and something a lot of people would give anything to have?"

"Oh, I want to go. More than anything. I wanted to go when I applied. Studying at Yale has always been my dream. But I never, for one second, really figured I'd have a chance. It's one of those things you fantasize about, like owning a yacht or finding a cure for cancer, you know?"

Caylee was so mature for her age, and so young, too. Such a contrast between owning a yacht and curing cancer. But she didn't point that out.

"You've got your answer," she said instead.

Caylee's brow creased. "I do?"

"Yes."

"What is it?"

"Think about everything you just told me, and you'll

know." Erin's father's words came back to her. She couldn't even remember the question she'd brought him during that visit, but she'd never forgotten the words, or the earnest look on her father's face as he'd gazed at her through the Plexiglas at the Illinois prison visiting booth.

Never forgotten, either, the sincerity in the apology that had followed.

It had been the last time she'd seen him alive.

After a few minutes of silence, Caylee's eyes brimmed with tears. "I don't know, Erin. I keep going around in circles. How can something so great be so wrong at the same time? How can the happiest day of my life be something I can't tell anyone about? Except you, of course."

With a sigh, Erin squeezed her hands into fists and wished she had the wisdom everyone seemed to think she had. "Life isn't easy, Caylee. Choices, answers, they aren't always clear-cut. And sometimes the best choice is the hardest one to make."

"If I go it'll kill Mom."

"You aren't responsible for your mom."

"I know that. But I can't just think of myself, either."

"No, but her inability to let Noah go, to move on with her life, is *her* issue. Her challenge. And, in a sense, her choice. That might sound harsh, like I don't care, but you know I do care, very much. And what I said is true. Noah's gone. You can't sacrifice your life because of that. Then there'll be two lives lost. Besides, he'd be really pissed if he knew that's what you were doing."

"So I should go?"

"I'm not saying that. All I'm saying is that you can't live other people's lives. Not Daniel's. Not your mother's. If you try, you're going to end up half-alive."

Please, don't let me be making a mistake.

"But I love them."

"Of course you do. And you want to spend your life with them and that's a great thing, but you still have to be *you,* or what do you really have to give them?"

"So what should I do?"

"What do you think you should do?"

Caylee's grin was weak, but genuine. "You sound like a shrink."

"You're a wise young woman, Caylee. Impressively wise. If you slow down, get outside yourself for a second so you can see the whole picture, you'll know what to do."

With her head bowed, her thumbs playing some kind of game with each other, Caylee held Erin's gaze.

"I have to talk to them," she finally said, conviction growing in her voice. "If they're going to be part of my life, if I'm going to be wholly in theirs, then they have to know about the scholarship."

Erin nodded.

"And they have to be part of the decision," Caylee added. "One way or the other."

Not quite the angle Erin would've taken, but assuming Patricia Fitzgerald and Daniel loved Caylee enough, Noah's little sister would be on her way to Yale this fall. Considering how much it meant to the girl, anything else would be criminal.

Most of the drive up the coast from Steve's place back to Temple was state highway—the two-lane kind that wound through the dark, wood-lined landscape with no signs, no homes, no lights.

The kind of road that was like Rick's life.

That thought crossed his mind and went on its way as

he made the trip back Thursday night. Rick was who he was. Steve's guardian.

He had everything he needed or wanted. Peace. Enough money. And proximity to Steve. He owned his own home—a small place that had been trashed and in foreclosure, which allowed Rick to pick it up for half its original value. He'd paid cash for it. He'd fixed it up exactly as he wanted it.

Not that he had to rush home. He could've spent the night on the sleeper sofa in Steve's apartment. That was why he'd bought that particular couch. But Steve cried whenever Rick left—unless he left when the older man was down for the night.

The tears didn't last long, or so he'd been told, but he hated being the cause of them. Why upset Steve's generally happy morning routine just because he was a little tired for the drive back to his place?

What a hell of a day this had been. Charles gone. Death didn't usually faze Rick a whole lot. It wasn't something he feared. Or thought much about.

But finding Charles that morning…in Temple. It didn't figure.

Who would want the man dead? And why? Charles was as close to under-the-radar boring as any man could be. A nice guy. But completely ordinary.

It didn't make sense.

Which made Rick's instincts crawl.

Overactive instincts, he reminded himself, his foot on the brake, arms holding the wheel steady as a deer bolted into the road.

If the four-legged creature had a death wish, he'd just missed having it granted.

Rick's hands still firm on the wheel, his nerves as steady as ever, he drove on. And was just nearing town when he noticed headlights pulling out of some trees behind him.

Depending on how quickly investigations happened in this town where shoplifting was big news, and on how quickly a crime scene was released, Rick might not be able to work the next day. In which case, he could've slept on Steve's couch. And saved himself this late-night trip.

The lights kept pace behind him and, as Rick sped up, maintained the same distance. He slowed.

And the car, a dark-colored sedan, slowed.

Was someone following him?

Turning before he'd intended to, Rick watched for the lights. And slowed when the car followed him around the corner.

In another time and place he'd have pulled a couple of fast ones and lost the guy. But that was then.

This was now, and if someone had business with him, he'd just as soon get it over with outside of town.

Still, his good mood diminished as the other car pulled off the road after him. Why would anyone here have business with him? He was a nothing handyman in small-town America.

Rick saw a man emerge and begin to approach him. The man had taken only a couple of steps when Rick placed him.

Huey Johnson. The county sheriff. Rick had seen him only that morning. And a couple of other times at the local tavern when Rick had stopped in for dinner.

Huey knew where Rick lived. And, after that morning at EMA, had his cell number, too.

Why not just call? Or stop by?

Opening his door, Rick slid out, meeting Huey at the bumper of his pickup.

"Huey? What's up?"

Out of uniform, the other man was wearing jeans and a flannel shirt under a half-zipped quilted vest. And a frown. He had his badge out. And a gun strapped to his hip.

"Rick Thomas?"

"Yeah." Rick frowned, too. What the hell was going on? This morning at the crime scene, Huey had slapped him on the back and thanked him for his help.

"You're under arrest for the murder of Charles Cook. You have the right to remain silent. Anything you say can and will be used against you in a court of law…."

You have the right to an attorney. If you cannot afford an attorney, one will be appointed to represent you…

Rick's brain recited the words silently, in unison with the sheriff.

Huey's voice faded and Rick faced him, quiet and unmoving.

"Turn around and put your hands up on the truck." Huey's command wasn't the least bit friendly.

Rick turned, lifted his hands and then swung his head back toward the officer. "What's going on?" he asked.

He was under arrest? *Here?* For Charles's murder? There had to be more to it than that.

"I just told you. Now get 'em up."

Rick complied, mostly to buy himself time to catch up with the situation. He'd let his guard down. The day with Steve. The deserted road and quiet drive…

"I didn't kill Charles," he said, staring at the ground between his outstretched arms as Huey patted him down.

He'd been with Steve so he wasn't packing. Thank God for small favors.

"Evidence says you did."

"What evidence?"

"Arms behind your back."

Mind racing, Rick followed orders. For the time being. Until he knew more.

He gritted his teeth at the weight of steel clasped around his wrists, and he heard the familiar click of the handcuffs closing down on his skin—a repeat performance he could have done without.

Leaving his truck at the side of the road, with only the crunch of Huey's boot steps and heavy breathing for company, he gave himself over to the mercy of a system he didn't trust and allowed the chief of police to lead him to the back of his unmarked car.

4

Erin watched the man. That was her job. To watch him. He knew she was there. Knew she was watching. She couldn't turn him in. Couldn't tell anyone what he'd done. He knew that. And laughed.

He wanted Erin to know what he was about to do.

She moved closer. The man's face changed. Now she was looking at an old man. With darker skin and different eyes.

His eyes were brown. She liked his eyes. He glanced at her and met her gaze. He shook his head, lifted his eyebrows, as though telling her to watch, and then raised his hand and whipped the back of it across the woman's cheek.

Erin couldn't stop him.

Then the face changed again. Became female, and young. With soulful blue eyes. Erin liked her eyes. The girl had money in her hand. She'd just been paid to do something and Erin had to watch. It was going to be bad. Really bad and—

Shooting up in bed Erin froze, waiting—for what, she didn't know. Confused by swirling thought, she couldn't escape the fragments of visions in her mind.

Was that what she did? What she'd become? Was she a voyeur to the bad and ugly? Someone who let bad people do bad things? Who watched it all—after the fact—and helped them get away with what they'd done?

Dripping with sweat, she shivered, scared to death.

She heard it again. The sound that had woken her. Her cell phone. On her nightstand. Right next to the clock with the big red numbers.

One-fourteen.

Boots, the five-year-old tabby cat Noah had given her for her birthday just weeks before he died, raised his head, looked up at her, as if to say "Aren't you going to get that?"

As if the ringing of the phone, the disturbance of his sleep, was her fault.

And she supposed it was. Boots didn't get a lot of calls.

On the next ring, Erin grabbed the phone, pressing the call button, while lingering images continued to float in and out of her consciousness. "Hello?"

Dreams. They were just dreams.

"Ms. Morgan?" She recognized the voice. It meant something. But what? From where?

Was he a client? Someone she'd set free? In trouble again?

A middle-of-the-night phone call wouldn't be a courtesy call. A thank-you.

"Yes."

"My name's Rick Thomas. We've never met. I need your help."

Erin clicked on the light, only vaguely aware of Boots's squinting, protesting eyes. "Where are you?"

"Sheriff's station. I've just been booked."

She'd been there the morning before. And that afternoon, too. And then she placed the voice.

"You're the man who found Charles Cook."

"That's right." He didn't ask how she knew.

"And now you're in jail."

"They think I killed him."

That was quick. And convenient.

"How'd you get my name?" Not that it mattered. But she liked to know.

"Huey Johnson." Sounded odd, not hearing him referred to as Sheriff Johnson. He was always Sheriff. Whether in uniform, at church or at the grocery store. He was the sheriff. Had been for decades.

"I'll call him about bail. You got money to post?"

"I can get it."

In that case, "My fee is two hundred dollars an hour."

"Are you that good?"

She had her AV rating. "Yes."

"Then get me out of here."

Erin tried to take offense at the man's high-handedness. Except that he didn't sound bossy or egotistical. He just sounded tired.

A man who didn't waste time on social games and niceties.

"One more question, Mr. Thomas."

She waited for a response that didn't come, then asked, "Did you do it?"

"No."

For now, and because the sheriff had told him to call her, she believed him.

And went to work.

"Okay, let's go."

Rick was just dozing off in the smallest cell he'd ever

occupied when Deputy John Wright, a young man from a neighboring city whom Rick had never seen before that night, was unlocking his door.

He stood. "What time is it?" They'd taken his watch.

"One forty-five."

Less than an hour since his one phone call? Erin Morgan was worth her two hundred an hour.

He hadn't met the woman, but picked her out immediately when he came around the corner from the now-empty cell block, consisting of six cells, and into the office area of the Ludwig County Sheriff's Department.

She was the only female in the room. The only other person besides the young man accompanying Rick and an older man who'd been working dispatch when Rick was brought in.

"Mr. Thomas?"

The woman was younger than he'd expected. And gorgeous. Two strikes against her. Rick didn't put any stock in looks—other than to recognize that they came in handy as a distraction—and at two hundred bucks an hour, he'd counted on the kind of experience that comes with age.

Still, she was all he had at the moment. And she'd managed to get him out of there. He nodded as they approached each other. Took the envelope of belongings she handed him. Noticed the small, soft hands with long slim fingers and evenly cropped nails.

"Do I need to sign anything?"

Ms. Morgan shook her head—a head bouncing with short, golden-brown hair.

"Let's go in here." Her voice, as soft and feminine-sounding as she looked, didn't ask. It instructed. She led him to a small door off the main office.

Once inside, she indicated which of the four chairs he should take at the round table in the middle of the room.

Because she'd just sprung him, because he might need her, he complied.

Dressed in brown slacks, a beige top and lighter brown sweater, with pumps that had enough of a heel to be dressy but not enough to be showy, she took the seat to his left. She opened the file she'd been carrying, detaching the pen hooked to the top of it.

"It says here you're thirty-seven."

"That's right."

She rattled off his birth date and social. Rick nodded. The same for his address. It was all common knowledge.

"I've never seen you around before."

"I've only been here a year."

"A year's quite a while in a town this size."

"I spend most of my free time in Ludington."

Still bent over her pages, she glanced up at him. "You know someone there?"

"Yes."

He didn't elaborate. Steve had nothing to do with this. She scored big with Rick when she didn't push.

Though the speculative look she sent him seemed to add an unspoken, *For now.*

"What are the charges?" He cut to the chase. Needed to find out everything she knew—information she'd have more access to than he would.

Erin Morgan might think she was there to defend him. In Rick's mind, she was there as a conduit between himself and whoever might be against him. She had the means to get inside information.

"There aren't any charges."

"Come again?"

"They can put you at the scene of the crime. And there's some pretty strong circumstantial evidence. Enough to bring you in for questioning. Not enough to detain you. As soon as I pointed that out, Sheriff Johnson had to let you go."

"So I'm free."

"For now."

"Right."

"They're going to arrest you again as soon as they have the evidence to make charges stick."

"There isn't going to be any."

"Sheriff Johnson thinks there is. He said they found some things at your place. They're just waiting on forensics."

"They searched my place?"

"They had a warrant for this afternoon."

"I wasn't home. The door was locked."

"I guess it isn't anymore."

So he had a door to fix before he could get some shut-eye.

"What does he think he found?"

Rick wasn't worried. There was nothing in his home in Temple that would identify anything about him or tie him to anything more dangerous than the local grocery-store dairy aisle.

And even if they searched the truck, he'd be safe. His locked storage was camouflaged as a second gas tank.

"They found the blade that killed Charles Cook in a register duct in your bedroom. They're just waiting on a match."

Rick's blood ran cold.

5

He was being framed.

A man had been killed when only Rick would have been around to find him. And the murder weapon had been planted in Rick's home.

He didn't panic. He didn't worry or give in to the cold knot of fear that occasionally took up residence in his gut. He just went from tired and irritated to focused.

During his fifteen-year career as a special agent, he'd been in far more dangerous situations.

"Who searched my place?" he asked the woman who managed to look fresh and perky at two in the morning.

Other than four years in the army, his work for the government had been covert. He'd been protecting national security. He'd used an alias. There should be no traceable record.

Who knew he was here in Temple?

Or was it Tom Watkins, his alias, they were after? And if so, who knew that Tom was Rick? That Rick Thomas was Tom Watkins?

Who planted a murder weapon in his home?

His new attorney was frowning. "The sheriff's department searched it at three o'clock this afternoon."

"Who specifically?"

"Sheriff Johnson was there. I don't know who else."

"Can you find out?"

"Yes." Her voice held questions that she didn't ask. He was making her suspicious.

Time to tone it down. He needed her. Needed an ear in the legal establishment. Just in case someone within local law enforcement had been hired to track him down.

And he needed a cover. Someone he could feed with information to pass on if necessary.

"I didn't do it."

"At the moment I believe you. I wouldn't be here if I didn't. You're cooperating fully. And the murder weapon was too conveniently placed for my liking. But if I'm going to do my job, I do need some help from you, Mr. Thomas."

"Of course." He tempered the aggression storming through him. "Ask me whatever you want."

He withstood her intense perusal with ease. He had a job to do now. And would call forth whatever persona he needed to get the job done. That was how it worked.

How it had always worked.

Didn't matter that he'd thought he was done with all that. Didn't matter what he wanted. What mattered was keeping himself safe. For Steve.

He wasn't above using this pretty attorney, or anyone else, to reach that end.

Erin Morgan studied the pages she'd brought in with her, moving through them quickly. Leaving the impression that it wasn't the first time she'd read them.

That was good. She was of no use to him if she wasn't sharp.

"It says here that you joined the army immediately after high school."

"That's right."

"You served four years."

"Yes."

"At twenty-two you sought and were awarded an honorable discharge."

"Correct." *That's it, Ms. Morgan, tell me everything that's officially available on Rick Thomas.*

Rick knew what information was *supposed* to be available. Knew what was supposed to be in his government record. Now he had to find out if something had been changed without his knowledge.

She glanced up. "What did you do after that?"

For a split second Rick thought of Brady. Or, more pertinently, of his comrade's death the year before. Brady Cardington, alias Jack Dunner. He should have investigated.

The first and only time he hadn't listened to his instincts.

Was he paying the price now?

Taking a calculated risk, betting that his cover was still intact, he said, "I was a contracted construction worker in the Middle East." It explained long periods undercover. And large amounts of money. And could be verified on his tax records.

He really had worked construction in the Middle East, should anyone want to check.

Most of that time, he *hadn't* been there—or at least not on construction sites. He'd worked as a member of a covert operations team for the United States government. His undercover persona, Tom Watkins, had specialized in illegal ammunitions running, doing jobs that could've landed him in prison any number of times.

Jobs the government would deny being aware of if he was ever caught.

"You worked in the Middle East for fifteen years."

"Fourteen. Yes."

"Do you have references?"

"Two," he said. "Jack Dunner." By rote Rick rattled off information that should lead her to a voice that would confirm his identity. A guaranteed benefit that had come with signing his life away to protect his country—and to make enough money to pay for Steve's care.

And then added the second name, Kit Matthews, the other man on their team of three agents overseen by Rick's army sergeant. Another alias. Tom, Jack and Kit. Three men who'd never really existed, but who'd risked their lives on a daily basis to help keep the country safe. The phone number he gave for Kit would lead to another voice confirmation of Rick Thomas's work in the Middle East.

A voice. He'd never met the person connected to that voice. Didn't even know if it was male or female, although he suspected it was some assistant hired by the Department of Defense.

And that person, who was probably well paid for answering anonymous phone calls, had no idea who or what he was. Just one more thing that had been "arranged" to cover for the members of the team.

Ms. Morgan nodded. "I'll give them both a call first thing in the morning. Now, what about personal references? People who'll vouch for you? Speak to your character?"

"Shelby Horne." An older woman who ran the boarding house in Maine that Rick had called home for most of the past fifteen years. He hadn't been there often, but enough to create an excellent character witness.

A carefully planned circumstance.

Tom Watkins had had a landlady, too. A room in a

boarding house. Different women. Different states. But identical characteristics. Identical plans.

Brady and Saul and their aliases had had the same.

Rick gave the attorney Shelby's number.

"Anyone else? Family, perhaps?"

"No." He shook his head. Portraying a sadness he mostly didn't feel. "I never knew my mother. I had a brother who is also deceased. And Dad died in a truck accident fifteen years ago."

He'd hit a tree roaring away from Rick.

"The same time you got out of the army."

"Just about." He'd already agreed to his future—had already agreed to be a member of the dangerous covert ops team being run by his sergeant. Because of his exemplary military record, Sarge had been promoted to lead the team and had carefully chosen the three men who would work with him.

"And that's it?"

"Yes."

"It says here that you've never been married. What about a girlfriend?" She flipped through a couple of pages, as though she'd find some woman lurking there. She didn't look over at Rick.

"No one significant. I couldn't ask a woman to be faithful to me and then leave her with no way to reach me for months at a time." He couldn't put another human being in danger. Associating with Rick—and by default with Tom—meant being exposed to danger.

If a job went bad, if Tom's cover was ever blown, if someone wanted to hold him hostage or blackmail him, a family member or loved one would've been the first weapon they'd use.

"What about friends? Army buddies?"

"There was one, but he died last year."

"What was his name?" No reason she had to know that. The man was dead, so he could hardly serve as a character reference.

"Brady Cardington." The real man behind Jack Dunner's alias. Dunner had been a well-known figure in the illegal drug business. When Brady was killed, there'd been a separate funeral for Jack.

"Where did you know Brady from?"

"Boot camp," he told her. They'd been the only two recruits who'd completed an unscheduled fitness challenge their first afternoon in. One that had been administered by a jackass.

Rick hadn't seen Brady after those grueling six weeks, until, four years later, Sarge had asked if he knew anyone he'd trust with his life.

He'd given the man Brady's name. Brady had found himself with a lucrative new career protecting his country in ways he'd never imagined.

And had ended up dead at thirty-six.

"This should help," Ms. Morgan said, looking over the short list she'd just made.

"Help?"

"Several things about you raised Sheriff Johnson's suspicions, which was one of the reasons he arrested you before he had enough evidence to hold you," the attorney confided.

And Rick was getting exactly what he was paying for. Inside information.

"What does the sheriff find suspicious?"

"You show up in town a year ago, a nearly middle-aged man with no family, no apparent ties to anyone or anything—and you've formed no close attachments since you've been here. Your previous career is unusual, to say the least. You have a substantial amount of money, although no one would guess that from how you live, and other than your social, there's no way to trace you."

That was it? He took an easier breath. Whatever the breach, apparently it was small.

"Forgive me for saying that the sheriff isn't much of a lawman if he jumps from Middle East construction worker to murderer just because I was tired of the constant risks and wanted to live a less complicated life."

It felt good telling what was mostly the truth.

"It's not quite that simple, sir."

"Please, call me Rick." *Sir* was just too much to swallow.

"Fine. I'm Erin."

Their eyes met and Rick almost forgot why they were here. Alone together, in the middle of the night, in a secluded room.

Almost, but not quite.

He nodded.

And she said, "You don't have fingerprints."

"I was born with a keratin 14 protein deficiency," he lied. But it was what had been added to his army medical record fifteen years before, though it would take some time for local law enforcement to gain access to that information. In reality, he and Brady and Saul Woodburn, the real man behind Kit's alias, had been administered a drug normally used on cancer patients. If it leaked from the right capillaries, it permanently erased a body's ability to produce fingerprints.

"Have you ever been in trouble with the law before?" Erin had moved on.

"No."

Rick hadn't been. And since Tom didn't exist…

Even if there was a record of Tom Watkins's existence,

Rick would've given his attorney the same answer. Lying didn't faze him.

It kept him alive.

"No bar fights? Nothing that might creep up later and show some latent aggressiveness? A temper? Fits of meanness? Even a random act of anger?"

"Nothing." Not as Rick Thomas. The little bits and pieces of life he'd spent as himself, Rick had either been working construction in the Middle East, getting some rest in his room at the boarding house in Maine or visiting Steve.

She looked him in the eye again. And Rick smiled. A wholly natural, unplanned, unwarranted smile. It caught him completely off guard.

And so did she.

When she smiled back.

6

Chandler, Ohio
Friday, October 15, 2010

This time when the phone rang, I recognized the number. The fact that Erin Morgan was calling me again so soon—just three days after our first phone call in a year—had me answering after the first ring.

She'd called my cell. But I had a feeling this wasn't strictly a "keep in touch" call.

"Can I hire you just to chat?" Erin asked as soon as we'd said our hellos.

"Excuse me?"

"I need someone to talk to. Someone who reads between the lines."

Interesting choice of words. Taking my pad, I moved over to my faded but still-colorful chintz sofa, kicked off my pumps and pulled my legs up beneath me.

"Reads between the lines?" I asked.

"You know, the stuff our subconscious hides from us. Or the stuff we block. The things we reframe but we don't know we're reframing. Misplaced perceptions. Motivations we aren't aware of."

I did know, but wasn't used to my clients summing it all up before we'd even begun. More often they were unhappy, depressed, afraid—ruled by negative emotions that were driving destructive behavior—and didn't think they had the ability to help themselves.

I tried to guide them in finding the internal mental and emotional resources they needed. And sometimes to organize those resources.

Awareness was the key that unlocked most mental doors.

Erin was already aware.

"I'm happy to talk to you. But you don't need to pay me."

"Of course I'll pay you. I'm not going to take advantage of our professional association for personal gain. I don't want you to think I'm using you. Really. I want to pay whatever your going rate is and—"

"Erin, it's okay. You aren't using me. I'm offering. From what I know of you, and what you said the other day, I don't feel you need my professional services. If I thought you did, I'd recommend you see someone local. If I start to think you do, I'll recommend someone to you."

"And I'd probably thank you and say no." Erin's candid response was part of the reason I felt comfortable with her. "But I'd feel better if you'd let me pay you," the other woman continued.

Clinging to independence, I jotted. And wondered if it was off-putting to be friends with someone like me. Who wanted to sit around over a glass-of-wine gab session and have someone taking notes?

As if all confessions would be recorded.

"I know what your expert witness charge is," Erin said. "Is it the same for private sessions?"

I had lots of friends. Like Sam. And Deb. And...oh, plenty of others around town. I knew practically everyone and...

"Tell you what," I said before I could analyze myself to death. "How about if we just chat and see how it goes."

"What do *you* get out of it?"

I recognized myself in Erin's independence. And wondered about her inability to let someone else do something for her.

I wasn't like that. Was I?

"Good conversation?" I replied.

"Are you in trouble? Do you need legal advice?"

I drew a circle. Dotted a couple of eyes in place. "No." If I did, there was always Sheila Grant, the local prosecutor I worked with on a regular basis. "You might remember, I live in a small town," I continued. "I've probably counseled half the people here—and the other half are related to them. Which tends to make socializing a little awkward." What was I saying? I socialized. Plenty. And embarrassingly enough, I kept talking. "Sometimes I feel like I'm quarantined. Or infectious or something."

I did not. My social status had never been a problem for me. I was content. Satisfied. Wasn't I?

I didn't want to own the words I'd just said. Or the feelings. And saw my name on them, anyway.

"I know the feeling, although not from the same source. Right now I feel like I'm the woman who puts the bad guys back out on the street."

She'd made a similar remark earlier. "For you, every day's a fight," I said. "That can't be easy."

"No. But it's not as bad as it sounds, either. Particularly when I'm helping someone who's been wrongly accused. That's kind of like saving lives."

"What was it you needed to speak with me about today? Did something happen?"

"Yes and no. I'm not sure how to describe it. I'm struggling, but I'm not. I'm confused, and yet I know what I'm doing. Maybe I'm crazier than I think."

"Seems to me that you're in a very normal transition period. What served you in the past isn't serving you now. Because you're moving on. Need more. Or somehow got off track."

"When I'm working, I'm okay. I seem to know what to do. But when I'm not, I'm second-guessing everything."

"Like what?"

"Like whether or not I can tell the difference between innocence and guilt."

"That's not really your job, is it?" I'd assisted many defense attorneys. I knew the score.

"Not in a legal sense, maybe. But certainly by my own moral code."

"Guilty people still deserve representation so their story is heard and punishment is just." I'd worked it all out years ago.

And knew that I'd simplified a deep and disturbing concept so I could live with the system until someone found a better way. I certainly didn't have one to offer.

"Right. But what if I've gotten so good at finding the loopholes that I'm really an accomplice?"

"Are you?"

"I hope to God I'm not."

"Then my guess is, you won't be. You care. You're on the lookout. I don't know what else you can do, short of inventing a lie detector that's infallible."

Erin chuckled. And I grinned, too.

"Have you considered changing sides?" I asked as the thought occurred to me. "Maybe all of this is your way of telling yourself to move on to another aspect of the law."

"No. I know it's not that. I'm where I need to be."

I didn't doubt her.

"I've got a new client," she said next. "A guy accused of murder."

With a steady beat I tapped my pen against the side of my foot. "Tell me about him."

Erin talked for a couple of minutes, filling me on her early-morning call and the subsequent interview.

"I have to admit that his life leaves room for questions. But, as he said, it's certainly not criminal behavior to do an unusual job. Someone has to," I told her.

"I know. And I believe him. I believe he's innocent."

"So what's the problem?"

"I'm suddenly wondering if I can trust myself to know the difference anymore."

"Why do you believe he's innocent?"

"At first, I just sensed that he was. And that's how it always used to be. I seemed to be able to tell. But now, I keep remembering this guy's eyes. They're dark and shadowed, but…I'm not sure. He…did things to me."

"Could you explain that?"

"I…I think I found him attractive."

"You *think* you did? Isn't that something you *know?*"

"Right. Yeah. Probably. I think I'm attracted to him."

"Enough so that it would be a conflict of interest?"

"Of course not! I'm not in the market for romance. Period. Been there. Done that. My heart was taken a long time ago and…"

Erin had talked to me about her Noah when we'd had drinks the year before. I understood that she'd loved the man, but Erin was far too young never to love again. She'd never even lived with him.

"And sometimes hearts surprise us by coming out of the deep freeze when we'd rather keep them in there, locked securely away," I said.

Erin's silence didn't seem to be an easy one.

"It's not a crime, you know," I told her. "Attraction is as instinctive as breathing."

"It's been so long since I've noticed a guy, really noticed him. And I pick now, when I'm already nervous about the path my career's taken. With my luck, this guy's a mass murderer and as long as he keeps smiling at me, I'll do my best to get him off so he can go kill some other unsuspecting person."

"You don't seem the type to fall for a smile. My bet is it'd take a lot more than good looks to pull a fast one on you."

"Yeah. I hope so."

"Look, you've got everything you need going for you here. You're doing the right thing, talking through your doubts. If you've somehow gone astray with your career choices, you'll know it soon enough.

"And in the meantime, my money's on you when it comes to this guy. Because of your current personal crisis, you're going to be looking at him, at the situation, more closely than anyone else will be."

"Even if his eyes are mesmerizing?"

"I'd say more so, precisely because of that. You're going to be extracareful. Extraobservant."

I had no idea if Erin's new client was a murderer or not. But I was pretty sure that if he was, she'd find out. And do the right thing.

We talked for a few more minutes and then I glanced at the clock. Deb had a couple of billing issues to go over with me and I'd been hoping to get home before Maggie did, at least one day that week. Since it was Friday, I only had one more shot. Not that I told Erin any of that.

Erin thanked me for my help and then said, "Hey, before you go, just out of curiosity, if you were going to talk to someone, you know, about yourself, what would you say?"

I was in a hurry. I had to go. And once again, my mouth turned traitor on me. "That I'm a new mother and have no idea how to be one."

I couldn't *believe* I'd just said that. Would never have voiced anything like that to anyone around me. Someone who was more than a voice on the phone.

"What?" Erin's shock was clear. "You had a baby? When? Why didn't you say anything? Did you get married, or is this something you did on your own? I mean, you couldn't conceive on your own, but after that?"

When I was fairly sure the questions had stopped, I said, "I didn't have a baby. I'm in the process of adopting a fourteen-year-old ward of the state," I said slowly. "She was my client until recently, when her mother was arrested for selling her into the illegal drug trade."

"Oh, my God."

I needed to talk. Okay, I'd admitted it. And with everyone here in town—well, my role was to be listener. That's how I liked it. But occasionally...

"What do you mean, she *sold* her to them?" Erin asked. "What did they do with her?"

"Used her to deliver their packages."

"Did she know what she was doing?"

"No."

"Is she...she wasn't hurt, was she? In my experience, with these types of guys...drugs is only part of it."

"She's okay." At least Maggie's physical health was

intact. "They kept her away from the stuff, for which I'm incredibly thankful."

"Did they…they didn't rape her, did they? Or…sell her that way? Child pornography is a huge business now that the internet's arrived."

"She says no. I can't really go into the details of the whole thing. It's complicated and, for now, I'm keeping her confidences."

"Did they get the guys?"

"One of them. He was a cop here in town. I'd known him for years."

"So he was someone in a position of authority. Someone a young person would trust."

"Right."

"Cops don't fare well in prison."

"This one's not going to prison. He's dead. Another deputy was close to catching him. He set a trap for her. She walked in to find herself facing the barrel of his gun. And managed to shoot first."

"Lucky woman."

"You'd have to know Sam." I switched my pen and, left-handed, drew guns. "Luck had nothing to do with what happened that evening."

Samantha Jones was a detective now. And newly married.

Which meant I was going to be the only female from our graduating class who wasn't married. Or hadn't been married.

I was mostly okay with that. My time would come. If I wanted it to.

"You said one of them. What about the others?"

"A second one died of an overdose. But the one they suspect as the ringleader is a lawyer here in town, and so far, he's still practicing law and going home to his wife and kids every night."

"They don't have enough to arrest him," Erin summarized.

"You got it."

"And the kid's right there in town, too?"

"Yep. But I don't think he's going to be stupid enough to try and see her. Sam, the detective I told you about, has him on a tight leash. And he knows she's looking for a way to connect the dots. He's not going to risk being seen with Maggie."

"Apparently he managed to see her before without anyone being the wiser."

"True, but no one was looking at him, either."

"So not only can't they tie him to the drugs, but they don't have enough to arrest him on contributing to the delinquency of a minor?"

"Maggie's mother insists he was her daughter's contact."

"I'm guessing that since she's also involved, her testimony could be too easily discredited for a grand jury to indict?"

"That's what I heard. Then there's the fact that everyone knows the guy. He's got a stellar record. Before all this, I would've bet my life that he was one of the nicest men I'd ever met. A paragon of virtue," I said dryly.

"Too good to be true, huh?" Erin's response came as no surprise. "How sure are they that it's this guy?"

"Sam's completely convinced." Which was enough for me.

"Then hopefully she'll get the goods on him."

That was my prayer. Every single night.

"What's it like, having an instant teenager?"

"She intimidates the hell out of me," I blurted, still thinking about my nightly worry sessions.

"Sounds like you're facing a transition period, too," Erin said, throwing my earlier words back at me.

She was right about that.

7

Not knowing what might happen to him in the coming days, Rick spent that Friday with Steve. He stayed the night, too. And had breakfast with Steve the next morning, followed by an hour of fishing. And when Steve went to the birthday party he'd been invited to—a thirty-year-old woman, victim of a skiing accident, whose time without air had left her with the mental abilities of a seven-year-old—Rick hugged him goodbye, an extra tight hug, and headed toward Grand Rapids.

He wasn't just out on bond. He was a completely free man—for now. He could still travel legally.

Pulling into the side parking lot of a Grand Rapids college, he locked the truck and strode to the library and a public computer kiosk he'd scoped out.

Five minutes later he was back on the road, with a confirmation number for the flight he'd just booked, and made it to the airport without time to spare.

In another minute or two, as soon as he slid Tom Watkins's driver's license through the magnetized slot at the check-in kiosk, he'd know if his problem was huge or merely big.

Tom checked in without a hitch.

Which meant that the government hadn't turned on him. Tom's cover was still good—at least where the United States government was concerned.

His problem wasn't huge. It was only big.

Rick allowed himself one shot of Scotch to celebrate on the three-hour flight.

Erin hated it when she couldn't find one of her clients. That topped her list of the many things that could go wrong in a case.

Not that Rick Thomas even had any charges against him at the moment. But he was going to. They both knew that.

So why wasn't he answering her calls? Or, on Saturday afternoon, her knock at his door?

She thought about calling Sheriff Johnson, in case something had happened to her client and he was lying dead on the floor of his home. A home he apparently shared with no one.

But she sensed that discretion was her best course of action at this point. If the man was dead, he'd still be dead tomorrow and the day after that. One thing she knew for sure, if the man was alive and in need of help, he'd make it to a phone.

And if he was alive and unconscious? And her decision not to call for help cost him his life?

Going around to the back of his house, Erin looked for signs of distress, of struggle or illegal entry. She'd been to enough crime scenes during her career to be fairly confident in her abilities to catch at least the basics. Nothing was out of place. There wasn't even an interesting smudge in the dirt.

There were two windows with blinds partially raised. Erin felt no compunction at all about peering inside.

And wasn't surprised when the inside of Thomas's home was as pristine as the outside. As unmarked.

The garage behind the house had a window, too. An uncurtained window. She had to park her car to the side of the garage to stand on, but once she did, she was glad she hadn't called the sheriff. Thomas's truck was gone.

She hoped to God the man hadn't skipped town.

That he wasn't gone for good.

Running was a sure sign of guilt.

And if he was guilty, Erin couldn't help him.

Technically Brady Cardington hadn't died. Jack Dunner had. And since Jack and Brady shared a body…

Finding Jack's grave wasn't hard. The mound of dirt in the Colorado cemetery was still fresh enough to stand out from the otherwise perfectly manicured green grass surrounding it. Rick had been told that Jack had killed himself.

Burnout. Couldn't stand the strain that was inherent in the things he'd been required to do.

One night, alone in his room in the boarding house Jack called home, Rick's buddy had taken his legally purchased hunting pistol and shot himself in the head.

An autopsy had confirmed that the wound had been self-inflicted.

The man who'd sent word of the incident to Rick had confirmed it, too. Rick had been somewhat detained back then. Or rather, Tom Harkins had been. Locked in a jail cell in Arizona, the result of a job gone bad, the only time in his fifteen-year career he'd been caught red-handed. So he'd been unable to get to Colorado.

The autopsy had also shown a heavy dose of painkiller in his friend's system.

Rick should never have accepted his source's word about the incident. He'd turned a blind eye for one reason only.

He'd wanted out. He'd made his plans while sitting in that Arizona hellhole. His thoughts had been on Steve. On building a future out of a nonexistent present.

He should've known it wouldn't be that easy.

You couldn't do the things Tom had done and simply walk away. Not with the number of angry people he'd left in his wake.

Someone had found him. Charles's death was his warning. He spared a moment to feel pity—and guilt—about that. Another unnecessary death…

If he was going to live, he had to find out who'd killed the security officer. And get to him before he got back to Rick. Before he struck again. Because one thing Rick knew: whoever had killed Charles *would* strike again.

The obvious place to start the search was with Brady. With Jack's death. His friend was dead for a reason. Rick had to learn what that reason was.

A year later, it was going to be a little harder to get to the truth. Not impossible. But harder.

Which meant more time.

Something he didn't have.

Erin tried to listen. To focus on the sincerely offered, heartfelt message the pastor was delivering with a grace and humbleness that should have held her attention.

Instead, sitting between seventeen-year-old Caylee and her father, Ron Fitzgerald, she had to concentrate just to keep herself in place. Noah's youngest sister and her father hadn't spoken a word since they'd all taken their seats. Instead, they both stared straight ahead.

Mrs. Fitzgerald sat on her husband's other side. And Daniel, Caylee's intended, flanked Caylee. He clutched the slender fingers of her left hand, not letting go even to hold the hymn book—as though, if he just held on, he wouldn't lose her.

Erin wanted to tell him that if he didn't want to lose her, he needed to let her go.

She'd never been much of a churchgoer. Kind of hard to do regularly when it was just you and a dad who cared more about football and horse races than the existence of any being higher than the bookie who owed him. Or, more typically, whom *he* owed.

But Valley Christian Church had been as much a home to Noah as the house in which he'd grown up. From before he was born his family had attended Sunday morning services together. Married siblings, their spouses and children, met in the Fitzgerald pew, which had grown to a Fitzgerald section, every single Sunday. Without fail.

As soon as the final hymn was sung, Erin turned to Caylee.

"I guess you told them?"

"Only Dad and Daniel," the girl leaned over to whisper. And then, as Daniel rose, stood with him. "I didn't tell them I talked to you."

She turned back as traffic cleared, allowing Daniel to exit the aisle, pulling Caylee behind him.

"You coming over for dinner?" Ron asked Erin as he followed her out of the pew.

She hadn't planned to. She had a list of questions to write for Clyde Sanderson's restraining order hearing in the morning. And a recalcitrant client to attempt to reach.

"It's been a couple of weeks since our last Sunday dinner together. I think it would do Mother good to have you."

"Sure," she said, promising to be over within the hour.

But first, after changing out of church clothes and into the jeans she loved and only got to wear on weekends, she was going to take another trip out to Rick Thomas's place. If the man was even half as smart as she'd given him credit for, his truck would be parked in plain sight, letting the world—and anyone suspecting him of anything—know that he was right where he belonged.

Letting them know he had nothing to hide. Nothing to run from.

The grave existed. Or at least a headstone did. Tom Watkins asked the yard keeper what he knew about the man who'd been laid to rest there. As a grieving friend, he wanted to hear anything the man could remember about the funeral. The people in attendance. If he'd seen the casket. Or, better yet, if there'd been a graveside service where the casket had been open.

Luckily for Rick, the graveyard keeper took pride in his job, a position he'd held for more than forty years. He took responsibility for every soul resting there. And he specifically remembered Jack Dunner because he'd been buried on what would've been the old man's fortieth wedding anniversary had his wife survived the pneumonia that had taken her the year before that.

"Kinda felt like it was me and him together that day," the wrinkled and weathered little man said. "He was leavin' the world mostly all alone, and I'm livin' in it that way. He was goin' to join my Greta and I figured maybe she'd know he came from my yard."

The kind of love the old guy wanted Rick to sympathize with simply wasn't in his realm of understanding. He tried to believe it really existed. Acknowledged that it did for some. But he never quite got there himself.

Rick had been born into the real world. It didn't include romance and fairy tales.

But he humored the guy. And then asked, "Why do you say he was going out of the world mostly alone?"

The guy shrugged, his flannel shirt at least one size too big for shoulders that were stooped with age. "Didn't have no service, just a graveside wake by Peter, the guy that runs the place. And only two folks showed up."

"What folks? What did they look like?"

The elderly gardener studied him, frowning. "Who'd you say you was?"

"Name's Tom. Tom Watkins. Jack and I…we've been like brothers since we were kids."

He'd thought himself an adult at eighteen, but compared to what he was now, he'd been such an idealistic kid back then.

"I was out of the country and didn't hear about his death until recently."

The man didn't look any less aged when the wrinkles of doubt left his lined face.

With both hands on the handle of his shovel, he leaned on it. "Rotten luck," he said, nodding pensively. "Them two folks who was here? A man and a woman. Didn't seem to know each other. The guy was like one of them folks who's always in charge of somethin'. Big guy. One of them buzz haircuts like in the army. He stood there real still, almost like he was the dead one."

Kit? "Did he have a tattoo on his neck?"

"Nope. No necktie, either. Just a jacket and slacks."

"Was the jacket black and the slacks beige?"

"Yeah, how'd you know?"

Sarge. Rick breathed his first truly easy breath since he'd faced Huey Johnson on the side of the road Thursday night.

"The guy's a friend of ours," he said now. Sarge didn't wear a tie—ever. He'd been captured in Kuwait, held with his hands tied behind his back and a noose around his neck. The rope had hung in front of his face, and during his many days alone, naked in captivity, he'd managed to work through it with his teeth.

Eventually he'd escaped and made it to the American embassy.

And the man who'd been Rick's sergeant for most of his time in the service always wore a black jacket with beige slacks. Though Rick had ribbed him about it a few times over a beer, he'd never found out why.

The old man leaned over, yanked up a couple of weeds not far from Brady's grave. "And the woman?" Rick asked.

"Sixty or so. Said she was his landlady."

"You spoke to her."

"She was pretty broke up," the man said. "I see a lot of that and figured I could help."

"Did she tell you how he died?"

"Nope. Didn't tell me nothin'. I told her about me and Greta's anniversary. She cried some more, then left."

A couple of minutes later, Rick left, too. But he didn't cry. Not for the loss of the only real friend he'd ever had. Not for himself or the life they'd lived.

Grieving didn't accomplish anything. Didn't solve problems or accomplish the business of living. It didn't undo what had been done.

8

There was no truck in the driveway Sunday afternoon, either. Or in the garage. Jumping down from the hood of her car for the second time in two days, Erin climbed back inside her Lexus and considered her options.

Her newest client wasn't answering her phone calls. Or her knock at his door.

She could hang on. Wait to hear from Rick Thomas.

Or drop the case.

Thomas was a free man. He could come and go as he pleased.

But he was also a suspect in a murder case.

The two of them should be going over details, solidifying alibis, lining up proof of his innocence to offset the arrest warrant they knew would be coming in a matter of days.

If he *had* alibis. If he *was* innocent.

She warred with herself all the way to the Fitzgerald home—a stately mansion on Main Street. But once inside the beautifully decorated house, she forgot about Rick Thomas for a while.

Janet Meadows, a tall, husky woman, didn't seem to let advancing age slow her down any. As soon as Rick

introduced himself—as Tom Watkins—she pulled him
inside, then had him sitting in a worn but clean and comfortable parlor with a cup of tea he didn't want in one
hand.

"You're the only person Jack ever talked about," the
landlady told him, sitting, legs crossed at the ankles, in a
wooden rocking chair that was easily as old as the house.
Her dress, a heavy, colorful material, hung down nylon-
covered calves that rasped when they brushed each other.
"At least, the only one he ever spoke of by name."

Rick told himself that Tom liked tea as he sipped a
liquid he'd never been able to acquire a taste for. The cup
gave him an excuse not to speak.

He could have closed his eyes and described his surroundings. All these rooming houses were carefully
chosen and basically the same. The layout might differ
some. The front room could be to the left of a foyer entry.
Or the right. The kitchen was always in the back. And
all the bedrooms upstairs. The quality of mattress might
change. The linens and curtains were different. And
the fabric on the worn, upholstered couches in the front
room.

But the basics were the same. Escape plans were the
same. There were certain things a guy had to know, no
matter who he was. He had to be able to get out immediately, no matter where he was.

Mrs. Meadows, a childless widow for thirty years, told
him about Jack fixing a loose banister rail, and coming
home one night after a couple of months on the road,
with a brand-new kitchen sink and drain, which he'd put
in for her. Her old drain had started to rust through, but
the bucket she kept underneath the stained and chipped
sink had worked just fine.

And Rick heard about the mouse Jack caught when her cat hadn't seemed the least bit interested in doing so.

"The best, though, was the dining room light," the woman said, the smile on her face not quite eradicating the sadness in her eyes. "My Walt and I picked it out together and when, after forty years, it shorted out, I felt like I was losing the final piece of him. And then I come home from the grocery one afternoon to find Jack in there, the light down and in pieces, all lined up in meticulous order across the table. I hadn't seen Jack in over a month. Had no idea he was going to be home. But there he was. And by the time I needed the table to serve dinner to him and the others, that light was back up where it had always been. And it was shining upon us once again." The hint of moisture in her eyes was Jack's eulogy.

Rick sipped. And nodded.

"I'm telling you, that Jack, he could do anything," Janet Meadows said.

Yes, he could. Which was why he'd been in the line of work he had. And why it didn't make sense that the man had taken his own life. Regardless of the problem, regardless of what had gone wrong, the Brady he'd known would've discovered a way to fix it.

Rick set his empty cup on the side table. "Who found him?"

"I did."

Her lips trembled and she clasped her hands in her lap.

Rick waited.

"He hadn't come down for breakfast." Her shaky voice drifted off. And then started again. "Jack was always on time for meals. Always."

"He liked to eat." There'd been an unofficial pancake-eating contest the last week of boot camp. Brady had consumed more than thirty flapjacks to ensure that the twenty-dollar pot the guys had collected went into his pocket.

Years later, Rick had still been talking about that morning, ribbing the man about feeding his appetite. And that was where the name Jack had come from. Brady, the flapjack king.

"He'd just come in the night before so I hadn't seen him, and when I knocked on his door several times that morning and he didn't answer, I sensed that something wasn't right. I went for the spare key…."

"Had anyone seen him that morning?"

"No. Only Bettina was living here then. She's a schoolteacher, third grade. She was just leaving for work."

"Is she still here?"

"Yes. Bettina's like me, alone in the world. She's been here over twenty years. She's family now. Just like Jack was…"

"When was the last time you saw him?"

"Three weeks before he died. I know for certain because he gave me six months' rent when he left, and I always log in the payments."

Six months' rent. It would've been in cash. And it meant that Jack was planning to be around. To continue working.

If his buddy had planned to get out, as Rick had, if he'd been having doubts about the job, he'd have saved that cash. Although he'd made enough money over the years to keep him for life, Brady was still that young kid who'd consumed thirty pancakes for a twenty-dollar pot.

"Three weeks." Rick focused on the task at hand. "You said he'd come home late the night before you found him?"

"Around eleven. He was quiet, but I heard him. I'd had the TV on in my room."

"So you have no way of knowing if he was alone."

Mrs. Meadows frowned. "No, I guess not," she said slowly. "But…he always was. Jack didn't ever…well, if he did…not in my house. He…never brought visitors here."

"Did you hear him coming up the stairs? Hear his key in his lock? Or did you just hear his door shut?"

"I heard him coming up the stairs. Bless his heart, he skipped the second-to-the-top stair, like he usually did. It squeaks."

"And it didn't squeak that night."

"No."

"So you listened to him climb the stairs."

"Yes. I counted the steps. And waited to hear his key in his door. I had to make sure it was Jack. A woman can't be too careful these days, you know."

"So you would've been able to tell if there were two sets of footsteps."

"I think so, yes."

"Did you hear anything else?"

"The plumbing in his bathroom."

"And then what?"

"I fell asleep."

"You never heard a gun go off."

"The police, they said he'd…used…one of those… silencer things. And…a pillow."

Rick couldn't think about his friend's brains blown all over a pillow.

"Could you tell if he'd been carrying anything? Did you hear him set down a suitcase when he stopped to unlock his door? Did the keys rattle? Or maybe there was the rustle of a bag, like he'd been to the store or some fast-food drive-through?"

"Jack always carried a duffel, slung over his shoulder. I heard it brush against the wall as he came up the stairs. And his keys—I only ever saw the two I'd given him. One for the front door and one for his room. He kept them on separate strings. I gave him a key chain one Christmas, but I never saw him use it. He didn't have a car, you know."

Rick nodded. Vehicles were messy. Too easy to trace. Too hard to dispose of. "He never learned to drive."

Tom's excuse for not having a car had been the environment.

"Luckily I'm right on the bus route," Mrs. Meadows said.

Luck had nothing to do with it.

"And he had his bike."

"Yes. He loved that bike. Washed it like my Walt used to wash that old car of his. Shined it, too." A sad smile spread across her face.

"What happened to Jack's bike?"

"It was taken, same as the rest of his stuff."

Every nerve in Rick's body buzzed. "Taken? Where? By whom?"

"Jack's uncle came for them. Funny, Jack never mentioned him. I didn't even know he had an uncle. Or any family."

The sergeant. Exactly as planned. Some of his tension abated. "They weren't close," Rick said, making it up. Then he steered attention away from Sarge, which he did as naturally as he breathed.

"Mrs. Meadows." He sat forward. "I realize this is difficult, but I have to ask. You knew Jack pretty well."

"Yes."

"Do you think he killed himself?"

"That's what they say."

"I know. And if he did, then I have to accept that. It's just that…"

"You don't believe it, either." The softness of the woman's words struck him.

"No, I don't."

"I wasn't allowed near the room," she said, her hands still in her lap. "At first…all I saw was a glimpse…of his body…and blood…and I hurried away and called 9-1-1. And after the police got there, they taped it off. By the time I could go in, Jack's uncle had taken all his things. And paid to have the room professionally cleaned and painted. Even put in new carpet."

Erasing all evidence of Jack's existence. Routine. Just as it should be. Keeping them all safe.

"The police had located the uncle as next of kin, and he'd arrived that same day. Took care of all the funeral arrangements, too."

So if there'd been foul play, any sign of it had come and gone within hours.

And that was what he would've expected, as well. According to the world they'd worked in. Lived in.

The world that had paid them well in exchange for their lives.

"I… You cared about him." Jack's landlady was peering at him with eyes that missed little.

"Yes," he admitted. "I did."

She stood then, as though coming to some decision. "I have something for you."

Janet Meadows left the room and Rick positioned himself at the side of the archway with his back to the wall, hand on the pistol beneath his shirt.

Didn't matter what town he was in, a guy like Rick always knew where to acquire a weapon.

And was always ready to use it.

"I have something for you" could mean anything.

Jack had died in this woman's home. She could've been involved.

Maybe whoever had been after Jack had been assuming Rick would visit here—and planned to get him in the same way. Maybe if he'd done so earlier, Charles Cook would be alive. And maybe Rick would be dead.

Maybe Janet Meadows had put something in his tea. And was waiting for whatever it was to take effect.

Maybe he was being paranoid.

A good thing. Paranoia kept him alert. Alive.

"Here it is—where'd you go?" Mrs. Meadows stopped midway in the room and turned.

"I was stretching my legs," Rick said, coming up behind her, his hand still inside his jacket, resting at the edge of his untucked shirt. "Long flight."

The perusal she gave him wasn't light, but Rick withstood it without a blink. He wasn't sure he'd convinced her he was the least bit trustworthy.

"Jack left this for you," she said, anyway, handing him a lunch-size brown paper bag, folded over on itself a couple of times.

Eyeing the small package, Rick asked, "How'd he do that if you didn't see him before he died?"

"He brought it to me the last morning I saw him. Three weeks before his death. He told me that if anything happened to him, I was to hold on to this. I wasn't to tell anyone he'd given it to me unless you showed up. And then I was to give it to you."

Frowning, Rick stepped forward. With his gun hand

on the bag, he didn't take complete possession of it. His gaze met hers. "You're sure?"

"Positive."

She could be lying. Rick didn't think so. He took the bag.

"You did the right thing," he told the older woman. "Thank you."

"You're welcome."

Rick was pretty certain she didn't entirely mean that. But he accepted her words with a nod and took his leave soon after. She didn't invite him back.

It was only after he'd returned to Grand Rapids, and was by himself in his own truck, that Rick pulled the folded brown paper bag out of his pocket and looked inside.

He'd carefully transported—through airport security and onto the plane—a faded, half-used matchbook. From a bar called The Resting Place.

9

Running her fingers through the thick layers of hair kept short for convenience, Erin stared at the one light bobbing out in the darkness beyond her window. She was in the living room, having dropped into a chair on her way back to bed. But she'd seen the same light from the dining room, too, both times she'd passed through to get a bottle of water from the refrigerator.

Bottle uncapped, she took a sip of liquid she didn't really need. The drink had only been an excuse to escape the torture she'd been experiencing in her losing battle with sleep.

The darkness beyond her wall of windows could have felt alarming. Frightening. Hiding all kinds of dangers. Instead, she listened to the waves hitting the rocks far below, taking comfort from their energy. Those waves, and that one light, were all the company she needed.

What a day it had been. The Fitzgeralds were the only family she had. Normally, their presence in her life was a godsend. A miracle. Until something happened that put the close-knit family at odds. Then it was like a person with a raging fever, a virus that caused every part of the body to ache.

Ron, who almost never asked anything of anyone, had asked Erin to talk Caylee into dropping "this Yale nonsense" before her mother found out.

The eldest Mrs. Fitzgerald had just been diagnosed with a liver disease that was exacerbated by stress. So far, and until more tests were done to determine severity, until more facts were known, Erin was the only one in the family, other than Ron, who knew about the diagnosis.

Although Erin had met Patricia Fitzgerald less than five years before, the woman was the only mother she'd really ever had. The reality that this petite and gentle woman could be facing a liver transplant or death was a crushing blow.

And now, more than ever, Erin believed Caylee should have her chance at a full and complete life of her own. The life her heart called her to follow, not the life her family wanted her to live.

Erin knew what it was like to lose a parent. To have to rely for your security—emotional as well as financial— solely on the life you'd created yourself.

But if stress was an escalator in Patricia's disease, Erin could be killing her almost-mother-in-law by encouraging Caylee to set out on her own.

Yet how could the choice to sacrifice Caylee's whole future be the right one?

"Caylee looks up to you, more than any of the others," Ron had said earlier that day. "She idolized Noah. He was her favorite. The one she ran to any time she had a problem. And you were Noah's choice. With him gone, Caylee has switched her loyalty to you."

Ron hadn't seemed displeased by his youngest daughter's defection. Quite the opposite, in fact. He'd just wanted to make sure that Erin was fully aware of her role in the family.

And fully aware of the responsibilities that accompanied it.

That light out there, shining in the darkness, seemed to be speaking to her. Or maybe she wished it would tell her what to do. She—

The ring of her cell phone pealed amid the comforting sound of crashing waves. She'd left it in her bedroom. Dressed in the thin white pajama pants and top she'd pulled on a couple of hours earlier, Erin hurried across the thick beige carpet to her room, wondering who was in trouble. And noticing that middle-of-the-night calls weren't as alarming when you were awake as they were when they woke you from a deep sleep.

Please let it be someone she didn't know, she half prayed, and then felt guilty for wishing misfortune on some unknown person as she reached for the phone.

She recognized the number. She shouldn't answer it. That was best.

"Hello?"

"I didn't wake you."

The man was observant. But then, she'd already realized that and so much more about him. "No."

"I apologize for calling so close to midnight."

"I answered." She'd had a choice. "I've reconsidered our arrangement. I don't think I can represent you. If you need a lawyer tonight I can recommend someone who—"

"I don't need a lawyer tonight."

For a second, she just stood there, taken aback by his words in a way she didn't understand.

"Then why are you calling me?"

"To ask a favor."

The man had gall. She'd hand him that. "I don't owe you any favors."

"I'm asking, anyway."

It was time to hang up. She positioned her thumb over the end-call button. "What?"

"I...found a matchbook cover that isn't mine, nor is it one I've seen before. I think it should be checked for fingerprints, but because we have no idea who planted that knife in my bedroom, I don't want anyone to know about this."

"Where did you find it?"

"It's right here."

"Where's here?"

"My home."

"In Temple?"

"It's the only home I have."

So he'd come back. He wasn't on the run. Slumping onto the edge of her bed, Erin stared at the red polish on her toes. And then slid backward, pulling her feet up as she leaned against the solid pecan headboard.

"Where've you been?"

"Tying up business. You intimated that I might not be a free man for much longer."

"We'll get you out on bail."

"But I won't be able to leave the state."

"You left the state?"

"Yes."

"What business did you have to tie up?" Her name was associated with this man. She had to know what he was into.

"I had a...woman...to see."

"You said there were no significant relationships."

"She's not significant."

With a second's worth of compassion for the unknown female, Erin asked, "You going to see her again?"

"No."

"Is she aware of that?"

"Yes."

She caught herself just before asking if he'd left a broken heart behind. The state of his ex-lover's heart was none of her concern.

But she did ask, "Were there any children involved?"

"No."

"Drop the matchbook by my office in the morning and I'll see what I can do."

"What time?"

"I'll be in at nine."

"Can the test be done quietly?"

"Yes." She had her sources. Any defense attorney worth her salt had to be able to get answers without alerting the world—or incriminating her client.

"And when Huey Johnson shows up here with his warrant, should I call you?"

When not *if*. And *here*. Rick wasn't running. He wasn't hiding.

Erin had to make a decision.

"Yes. And don't say a word to anyone until I get there."

Rick slept through the night and was still at home, uninterrupted, Monday morning. He celebrated with a bowl of sugared flakes and a pot of really strong Colombian coffee. Just the way he liked it.

And then he showered and headed out.

He had a couple of hours before he could deliver Brady's last offering and wanted to ensure that he was free to do so. He wanted to live, and so had no choice but to play this thing to the end—to learn who was out to get him and get them first. But that didn't mean he was going to be waiting.

Waiting would put him on the defensive.

He'd preferred to play offense. In his type of work that was how to stay alive.

And so, in jeans, a flannel shirt and a black leather jacket, he donned work boots, grabbed his gun, loaded it, stowed it and went for a drive. A long drive. He kept moving.

Until he passed through a town with a gas station that advertised prepaid cell phones. Rick stopped then. Paid cash for a phone.

Back in the truck, he dialed a Laundromat in Kansas City. And when a woman answered he told her Tom was calling to say he wanted his shirts starched. She told him she'd be happy to take care of that for him and hung up.

Rick stopped a second time. Dropped the phone behind his tire, backed over it, picked up the remains and tossed them in the next roadside Dumpster he passed.

Assuming he was still a free man, and Sarge was able to get to Michigan, he should be meeting him out on the lake sometime after midnight. That was the plan. One Rick had hoped never to need.

And if Sarge didn't show Monday night, Rick would return on Tuesday, renting boats from marinas that he didn't frequent. Different boats. Different sizes. For un-specified periods of time.

Paying cash.

Using fake IDs.

No pattern. Nothing to trace.

In his life as Tom, that was how it had to be.

Erin was in her office by eight. The navy slacks and jacket, the silk blouse and matching pumps, the pearls in her ears and at her throat, the carefully applied make-up and the extra time she'd taken to ensure that her hair maintained the casually windblown look, were all for her court appearance on Clyde's behalf. Not to impress her newest client—the one who'd be dropping by with a small package.

She did her hair and makeup every day. Hadn't been seen without eyeliner by anyone but her reflection in the mirror—and maybe her cat—since Noah died. Today the application had taken longer because of a sleepless night that had left her hand a little shaky.

She didn't need to attract attention to herself. She had no one to convince that she was on top of her game.

By eight forty-five she'd confirmed final arrangements for a settlement conference with Clyde and his wife, Laura Jane, that afternoon. If all went well the man would be protected by nightfall. The restraining order against Laura Jane wasn't going to do it. The one against Clyde would. If he stayed away from the woman, she wouldn't be able to manipulate him.

He loved her too much to keep his distance when she reached out to him, which she did each and every time he tried to free himself from her abusiveness. Erin hoped a court order would be enough incentive for him to hold out against her pleas.

Her stomach jumped when the outer door of her office jangled at eight fifty-five. The receptionist she shared with a family court attorney on the opposite side of the building wasn't due in until nine.

"Mr. Thomas?" she called as she went out to the deserted lobby.

"Rick." With that deep, assertive voice, he put more into one syllable than most people managed to cram into a paragraph.

Not that she was open to anything from him other than the facts that were going to help her win his case.

If there was one.

There'd been no message from the sheriff that morning.

Without another word, Rick handed her a folded brown bag. And, as she took it with a tissue between it and her hand, Rick Thomas nodded and turned to go.

"Wait." He couldn't just walk out on her like that.

Well…he could, of course. But they had to talk. If she was going to defend this man against a murder charge, she needed answers. A lot of them.

He was watching her.

"I… Where will you be?"

A raised eyebrow was the only answer she received.

"You aren't leaving town again, are you? I'd advise against it."

"I'm going to work." The hand he slid into his pocket stretched his jeans taut. "Until I'm told otherwise, I still have a job."

She had to figure this man out. *Now.*

"And if I get there and find out I don't, I'm going fishing."

"Locally?"

"For now." And then, "I'm not guilty, Erin." She'd given him permission to use her name. She hadn't expected it to sound so…so…deep. So— "If they indict me, I'll be here."

"Okay."

"I'm counting on you to do the rest."

"I'll need your help."

"Of course."

"We need to talk. There are things I need to know."

"If I'm indicted, we'll talk."

If this morning. Not *when*.

The man wasn't giving her anything he didn't have to.

"And when I get an answer on the prints?"

"Call my cell."

"Should I leave a message?"

His eyes narrowed and she was left feeling as though she'd just gained something, though with him it wouldn't be much. Or change much.

"No."

She nodded and didn't try to stop him a second time when he turned to walk out her door.

10

I'd seen David Abrams—the attorney I used to consider one of the good guys—at the local discount department store on Saturday. I'm not sure whether Maggie saw him or not. She didn't seem to. But I didn't take comfort in that. Maggie was skilled beyond her years at looking peaceful while tempests raged inside.

The man who'd had sex, multiple times in one day, with my fourteen-year-old foster daughter saw us. And immediately exited the premises—as was mandated by the strongly issued warning Samantha Jones had given him to stay away from Maggie. But I caught a glimpse of a certain something on his face as he saw Maggie— longing, maybe, or ownership—and I hadn't been able to relax since.

I didn't believe, as Maggie did, that David Abrams loved her. I knew better. A thirty-something father of four did not take the virginity of a fourteen-year-old girl he cared about.

I was not going to allow that man to sway my sweet girl

a second time. I wasn't mercenary as Maggie's biological mother had been. Nor was I desperate. I wasn't afraid to take him on. I didn't care who he knew, or where he had friends.

I did care that I couldn't be everywhere at once. I couldn't shadow Maggie at school, couldn't follow her every time she stepped foot outside our home. Even if I could make the physical arrangements—and I'd been tempted to try—I couldn't do that to the girl. I couldn't make her a prisoner in her own life or take away a trust she hadn't abused.

Camy, my doubly spoiled toy poodle now that Maggie had joined us, sat on the chair opposite me at our kitchen table, watching intently as I finished my tuna salad. I didn't always get home for lunch, but when I did, Camy liked to make me believe she should eat, as well.

I thought of her little heart, which would be overtaxed if she was overweight—and of the fact that poodles were prone to heart disease—and gained strength to withstand the pressure.

And was relieved when my phone rang. I grabbed it, eager when I saw the name reflected on the screen.

"Hello?" I didn't trust caller ID enough to offer a familiar greeting. There was always that off chance that someone else was using my contact's phone. The cops, maybe.

"It's Erin Morgan. Are you busy?"

Funny how the woman had called while I was talking myself into circles.

"I'm thankful for the rescue," I told her. "I'm in the middle of counseling myself."

Her burst of laughter made me smile, too.

"I take it you aren't a cooperative client?"

"I'm getting dizzy keeping track of who's talking."

"Sounds like you need a mediator."

"Or a rule book on the differences between counseling and parenting."

"Tell me about it." She groaned.

I picked up a pen from the middle of the table. Scribbled Erin's name on my napkin. "You've got parenting problems?" I asked. Erin had never been married. And as far as I knew, had never had a child, either.

But then, neither had I.

"I've got a question for you," the other woman said instead of responding. "But before I ask it, I want you to let me hire you…."

"You want me to hang up on you? Is that what you said?"

She sighed, and I understood. For some people asking for help was too easy. And for some of us it was pretty much like walking barefoot through fire.

I waited, hoping Erin would just ask her question.

"What did your counselor have to say to you this morning?" And the question gave real meaning to the cliché *Be careful what you hope for.*

"I'm not sure I was listening well enough to really notice," I said.

"What did you talk to her about?"

I thought for a second. I didn't confide in anyone. Never had.

But I was in over my head. If it were just me, I'd tough it out. But it wasn't just me anymore. I had a hurting and confused fourteen-year-old girl relying on me for… everything.

"Remember that lawyer I told you about?"

"The one your policewoman friend suspects is a drug lord?"

"Yeah. He…" There really were some things I couldn't

say. "I saw him during the weekend. At a store. I'm… afraid he wants Maggie."

"Does Maggie know?"

"I hope not."

"Did you warn her about him?"

"Not this time. She knows how I feel about him."

"And she knows to stay away from him, right?"

"Yes, but that doesn't mean she will."

"You don't trust her."

"I do." As I said the words, I recognized that they were true. "It's just that she really thinks she's in love with this man. She believes in him and thinks we're all lying about him because he's older than she is."

"And at fourteen, when you know everything, concern about the age difference appears grossly overblown."

Erin handled a lot of juvenile cases. And I remembered she'd had at least one case involving statutory rape. She'd told me about it the year before.

"Right," I said, glad to have my own thoughts reaffirmed. "But she *definitely* knows how I feel about him. And she knows I've forbidden her to see him."

"House rules."

"Uh-huh. But if I don't trust her, I'm sending her the message that she's not trustworthy," I said. "As a counselor, I'm supposed to question. As a parent, I need to give her my trust. Unless she proves otherwise…"

"I might be out of line here, but didn't you stop being her counselor when you became her parent?"

I dropped my pen. Could it really be that simple?

And that difficult, too. Because it meant I had to keep a vigilant watch over my young charge, but let her live her life, too.

"It would all be much easier if I could just live her life *for* her," I grumbled.

"Would it?" Erin's question had a serious tone. I picked up the pen. "It's one thing to make wrong decisions for your own life. Think how hard it would be to live with yourself if you made wrong choices for someone else."

"But can we ever really make choices for someone else if they won't let us?" I asked her. "I can tell Maggie what I want her to do. I can threaten. I can punish. But in the end, personal choice will always prevail. We each make our own choices—even the choice to let someone else make our choices for us."

The chuckle on the other end of the line made me smile again, too. I was still caught in my circles.

And then Erin said, "I have a question."

And I remembered she'd had a specific reason for calling. "What's that?"

Don't let friendship cloud your judgment, I jotted down.

"When is it selfish to go after what you want at the cost of others, as opposed to standing up for yourself and what *you* want and need?"

Ah. The fine line between emotional and moral health. And the inescapable fact that sometimes there was no line.

"My immediate, and not professional, answer would be that each situation has to be assessed independently."

"I gave you a simple answer to *your* dilemma," my new friend replied, half teasing.

"I know. But then you were familiar with some of the details. So…give me details."

After another brief pause Erin launched into a rundown of Noah's family situation.

Is Erin happy with the status quo? I wrote. And then Erin said, "Caylee is coming to me for advice. And her father just told me on Sunday that Caylee has started trusting me in place of Noah, and that he's okay with it. He's expecting me to convince Caylee to give up the scholarship.

"I don't know what to do," she said. "Is it best for the child to pursue her own personal desires or to serve her family? Which benefits her more in the long run?"

I wasn't Erin's therapist. And as with Maggie, I realized I had no idea how *not* to be one.

"If this was your decision, if you had to choose for yourself between the scholarship and your mother's possible well-being, what would you do?"

"I'd find a way to do both."

We talked about Caylee, about her options. And I wondered about Erin. After four years, her only life outside work was still as a member of Noah's family. Was that because of love or habit? Survivor's guilt or fear? Or some combination of all those emotions.

"How's work?" I asked when we'd agreed that life was damned hard and got stuck there.

"Fine," Erin said quickly. After a moment she added, "I've decided to keep that case I was talking to you about."

"Have they charged him, then?"

"No. I'm guessing they're still waiting on forensics. It isn't like New York City out here. We have one official lab that serves several counties."

"What made you decide to defend him?" I asked.

"There wasn't any one thing." Erin's hesitation struck a chord in me. I was learning just how cruel self-doubt could be. "I hope to God it's not his eyes."

"Well, as the cliché has it, sometimes a person speaks through his eyes."

"Yeah, and sometimes those eyes can lie very convincingly."

"If you think he's lying, why not turn him over to someone else?"

"Because I don't think he's lying."

"But you're not sure?"

"How can I be? What I'm *really* not sure about is why I'm suddenly not confident in my own judgment."

"Like I told you last week, questioning yourself isn't a bad thing. It's healthy. And wise. Just make sure you listen when you answer yourself."

A piece of advice I knew I needed as much as Erin.

Rick still had a job, but not because the agents working at the Temple EMA office wanted him there. If he had to guess, he figured his continued presence at the murder scene was a result of the red tape required to relieve him—a man who hadn't been charged with any crime—from his job. As he torched copper pipes, slathered them with plumber's putty and soldered their joints, Rick watched his back. And kept Charles's temporary replacement, a guy who'd introduced himself as Robbie Greene, under surveillance—by sight or sound—at all times. He didn't want another dead guy on his hands. And he didn't plan to be one, either.

Greene was easy to watch. He constantly asked what Rick was doing and Rick suspected the unsmiling man was guarding him on orders.

So he finished the bathroom plumbing. Turned on the water supply, satisfied when there were no leaks. And then he caulked. Spackled the drywall that would eventually be painted—by him, or so he liked to think. After lunch, a peanut butter sandwich he'd brought from home, he started cutting two-by-fours to frame the wall that would divide the rest of the space into two offices.

And he thought about the matchbook, considering it

from every conceivable angle. Brady wanted Rick to get a message from that innocuous little package.

Brady's prints, like Rick's, wouldn't be there—because they didn't exist. If Janet Meadows's were there, that would tell Rick something about the woman.

And what would she think if she'd looked inside the bag? Would she tell someone? More importantly, *who* would she tell?

What message could anyone get from a half-used book of matches?

The matchbook could be construed as a memento.

A couple of years earlier, during a rare few days filled with pleasures of the flesh—good food, good booze and a woman—he and Brady had taken a cruise on a luxury yacht provided for them through Sarge. It wasn't unusual for opportunities like that to appear for the use of the covert ops team members. While the government couldn't formally or openly acknowledge them, it did take care of them. A lot of the time through highly positioned businessmen who donated liberally and who sometimes pulled seemingly impossible strings so a job of critical importance could be done.

Men who, Rick figured, also had a lot of say in what governmental decisions were made.

He and Brady had assumed that yacht trip had been one such donation. Rick had just finished a two-month undercover expedition that had almost cost him his life. Brady had also completed a particularly grueling job involving Mexico's largest drug cartel.

During that one brief respite in fifteen years of service, he and Brady—as Tom and Jack to the world, Rick and Brady to each other—had pulled into a harbor in the Bahamas one night and smoked a pack of cigarettes between them at the beach bar named on the matchbook—The

Resting Place. At the end of the night, they'd tried to pay their tab, but were told it had been taken care of. Though they'd pressed the bartender, he'd never told them who their benefactor had been.

Brady was a man who, by necessity, had to travel lightly, a man of few possessions; he could have pocketed the half-used matchbook, a small memento, out of fondness for the good time. He could have passed it on to Rick for that reason—a reminder that there were enjoyable moments in life.

Or a reminder of the brotherhood the two loners had shared.

To Janet Meadows and anyone else who might know that Brady had given it to Rick, that parting gift could simply be a memento.

It *was* one.

But it was something else, as well.

Something Rick had yet to identify. What was its significance? As a code of some kind? A warning? A clue?

Metal joists were in place and drywall was up before Rick left that afternoon. Earlier than he'd planned. And not of his own accord.

Without being allowed to clean up his tools, he was escorted out just after three by a grim-faced sheriff with fully armed deputies flanking both sides.

11

"Who's Steve?" Erin was pissed off. She paced in front of her client as he sat slouched in one of two maroon upholstered chairs opposite the desk in her office. His worn jeans and untucked flannel shirt, his long hair and lazy posture, should have made the man look more like the criminal he might be. Or at least lazy and uncaring.

Instead, Erin felt as though she was facing a snake that could whip out and strike at any moment.

"I asked a question, Mr. Thomas."

His silent stare was a pretty unmistakable answer. And at eight o'clock on Monday evening, after a sleepless Sunday night, Erin was out of patience.

So she took a deep breath. Leaned against the edge of her desk and softened her tone.

"Rick, you had to know that when you gave me the information to post your bail, I'd find out that someone else's name was on that account."

"I'm paying you well to clear my name," he said.

Erin's feet hurt. Still in the suit and pumps she'd worn that morning when she'd met Rick to take delivery of the evidence he found in his home, she had yet to have dinner.

She hadn't eaten lunch, either. Unless granola bars counted.

But Clyde was home—all charges against him dropped. He wasn't allowed within five hundred feet of his wife, under the temporary restraining order that had to wait a week before it could become a permanent order. But Laura Jane wasn't allowed near him, either.

Caylee had called. And Ron, too. Both were upset and expecting her to call back. She understood. Luckily Caylee was a late-night person.

"I can't clear your name when you're withholding information from me," Erin explained. She would *not* get a headache. Not tonight.

"I'm withholding nothing that matters to you. Nothing that could possibly be tied to Charles's murder."

"How can you be sure of that? Until we know what happened, we don't know what's pertinent."

"Agreed. But the money I used to post bail has been sitting in an account that has existed for fifteen years. There is no connection."

She wanted to help this man. And had to assume that he had no idea how difficult he was making her task.

"You're going to have to trust me, Rick."

He blinked. "I do."

Uh-huh. "Then tell me who Steve is. Trust me to figure out what's pertinent and to leave the rest alone."

"You will leave Steve alone. Period."

"His last name is different from yours. Is he family?"

She got what appeared to be Rick Thomas's standard answer. A silent stare that made her feel smaller than she was.

"Sometimes the less said, the better," Erin said, crossing her ankles. "Like when you're talking to anyone but me. But right now saying less could very well get you convicted."

"I have no motive."

"They'll find one."

"There isn't one to find."

"Then they'll make one up."

Because the justice system wasn't always about truth, it was about who could come up with the best argument…

Erin halted that thought. Filed it away for later. Maybe.

"I'm going to do a search on a secure database I have access to."

"Not on my dime, you aren't. There'll be hundreds of Steve Millers."

"Then save me the time. Because I can guarantee you the other side will want to know who paid your bail. They'll want to know everyone you're connected to. Which leaves me ill-prepared and unable to defend whatever suppositions they present."

The man must be a masochist. He must want to shell out thousands of dollars to Erin for a long-drawn-out trip to life in prison.

"They'll subpoena the bank records of the account the bail was drawn from."

"It's not in my name."

"It's an account *you* just used. Your name is on a debit card attached to it. Remember, they're going to be looking for motive. Money is a good one. Could be someone paid you to make the hit on Charles."

"I did not kill Charles."

"But a warrant to access records to search for a large deposit will be granted."

Chin raised, he peered at her. "Let them search. There's nothing for them to find."

Sitting forward, Rick reached around her, tore the top sheet off a notepad on the edge of her desk, his arm almost touching her hip as he grabbed the pen in the note holder. He sat back and wrote a few lines on the paper.

"Here," he said, handing her the note. "There's my banking information. Bank. Online user ID and password. You go ahead and have a look. You'll see every deposit I've made, every bill I've paid, how much I have in savings, and how often and where I use my debit card. Plus how much I've withdrawn. It's all there. Have at it."

Finally. Information she needed. Given freely. So why did Erin feel as though she'd somehow violated this taciturn man as she took the paper with the full intention of visiting the site before she slept again.

And still he was hiding something. She had to know what. And why. And to assume that the prosecution was going to find out whatever it was.

"You said you don't have any family."

"Have you heard anything back on the prints?"

"Not yet. Who's Steve?"

"At the arraignment, the judge read the charge as second-degree murder. Did the grand jury receive any evidence other than the report on the knife found in my home?"

"The knife found in your home was the murder weapon."

"Without my prints."

"You don't have prints. Who's Steve?"

"What else does this prosecutor, this Christa Hart, think she has?"

"You know everything I know at this point."

"What about this woman, Hart? What's she like?"

"Plays by the book. Until she can't win that way and then she doesn't."

"What about our judge? Castillo?"

"Hard. Nothing lenient about him. But fair."

"I didn't expect to have to post a cash bond."

Which explained the use of a bank account he didn't want to discuss. "I think the idea was to keep you in jail."

"Then why offer bail at all?"

"I'm not sure," she admitted. "Frankly I expected to have to fight for you on that one."

"I didn't do anything wrong."

"We have to prove that."

"What happened to innocent until proven guilty?"

Nice words. Erin defended them on a daily basis. But the system she worked with tended more toward guilty until proven innocent.

Right until cases went out to their juries.

"Don't worry, counselor," Rick said, drawing out the word as if they were on some television law drama. "I know the score."

She doubted it. He'd be a hell of a lot more worried—and more cooperative—if he had any idea how determined Johnson and his people were to get him for the death of a Temple native.

"Who's Steve Miller?"

He stood. "Call me if you hear anything more. I've got things to do."

"They're going to find him."

He didn't respond.

It might be dark and cold and after nine, but Rick's day was far from over.

He retrieved his truck, which had been towed and

conveniently parked in a private lot behind the jail, probably with Sheriff Johnson hoping he'd soon have the go-ahead to sell the vehicle. Then Rick stopped by the EMA office. The building was manned around the clock and he wanted his tools.

Turned out he didn't have to interrupt whoever was on duty inside. His belongings were tossed haphazardly out the back door. The blade on his jigsaw was busted. His table saw on its side. The electrical toolbox was open with the color-coded connectors on the ground rather than stored neatly in their plastic compartments. The plumber's toolbox was relatively intact, though. All the compression fittings were in their slots according to size.

It took him only a couple of minutes to verify that nothing was missing. Not even a tape measure.

And another twenty to pack everything into the back of his truck.

He thought about knocking on the door to let whoever was on duty know he'd been by, but didn't bother. Chances were the guy had been watching him since he'd pulled into the lot.

And if he hadn't, he should've been.

After all, Rick had just been charged with the murder of one of the guy's associates.

So why was he out on bail? Granted, the amount had been high enough that no one had expected him to be able to ante up. But whoever was behind this was no amateur. He'd been found.

Someone from his past had to be orchestrating the whole thing. The setup. Charles's murder. The knife in Rick's home. Someone from his past had found him. And whoever had managed to do that, had to know his net worth, as well.

Which brought him back to the original question.

Why was he out on bail?

There was only one obvious answer. Because he—or they—wanted Rick to do something. Or appear to do something.

So…was he supposed to lead them to someone? Or something?

Was he going to be contacted? Threatened with life imprisonment, or worse, if he didn't do a job for someone?

Or… With a grim face he drove out of the EMA lot. Or was he being set up to take another fall? A bigger fall? One he couldn't be blamed for if he had an alibi—like jail.

Rick pulled his cell phone out of the pocket of the leather jacket he'd put on after loading his tools. Hit speed dial. And asked for Angela Markham.

"Hi, Mr. Thomas, is everything okay?"

"Fine, Angela. How's Steve?"

"Sleeping soundly. He had a busy day. Jill helped them make kites. Steve was the first one to get his airborne and was out there all afternoon. We had to bribe him with chocolate cake for dessert to get him to come in and eat dinner."

Rick wouldn't have used a bribe. He'd simply have told Steve it was time to go in. Period. And that if he didn't, he would not be flying his kite tomorrow. Once Steve knew there was no room for negotiation, he was generally amenable.

Jill and Angela and everyone else he'd met at Lakeside Family Care just wanted to keep Steve happy. They were good people. Kind. Most importantly, they cared about Steve.

"I need you to do me a favor."

"Sure," the young woman said. "What is it?"

"I was arrested today." Rick stated the facts with no emotion attached. That was the way he got through life. "I'm innocent and they're working on clearing things up quickly, but in the meantime, I don't want any word of this to get to Steve. It probably won't hit the news, but I'd appreciate it if you could block the news stations on his television for the moment."

"He doesn't watch the news, anyway, but I'll put in an order in the morning."

"And if someone comes to Lakeside asking questions, keep him away from Steve. I don't want anyone, except staff and residents, anywhere near him."

That meant Steve would have to be kept in a restricted area for now, but so be it. Lakeside was a secure facility, which was one of the reasons Steve was there.

"Got it."

Steve Miller—as Erin was probably going to find out since she had the actual account number—was the full beneficiary of monies that had been put in a trust.

Rick managed the trust. But his name was privileged information. Sarge had arranged that when Rick left the army.

Even so, he didn't like the fact that there was any connection to him at all, but the money had to be in Steve's name to insure that the man was cared for in the event of Rick's untimely death.

And Rick had access to that account for one simple reason. He didn't trust another living soul with the management of his money.

"I don't think they'll bother him," Rick told Angela. He and Sarge had made damn sure no one would make the connection between him and Steve. And in fifteen years, no one had. "I don't want to take any chances," Rick added.

Chances, like he'd taken that afternoon, drawing on the account he'd set up for Steve's care. But it was the only one that had the amount of cash he needed. Even if they got a judge to issue some kind of special clearance that would reveal Steve's identity, his address would tell them that Steve was of no use in court.

Rick knew that.

He was just being paranoid. Overprotective.

For the first time as an adult, Rick wasn't in complete control. There were always unknowns in life, but Rick was usually one of them—not a victim of them.

Until he figured out what was going on, if his identity had been breached, if someone knew that Rick Thomas and Tom Watkins were the same man, until he understood why he was suddenly faced with defending himself against a murder he didn't commit, he was going to act as though the worst had happened.

That one of his many, many enemies had found him.

And would stop at nothing to make his life a living hell.

One thing was certain. If they'd simply wanted him dead, they'd have killed him by now.

"And, Angela," he said just before he hung up. "If for some reason I don't make it by, tell Steve I'm working."

"We always do," the woman said, her tone filled with as much compassion as cheer. "When he's missing you, it's the one excuse that seems to appease him, to make sense to him."

With Steve's lack of ability to discern the passage of time, he could be missing Rick ten minutes after a visit. Or go ten days without asking about him.

"I know you do." Rick spoke softly, though he was alone in his truck. "I'm saying that if I don't make it by again—ever—tell Steve I'm working."

Steve's bills would be paid. Permanently. Rick had already made that arrangement a long time ago.

"Are you sure you're okay, Mr. Thomas? Is there someone I can call? Something we can do?"

"I'm fine," he assured her, ending the call as he turned off toward the privately owned marina he'd visited the day before, to prepay, in cash, for a boat that would be waiting for him. If he hadn't shown up tonight, the guy would've kept the cash.

The keys to the small motorized fishing boat were exactly where he'd been told he'd find them. The gas tank was full.

A can of fresh worms waited in the bottom of the boat. Grabbing his rod and tackle box from the truck and exchanging his leather jacket for an insulated hunting suit, Rick set out for a night of fishing—and a rendezvous.

12

Rick Thomas was playing the stock market. And doing quite well at it. In her favorite soft robe and big furry slippers, Erin lounged in the corner of her sectional couch, looking out over the darkness of the lake beyond, listening to the sound of the waves through the window she'd opened a crack. Studying the screen on her laptop, she followed his buying and selling patterns over the past year.

He'd started with a conservative ten thousand dollars. Had withdrawn twenty-five thousand. And still had eleven. Not bad for a construction worker in a down economy.

Erin reached for the toast sitting next to her on a paper towel. Toast with peanut butter might not be a balanced meal, but it had protein. And it suited her just fine.

Especially since the glass of wine was covering the fruit and vegetable group.

She had a call into Caylee.

She was also running a program, on another screen, that gave her a list of Steve Millers. She was trying to narrow her search to those with connections in Chicago, since the bail money had been drawn from a Chicago account.

You could tell a lot from a man's bank account. Like the fact that he was responsible. Organized. Paid his bills online on the same dates every month. He kept two hundred dollars in his checking account and, if he made extra in a week, moved it into a savings account that was substantial enough to carry him for a year or more.

He had no frivolous expenses. Not even cable TV, although the amount he paid for his cell phone indicated that he probably had online browsing services.

Utilities were about the same every single month, not fluctuating much between summer and winter.

He did his grocery shopping every two weeks, spending between seventy-five and one hundred dollars every time.

His bar bill was a little more sporadic; sometimes he drank twice a week, sometimes not at all. And his tab was never more than twenty dollars.

He didn't seem to carry much cash with him.

And didn't do a whole lot for entertainment, either. Except rent a boat now and then. Or buy fishing bait.

So what did the guy do with his free time? He didn't go anywhere. Didn't do anything except fish. He didn't even sit at home and watch sports channels, since he didn't subscribe to any.

So if he did kill Charles Cook, money was probably not the motive.

He could have an offshore account. Could've made a big deposit there if he'd received payment for a hit—

Erin stopped those thoughts. She'd agreed to defend Rick, not to doubt him.

She scrolled through more search results on Rick Thomas.

And froze, just as the phone rang.

It was Caylee.

A call she had to take.

Rick welcomed the cold, the fresh air, as he bobbed quietly in an alcove not far from the lighthouse that marked the cliff bank where Sarge would be if he'd been able to get away.

Rick's line was in the water. He watched the bobber when he could make it out in the moonlight.

He'd pulled in a decent-size smallmouth bass. And a few blue gill. He'd kept the bass. They were good grilled. And proof that he'd been fishing. The blue gill he tossed back.

And he focused on the murder of Charles Cook—listening not so much to the words in his head as to the feeling in his gut.

He tended to assume the worst. He'd found it a prudent way to stay alive.

But if he wasn't careful, it could also blind him to the truth.

This whole setup, Charles's murder, the weapon planted in Rick's home, could just be some local yokel who had it in for Charles and saw Rick—a loner construction worker with no history in town—as an easy target to take the fall for him. And that person would've had no way of knowing that Rick was anything other than what he seemed to be.

So why had they stipulated a cash bail? If they'd thought he was a construction worker with a blue-collar bank account, and they'd wanted to keep him in jail, simply setting such a large amount of bail would've served that purpose. As Rick Thomas, he didn't have enough assets to use as collateral to raise that amount of money. If they'd just been dealing with Rick Thomas, there would've been no reason to stipulate a cash bail.

At least, not that he could see.

And if the hit wasn't a professional job, not a ghost from Tom's past, then someone from the sheriff's office would have to be in on the scheme. How else could the perpetrator have gained access to Rick's bedroom to plant that knife?

There'd been no sign of forced entry.

But why would someone want an under-the-radar guy like Charles dead?

Who stood to benefit?

Forgetting his bobber, Rick turned to the touch screen on his phone, accessing the internet and typing in the name Charles Cook. With his membership on some intelligence websites, a once-a-year investment, he had access to public records.

He knew Charles wasn't married. Apparently never had been. Forty-five years old and the man had only had two addresses. The home in Temple he'd been born in and the one that was now owned by his estate, which was now in limbo, since he'd left no will—or any apparent heirs.

There were no bankruptcies or foreclosures. No court cases. No criminal records.

When he did a general search he found a copy of a local newspaper article naming Charles as a member of the parish committee that had been in charge of bringing in a new minister to a local church.

And that was it.

But Rick needed more.

His life could very well depend on it.

"Noah used to tell me that in any situation, if I listened to my heart, I'd never go wrong."

Standing in front of her wall of windows, gazing out into the darkness, Erin rubbed the back of her neck. She and Caylee had been talking for more than half an hour, with Erin doing a lot of listening and mostly giving placebo responses.

Because she didn't have answers.

Or because she was afraid to give them?

"Sounds like good advice," she said now. Ron Fitzgerald had trusted his son's judgment.

"Yeah, well, the problem is that I am in love with Daniel, who doesn't want me to pursue any kind of college education, let alone one at Yale. I love my mother, and we both know what she wants. So I try to listen to that love. To find peace in the idea of staying in Temple, marrying Daniel and having babies. But I start to panic before I even get to the wedding."

"I don't think listening to your heart means simply following the dictates of those you love."

"What *do* you think, Erin?" Caylee asked in exasperation. "All this talking and I still don't know. What would you do if you were me?"

"I'm not you," she said. "You guys are all the family I have, Caylee. You know that. And I love you all so much. This rift between you and your dad, and maybe your mom... I don't know what to do. I didn't grow up in a big family. As a matter of fact, I didn't have much of a family at all. Just me and my dad. And then just me."

"That's exactly why I want to hear your thoughts." The young woman's words didn't ease Erin's tension. "You have a different perspective. You aren't so tied down by generations of one pew at church. I can't seem to separate myself from the obligations I've grown up with. I can't figure out if I'm just being selfish by needing this opportunity at Yale or if, by passing it up, I'd be unhappy and dissatisfied for the rest of my life."

Go. Erin almost said it. But she didn't.

What if her response contributed to the eventual death of Noah's mom?

What if, when Caylee got to Yale, she found that she didn't fit in? What if the girl really did belong in Temple? What if her happiness was right here? What if the people who loved Caylee knew that about her?

"Erin? You still there?"

"Yes." Turning, Erin settled on the couch, resting her head against the back cushion. Her conversation with Kelly Chapman came back to her.

"What I'd do, if I couldn't give up on either option, would be to find a way to make both work," she said.

"Go to Yale *and* stay here and get married? How on earth would I do that? Cut myself in half?"

"I don't know how to do it, Cay, or I'd tell you."

"So you don't think I should go to Yale?"

"I didn't say that."

"Then you think I should."

"I didn't say that, either."

"I know. You aren't saying anything. What I don't understand is why not."

Erin didn't understand herself. She knew what she'd do. She could tell Caylee.

But she didn't.

Erin had barely hung up—hadn't even pulled her computer back on her lap—when the phone rang a second time.

Rick Thomas. At eleven-fifteen at night.

"What's up?" she asked as she pushed the call button on her smartphone.

Smartphone. At least there was something about her with a semblance of intelligence.

"What do you know about Charles Cook?"

"He worked hard," she said. "Took good care of his house. Liked to hunt and fish. That's about it."

"Can you do some checking? Find out if maybe the guy was into something that pissed someone off?"

"You mean, find out who really killed him?" she asked.

"Yes."

"I've already got someone working on it," Erin said. She'd made the call that afternoon—and would've told Rick if he'd hadn't walked out of her office.

"Who?"

"A guy from Reed City. He's done some work for me before. I trust him."

"Any ties to Sheriff Johnson?"

"No."

"Or to any of his deputies?"

"No."

"Fine, then. Let me know what you find out."

"I planned to."

"And send me the bill."

"I intend to."

"Thank you. Good night—"

"Wait—"

Erin stared at the display on her phone—at the little letters call disconnected.

He had until tomorrow. And then he was going to tell her who Steve Miller was.

Tonight she'd give him a break because it was late.

And because she'd just found out that he'd lost his only brother in the same accident that had killed his father. He'd been eighteen at the time.

* * *

Rick hadn't really expected to see the nondescript aluminum boat come around the ridge. But he stood, letting the hand on his gun drop when he saw Sarge give him the familiar salute—the only form of greeting the man ever gave.

Rick, who hadn't seen his sergeant since before he went to prison, returned the gesture. And waited, without a word, as the older man, dressed in his usual black jacket and beige slacks, boarded Rick's boat and took a seat.

With one hand on the wheel, he let the engine idle and guided the boat along the cliff—far enough away to keep afloat, but close enough to stay hidden from above.

And then, in two sentences, he gave his report.

"Shit." That single word, instead of the colorful string of curses the sergeant would more typically have uttered, was not a good sign.

"Tell me," Rick said, frowning as he and Sarge looked at each other.

Two hard men, trained in special operations—men who'd killed and had blood on their souls.

"Woodburn is dead." Saul. Which left Rick the only living member of their team of four. Besides Sarge, of course.

Rick felt nothing. The same nothing he'd been feeling since he'd seen Charles Cook's dead body on the floor at the Emergency Management Agency and Homeland Security office.

His mind cranked up, thoughts flying rapid-fire, organizing themselves into lists of suspects. Motives. Safety measures.

"Someone knows about us."

Sarge didn't say anything. His pursed lips and unblinking stare were answer enough.

"When did Woodburn get it?" Jack had been dead for more than a year.

"Three months ago. In Tennessee."

In Tennessee. Another boarding house. Another widow in another town with another room to let. In Tennessee—Kit Matthews's residence, not Saul Woodburn's.

"Did you find anything?"

"No."

"How'd it happen?"

"Drove his car over a mountain. Sheriff's report said he was drunk. But I didn't find any alcohol or bar receipts when I collected his things."

"Woodburn didn't drink."

Not ever. How the man had survived the life, slept at night, without a little whiskey now and then to drown the memories, to slow down the instincts, Rick had no idea.

He hadn't known Woodburn all that well. Saul—Kit—had specialized in human trafficking, and their paths hadn't crossed as often as his and Brady's had. Sarge had been the only one Woodburn had ever warmed to.

"I'm sorry," Rick said now. Rick had lost a work associate. Sarge had lost another friend.

"It happens," was all the man said. His bent shoulders, the glistening eyes, told another story.

One of which they wouldn't speak.

"You talk to Sharon Hampton?" Rick asked. Kit Matthews's landlady.

"Yes."

"She didn't say anything? Have any message for you?" Rick thought of the matchbook. A message from Brady? Until he knew for sure, he couldn't say anything to anyone about that matchbook. Brady had left it to him—specifically—and only to him. Their covert team protocol stated that he couldn't talk about it until he knew he wouldn't be putting other lives, including Sarge's, in jeopardy.

"No."

"Was she suspicious?"

"No."

"Maybe I should pay her a visit."

"Couldn't hurt."

They were getting a little close to shore. Rick steered the boat out several feet. "What's going on, Sarge?"

"I wish to hell I knew."

13

"If someone wants us all dead, why take us out a year apart?"

"Why kill the others and frame you?"

"And what are their plans for *you?*"

"We have to assume that our cover is blown. Someone is on to us." The sergeant's voice was low. Gravelly. And calm. "Brady and Saul were still working as part of the team when they died, but you've been out for a year. The fact that you're the target tells me this goes way back. We have to assume you're next."

"Agreed."

"And that whoever's after us is as sophisticated, as highly trained, as highly connected, as we were."

Rick had already come to that conclusion.

"We're on our own. Chances are they're not."

"But do we have to be?" Rick hadn't just called Sarge to commiserate. And he'd long since passed the day when he asked anyone for advice.

"What does that mean?"

"Call our people. Get us connected again." Sarge was the only one who could. He'd been the point man. The only visible member of their team. The contact with "their people."

Sarge just stared at him.

"What?"

"I quit special ops right after Kit died. The team was gone and I wasn't going to start all over. I'm just regular army now."

Shit. "Get back in."

"I can't. You know that."

"Call someone. My God, man, you have connections to the top."

Sarge shook his head. "Now that we've disbanded, the new secretary of defense isn't acknowledging that our team ever existed."

And a new president had taken office just before Rick had quit. One who probably hadn't been briefed on their small task force.

"I had a secure line. I no longer have it," Sarge added.

"What about outside connections? Businessmen with clout?"

"I was never directly connected to any of them."

"What about the yacht? The little vacation Brady and I had…"

"I don't know who owned that yacht."

"You said it was Roberts." A rich businessman they'd once investigated for large-scale drug and illegal weapon trafficking and had ultimately saved when they discovered he'd been set up by his disgruntled son. Roberts, Junior, had been in the trafficking business and was now, thanks to them, serving several life terms in jail.

"What I said was that a benefactor had provided the yacht.

Rick thought back. A benefactor. The mysterious

Roberts had been that. Had he made an incorrect assumption?

But Brady had, too. They'd referred to Roberts during those few days. Toasting him.

"I let the powers that be know that I needed a yacht and a few days of protected R and R for the two of you," Sarge said.

"Protected?"

"That's right. You were guarded the entire time."

"And the woman Brady took up with?"

"She was provided, too—by the owner of the yacht, I assume. There was also supposed to have been one for you."

Rick shrugged. As he recalled, Maria, Brady's companion, had had a friend. Rick hadn't been interested. "Why?"

"Brady had just killed a young kid, a girl. Did you know that?"

"No."

"He'd been shot at in the Mexican desert, was returning fire when a four-year-old girl came running out from what was supposed to have been a deserted building."

No wonder Brady had been so set on staying drunk.

"He wanted out right then and there. I knew if the two of you were together for a few days, Brady would pull through."

"I had no idea."

"You weren't meant to."

But Brady had saved a matchbook they'd used during those days of R and R, his days of recovery. So maybe the matchbook really had been just a memento. A thank-you.

Rick would bet his life it was not.

"Who else knew about that trip?"

"Other than the agents who made sure no one messed with you, only the two women." Only one of them had ever been to the yacht. Brady's woman. Maria.

What about that trip was so important to Brady? Something he'd expect Rick to know about...

Rick had to find the woman.

And they needed access to inaccessible information. Secure information. Who owned the yacht?

"Surely, after fifteen years, there's *someone* you know. Someone you can call."

"I've already made a couple of calls," Sarge said.

Rick waited.

"After I got your message I put in a call regarding the Temple EMA office."

"And?"

"Word is there've been a couple of emails removed from the secure server."

"Removed when?"

"Over the weekend."

"To frame me?"

"Could be. Doesn't look like it. If it had been before the murder, maybe. But afterward, you damned sure couldn't get into that building."

"Who did?"

"It's not so much access to the building that was necessary. Whoever removed the posts had to have access to the secure server *after* the murder, which you didn't."

Frowning, Rick eyed his sergeant. "Something's going on inside Homeland Security?"

"Could be."

"You're thinking terrorist threat here?"

"I'm thinking I don't know."

"And that we're somehow tied to it?"

"It's conceivable. Collectively, with the human trafficking we've exposed, the drug cartels we've broken, the weapons we've confiscated, the four of us have done a lot of damage to a lot of people."

"I know Tom Watkins's contacts. Do you have a log of the rest?"

"Not officially, no."

Of course not.

"I'd say that's where we need to start."

Reaching into his pocket, Sarge pulled out a flip phone and tossed it to Rick. "It's scrambled," he said. "I'll call you with a list of names. Don't answer. I'll leave a message you can decipher. And then pray like hell."

Erin had a felony assault case Tuesday morning. She met her client, a young man who'd gone after his sister's ex-boyfriend when he'd found out that the man had date-raped her. It only took Erin half an hour to work a deal, getting him down to misdemeanor assault with six months' suspended sentence and a year's probation. If he stayed clean, his record would be expunged. The ex-boyfriend had been charged with rape.

The twenty-year-old, his mother and his eighteen-year-old sister were all in tears, and his father looked close to them, as they thanked her and said goodbye outside the Ludington courtroom.

She was on her cell, calling Ben Pope, the private investigator in Reed City who was as discreet as he was good at ferreting out information, before she got to the bottom of the courthouse steps.

Pope called her back an hour later.

"I've barely begun, but I got a hit already and it's pertinent enough to let you know right away."

Erin, who'd just arrived back at work, shut the door of her office. "Thanks, Ben. What've you got?"

"I showed Cook's picture to a guy I know. He recognized it. Said Cook bought a semiautomatic nine millimeter a couple of weeks ago."

"He's with the office of Emergency Management. Wouldn't he have access to weapons, anyway?"

"Not Cook. He was an emergency management technician. His primary job was to manage sites during emergencies. Winter weather emergencies, for instance. Natural disasters. That kind of thing. He was responsible for setting up aid sites, coordinating agencies, keeping the government informed. He had EMT training. No weapons training. He could be sent anywhere, but never actually left Michigan. During nonemergency times he was supposed to check incoming data and so on. And beyond all that, he didn't buy this gun legally. That's what caught my attention. He didn't want anyone to know he had it."

"He was afraid of something."

"Maybe. Or angry with someone."

"Charles didn't seem the type."

"I'm not deep enough into this to know his 'type.' Not yet. I'll get back to you when I do."

"Thanks, Ben."

Hanging up, Erin started to dial Rick Thomas and then, remembering the night before, when he'd ended the call so abruptly, she stopped. Clearly, if she hoped to get answers to her questions, she had to meet with her very frustrating client face-to-face.

Rick stayed on the boat most of the night. He wanted to dock, with a line full of fish, after the marina caretaker had arrived at work to ensure his alibi. He also wanted to give Sarge time to get out of the state.

And he needed the peace.

With the temperature dropping to forty-five degrees—

downright balmy—he even managed to doze for an hour or two.

He caught another hour on Steve's couch while Steve went to an occupational therapy class. They were teaching him how to do simple assembly jobs.

He spent the rest of the morning flying a kite Steve helped him make, smiling as the older man took such obvious pleasure from making it soar.

When lunchtime rolled around, he walked Steve to the cafeteria and said goodbye. Having noticed the brownies he was getting for dessert, Steve didn't cry.

Before Rick left, he returned to Steve's room to grab the jigsaw puzzle he'd hidden in the back of his closet more than a year ago.

Watching his rearview mirror as he took side roads back to town, Rick ran a mental check, again, on all the jobs he could remember over the past fifteen years. Focusing on those that were out of the country, but not bypassing the domestic jobs, either.

He was looking for anyone who might have a grudge. Anyone who might be suspicious. Anyone who'd want him dead.

Making a list of jobs that fit those criteria wasn't hard.

Harder was finding ones that didn't.

Tom's work, whether infiltrating a business, becoming part of it to gather enough evidence so someone else could come in and make arrests, or outright stealing things from those who trusted him, hadn't been nice. If the job had been easy, anyone could've done it. Which was why Steve Miller had a bank account that could take the outrageous bail hit without much pain.

The tires whirred a steady rhythm as he drove.

His attorney should be getting some information on

Cook for him. And he'd have a coded list from Sarge within hours, as well.

He drove straight through town, slowing down on Main Street to make sure he was seen, and then turned toward his place. It was a quiet, sunny Tuesday afternoon. The type of day that bothered Rick.

Because it could lull you into a false sense of security.

Because he couldn't see what was happening in the dark corners.

Because something always was….

His fingers tensed on the wheel as he pulled into his drive. Someone had been there in his absence. There were fresh tire marks in the dirt an inch to the left of the tracks he'd made the day before.

Tracks that were as large as his.

The front of the house appeared undisturbed. The small clear plastic bag with the advertising flyer was right where he'd last seen it—hanging from the screen door handle.

Someone had been in the back. Sometime the previous night, before dew had gathered in the grass, based on the moisture pooled in one set of male-size footprints. Maneuvering his truck slowly, Rick steered with his right hand, opening the panel behind the driver's door with his left. Seconds later, his hand wrapped around the barrel of his loaded gun.

Whoever had driven up here and walked across his lawn toward his home could have come and gone.

Or a vehicle could have dropped someone off, left him behind.

If someone was there, chances were he knew Rick was outside.

Crouching as he put the truck in park, in case of a flying bullet, Rick kept the vehicle running and opened the door just enough to slide his foot down to the ground. With the door shielding his back, he pointed his gun through the truck to the house, and looked to the left, surveying the ground in that direction and then, through the side mirror, the area to the right.

Slowly, moving in small bursts, hiding first behind steel and tire, and then trees, he made his way toward the house.

He was one tree away when he heard something. Barely discernible. Maybe the rustling of a slight breeze in the bare twigs on trees that had shed their leaves weeks ago.

Or someone moving.

The side of the house was two feet away. With his back to the tree, his gun held at chest level and pointed straight out, Rick rounded the truck. Bringing the gun closer, he darted over to the house. He looked right. Left. And keeping his body against the house, he let his gun lead him to the door.

It was undisturbed—the screen door not quite latched, just as he'd left it. Switching his gun to his other hand, still aimed, he pulled the aluminum handle, held the screen with his foot and yanked his keys from the back pocket of his jeans. Key in the lock of the heavy wooden door, he turned slowly. Then he gently pushed the door with his toe, edging into the mudroom at the back of his home.

A drawer in the storage cabinet was a quarter of an inch out of place. Steaks were on the left side of the freezer instead of the right.

The kitchen faucet was turned to the right. Rick always kept it to the left.

It was the same throughout the house. A rug was slightly askew. The pull handle on a drawer in the living room was hanging down instead of facing up as he always left it. For just this purpose.

Clues to tell him that someone had invaded his space.

And there were jimmy marks on the bathroom window.

A pair of his shoes had been removed from the metal shoe tree and put back—toes straight up instead of slightly in.

But the security alarm hadn't been triggered. Not that *that* meant a lot.

A professional, someone like Rick, could have dismantled the thing in any number of ways. He didn't rely on it.

He'd had the alarm installed for much the same reason he wore his seat belt. A little extra precaution just in case.

Rick didn't need long to check the house. Whoever had been here was gone.

There'd been nothing for them—the person or persons who'd broken in—to take.

He figured they'd accomplished exactly what they wanted—they'd told him they knew where he lived. That they could invade his space, get to him whenever they wanted. That they could run their hands over his things. Look at everything he had. He was theirs.

They'd let him know without giving him anything to report to the authorities.

He'd rather have come in to find guns pointing at him.

14

Rick was in no mood for a second visitor that day. He'd popped the top on a beer and, jigsaw puzzle in hand, was sitting down at the table in what was designed to be a formal dining room but was now just a room with a table in it. He'd almost begun to relax—as much as he ever did—when he heard tires crunching along his gravel drive.

Storing the puzzle back on the shelf of his coat closet, Rick glanced out through the living room drapes that came with the house.

He'd seen the four-door dark blue Lexus before. Parked outside Erin Morgan's office.

And outside the sheriff's office, too.

Lowering the hand that had been poised by the gun holstered beneath his flannel shirt, Rick debated whether or not he was going to open the door. Even while he knew he would.

He had to. The bad news was that, right now, he needed Erin Morgan far more than she needed him.

Not a position Rick Thomas ever allowed himself to be in. Not a position he could tolerate.

But there it was.

* * *

He opened the front door just as she raised her hand to knock. Quelling the butterflies in her stomach, Erin dropped her shaking hand. What was the matter with her?

She didn't scare easily.

And after years of dealing with prisons and criminals and facing judges, she didn't get nervous, either.

Rick Thomas was dressed almost identically to the day before, except that the red plaid shirt had been exchanged for a blue one and his jeans were newer, a little less faded. He stood there without greeting or acknowledging her.

"Can I come in?"

He hesitated and she wondered what he had to hide. What had he been doing? What was going on inside that quiet nondescript house?

The lock on the screen door clicked and she stepped back as it pushed outward. And then stepped inside.

The place smelled…sterile. No cooking odors. No coffee. No pets or room deodorizers. Looked sterile, too. White walls. No adornment. Anywhere. Not on the walls. Or tables. Hell, there wasn't even a piece of lint on the plush beige carpet.

He led her down a small foyer to a living room that boasted a couch, a chair and a couple of matching end tables. The couches were sandy brown, microfiber. The tables solid wood stained to match. A small flat-screen television sat on a cart, made of the same wood as the tables—and that was it. No pictures or magazines. No movies on the cart. No cable or satellite box. She already knew he didn't subscribe to a television service. And now she knew he hadn't tapped into an existing line illegally, either.

If the television had a remote control, it was put away somewhere.

"Nice place you have here," she said before she could stop herself. She'd die if she had to come home to this nothingness every night. It would suffocate her, deny her need for beauty. For individuality.

"Thank you."

He hadn't seemed to notice her sarcasm. Thank goodness. It wasn't like her to be rude.

Whether it was the doubts that were driving her to act so out of character, or this man, she didn't know. But she wouldn't do it again.

He didn't invite her to sit, so she chose the chair. Set her purse down beside her and opened the leather-bound folder that held her legal pad and the pen she'd been using since before she'd started law school.

It had been a gift from her father. Purchased online with the minimal funds he'd earned working in the prison kitchen.

"Who is Steve Miller?"

Hands in his pockets he stood over her. Erin didn't care. She wasn't leaving without answers.

"I cannot represent you if you're going to keep secrets from me." She repeated the mental conversation they'd had on her way over.

"You can rest assured that I'll tell you everything you need to know."

"Based on my assessment or yours?"

His silence wasn't going to win this time.

"If you want me to continue representing you, it has to be based on *my* assessment of what I need to know."

Still nothing.

She clipped her pen to her folder. Closed it. Picked up her purse and—

"Okay."

"Okay what?"

"I'll tell you everything you feel you need to know. Based on *your* assessment."

He was staring straight at her, those dark eyes seeming to penetrate hers. His face was shadowed, like he needed to shave, but it had looked exactly the same way each time she'd seen him.

Everything about this man was dark. Shadowed.

Or was it just her? With her perceptions about her own life these days.

Was her reaction to Rick Thomas due to the fact that he was the player on the stage of her personal crisis? Or was it the man himself?

"What I need to know, first, is who is Steve Miller? And why was he willing to risk such a large amount of money to get you out of jail?"

Rick turned away. Walked over to the window. But rather than standing right in front of it, gazing out, as she would have done—as most people would have—he stood to the side, peering through the small space left between the edge of the drape and the wall behind it.

She waited. She was curious. And…more.

The man had the nicest backside. Tight. Perfectly shaped. Not too flat. Not too round.

Her eyes rose to his shoulders. She wanted to ease their burden.

Erin straightened. Where the hell had *that* thought come from?

For that matter, who'd put the other ones there? Erin didn't go around looking at men's asses. And if she happened to notice one, she glanced away. Quickly.

It was a butt. Everyone had one.

Everyone had shoulders, too.

When Rick turned, the resolute expression on his face caught her attention. Her stomach tensed. He sat on the end of the couch closest to her. Sat as though he owned the couch, which presumably he did. But not like most people sat on their own furniture. Not as though he was comfortable sitting there. More like he was the boss.

Of it.

Of his space?

Of her?

"What I am about to tell you has to be held in the strictest confidence." His words elicited a sharp jump in her heart rate.

She nodded.

"I mean that. If you are not prepared to uphold client-attorney confidentiality, regardless of pressure, in all matters pertaining to me, then you know where the door is."

Erin didn't move. "Look, Rick, it's clear that you have trust issues. And I don't blame you. If, as you say, you didn't kill Charles Cook, then you have reason to be suspicious of everyone. But it also seems clear that you need someone on your side."

His hard stare could have unnerved her. It didn't. It made her want to help him.

"You can trust me."

"Steve Miller did not choose to pay my bail. I paid it. I am the trustee for that account with all rights and privileges. I am entitled to spend that money however I see fit."

Her blood ran cold. She couldn't do anything about what he was telling her. They'd just established that. No one could touch him based on any information given by her. Even if he was guilty of criminal activity—if he'd stolen from this account.

But…

"You spent someone else's money without his knowledge?"

He frowned. And seemed to consider what she'd said. What was he doing? Concocting some story that would appease her now? Wasn't that what all criminals did? Went from one lie to another to cover their tracks?

But then, he hadn't lied to her yet, not technically. At least, not that she knew of. "You want me to trust you," she said, "but you keep too many secrets."

"Such as?"

"You didn't tell me your brother died, for one."

"You didn't ask."

"I came across a newspaper article. It says your brother was a passenger in the truck when your father was killed."

"That's right. But that has nothing to do with Cook's murder."

"I disagree. It's an incident that had to affect you in some elemental way. I'm representing *you,* Rick. I have to know all about you to do that."

When he said nothing, Erin pushed.

"Your father had been drinking."

"Yes."

"A lot."

"Yes."

"You were the one who found them."

"They were yards from our house."

"That must've been hard. To lose your whole family at once. You were so young to be all alone in the world."

Was that why she was defending him? Because she felt sorry for him?

Or was it because Johnson and his people had yet to

come up with enough evidence to prove to her that she couldn't win?

Her client shrugged. If she'd hoped to evoke any show of emotion, she'd failed.

"Who's Steve Miller?"

"A...friend."

"Why are you the trustee for his money?"

"Because he can't manage it himself."

"Why not?"

Rick's chin stiffened, as though he was gritting his teeth. She didn't think he was, though. No, a guy like Rick would just will his chin to be solid and firm and intimidating.

"Is Steve Miller alive?"

"Yes."

"How old is he?"

"Thirty-nine."

She could play this game all night.

"Have you known him long?" she asked.

"Most of my life. We grew up in the same neighborhood outside Chicago."

Whoa. *Two* pieces of information. She was making progress.

"What does he do for a living?"

"Nothing. He's independently wealthy."

"How did he come by his wealth?"

"It was given to him."

"He inherited it?"

"You could say that."

"Uh-uh, Mr. Thomas. I could *say* anything. But I'm asking for the facts. Did someone die and leave Mr. Thomas that money?"

"No."

"So how'd he come by it?"

He sat forward, rubbing his hands together. Seeming almost…vulnerable. Odd. That had to be pure fantasy on her part.

When he looked at her, his head was still lowered. "In strictest confidence."

"Of course. I give you my word. I would go to jail before I betrayed the trust of a client." Because either way, jail or not, her life would be done. If she betrayed a client's trust, she would lose her job. And defending people—people who deserved it—was the only life she could imagine.

That thought came out of the blue.

And it was completely true.

She'd known that about herself once.

How had she lost that piece of self-knowledge along the way?

"I gave it to him."

She wasn't sure she'd heard him correctly.

"What?"

Rick Thomas looked her straight in the eye.

"I said I gave it to him."

15

Rick had felt less trapped with his hands and feet tied together and his body in between two blocks of cement with cranes pushing in on both sides. Enemies of a gun-runner he, as Tom, had befriended five years before had left him for dead. He'd thought those sixteen-foot-tall blocks were going to crush him before he managed to use their leverage—to push against them with his elbows and shimmy to the top.

The two men who'd put him, bound and gagged, between two pieces of moving concrete had been surprised, later on, when they'd found themselves on the wrong end of Rick's gun.

"You gave a friend more than a million dollars?"

More like ten million, actually. She was obviously guessing based on the amount of his bail.

"Yes."

"Where'd you get the money?"

"I worked damned hard."

"Enough to make that much money?"

"I invested some of it. My portfolio is in a safety-deposit box in Ludington, if you want to check it out."

"That won't be necessary."

Why not? She wanted to know every other damn thing about him.

He'd want to know just as much about Erin Morgan if he was in her position.

"But…why would you give so much money to a friend?"

"He needs it more than I do."

"Why?"

In fifteen years of undercover work, Steve had never once been put in a position of vulnerability.

And now this.

Because Rick had had to get his ass out of jail in order to save his own life. If he'd known it would come to this, he'd have stayed in jail.

At least then Steve wouldn't even be a possible factor.

He'd gotten soft. Made a mistake.

And mistakes got people killed.

Rick assessed the woman sitting in his living room. The only woman who'd been there since he'd purchased the place the year before.

The consummate professional, she was everything he was not. Classy. Refined. Protected.

She probably ate balanced meals off real china. And had four servings of vegetables every day.

And, like him, she was smart enough to figure out more than most people did.

She was also beautiful. A problem he didn't need.

He was going to have to take care of this himself. Find out who wanted him, what they wanted—and give it to them.

"Steve Miller is a permanent resident of Lakeside Family Care in Ludington." The words burned Rick's throat. But he had to have an ear in the legal system. And keep Steve out of it. "He fell when we were young. He's mentally challenged."

"Fell? How? From where?"

Were you involved? Was there trouble?

He could almost read her mind. After all, why would Rick hand over so much of his money to a nonfamily member if he weren't somehow to blame?

"He fell from a roof."

"Were you there?"

"Yes. And no, I didn't push him."

Her eyes widened. "I never thought you did."

He believed her. Had misjudged her. Rick didn't like that.

She hadn't written anything in that notebook of hers yet.

"You said, during our first meeting, that you spend a lot of time in Ludington. Is that where you go? Lakeside?"

"Sometimes." Enough was enough. "Mostly I fish."

"Even in the winter?"

"Even in the winter. Ever hear of ice fishing?"

She couldn't have lived in the area long and not known about it.

"Charles Cook purchased a nine millimeter less than a month ago," she said.

Rick settled into the couch. The strap of his holster felt reassuring against his back. "Not a hunting pistol."

"Nope."

"Did he come by it legally?" He'd seen no record of a gun license, although that could be the result of less-than-pristine paperwork. Or time.

"No."

"He was afraid of something. Or someone."

"That would seem to be the case."

"We have to find out who. Or what."

"My guy's on it as we speak." She glanced around. "How do you stand this quiet?"

Not a question he'd been expecting.

"I'd be interested to learn your assessment of that information. Is it something you need to know?"

She grinned. And Rick felt an answering twinge of desire beneath the fly of his pants. One he immediately ignored and extinguished with the mental control that served him well.

"I don't need to know," Erin said. "I just wondered."

"I like quiet," Rick told her. Noise around him camouflaged what might be going on. The approach of death was often stealthy, secretive, so the quieter his surroundings, the better.

"I have a house on the lake," she said, although he hadn't asked. He didn't particularly want that personal picture of her to carry around in his head. The image could do nothing but distract him.

And Rick couldn't afford distractions. Maybe last week. Certainly not this week.

"I can hear the waves from every room," she was saying.

Repetitive noise camouflaged sound.

Which made her easy prey for anyone who wanted to get into her home. To sneak up on her without her ever knowing she wasn't alone.

"They're way more effective than sleep aids," she said, with another small smile.

She was trying to make things between them more comfortable. To meet him on a human level. Rick understood that.

He just didn't want it.

Or, more accurately, couldn't afford it.

What he *wanted* was irrelevant.

His life was about being prepared. Making the wisest choices. Like buying a black vehicle because it was easier to hide in a clump of trees or drive unseen in the night as long as he kept the headlights off. And a truck because it could manage more types of terrain, withstand heavier hits. It put him higher off the road in case of gunfire. Towed bigger boats. And held a lot of fishing tackle.

"Charles mentioned a woman once," Rick said. "Maybe he corresponded with her. I don't know. I got the feeling she might be in prison. Or in a convent…" His lies were fluid. Natural. "Maria Valdez." He named the woman Brady had slept with one night on that yacht. The night Rick could have had her friend. He'd tried to play along. But he hadn't been interested.

"I'll check her out," Erin Morgan said, crossing one long leg over the other as she jotted on her notepad.

And Rick reminded himself once again that a woman like her was out of his league. Out of his world.

When he wanted sex, he settled for women who didn't mind cheap hotels, first names only and no second visits.

Chandler, Ohio
Wednesday, October 20, 2010

I'd been a mother for two weeks and two days, and so far my kid was still alive. Physically healthy. Attending school. Eating her meals.

Maggie had her period that morning. After helping her with the supplies she needed, I actually stopped, in the middle of my room, and thanked God. We'd just had final confirmation that there was no pregnancy. The lies and deceit perpetrated by the girl's biological mother wouldn't have that kind of repercussion, anyway. Others but not that.

Once I was sure Maggie was feeling okay, I sent her off to school. I was going to court later that morning. I'd debated taking Maggie with me—or at least telling her I was going. But in the end, I chose not to.

I'd made a parental decision. Right or wrong.

Erin Morgan called as I was giving Camy her treat so she'd let me leave the house without throwing a huge splash of guilt in my direction. Odd, Erin calling now right now, just as I was struggling with a personal decision of my own.

Her timing was coincidental. I knew that. But I took comfort from it, anyway.

"Hello?" I said, answering in spite of the fact that I was juggling my leather satchel, keys, purse, phone and garage door opener.

"Kelly, is this a bad time?"

"No. Quite the opposite. I have Maggie's mother's sentencing in an hour and I'm nervous as heck."

I was in my Nitro by now, my things on the seat beside me.

"Didn't you say she pled out?"

"Yeah. Two weeks ago. They made the deal the day after they booked her."

The Nitro started with a purr before the garage door was even fully open.

"Then sentencing's more of a formality than anything else. Nothing to worry about."

"I'm not worried about the sentencing. I have her daughter. And I'm in the process of taking Maggie from her legally. Permanently."

"If the state's going to sever the woman's rights, they'd do it whether you were waiting in the wings or not."

"I know. But I still keep thinking she'll be able to do something to prevent me from keeping Maggie."

"If the woman loves Maggie at all, she should be grateful to you for taking her in. Giving her a decent life. Loving her."

"Yeah." My head told me the same thing. My heart just wasn't cooperating. "She told Child Services that she wanted Maggie placed with me, but that was two weeks ago. The night she was arrested." Things had changed since then. After a couple of weeks in a jail cell, Lori Winston was angry as hell and blaming me for everything.

She was playing the victim. Needed a scapegoat. And I was it.

Which was fine. I'd been worse.

I backed out of the drive.

I could handle the weight of Lori Winston's blame. What made me nervous was knowing that a woman Maggie loved hated me.

"Is Maggie with you?" Erin's tone had softened more.

"No."

"That's probably good."

I hoped so. Talking on the phone while operating a car was still legal in Ohio, but I had a hands-free device, because it was safer.

"How are things in Michigan?" I asked, driving toward my office near the courthouse. A half hour in my office, sitting on my old sofa, with a can of soda and a granola bar were just what I needed. I'd walk to court from there.

"Cold," Erin said.

"Here, too." If it hadn't been so darned cold out, I'd have gone skating that morning. I got a lot of clarity—

calmness—when I could skate and meditate about the things that were bothering me.

And I figured Erin wasn't calling to discuss the weather.

"How's everything with Noah's family?" I asked.

"I don't know. I feel like I let Caylee down because I didn't give her the unequivocal answer she wanted from me. I let Ron down, too, because I didn't tell Caylee to forget the scholarship. And I'm worried about Patricia."

"What about *you?*"

"This isn't about me."

"Everything that happens to you is about you in some fashion."

Pulling into my parking space in the little lot behind the downtown building where I rented my office, I waited for Erin to say something. And when she didn't, I asked, "You didn't do what *they* wanted you to, but did you do what *you* thought was right?"

"I… No, I don't think I did."

I took a pen from the console and grabbed a napkin to write on, holding it against my purse.

"How so?"

"Caylee asked what I'd do if it were me. I wanted to tell her. I didn't."

"Why not?"

"I don't really know."

I could tell her what I thought about it. But, unlike Caylee, she didn't ask. And I didn't want to tell her. I wanted her to get there on her own. She seemed to want that, too. I drew a three-dimensional question mark on the napkin.

"I'd like to ask your opinion on something."

"What's that?" A smiley face joined the question mark.

"This new case. My client, Rick Thomas, doesn't have fingerprints." Erin explained about the protein deficiency.

"I'm familiar with another case where a lack of fingerprints was an issue."

"I had a call from the prosecutor on the case, Christa Hart, this morning. She was writing a motion to subpoena Mr. Thomas's DNA. I fought that because there's no DNA evidence from the crime scene. They didn't get anything off the knife used to kill Charles Cook. And that knife was the only evidence at the scene."

"Did you win?"

"Yeah."

Sitting in my Nitro, talking to my friend, was better than sitting alone on my couch, no matter how much I liked my office.

"So what's the problem?"

"I want to run his DNA." Erin said the words quickly. Almost as though she was ashamed of them.

"You think you'll find something in the system on him? He'd have to be a convicted criminal for anything to show up."

"I know."

Uh-oh.

"So why do you want to check?"

"Christa's going to do everything she can to learn whatever she can about him. If I'm going to defend him, I have to know what she might find."

"Sounds reasonable." And it did. But I figured there was more. "What does he say about it?"

"I haven't asked him. If I ask and he says no, I can't do it. And I'm about ninety-five percent certain he'd say no."

I was beginning to understand her dilemma. "Are you thinking about doing it without his knowledge?"

"I could offer him a cup of coffee. And have a friend of mine look for a match—unofficially."

"You want to tell me the real reason you believe you should do this?"

"Because I think he's hiding something from me."

"Something that could affect the case?"

"Yes."

I thought about what she was saying. Not from a legal standpoint—that was her specialty. And, I hoped, not from the position of a therapist, either, but as a friend.

Look out for the other. Look out for self, I jotted.

And then Erin started to talk again. Softly. Hesitantly. "I'm afraid that he's leading me into something. I don't know what. I need to be aware if I'm walking into danger. And beyond that, I'm afraid if I don't find out what he's hiding, I won't have any hope of helping him. I won't be able to win the case."

I remembered our first conversation the week before.

"And winning the case is important."

"*Helping* him is important," she said. I believed her.

"And beyond helping him? Do you want to know about him for personal reasons?"

"How can I tell? Defending him, winning, wanting to help him, they're all connected and they're all part of me. So that makes it personal, doesn't it?"

"Yeah," I said. "But are you curious about what you'd find because of the case, or because, case aside, you want to know?" I wasn't sure it mattered, in the end, to the question Erin had asked. But it seemed to me that she should be clear on her reasons.

"Is it him you're trying to protect? Or yourself?"

"I like him," the attorney told me, as though confessing some great sin, and I felt her struggle acutely. One woman to another.

"The attraction…it's not lessening," I suggested.

"No."

"Is it growing?"

"Probably. I'm trying to ignore it."

"Trying to protect your heart isn't a crime," I told her. "Particularly in a situation like yours where you've already been so badly hurt."

"I really do want to run his DNA for the case."

"I believe you."

"So?"

"What?"

"Your opinion…"

"I'd run it," I told her. "He's made the choice, for whatever reason, to be secretive. You're treating him accordingly."

Erin was quiet again.

"You need the information to do your job to the best of your ability."

"I think I do. I'm just afraid I'm talking myself into it because his secrets are driving me crazy. Am I justifying an action I want to take?"

"That's something we all do every single day, Erin. It's called living. We want to do things. We justify them. Or not. And we do them. Or not. From having that extra cup of coffee to going to bed early. It's like I told you last week. Pay attention to your doubts. And listen to yourself for the answers."

"I think I did. I called you."

She'd just made my day.

16

The pieces of the bass fish jigsaw puzzle were coded on the backs, a chronology of every job he'd ever done. That was the beginning of Rick's list. Or rather, lists. Sarge called, adding another ninety-seven potential enemies. Rick spent Tuesday night and Wednesday morning working on his lists. Starting with parts of the world. Using the wireless internet function on his phone, he looked up current political conditions for every place he'd ever been.

And then he listed jobs by people.

By date.

By number of deaths that occurred.

He made a list of people who were the target of more than one job.

And a list of jobs that had more than one target.

Jobs during which he'd made friends—and possibly still had an undercover contact.

Jobs where he'd worked completely alone, like the Arizona hit. That job had been wrong from the beginning. In the first place, it had been a drug job—Brady's specialty, but Brady had already been working an undercover project. One he'd been at for weeks. Calling him in would have jeopardized that mission. And the Arizona problem had only needed a quick, one-hour fix. Or so he was told. It had required someone to get in and out of a government building, a government office, in the middle of the day without being seen.

Rick was the best on the team at getting in and out of anywhere. With just about anything.

He looked at his lists. He'd separated the jobs that were stateside from those that had gone down on foreign soil.

Jobs involving large sums of money were in a category by themselves.

Those involving drugs.

Weapons.

He showered, shaving without a mirror while under the spray. He shook the water out of his hair, put on clean jeans and a black sleeveless T-shirt, strapped on the holster that crossed his chest and slid his arms into an unbuttoned, long-sleeved denim shirt he'd picked up locally for less than twenty bucks.

And he thought about the woman on the boat. About Brady's matchbook.

He went back to his lists, looking for anything there that would tie in to those few days filled with too much alcohol and not enough hours to spend with the only real friend he'd ever had.

At noon, Rick stopped for a bowl of sugared flakes, adding the emptied bowl to the other three that were piled in the sink, and made a mental note to get some protein into his system. He had to be ready for full performance with no sustenance for an extended length of time.

Just in case.

When he'd made every list he could think of, then cross-referenced, studied and honed, he ended up with nine equally weighted people as the most probable suspects.

And he had to find them without leaving the area or he'd risk losing hundreds of thousands of dollars of Steve's future support. Risk sitting in a jail cell instead of finding his killer. Which left only his wits, his attorney and a phone to save his life.

After burning the lists, Rick took the puzzle apart, carefully gathering the pieces into their plastic bag, putting it back in the box and sealing the box with tape. Before he'd quit his job, he'd bought the puzzle, put it together, turned it over and coded each job on a separate piece, starting with the first job on the top left puzzle piece and working his way around. Then he'd handed over his records—and destroyed what he didn't give back.

He'd visit Lakeside, put the puzzle back and spend the evening, and quite possibly the night, with Steve. On his way—out of his way, really—Rick pulled into a small gravel lot in front of a rundown little building with a barely discernible sign advertising boat rentals. Slapping down a twenty-dollar bill for a rowboat that looked like it might last half an hour without sinking, he rented a rod, then rowed out on the decent-size fishing lake. He put a line in the water, pulled out the phone with the scrambled line and called Sarge.

They discussed the names Rick had come up with. Sarge added half a dozen of his own to the list. And they divvied up search assignments. Rick, by necessity, had most of the online searches. Record searches.

Sarge's included travel.

"First place to look is anyone who's got current contacts in Michigan." Rick spoke softly into the scrambled phone. His home might be bugged. His truck certainly could be. He'd briefly lost access to both while he was in custody. But there was no way that old boat could have any listening devices. Still, habits died hard. "Anyone who's traveled to Michigan," he said. "I'm here. If they want me, they're going to have to show up here, too."

"Eventually," Sarge said. "Right now, we have to find the bigger deal. What's going down, where, that involves either one of us. Or all four of us. In order to find out *who* wants us, we have to find out *why*."

"About that Cook guy," Rick said. "I can't come up with any connection between what I know about him and any of the names on our lists. But he just acquired a nine millimeter."

"He was on to something."

"Those missing emails?"

"We've got seven jobs that involved weapons and known terrorist connections. Those were the most obvious threats to Homeland Security, the most obvious explanation for missing emails. Maybe a new cell in one of the organizations we brought down is behind this," Sarge said.

"Let's start with those. But what Charles Cook did or didn't know and who wants us dead could be unrelated."

"The coincidence bears checking out. I'm monitoring HS as well as I can, but my access isn't what it used to be."

That weekend with Brady kept coming back to Rick. Because of a matchbook from a guy who'd killed a kid and hadn't even told him. He needed to tell Sarge about the matchbook but he couldn't. Brady had left it specifically for Rick for a reason. Perhaps because whatever it meant would risk Sarge's life if he knew. So whatever it meant could get Rick killed, too.

His life was more expendable than Sarge's. Brady understood that. So did Rick. They'd all known that. Sarge was the one protected by the government. He was the one who knew all the jobs. The overseer.

Until Rick discovered why Brady had left him the matchbook, he had to keep its existence to himself.

But he couldn't keep his leader totally in the dark.

"I'm going to see if I can learn who owned the yacht Brady and I were on," he said. "That was the last time I saw Brady. Maybe there's something there."

"Good idea. I was never told the name of it. Just to send you to slip eighteen."

"I remember the name." *The One That Got Away.*

Water was coming in at the bow. He probably had another ten minutes or so to get back.

"Why didn't they just off me last week instead of framing me for murder?" he asked out loud. Only with Sarge would he ask. Rick had never discussed an ongoing job with Brady—not unless they were working together. He didn't talk to anyone but Sarge.

"Obviously they want you alive. For now. We have to find out why. And make damn sure they don't get what they want and decide you're no longer worth the air you breathe before we figure it out."

"Or that you aren't worth the air you breathe."

"I'm with you on that."

"Watch your back," Rick said, assessing the rising water level in the bottom of a boat that should have been firewood years ago.

"Watch yours, son."

The phone clicked and Rick was alone on the water again. But he didn't *feel* quite as alone.

Erin heard from Ben Pope Thursday afternoon. She could have called her client, relayed the information. She didn't.

She couldn't offer him a cup of coffee over the phone. And after two days of thinking about it, she'd decided to run Rick Thomas's DNA through the system.

She'd have the test done quietly—for a hefty price that she'd foot herself. In cash. And then have it unofficially checked against national databases.

Nothing that would hold up in a court of law. But then, she wasn't planning to fight Rick in court.

She was planning to fight *with* him. For him.

And win.

Which was why she was going to run the test. Ultimately, it was for his own good.

Unfortunately, he didn't answer his home phone. Or his cell.

She left a message on both.

Any man who'd give most of his fortune to the care of a mentally disabled childhood friend, who bothered to visit that friend, even infrequently, was a man with character.

A man who looked at her with haunted eyes and still compelled her to believe him was a man she had to try to help.

She just hoped he hadn't skipped town again.

Paranoid was good. Insanity was not.

"Yum. I love brownies. You love them, too, huh, Ricky?"

On the floor with Steve, an Erector set and plate of brownies between them, Rick said, "You bet I do, sport."

"Then come on, have another one."

"I've already had two." Rick grinned at the older man. A real grin. Steve was just so damned happy most of the time.

And that was as life should be.

"Will Angela get mad at you if you have some more? I won't tell her, I promise."

"Hey." Leaning on his elbow, Rick grabbed Steve's hand, waiting until Steve was staring him in the face wide-eyed before he continued. "You tell Angela everything, you hear me? Everything. You notice anyone breaking any rules, any rules at all, you tell her."

Steve's mouth agape, he nodded, never moving his gaze from Rick's.

"I mean it, big guy. Everything. You don't ever keep secrets from Angela or Jill."

"Or you."

"That's right. Most of all me." And then Rick grinned again. Picked up a brownie he absolutely did not want and took a bite. "Come on, let's get to work or we'll never have it finished by bedtime."

And that easily, Steve's attention was diverted as they went back to the robot Steve had wanted to build when Rick had arrived with the new set that afternoon.

Rick wished he had the same ability to let things go. There'd been a man standing on the beach that afternoon. He hadn't even been on Lakeside property. Nor did he seem to be watching the couple of residents who'd been down by the water.

But his presence bothered Rick. Because shouldn't the man have been at least a little curious to see adult-size children playing in the sand?

Maybe the pressure was getting to him and he was seeing bad guys everywhere. Was he was crossing the line from careful to insane?

Erin was in a hotel ballroom in Ludington, at a professional gathering of judges and attorneys. She was listening to a judge at her table espouse the values of settlement conferences when she felt her phone vibrate. With a discreet look, she saw who was calling. And immediately excused herself.

She was sitting in the back. Intentionally.

"Rick, hi, thanks for getting back with me," she said before the door was fully closed behind her. She didn't want him to hang up. Didn't want to wait for him to decide to call her back. "I have some information for you. Are you free tonight?" It was just past eight. Not too late for a man who'd called her close to midnight the other night.

"I'm free now." The man's voice always had that slow, steady tone. Whether he'd just been charged with murder or was sitting in his own living room. Calm. Like he could handle anything at any time. "What have you got?"

"Actually, it's more than information," Erin said, feeling in her purse for her keys as she headed out to her car. She'd apologize to her peers later for deserting them without a goodbye. "I talked to Christa Hart today. She's hard at work trying to convict you of murder. I need a plan here. And I'm assuming—correct me if it's a wrong assumption—that you don't want to sit back and let me handle everything."

"You are correct."

"Can you spare a couple of hours, then? Meet me at my office? Or I can come to your house. Give me half an hour to get back to town."

"Where are you?"

"Ludington."

"As it happens, so am I. Have you eaten?"

"I'd just taken two bites of rubber chicken when your phone call rescued me."

"You left a dinner to take my call?"

She needed this man to trust her. She needed to trust him. "Yes."

"I've had nothing but brownies since lunch." He mentioned a bar not far from the two-lane state route they'd be taking back to Temple.

Erin agreed to meet him there in ten minutes.

She wondered how she was going to get a glass or fork from the place into her purse without his knowing.

The idea that she was contemplating theft hardly fazed her at the moment.

She needn't have worried.

George's Place was as plain and nondescript on the inside as its gray weathered siding promised from the exterior. Considering that Rick Thomas had suggested the place, she should have expected the dim lighting. Dim not in a romantic way, but in a dark way. And where it wasn't too dim to see anything but shadows, everything was red. Red booths. Red Formica flooring. Red Formica-topped tables with red faux leather chairs.

The bartender glanced up as Rick followed Erin inside. He saw Rick, waved and went back to work.

No one else seemed to notice them. There was no hostess to seat them. No waitress to bring menus.

Rick chose one of the four empty booths—the one in the far corner—and took the side with his back to the wall. He slid all the way in, with his left leg up on the seat beside him.

Erin slid in across from him and had barely removed her calf-length black coat and placed it beside her purse on the seat when the bartender was at their table, setting a cup of beer down in front of Rick. A plastic cup of beer.

One problem solved.

"What can I get you?" the fiftyish man asked. He was tall, husky and had a beard.

She wanted a glass of wine. But was afraid to chance

what she might get in this stellar establishment. "Light beer, please."

She'd sip slowly. She was driving.

"And can you get us a couple of steaks, George?" Just steak. No particular cut.

"Sure thing." The man wrote nothing down. And didn't ask any other questions, either, like how she might want her steak done. Or if she wanted anything to go with it.

George left and, with the rumble of conversation around them, Erin looked at her client. He'd downed a quarter of the beer in one long swig. His chin was shadowed again, as though he needed a shave, but there was no stubble there.

His glance was lazy as he took in the room. More than half the booths had been filled when they'd come in. All the tables except one by the door were occupied. She'd seen only one vacant stool at the bar. Not bad business for eight o'clock on a Thursday night.

George returned with her beer, set it down and left without a word. She understood why Rick Thomas frequented the place.

Erin had never been in a bar or restaurant quite like it. But she didn't feel unwelcome there. Or particularly uncomfortable, either.

A little nervous, maybe. But that, she feared, had nothing to do with the establishment—and everything to do with the man who lounged across from her.

He hadn't worn a coat, just an untucked denim shirt over a black T-shirt and the inevitable jeans.

Had any woman ever had the right to see that chest naked? To run her fingers through the hair she'd occasionally glimpsed?

Was Erin losing her mind?

"Maria Valdez was in prison," she blurted, although she managed to keep her voice low.

"Was?"

Nodding, Erin said, "Drug trafficking, although there was no record of who she ran for. She also had prostitution raps in several different states. But only one attorney, a Ralph Guardano. I looked him up. He practices out of Florida but doesn't seem to have much in the way of big wins. Or big clients."

"Was?" Rick asked again.

"She's dead."

He blinked. And then his gaze, which had been casually roaming, locked on Erin. "Dead."

She nodded again. "Considering the life she was leading, that's not all that surprising."

"When?"

"Six months ago. She was involved in an altercation in prison. Another inmate stabbed her."

He didn't say a word. Just stared at her.

"How long ago did Charles Cook mention her to you?

He didn't answer.

"I wonder if he knew she was dead. And how he knew her in the first place. Charles didn't do drugs. In a town the size of Temple something like that wouldn't have passed unnoticed. Besides, he'd have gone through random drug testing for his job."

Rick Thomas watched her. And, completely out of character, Erin continued to babble. "I was thinking maybe he hired her…you know…services. Maybe Cook was into ladies of the night."

Ladies of the night. Great, Morgan. A phrase from the gangster movies of childhood days spent with her father.

"Maybe."

"I'll put my guy on it. See if anyone on the streets recognizes him. He never married. Never even had a girlfriend that I know of. It's not impossible that he bought sex partners and had some pimp after him."

"Or that he was gay."

"You think Charles Cook was gay?" she asked skeptically.

"I don't know. But I wouldn't rule out the possibility."

"You think his death was somehow attached to that? Maybe someone found out? A wife or girlfriend, maybe?"

"There are a lot of small-minded people in Temple."

She didn't agree. Temple was a conservative town, but the citizens there were basically open-minded.

"Could also have been a lovers' tiff," Rick added. "The one thing I've learned is that everyone has secrets." He was staring straight at her.

And Erin burned from the inside out. He couldn't possibly know what she was planning to do.

And then another thought occurred to her. He didn't know about—no one in Temple knew about—Erin's past, about her father, about staying under the radar until she was eighteen so she didn't become a ward of the state. She hadn't told anyone, not even Noah.

Not that she had anything to be ashamed of. But old habits died hard. And…she hadn't wanted anyone to think there was anything different about her. Anything odd.

She hadn't wanted sympathy.

Or raised eyebrows.

All she'd ever wanted was to be accepted for who she was. Not to be judged by what she'd come from.

Her father had paid that price for both of them.

She stared back at her client. Afraid of what he knew.

And then her mind caught up to her.

This wasn't about *her*. He'd just admitted *he* had secrets.

And, that quickly, Erin was back on her game.

"Tell me, Rick, what are your secrets?"

"I sleep in the nude."

He'd obviously meant to unnerve her. He'd succeeded. Damn him. Erin didn't want to think of him nude. Didn't need any push in that direction at all.

"I remembered something else Cook talked about." Rick's tone had changed, lost that hint of the personal. "There was a vacation. I'm not sure when. He never mentioned with whom. I was going fishing after work and he said he'd gone deep-sea fishing once. Caught some fifty-pounder that broke his pole, but the line held. He was on a yacht called *The One That Got Away*. Can you check that out? See who owns the boat?"

Pulling a notepad out of her purse, Erin jotted it down.

"We can't ignore another angle," she told Rick. "Cook worked for Homeland Security. Maybe there's something going on there."

"I assumed Johnson's looking into all of that. You said he was searching Cook's place and his things."

"According to Christa Hart they haven't found anything, but we can't expect them to do our job for us. They aren't going to be looking for any other suspects. They believe they have their man."

Him. His gaze shuttered, Rick finished off his beer just as George reappeared with another. And a tray with two plates containing the thickest, juiciest-looking T-bone steaks Erin had ever seen, each accompanied by a baked potato big enough for two with sour cream and real bacon bits and a tossed salad with eggs and croutons garnishing it. George plopped a couple of small plastic lidded containers between them.

"Ranch dressing," he said.

Rick nodded. And Erin was glad she hadn't preferred honey mustard.

Before she'd even cut into her steak, George was back with a cup of water for her, not that she'd asked for it, and a plastic basket of warm bread.

So while Rick Thomas went for simple in some things, apparently he also appreciated quality.

17

The steak was as good as usual. George didn't miss a beat.

The woman across from him had missed several—just in the half hour they'd been at the bar. She was hiding something.

Rick didn't like that. Not with his future resting partially in her hands.

He liked how she ate, though. With attention. No nonsensical chatting. Rick liked to treat a good steak with reverence. It was one of the few pleasures in life he could count on.

Halfway through her meat, Erin Morgan put down her knife and fork. "That was excellent."

"You were hungry."

"Yeah. I forgot lunch today."

Rick caught George's eye and signaled for another beer. He was going to be there a while tonight. Now that he had a scrambled phone and time to think, he had phone calls to make and didn't trust them to his truck or house. Nor did he relish walking around out in the cold.

George's Place was noisy enough to allow for private

conversation as long as Rick was in the back booth. And George took good care of Rick.

Erin reached for her purse. Fine with him if she left. He could enjoy a couple more beers before getting to work.

Her breasts pulled against her jacket as she turned back. She was too gorgeous and fragile-looking to be running around alone at all hours of the night.

And too much of a distraction to Rick.

She handed him a familiar, folded lunch-size brown bag. "I didn't know if you'd want this back."

His matchbook. Rick took it. Slid it in his shirt pocket.

"There were no prints on it at all. Which is odd if it just fell out of someone's pocket."

He'd figured there'd be nothing. But he'd had to be sure. "Unless whoever was using the matches wears gloves. Or at least he did the last time he used them."

"Why would someone wear gloves to light a match?"

Shrugging, Rick could come up with any number of scenarios. He settled on the most innocuous. "Maybe he camps and used them to light his campfire on cold nights."

"I was hoping there'd be something to lead us to Cook's real killer," Erin said, pushing her plate to the edge of the table and setting an open notebook in front of her. "Christa Hart is working hard to build her case against you, Rick. We've got to have answers."

He frowned, wishing she'd let him drink another beer or two before reminding him that he was sitting with murder charges on his back. Or given him ten minutes for the steak to digest, anyway. But he applauded her, too. Get business done and get out. Good motto.

"She wants to go for capital murder. The murder weapon wasn't something that would've been at the EMA office. Nor was there any sign of struggle. Charles Cook's murder was obviously premeditated."

"All supposition."

"And all she has to do is convince a jury—not provide irrefutable proof."

"Convince them beyond the shadow of a doubt if she's going for capital murder."

He couldn't believe he was even discussing such a thing in regard to himself. Capital murder? It was…

Possible.

Rick had blood on his hands. But not Charles Cook's.

"Exactly. And right now, I don't think she has enough to do that." Twisting the pen she held between the thumbs and forefingers of both hands, Erin leaned forward, her gaze locked with Rick's.

"Here's what I'm looking at," she said, her voice clear. Confident. "The most significant piece of evidence is the murder weapon. Cook's blood was on the knife and Hart has a statement from the coroner saying the incision matches the blade. The knife was found in a register duct in your bedroom.

"You have no alibi. Your own phone call puts you at the scene around the time of the murder. And you had plenty of opportunity to get home and hide the weapon before the sheriff got his search warrant."

"Anyone could've hidden that knife there. Hell, there was an entire crew of people traipsing through the house, judging by the footprints."

And all his things that had been moved out of place. Things Rick had taken the time to meticulously right. His order was a layer of protection he'd learned at the hands of a master.

"I realize that, and believe me, I intend to drill that point home. But fingerprints on the matchbook would have helped. One of the sheriff's deputies could've dropped it during the search and that wouldn't have done much for us. But I was really hoping that whoever was there before the sheriff, whoever planted the weapon there, had dropped it."

She'd been resting his defense on a lie he'd told her. On a matchbook that had come from a beach island via Colorado—not from his living room floor.

"I called the references you gave me. I had to leave messages but they called back. And vouched for you."

Rick wasn't surprised. But it was nice to know that the precautions they'd taken, measures they'd put in place, were still functioning.

It meant the U.S. government wasn't involved in whatever was going on.

Or…maybe they were. Maybe they were lulling him into a false sense of security. Had Rick and his team been sacrificed to protect the government they'd served?

They'd always known it could happen.

"Right now Christa's got to be scrambling for a motive," Erin continued. "She's creative. And smart. She can put two and six together and get four every time. I can, too. But I have to know everything there is to know. Everything she might learn."

"You know it all." She knew more than Christa Hart was ever going to find. Because most of Rick's life didn't exist.

"Then we have to find out what Charles Cook was up to. As it stands, if Christa hasn't got anything else, I'll probably be able to talk her down to a reasonable plea. I should be able to lay enough doubt to convince her not to go to trial unless she has more. But if you didn't kill Cook, I don't want a plea bargain. I want you free."

If Rick didn't know better, he'd say that Erin Morgan

meant what she said. That *she* wanted him free. That his freedom meant something to her. Personally.

Pressure mounted between his legs. He shifted. Forced himself to think of his months in a prison cell in Arizona.

And when that didn't work, he took a mental journey through different jobs he'd done.

He couldn't afford a distraction. Not now. Not with her.

"Think about Cook. About every innocuous conversation the two of you had. Did he ever mention anything that could be perceived as valuable to you? Anything he might have repeated to someone else that could make you seem like a threat?"

Rick Thomas? No. He shook his head.

Now, Tom Watkins—definitely. If Cook had been involved in something going on within Homeland Security, as Sarge's missing emails might suggest, and if Cook had had any idea that Rick was Tom, then yes, Cook should have felt threatened. But Cook was dead.

And Cook couldn't have known. He just wasn't that savvy. Or that good an agent.

Over his years in the field, Rick had developed almost a sixth sense when it came to his cover, to knowing if anyone was doubting him. He'd extricated himself just in time on more than one occasion. Bottom line, if Cook suspected anything, Rick would've been aware of it.

"He bought a gun for a reason," Rick said now. "We need to know why. Maybe your guy's source has some idea."

Erin wrote that down. "I'll ask."

"I'm assuming you've seen his bank records?"

"I'm waiting for Christa to send certified copies, but she's already told me there's nothing there."

Her face was earnest, her brows creased over features that were lovelier than anything Rick had seen in a long time. The short hair accentuated the intense expression in her eyes.

Rick needed her to go. He had to stay focused. To make phone calls. To find someone who knew something. About missing emails. A hit on him. Or an upcoming job.

Was it drugs? Terrorists? Or simply revenge for past sins? Not that there was anything simple about revenge. Drugs, terrorism—those were predictable. Revenge, which was driven more by emotion than greed, was not.

The woman closed her notebook with fingers that were slender, feminine, tipped with manicured nails.

It'd been years since he'd noticed a woman's hands and he had more than passing thoughts about how those hands would feel on his skin….

"I'll be back," he said abruptly, heading to the men's room.

In the end, getting a DNA sample had been almost easy. While Rick was in the bathroom, George returned with another round of beer and offered to clear away the remains of their dinner as he delivered the bill. She'd had some beer left in her cup, Rick had had some in his, and she'd combined the two, giving George her empty cup to take away with the rest of their dishes. Then she paid cash for dinner.

She'd gulped down enough beer from one of the new glass to let her pour the old stuff in and then, turning her back to the room, she'd wrapped Rick's cup in her napkin and had it safely in her purse before he returned.

When Rick came back a minute later the table had been cleared, and Erin sat with her coat on her lap. "I've got to get back," she said, pushing both new cups of beer in front of him. "I paid for dinner."

"Bill me."

"If we win." She grinned. And he thought about her going out into the dark alone. Driving along the deserted highway alone. Arriving at an empty house on the lake with walls of windows and sound cover that would allow someone to creep through her house without alerting her...

"Why are you alone?" He hadn't meant to ask.

"Excuse me?"

"You're young, beautiful. Successful. Living in a small town. I'm sure I'm stereotyping, but you being alone doesn't make sense to me."

She didn't say anything and he didn't blame her. The question had been out of line. Completely inappropriate. He wished he hadn't asked.

"I assumed you'd heard." Her chuckle lacked humor and she didn't meet his eyes. "Living in a town like Temple, you get used to everyone knowing everything about you." She looked up at him. "I forget sometimes that not everyone does."

He wasn't going to ask what he was supposed to know. He didn't make the same mistake twice.

"I was engaged to be married," she said, and the way her eyes softened struck Rick. Not emotionally. But he noticed. *How odd to be so loved* was his thought.

In his world, he didn't see much of the gentler side of life. The only real family he'd spent any time with had been on sitcoms. Especially when he couldn't sleep at night and needed the irritating laugh tracks to bore him to sleep.

"We met in college. Dated on and off while I was in law school and then more seriously afterward. But I was in Grand Rapids and he was here. Until he asked me to marry him. That's when I moved to Temple. Because Noah's family was here."

"What about your family?"

"What family? It was only me and my dad, and he passed away when I was twenty."

They had something in common.

"What happened between you and your fiancé?"

"Noah's family owns the local hardware store. He worked for his dad, but he also volunteered with the Temple fire department, which mostly meant rescuing cats from trees."

The whole department, including the chief, was on volunteer status. Rick had known that from the first day he'd read about Temple, Michigan, while sitting at a computer in the jail library—if you could call a corner of the TV room a library—planning a future he wasn't sure he'd ever see.

"Then one night there was a huge fire. One of the big, three-story houses in town. Had to do with an electrical system that hadn't been updated to code. Anyway, a little boy had been trapped upstairs on the third floor. In spite of orders to the contrary, Noah couldn't just let the little boy go down with the house. He went in."

And died with the child. Noah Fitzgerald. Rick had read about it. And wondered if he would've done the same.

"That was almost five years ago," he said now. And at her look of surprise, he added, "I heard about the fire. I didn't know you were engaged to the firefighter who perished."

She nodded. And stood. "It's been a long day," she said. "I've got to go. I'll check on Charles Cook's sex life, the yacht and the gun dealer." She buttoned her coat. "You be careful driving home. We don't need a DUI added to our battles."

Rick almost saluted her. He'd had just enough beer. But he didn't want to be rude.

He liked how she'd said "we."

Erin had two missed calls on her cell phone. One from Caylee and one from Ron Fitzgerald. They'd both left messages. She didn't return either.

Instead, she called a forensic technician friend of hers. He lived in Ludington, had graduated from a local college. He was the oldest sibling of the little guy Noah had tried to save in the fire that had killed him.

"Chip? I need a favor...."

Half an hour later, Erin had dropped off the beer cup she'd shoved in her purse while Rick Thomas used the restroom, and was on her way home. It would take some time, but eventually she'd know if Rick Thomas was holding out on her.

The man had secrets. He'd as much as admitted it tonight, but he hadn't had to. She knew. Her instincts were screaming loud and clear.

But they were telling her he was innocent, too.

"Eddie? Yeah, man, it's Tom. Tom Watkins." Cell phone at his ear, Rick slouched in the booth, back in the corner, feet up with ankles crossed on the bench.

"I thought you was in jail, man." He'd met Eddie through Brady, while helping his teammate run a two-man job. They'd been playing one drug cartel against another. Eddie's boss at the time had gone down.

No one had ever known that Brady or Rick had been instrumental in making it happen.

"Nope. Been out for a while."

Eddie was a drug man. Maria had been jailed for drug trafficking. It didn't matter to Rick that Maria had been on a southeastern island and Eddie was in Arizona.

Businessmen were businessmen. And successful ones like Eddie knew their trade.

"I'm looking for work," Rick said. "I need cash. Big cash."

"What kinda time you got?" Eddie asked.

"A lifetime of it."

"I might be able to find something," the other man said. "Where can I reach you?"

"Nowhere, man. I'll call you. Two days from now?"

"Can't make no promises."

But Eddie would put the word out.

He owed Rick. Or rather, Tom. During the bust, Eddie had almost been killed. They'd needed Eddie alive to get incriminating evidence about his boss on tape. They hadn't been after the young man; Eddie wasn't a threat to national security. If Eddie had died, six months of undercover work would've been blown. Tom had saved the man's life—jumping in front of a bullet and getting them both to safety.

If anyone in the drug world had a hit out on Tom, Eddie could get the facts. Sooner or later.

"I got it, man. We'll be talking."

Rick hung up. Dialed again.

"Sophie, sweetie, Tom Watkins. How you doin', baby?" He tried to bring the black-haired beauty's features to mind. And saw, instead, short amber hair tickling a long slim neck. And dark brown eyes that had a vocabulary all their own.

"Tom? You in town?"

"Not yet, baby, but I might be." Sophie Segura was a Costa Rican beauty. "You got time for me?"

"Mmm." Her voice would have been delicious. If he hadn't already tasted everything Sophie had to offer. Still, she'd been accommodating. And…pleasant. "For you, lover, I'll make time."

"What about that old man of yours?" Hernandez Segura. An ammunitions specialist who'd walked after Rick had spent six months infiltrating his organization. Rick had always suspected the man had contacts. Government contacts. Sarge's team wasn't given the clean jobs. Still, he'd managed to shut down Segura's illegal gunrunning business. At least for a while. And to get out without blowing his cover.

"He's…busy."

"How busy?"

"Very." The bastard was running guns again. Rick had known it would only be a matter of time.

No matter how hard they fought, how many lives were sacrificed, how many scum they either killed or put away, there'd always be someone to run the guns.

And the drugs.

Someone to clear the way. Because of the money. In the end, it was always about the money.

Rick swallowed. Put as much pleasantness in his voice as he could.

"You think you can get me some work?"

"You'll…visit me?"

"You can count on that, sweetheart…." He spoke from deep in his throat.

"I'll talk to him."

"Can I call you again tomorrow?"

"You better. And, Tom?" Her voice grew husky. Clothes rustled and he didn't have to wonder what she was doing to herself.

"Yeah, baby?"

"I'm in the pool house all by myself. All I have on is a sleeveless dress and panties. The night air is cool. Nice. Just like when you were here with me. I need you here now, Tom." Her breathing grew louder.

He watched George pour a beer. "I'm right there, sweet thing."

"Help me, Tom. Please." She moaned. "Oh, Tom, I need you."

His glance around the bar was desultory. And then, in a firm tone, he said, "Pull down your panties and spread your legs…"

Luckily Sophie was easy. A couple of minutes, a few more commands, and he could end the call.

The conversation with Sophie left him cold. And bored. And trying not to think about Erin.

18

Erin waited until Caylee would have left for school and Ron would be opening Fitzgerald Hardware before she pulled into the short drive beside the Main Street mansion where Noah grew up.

The first time he'd brought her there she'd felt so nervous she'd been too nauseous to eat the Sunday dinner she'd come to share with the family of eleven. The closest thing she'd had to a family dinner growing up was boxed macaroni and cheese eaten off trays in the living room in front of the television set. That was when her father was present.

Mostly, from the time she'd been about seven, she'd fended for herself. And eaten her meals alone.

By the time she was seventeen, she'd lived alone in her father's house.

Remembering that twenty-six-year-old who'd accompanied her fiancé home to make the announcement of their impending marriage, Erin wondered if she'd really come as far in life as she'd thought.

Judging by the state of her stomach, she didn't think so.

She'd hoped Patricia would notice her car and come

to the door. No such luck. Standing at the back door, she lifted her hand to knock, something she hadn't done since that first Sunday meeting. Erin let her hand drop. She pushed open the door to the kitchen instead, calling out.

"Mom?"

No answer.

The kitchen was clean—no sign of breakfast dishes. But there was still warm coffee in the pot. Erin poured herself a cup.

"Mom?" she called again, moving through the dining room to peer into the living room and on to the family room. Patricia liked to catch a morning news show.

Unless she was sewing. Patricia Fitzgerald, a renowned quilt-maker, created magic with the machine her husband had bought her twenty years before.

"Mom?"

When she didn't find the older woman in any of her usual spots, Erin checked the garage for Patricia's van. The maroon vehicle was there. Ron's truck was gone, which of course made sense.

Back in the house, she made her way through the rest of it. Maybe Noah's mom was changing sheets. Or doing laundry. Erin called, to no response, as she went up a flight of stairs. And then another. Until she'd reached the converted master suite on the third floor.

"Mom?"

"Erin?" The voice came from behind the bedroom door. Erin knocked, then entered the room.

Patricia sat in one of two black wrought-iron chairs at a round table set by the bay window. She had a cup of coffee in front of her and a crossword puzzle in her hand. Classical music was playing. A pair of jeweled gold-rimmed glasses sat on the end of Patricia's nose.

"Hey, am I interrupting?"

"Of course not, dear. Come in." Patricia smiled. "I just love it back here when the sun's shining," she said, glancing out at the bare trees down below her window. They surrounded a small but exquisitely kept rose garden. "You've found me out." The woman smiled again. "I've been stealing half an hour up here for years once everyone leaves, before I start my day."

"I can go…."

"Of course not. I wouldn't hear of it. You've got coffee. Have a seat."

Erin sat. And hoped she could sip her coffee and actually keep it down.

"I'd much rather share my peace with you than a crossword puzzle," Patricia said. "We never have time alone, just the two of us."

Something Erin regretted.

"I need to talk to you."

Patricia's smile was filled with understanding. With a perceptiveness Erin had envied many times throughout the five years she'd known this family. "I figured as much," Noah's mom said in that soft way of hers.

"First, I want to know what you learned at the doctor's office yesterday."

Patricia flinched slightly. But she didn't look away. "Ron told you."

"Yeah."

"Did he tell any of the others?"

"I don't think so."

The woman nodded. "We'd decided to find out the details and then tell them together. Which we're going to start doing, a couple at a time, tonight."

"And?"

"It's not as bad as it could be."

Relief flowed like a river. And then slowed. "But?"

"I have something called primary biliary cirrhosis. It's incurable."

Oh, God, no.

"I don't understand. I've hardly ever seen you drink."

"An occasional glass of wine on special occasions," Patricia said. "This isn't alcohol-related. Or hepatitis-related, either. It's a degeneration of liver tissue. Kind of like scarring. But it's not hopeless."

Was Patricia's sense of peace due to shock? To resignation? To emotionally moving on to another place? Or was it because she was telling the truth—it wasn't hopeless?

"There's medication I can take. If I respond well to it, and many women my age do, I could go into remission. There's no healing the tissue that's damaged, but it could stop any further damage."

"So you could live a normal life span?"

"Yep."

"And if the medication doesn't work?"

"Then we consider a transplant. With a family donor, and my good health, my chances of success are excellent. And the best thing is that a healthy liver regenerates. Which means that whoever donates would still have a full liver."

Patricia was certainly not without donor options. "Ron wants to talk to all the kids and have tests run now, have them all think about the idea, and see if anyone's willing to donate should the need arise."

"They'd all be willing," Erin said confidently. Heck, *she'd* be willing.

"Personally I think Ron's rushing things a bit. It'll be at least six months, and probably longer, before we know how well the medication is going to do. There'll be plenty of time to worry about donors after that. But that's my

Ron. He needs to make sure his family's ducks are all in a row."

Yes, he did. Which was part of the reason Erin was there.

"Are you scared?" Erin asked.

"Nope. I've been richly blessed in my life, Erin. And I've suffered great loss, too. What's meant to happen is what will happen. And those who are left will go on."

True. And yet… Erin wasn't as accepting. She wanted more say in what would happen. At the same time, maybe she'd done the right thing, coming to Patricia. It sounded as though Noah's mother could handle more than her family gave her credit for.

Which included moving on past Noah's death.

Still, telling Caylee's news wasn't for Erin to do.

"Now, what did you need to speak with me about?"

"Your liver, mostly," Erin said. She'd had to know. For herself. And before she could speak with either Ron or Caylee again.

"Something else is bothering you."

Was she that transparent? Or had she become enough of a daughter that Patricia's maternal intuition had kicked in?

"I loved your son more than I've ever loved anyone. Ever. In my life."

She hadn't planned to mention Noah. This concerned Patricia. And Caylee. And Ron.

But it also concerned Erin's place in the family. And the position two members of this family had put her in.

"I know that, dear." Patricia's eyes filled with pain. But with compassion, too.

"And this family. You're all my family."

"You bet we are. You're as much one of my children as anyone who sits at our table."

Or at least as much as any of the spouses of her biological children were, which was enough for Erin.

"That means the world to me."

"And to us." Leaning forward, Patricia took Erin's hand in both of hers. "Love knows no bounds, sweetie. And family isn't about birth. It's about heart."

Erin's throat was so tight she could hardly speak. "I never knew that until I came here."

Patricia sat back and Erin started to breathe again. "You don't talk much about your own family. About growing up in Detroit."

"There's not much to tell."

"Noah said your mother died when you were a little girl."

That story was as good as any. "I never knew her," Erin said.

"And your dad never remarried. Never had any more kids."

"Nope."

"He was an autoworker, right?"

"Right. A floor supervisor."

"But he worked first shift so he could be home with you?"

All things she'd told Noah. All things he'd repeated to his family when Erin wasn't around. But she'd known he'd told them about her.

"Most of the time," she said now. "When I was really little he worked second shift. He hired a woman to stay with me, but I was asleep most of the time she was there. And that way he had all day to be with me, to raise me. And he was home in the middle of the night to scare away the bogeyman."

Her father had told her that. Every night before she went to bed—even when she'd grown into a more independent teenager. He'd told her, as he kissed her good-night, that he was there to chase away the bogeymen.

Until he hadn't been.

"What's bothering you, Erin? I've never seen you look so serious. So...worried."

She'd never felt so worried. Not for herself. Not in many, many years.

"I don't want to lose you all. I don't think I could bear that."

"You aren't going to lose us."

If she misstepped with Caylee, Ron would do what he had to do in order to protect his family. And if she became Ron's puppet, she'd lose the respect of Caylee and eventually her siblings.

And if she...

"Noah's gone," she said.

"Yes, sweetie, he is."

"And I..."

"You've met someone." Patricia sounded...less peaceful than she had when they'd been discussing her liver disease. Almost as though the idea was one Patricia was familiar with, had worried about.

"No!" Shocked, Erin stared at the older woman. "Of course I haven't. Come on, this is Temple. Who would I meet?"

"You work in Ludington as often as here," Patricia pointed out.

Well, that was true. And she knew a lot of people the Fitzgeralds knew nothing about. People who knew nothing about them, either.

"I'm not seeing anyone, I swear." The picture of Rick Thomas that came to mind was an intrusion. One she didn't welcome. Or need.

"Then what's the problem?"

"I… If I'm going to be a real and true member of this family, I have to be myself."

"No one expects you to be anything else."

"What I mean is, my life has to be part of the mix."

"Has someone said something to you? Done something? Because if they did, they'll have Ron and me to answer to. We are the heads of this family. And if we say—"

"No." Erin cut Patricia off. "No one's said or done anything. You all love me far more than I ever thought possible. I love it here. I love all of you. It's just that…I have to live a full life. *My* life. So do all the other kids."

Namely Caylee. Being a Fitzgerald child was wonderful. Miraculous. And also extremely difficult.

"You're absolutely right about that," Patricia said. "It's what we've told all our kids, from the time they were little. They didn't have to be in Scouts or dance or sports, and they didn't have to work at the hardware store, unless they wanted to. But they had to get good grades. And to work at *something*. To love and care about one another and others outside our home. And to grow up to be contributing citizens in the good Lord's world."

Patricia's comments gave Erin a natural segue to her real question. "And if that meant being called away from Temple?"

Patricia's horrified frown was more in line with what Erin had been expecting when she'd pictured this conversation in the shower that morning. "You're moving?"

"No, I'm not moving, Patricia. Not ever. I love Temple. And my house. And all of you. I'm happy here. But if I wasn't and I did have to move…I'd still want to know my home was here."

"And it would be."

Erin felt only marginally better. Which didn't make sense.

She nodded. Got ready to leave. And said…

"And if…someday…I meet a man—not that I have—a man who, you know, attracts me?"

"Then you must explore the possibilities," Patricia said.

"Even if that means he takes Noah's place in my life?" What was she saying? She was practically kicking herself out the door when she'd just spent the past half hour making sure she was fully inside.

"We'll cross that bridge when we come to it," Patricia said. And Erin was reminded of her earlier statement about those being left going on. "He might have a family of his own to bring you home to."

So it was as she'd feared. Her place at the Fitzgerald table was conditional. As long as she stayed true to a man who'd been gone for four and a half years, she could remain a member of the only family she'd ever really had.

And if she betrayed Ron and maybe Patricia by encouraging Caylee to follow her heart?

What then?

19

Rain threatened on Friday, but held off, allowing Rick to take the walk he'd planned. Another person might have enjoyed the balmy sixty-five degree Michigan weather, the fresh air in his lungs. Rick barely noticed.

He got far enough away from any place that could be bugged and dialed the scrambled phone Sarge had given him. He had to get Sophie when she was just waking up. He needed her sober.

"Hi, angel, you awake?"

"Tom-m-m?" The rustle of her sheets brought to mind an image of the whitewashed four-poster bed with its mirrored canopy.

Rick had seen his own likeness, buck-naked and hard with desire, reflected on that ceilinged frame, but suspected the mirrors were really there for Sophie's own pleasure—when she was in the bed alone.

"How was breakfast?" Without fail, no matter what else she had going on in her life, or who she might have snuck into her room for the night, Sophie met her husband in his suite of rooms for breakfast at seven o'clock every morning. After which she went back to bed. Or sometimes just to bed, depending on the night before.

"He was in a surly mood," she said now.

"I'm sure you took care of that."

"Of course."

Sex with her much older husband might bore her to tears, but Sophie knew how to earn her keep.

"I did it while he was sitting at the table and thought of you the whole time."

A car passed, and then another. Rick was walking on the edge of a two-lane state route without sidewalks.

"What about his breakfast?"

"The eggs got a little cold. He didn't seem to care."

A field to his right had recently been mowed. The trees across the road, on his left, were another story; anything or anyone could be hiding there, lying in wait. Or just watching.

"And?"

"I told him Carla's brother was coming for a visit." Hernandez Segura believed Tom Watkins was half brother to a friend of his wife's. If he'd done any checking, which Rick was sure he had, he'd have found verification of the identities in question. What he didn't know was that Sophie's friend Carla existed only on paper.

Sophie thought lying to her husband, getting "Tom" an in with her husband, had all been her idea.

But then she thought meeting Rick on the beach one night had been fate, too, instead of the carefully orchestrated event that had actually taken place.

"What did he say?" Rick asked.

"To let Carla know that if you wanted work, to get in touch with him."

Two scenarios immediately occurred to Rick. Either his cover in the business of illegal arms distribution was still intact. Or Hernandez Segura was inviting Rick to his own execution.

"That means you can stay for a while, lover. Longer than last time. I'm wet just thinking about you…."

"Tell me…" Rick dropped his voice, his gaze constantly on the move, aware of every movement of every leaf in his vicinity.

The sexy words dripping from Sophie's tongue were better than any 900-number. Rick missed half of them. And disregarded the other half.

"I'm hard enough to burst," he told her, completely by rote.

"Do it now, baby. Do it for me."

"Ah, baby." Crossing the road, darting in between trees, he put just the right amount of breathlessness into his voice. "It's good…mmm…so good."

A dark blue SUV sped by for the second time. Rick stopped, his back against a tree, and waited.

"Tell me about your hand on your cock, lover. Tell me what it's doing."

Rick could play the part if he had to. When he was actually with Sophie he could get hard and spill himself. Today, he didn't have to.

He just had to talk the talk. Which he did adeptly enough to satisfy Sophie.

"Mmm. That was good, lover." Sophie's accented husky tones filled his ears. Not his senses. "How long's it been for you?"

Rick wasn't sure he remembered the last time. It certainly hadn't been memorable.

"Too long, Soph. I need you. More than you'll ever know…" That tiny sliver of truth gave credibility to the lies.

"Then come to me, Tom."

"I will."

"I'll be waiting."

"You better be. I want you naked and spread." Sophie liked to be handled.

"Tom?"

"Yeah?"

"Hurry…"

Erin didn't like unexplained absences. Not in her clients. And not in deputies' names on reports, either. Maybe she was making something out of nothing. She'd looked at the Cook/Thomas case files so many times she could be overanalyzing. Or maybe she *was* missing something.

In her office on Friday afternoon, she listened to her instincts and called the sheriff's direct line.

"Erin, how are you? I ran into Ron at the store this morning and he told me about Patricia. I guess they're telling the rest of the kids this weekend, but he said you know."

"That's right." Erin's nerves began to settle just a bit as she relaxed back into her chair. Sheriff Johnson and Ron Fitzgerald had graduated from high school together and remained friends in all the years since. Through the sheriff's divorce. And remarriage to a woman half their age. Through elections and hard economic times.

Through the invention of the internet and the subsequent change it'd brought to small-town life. No one was secluded anymore. Not really.

The sheriff had been the one to tell them about Noah. He'd been there. Had watched Noah run in…and then saw the building collapse.

He'd delivered the eulogy at Noah's funeral.

"I saw her this morning," Erin said slowly. "She says she's going to be fine."

"Ron said the same," Sheriff said. "Still, kind of a shock to think of Patricia sick…"

Erin wanted to ask if Ron Fitzgerald had mentioned his youngest daughter to his friend. Mentioned that she'd won a full scholarship to Yale. News most parents would brag about.

But she didn't ask. She didn't need the sheriff pressuring her to talk to Caylee, too.

"I, um, I'm calling on a business matter," she said instead. "I'm going over the Cook case, and I noticed that Bruce Halloway isn't listed as present during the search of the Thomas residence."

"That's correct."

"He wasn't there?" Bruce Halloway was a hometown deputy.

"No. He was on another call when the warrant came through."

"Something bigger than the search of a possible murder suspect's home?" First-degree felonies didn't happen often in Temple. A murder right in their town? Everyone who'd even thought about being a cop would've been in on the investigation one way or another.

"Listen, Erin." Sheriff Johnson lowered his voice. "Halloway's going through a rough spot right now. He's involved with some woman in Ludington. His wife found out. Left him. Took the kids. I've been cutting him some slack."

"So he wasn't at work the day Charles was murdered," Erin said.

"You guessed it."

"Do you know where he was?"

"Home. Drunk."

"Is he getting help?"

"Yes. I gave him a choice. Either get help or lose his badge. Permanently."

Erin thanked the sheriff and hung up, not really feel-ing any better, even with answers.

She and Noah used to play cards with Halloway and his wife, Michelle. Life was just plain hard all the way around.

Ben Pope called a few minutes after Erin left the office on Friday afternoon. She took the call, anyway; it let her procrastinate a little longer. Sometime that day she had to return Caylee's phone call. Erin might not know how to handle the situation with Caylee, but she did know that ignoring the girl's messages was wrong.

Flipping open her phone, she said, "Erin Morgan."

"I found the guy who sold Cook the gun."

"Could he tell you anything?"

"Cook wanted a gun for his own personal protection. Something powerful enough to kill with one shot, even if the shot wasn't straight to the heart or the brain. I guess the guy didn't trust himself to get it right."

"Sounds like he was planning to shoot first."

"He was scared."

"Do we know what he was scared of?"

"Nope. Not a clue."

"Was it job-related?"

"He didn't say. But I can tell you this. From everything I've learned, Cook wasn't the aggressive type. He didn't go looking for trouble. But if he was pushed, he was no coward."

The description fit what Erin had heard about him. So what had scared the man so badly he felt he had to arm himself?

Charles Cook had only just bought the gun, so what-ever had frightened him was fairly recent.

Erin hoped to God the source of Charles's fear didn't have anything to do with her client.

"Thanks, Ben," she said aloud.

"There's more." The man's voice held no intonation at all. He sounded too much like Rick Thomas for Erin's comfort. "The yacht, *The One That Got Away*..."

"Yeah?"

"There was an explosion at sea. Caused by a gas leak."

"What about the people on board?"

"No one seemed to know who'd taken the boat out that day. Apparently many people had access to it, but they were all accounted for."

"What about missing persons reports at the time?"

"Miami police looked into it. Didn't find anything."

"And the owner?"

"It's registered to the U.S. Department of Defense."

"*What?* Why would the government own a pleasure yacht?"

"My guess would be to have meetings that they wanted to keep quiet. Or to be out on the water in an unmarked boat. I'm sure the government owns more than one."

"So Cook's vacation wasn't really a vacation? He was working?" The man was employed by Homeland Security. Maybe he'd been involved in some project with the Department of Defense.

But then why had there been no record of any involvement?

"Or it was genuinely a vacation. It's possible that the yacht was used for incentive rewards. Do you know when he supposedly took this vacation? Or who he was with?"

"Nope. It was just a comment made in passing."

Another dangling piece of information that did nothing but create more questions.

And then Ben told Erin something that picked up her day a bit. Something that had her calling Rick Thomas rather than Caylee as soon as she hung up.

20

Rick saw Erin's number show up on his phone screen. He waited for the call to switch to voice mail. Waited for her to leave a message.

"It's ringing." Steve stared at the phone. And then at Rick. "It's ringing," he said again.

"I know, sport. It's business. I'll get it later."

Nodding, Steve rolled the dice and moved his cardboard figure over the colorful trail on the board, which lay on the floor between them. It was an educational game he'd bought Steve. Rick counted silently, watching every move.

Steve, who'd been lying on his stomach, sat up. "Gotcha," he said, sending Rick's figure back.

"Ah, no," Rick groaned. And he cheered, too. Steve had counted correctly.

He took his turn, teasing Steve, trying his best to make the game half as much fun as the kite-flying he'd put a halt to half an hour before. He'd seen someone on the beach again. Couldn't tell if the person was male or female, but he or she had definitely been facing the Lakeside residents on the beach.

He'd accidentally-on-purpose tangled his string with

Steve's, and then stepped on their kites, breaking them, soothing Steve with promises of a trip to the toy store the next day, as he'd rushed Steve back inside.

Rick was afraid he'd been seen.

With Steve.

"I told Angela about the three brownies." The random announcement was issued with a bit of trepidation.

It took Rick a second to follow Steve's thought process, not sure why brownies would upset him. And then he remembered the night he'd eaten the extra brownies at Steve's urging. And Steve's promise not to tell Angela.

"That's good, sport," Rick said now, looking Steve in the eye. He smiled. And rubbed Steve's shoulder. "You did exactly the right thing."

"That's what she said, too."

"Well, she's absolutely correct. I'm proud of you."

Steve was still frowning. "And you didn't get in trouble?"

"Nope."

"Did she yell at you, though?"

"No. She said it was okay because you and I were having fun."

"Maybe next time we have brownies for dessert I can have three, 'cause it'll be fun."

"No way, sport! You have to eat your dinner first. You know the rules. And you know what happens if you eat too many brownies after dinner."

"I throw up!" Steve laughed. And then sobered. "Or get the runs. I really hate that."

"Everybody does," he said sympathetically.

Rick's voice mail message flashed. But he waited until Steve had fallen asleep and he'd tucked him into bed before making his exit.

And he stopped to speak with Angela on his way out,

as well. Making sure that Steve would be kept under lock-and-key surveillance anytime he wasn't with Rick. At least for the time being.

Until Rick could figure out whether he was being paranoid or he'd been followed.

He used his scrambled phone to return his attorney's phone call.

"It's Rick," he said as soon as she identified herself. "You said you had something."

She told him about the yacht. Tried to engage in dialogue regarding the boat's ownership, to come up with possible scenarios. Rick didn't want to.

Department of Defense made perfect sense to him. Relieved him, actually.

And the reason for that was something she could never, ever know about.

"Charles talked to you about the trip," Erin persisted. "Did you have the feeling that he was really on vacation? Or was he down there on a job?"

"I didn't have a feeling one way or the other." Because Charles had never been on *The One That Got Away*.

"I think we need to dig deeper. Try to find out what he was working on, if maybe he was involved in something classified or—"

"You'd know it by now if he was," Rick said, driving around the Lakeside Family Care grounds, perusing every inch of every acre, looking for anything different. "Someone would've shown up to investigate. Or to offer some explanation about Charles's life that would keep us from looking any further."

"You sound like you know what you're talking about."

Damn. He was getting sloppy. Or too comfortable with

his oh-so-feminine attorney. "I was in the army," he said. "You hear about all kinds of things when you're on the inside."

"I'll ask the sheriff what he's heard...."

"Was there anything else?" Rick pulled out of the care facility, turning right. A couple of times around the perimeter and then he'd head home.

And in the morning he was going to hire twenty-four-hour private security for Steve.

"Yes, as a matter of fact, there was."

Holding his phone a little tighter, Rick tuned in. "What?"

"Charles's sex life."

"He's gay?"

"No. He had a lover."

"What? Where?"

"A small town called Baldwin. Pope found gas receipts—I don't know how and didn't ask—that showed Cook filling up with gas in Temple every Tuesday afternoon after work. And then he'd fill up again Wednesday morning before work."

"He drove a tank of gas every Tuesday night."

"Right. But there were a couple of times he didn't fill up before he left town."

"He got gas in Baldwin."

"Yeah. Pope spent this afternoon there, showing Cook's picture around. Everyone knew him. Put him with a woman they thought was his wife. Her name's Bea Wagner. Turns out she's from Evart. Her husband, Paul, believed she was staying with her sister every Tuesday night. Instead, she and Cook rented a one-room apartment there. I guess she visited it other times, too."

"With other men?'

"It doesn't appear so. Pope spoke to her and is convinced she really loved Charles. He's also convinced she's scared to death of her husband."

"Did Paul Wagner find out about Cook?"

All the streets around Lakeside were quiet. Rick turned haphazardly, and illegally, to make sure he wasn't being followed.

"Yeah, the woman—Bea—thinks so. A couple of weeks ago. Right about the time Charles bought the gun."

"Where's the husband now?"

"He works nights. At some car plant in Evart. Sheriff is going to pick him up for questioning."

"You called Huey Johnson?"

"Of course. The sheriff's not out to get you. He's out to get Charles's killer."

Could it be that easy? Could Cook really have been murdered by a jealous husband?

And his fears, and Sarge's, the suspicion that a person was watching Steve—were then all conjured up by overactive imaginations and too much adrenaline pumped up over too many years?

But how did that explain Brady's and Kit's deaths? And Maria Valdez's murder? And what about the stolen and destroyed yacht? Had that really been an accident? And someone had been in his home the night he'd been out on the boat with Sarge.

What about the missing Homeland Security emails?

Too much to be explained away by mere coincidence. Or paranoia.

Still… Rick turned the truck toward home. If he could be cleared of Charles's murder he'd be free to travel wherever he needed to go to figure out what had gone wrong with the unit that had been his family for fifteen years.

He'd be free to slip back undercover and enter the world that was home to him.

Rick slept Friday night. Well enough that images of a certain serious-faced female with flyaway hair intruded into his private spaces. He woke up with a hard-on.

And helped himself to a cold shower. He was not going to use his attorney to get his rocks off. With *or* without her knowledge.

It was obviously time for him to visit the city. Didn't really matter which one. And a side of town that existed in every city he'd ever been in. Time to find a woman willing to spread her legs for a few kind words and a free dinner.

But the idea didn't appeal to him.

It was Saturday. Two days since his call to Eddie. Tom Watkins needed to follow up.

He did while Rick waited for his coffee to drip.

Holding the scrambled phone to an ear partially covered by his wet hair, Rick stood outside his back door. Far enough to be missed on any bugging devices that might have been planted in his home during the last invasion of his privacy. He'd checked. Hadn't found any. But he wasn't taking chances.

"Eddie, my man, Tom here."

"Can't talk to you, man." Eddie's voice was low, rushed, imparting a sense of urgency to a Saturday morning that had started out not half-bad.

"You busy?" Rick asked.

"You're death, man. I got a wife now. A kid on the way. What you did for me before, savin' me an' all, I owe you, but I ain't goin' down for you."

Skin cold, Rick backed up to a tree. "What are you talking about, man? I'm asking for work, Eddie. That's it."

"Someone's put out the word 'bout you, Tom. You're all washed up. I ain't sayin' nothin'. Not judgin' you, man. But I worked hard to get where I am. I can't be lettin' my reputation go down with you. Sorry, man." Eddie's last words had a definite note of finality. And Rick was left with dead air.

"Rick, can I speak to you?"

Stopping in the middle of the richly appointed foyer at Lakeside, Rick turned and faced Jill Williams, social services director and one of Steve's favorite people.

"Sure, what's up?" he asked. Hands in the pockets of his Levi's beneath the tails of the flannel shirt that covered his holster, Rick was sure he seemed the epitome of calm.

He had to get Steve out. At least for the day. Lakeside had security. Steve was being kept in the ward. But…

He had to keep the other man from hugging him, too. Steve would freak out if he realized Rick was carrying.

But until he knew more, he wasn't taking any chances with Steve's safety.

"I don't know." Jill was frowning. Not good. "Maybe nothing. But…"

Just say it. Rick didn't utter the command. He waited.

"A guy approached Steve this morning. I didn't recognize him and—"

"I gave explicit orders that he was to be kept under guard. No one other than Lakeside personnel and residents are to be anywhere near him. No outings, no—"

"I know." Jill's nod, her hand on his forearm, stalled Rick's tirade. "He had a badge. Said he was a sheriff's deputy. Mandy let him in."

Mandy, the weekend receptionist who checked in guests.

"What happened? Where's Steve?" Rick strode forward.

"He's fine." Jill kept up with him. Didn't try to slow him down. Rick respected her for the quick decision. "I saw what was happening and got Steve out of the room right away."

"So the guy didn't talk to him."

"He did. But only for a second."

"Did you hear what he said?"

"He told the guy he doesn't talk to strangers. That's all."

Okay. Good. But he still had to get Steve and go. Find another home for him.

Which would terrify Steve. He needed routine. The people he was used to. Familiar things. Security was everything to him.

And until Rick found a new home for him, there'd be no one to care for Steve while he hunted down whoever was after him. No way to work.

"Did you get a look at the guy?" Rick asked. "Get a name?"

"Of course." Jill handed him a card. "He gave me this. He's from Temple. I thought maybe you'd know him. He didn't have a warrant, and I thought maybe you were aware he was coming. But since you hadn't left word, I had security escort him out."

Bruce Halloway. Deputy. Rick saw the county seal. He knew Halloway. The guy drank too much. But Sheriff Huey Johnson stood by him. Vouched for him.

"Thanks," Rick said, his mind racing. "I do know him. But you did the right thing." He spotted Steve in front of the television with a couple of other residents. Steve was laughing. The woman sitting next to him was looking at Steve.

The woman whose birthday party Steve had recently attended. The skiing victim. She had the mind of a seven-year-old and the body of a thirty-year-old blond bombshell.

Steve hadn't seen him yet, so Rick ducked into a corridor, and then into the room that held the Jacuzzi tub that was used for therapy. He hit speed dial before the door shut behind him.

"Erin Morgan." Getting ready to meet Caylee Fitzgerald for coffee, Erin picked up the call that came in over her cell when she saw the name on the screen.

"I need you to get over here."

Picturing the man in a jail cell, Erin got into her car and prepared to drive to the sheriff's office. "What happened?"

"Bruce Halloway approached Steve."

Steve Miller, she assumed. She'd never heard Rick so agitated. Not even when he'd called to tell her he'd just been arrested. Either time. Certainly not when he'd called to report the murder of Charles Cook.

Erin's heart pounded. "Did you hit him?" she asked, immediately working up a self-defense theory. Because Steve couldn't defend himself—

"No!" Now he sounded affronted. And far too impatient for someone who'd told her pretty much nothing. "He had no right to be here. No warrant.

"Listen, I'm sorry," he said before she could respond to his rudeness. "I don't know what's going on. Why would Halloway show up here? Harass a helpless man who had nothing to do with anything?"

Show up here? "Where are you?"

"Lakeside Family Care."

"In Ludington."

"Yes."

"You want me to come there?"

"Yes. If you can. Please. I just arranged for a private security guard for Steve, but I don't want to leave him. Not until I know what's going on. Until I know he's safe. And I can't take him anywhere else. Not without upsetting him." He took an audible breath. "Find out what Halloway was doing here."

She forgave the man his terseness. Forgave the fact that he was ordering her more than asking, regardless of the words he'd used.

Telling him she was on her way, Erin hung up and dialed Caylee, canceling their morning chat session.

Then she called Sheriff Johnson. And started her car.

21

"Who is she, Ricky? I don't want her to come here. Why can't it be just me and you?"

He'd put *Toy Story* in the DVD player, but Steve was ignoring the thirty-two-inch LCD flat screen in his small apartment. He paced back and forth in front of the television.

"Come here, sport. Sit with me." With his arm along the back of the couch, Rick patted the cushion.

He hated that he'd had to ask Erin there. Steve didn't like new situations, or new people in his space. And Rick didn't actually *want* Erin there. Didn't want anyone to meet Steve—with him.

Steve's safety was in not being associated with Rick.

"I thought we were going to have fun today. And that's not fun," Steve whined. "Why did you have to ask her, anyway?"

"You're going to like her, buddy."

Impatient for Erin's arrival to get the meeting over and done with, Rick glanced at his watch again. He had to be able to look her in the eye when she was talking to him. A phone call wasn't good enough. He had to know— from her face, her expression, her body language—that she wasn't lying. That he could trust her. And he had to be sure no one else heard their conversation. For all he knew her phone could be bugged.

He had to find out what Bruce Halloway wanted with Steve.

And he wasn't going to leave until he knew what was going on.

"No, I won't like her."

"You like Jill, don't you?"

"Yeah."

"And Angela?"

He had to think. To figure out where these questions were leading.

"Yeah."

"Erin's just like them."

"No, she's not."

"How do you know that?"

"Because she's not my friend."

"Maybe she wants to be."

Steve stopped his pacing. "Did she say that?"

"Yes." Lying to Steve hurt. Every single time.

"Well, I might not like *her*." The words weren't promising, but the sulky tone had lessened.

"If you don't, we'll tell her to go away. How's that?" Rick bartered.

Steve stared at him, his chin and nose scrunched up with resentment. An expression Rick remembered from their youth. Except the memory evoked a much smaller, pudgier nose.

"You promise?" Steve asked.

"Yeah, sport, I promise."

But he wanted Steve to like Erin. Which made no sense at all.

"Okay." Steve plopped down next to him, flinging his

leg over Rick's. And, with his arms crossed over his chest, gazed at the TV. "I guess I'll see if she's nice."

The place smelled like…home. Flowers and chocolate chip cookies. After showing her identification and signing in, Erin followed the directions she'd been given, walking down a hallway that reminded her of her college dormitory, to the numbered door she'd been told to knock on.

A man wearing a khaki shirt and pants stood just outside the door. His hands were clasped, one over the other. He nodded as she approached but didn't move.

And she realized that Rick had someone guarding Steve's room. Rick's guard had already arrived.

"I'm Erin Morgan," she said. "Rick's expecting me."

"Can I see some ID?"

She'd just shown it at the front desk, but Erin pulled her weekend purse—little, black, embellished—from her shoulder a second time and produced her driver's license.

Surprised by the relief she felt when Rick Thomas opened the door, Erin worried that her smile was maybe a little too warm. Too familiar.

It was just good to see him. Standing there in his jeans and flannel shirt.

And not in jail.

And then she saw the man just behind him, huddled up to her client, with his big hands on Rick's back, peering over his shoulder.

"Erin, this is Steve," Rick said, not moving as she stood in the doorway, not stepping back to welcome her in.

"Steve Miller?" she asked, looking directly into the other man's eyes.

"She knows my name." The words took her aback,

unusual because of the contrast between their childlike accusative tone and the deep, masculine voice.

"I told her all about you," Rick said. He reached behind him and held the other man's hand. "I explained that, remember?"

Steve nodded. Stared at her for an uncomfortably long moment, and then slowly appeared from behind Rick Thomas.

The man was gorgeous. And had drool in the corner of his mouth as he gave her a wide grin.

With an eye on Steve, who was sitting on the floor by the blaring television playing an interactive video game, Rick stood just inside Steve's bedroom, facing his attorney.

Jill had freshly baked brownies in the kitchen if he needed them to distract Steve. So far the game was working.

As long as Steve could keep Rick in sight. Which was fine with Rick. He wanted Steve in sight, too.

"Your guard got here quickly." Erin started the conversation.

He'd never seen her in anything but suits and much preferred them to the form-fitting jeans, black sweater and black heeled boots she was wearing this morning. She looked completely different. Too approachable, warm. Sexy. And beautiful.

A distraction he couldn't afford.

"He'll have twenty-four-hour surveillance until further notice." Rick had confirmed the presence of the private security company on his payroll as of that morning.

"Won't that upset him?" She was watching Steve, but didn't seem put off by him.

"Not if he doesn't realize the man is there because of

him. As long as the guards don't talk to him or upset his routine, he'll be fine."

"I spoke to Sheriff Johnson. Halloway was here with his authorization at the request of the county attorney's office."

The prosecutor was using Steve to try to build her case?

"Steve's protected by the same laws that protect underage children. He can't be questioned without custodial consent."

"I know. The sheriff apologizes for that and wanted me to assure you that no one will be coming anywhere near Steve again. Halloway was only supposed to confirm Steve's identity and verify that he actually lives here. He wasn't supposed to speak with him."

Rick met her gaze. Held it. And saw more than he'd bargained for. He saw a person. Feelings.

He also saw honesty.

And that was why he'd had to see her rather than just speak with her on the phone.

"Halloway—he's going through some hard times. Sheriff Johnson's been limiting his duties, but doesn't want to make him go on leave because he needs the money. He's used up all his vacation time and paid leave. He thought this morning's assignment was a no-brainer. Truly."

Rick believed her. And, overall, the news was good.

Great.

Whoever was after him hadn't found Steve. Christa Hart had traced him through the bail money.

She didn't know about Tom.

Because she sure as hell wouldn't need Steve if she did.

He could handle having someone out to get him. Having someone after Steve was another matter entirely.

"So…do you want me to press charges?"

"What?"

"Against the sheriff's office? Did they upset Steve? Compromise him in any way? We can press charges…."

"Hell, no." Rick frowned at her. Steve's name was not going on any court document. Until now, no one else, except for Sarge, had even known that Steve existed.

"I can get an emergency injunction from the judge, kind of like a restraining order, until we can face them in court on Monday."

"Do you believe the sheriff's assurance that Steve won't be bothered again?"

"Absolutely."

"Then that's good enough for me. I just want them to leave us—me and Steve—alone."

"Done. I asked the sheriff about Paul Wagner, the husband of Cook's lover. The guy hasn't been home or shown up for work all week. His wife hasn't heard from him. They've got an APB out on him and they're in the process of getting a warrant for bank and credit card statements and phone bills."

Today was a good day, after all.

Rick heard the downward spiral of music that signified the loss of a round in Steve's game. Steve glanced at the two of them. Rick started to nod reassuringly, but Steve wasn't looking at him.

He was smiling.

At Erin.

And when he turned, Rick saw her smiling at Steve. That smile made Rick's heart jolt in a way he didn't recognize. He'd never seen anyone look at Steve with such softness. Such compassion. Such…acceptance.

Jill cared about Steve. Angela and the others did, too. But Steve was a job to them. Always a job.

It had to be that way or they wouldn't be able to do their work.

Rick understood that.

He just hadn't understood that there were other human elements Steve was missing by living in a place like Lakeside and associating only with caregivers and other mentally disabled people.

"Can I go again, Ricky?"

"Sure, sport."

With both hands already on the controls, Steve turned back to the game.

Ricky. Erin held back tears. And swallowed.

"If you aren't going to press charges, I should go," Erin said. She'd assumed she was there to get Rick's signature so she could proceed with a complaint against the sheriff's office.

"Would you mind waiting just until he finishes this round? He'll cry if he doesn't get to say goodbye, and it's easier if you don't interrupt him once he's focused."

"Especially if he's doing well?" Erin asked, thinking of Noah's brothers and their addiction to video games. She'd learned a lot about boys in the past five years as a member of the Fitzgerald family.

"Yeah, he hates to lose." She wasn't sure what Rick's pointed stare meant; his expressions changed through the course of conversations, but none of them gave much away.

They moved into the sitting room and watched Steve's game. The man was proficient. He made it through several levels, his tongue sticking out of his mouth the whole time, before he finally lost.

And then, with the exuberance and short attention span

of a young child, he flung away the controls and, standing, spun to face them.

"Are you leaving?" he asked.

"Yes. It was nice meeting you Steve."

"But…" His face started to crumple.

"What is it, sport?" Rick asked, his voice kind, but without coddling.

"I didn't get to be her friend. Only you did."

"Erin's a busy lady, Steve. She has other people to see today and you and I are going to—"

"Can't she have lunch with us?" Steve interrupted. "Please? I thought she was going to have lunch with us. Can you?" He looked at Erin.

"Well…I…" Erin glanced at Rick.

"You told Jill we might have a guest for lunch," Steve blurted. "That's why she's bringing it here, 'member, Ricky? Salads, you said, except I get a peanut butter sandwich, 'member?"

Rick looked uncomfortable and Erin smiled. "Since it's already been ordered, I'd be happy to stay for lunch," she told Steve, hoping she wasn't annoying her client. The truth was, she *wanted* to stay.

Steve asked to play another video game and while they waited for lunch, Erin sat on the couch and watched as Rick and Steve raced cartoon cars over trails on the television screen. The expressions both men wore were concentrated, engaged.

They were like two little boys sitting there.

And were equally matched as they played.

"Got you, Ricky!" Steve whooped when the round finished. And Erin laughed out loud.

She'd never been in the room before that day, never met Steve before, and yet she felt as though she belonged.

As though Rick and Steve were hers. As though she was at home.

She felt that way for a split second. It was almost like… being in an alternate universe. Or experiencing a moment of insanity.

Until she crashed back into reality.

Yes, Rick was hers. Her *client*. And today, Steve had become a person of interest to her because her client needed her to help protect him from any of the fallout of Rick's arrest and subsequent charges.

That was all.

By the time lunch arrived and they were seated, she and Rick on the couch leaning over the coffee table, and Steve on the floor, his food on the other side of the table, she had herself firmly in hand.

"You gonna be our friend?" Steve asked, peanut butter from his sandwich smeared on his face.

"I hope so," Erin said when Rick didn't speak up.

"We're best friends, huh, Ricky?"

"That we are, sport," Rick said, nodding at the other man. "Very best friends." And then Rick turned to her as he continued. "I already told Erin that, didn't I?" His look was expectant. Intense.

"Yeah, you did," she said, holding his gaze.

Lunch was almost over and Rick had survived. As a matter of fact, sitting there in Steve's room, with a guard outside the door and his attorney next to him, eating freshly prepared food and watching the smile on Steve's face, Rick felt pretty good. As relaxed as he ever got.

"You're pretty," Steve said. He'd been staring at Erin, but she didn't seem to mind. Or seem the least bit uncomfortable with the attention.

"Thank you." She smiled again, an expression that seemed to convey personal caring. Warmth.

"Your hair's like that other lady," Steve was saying.

"What lady?" Erin glanced at Rick, her eyebrows raised, but he shook his head. Could be anyone from an actress on TV to the nurse giving flu shots a week earlier.

"From before. When I lived with Dad. You remember her, huh, Ricky?" Steve's nose wrinkled as he spoke to Rick.

"I—"

"'Member? You got all mad 'cause I told you my dad told me to take off my clothes and she liked my pee-pee and—"

"Steve." His voice wasn't harsh. Or loud. But it brought immediate silence to the room. "I remember, buddy," Rick said, his tone softening. "But nice guys don't talk about certain things in front of women. You know that."

"Like pee-pees."

"Right."

Steve's head dropped. "Sorry."

"It's okay, Steve." Erin touched Steve's hand on the table and Rick was…envious. "Rick said you grew up without a mom just like he did."

"Uh-huh."

"Me, too. I grew up without a mom. It was just me and my dad, so I got used to the way guys talk."

Rick wanted to know more. And needed to know less.

Jill came to pick up Steve for the ice cream social they were having for all the residents of his hallway, and Rick watched as the guard he'd hired followed them down the hall. Steve jumped every second step.

He was happy.

Which was all Rick wanted *or* needed.

"I really like him." Erin's voice reminded Rick that he had to get rid of her. Before Steve came back. He'd cry if he had to tell her goodbye.

Even more than that, Rick had to get rid of her before he could spend any more time with her. Get to know her any better. Like her any more.

But her purse was still inside the room. Rick followed her back in and stood, waiting for her to grab the bag and leave.

"His dad abused him, didn't he?"

"Neglected him is more like it."

She was standing there, her forehead drawn, looking at him. Not grabbing her purse. Not leaving. "And the woman? The one he still remembers after all these years?"

What would it hurt to tell her the truth? That was what she wanted from him. The truth.

"She was his father's girlfriend. It was while I was in the army. I came home on leave and knew something was wrong the second I saw Steve. He was twenty-four at the time. And as you can see, he's a good-looking guy. At twenty-four even more so. His dad had him doing manual labor. Anyway, the two of them had been using him for a threesome."

"His own *father?*"

"The old man didn't do anything but watch." Watched and laughed.

And if he hadn't had to keep himself out of jail to make money so he could get Steve away from that bastard, Rick would have killed him. Without remorse.

"Did she have sex with Steve?"

"Yeah. In every imaginable way."

"Oh, my God." Arms crossed over her chest, she asked, "How was Steve with it all?"

"He was Steve. Took it in stride because his dad was there. It wasn't like he got any real pleasure out of it. Steve's like any five-year-old kid." Rick didn't spare her, almost as though to punish her for her nosiness.

Any other reason, like the fact that he'd never had anyone to talk to about such things before, was irrelevant, he told himself.

"He can be stimulated, he can get it up, but that's about as far as it goes. There's no mental process to take him any further."

"So she used him and that was it."

"Pretty much."

The guy had wet dreams sometimes. But not often. Thank God. They upset the hell out of him.

Rick felt he needed to wash his mouth out with soap, speaking to a woman of Erin's caliber like this. It wasn't anything he'd done before. Ever.

"If Steve was twenty-four, that would make you twenty-two."

"Right."

"Which was when you left the army."

"I needed to make more money."

"To take care of Steve."

She was astute. "Yeah."

"What about his father? Is he still alive?"

"Nope." The bastard died right after Rick had made him sign over legal guardianship.

"How'd he die?"

"He was in the truck with my father and brother, just as drunk as my old man was when it hit that tree. He was the neighbor mentioned in the article. The one not named until next of kin could be notified."

"Right."
"Was your brother drunk, too?"
"No."
Time for confession was done.

22

Maggie and I were in her room, painting the walls, when my cell phone rang. For the past ten years, I'd welcomed my phone ringing on Saturday. Welcomed being needed.

Now the intrusion made me tense. I needed to answer the call. And I needed to spend uninterrupted time with my new daughter. Maggie deserved to come first with me.

"You'd better get that," the girl said, a blotch of butterscotch-colored paint on her cheek. She refilled her roller and continued covering the largest wall of the room that, by that night, would be butterscotch and off-white.

Those four words—"You'd better get that"—were the first four words the girl had spoken since we'd opened the can of paint twenty minutes before.

I'd chatted. She'd grunted.

Politely. But still just grunted.

I let the phone ring.

"Maggie, you don't have to live here, you know."

The girl turned, calm as always, but I was pretty sure I'd seen fear in her eyes. "If you want me to go, I understand."

My phone beeped, signifying that I'd just received a voice mail.

"I don't want you to go," I said, standing there in sweats and a T-shirt. "I want to be your permanent guardian, just like we talked about. But not if you don't want that, too."

The teenager looked me straight in the eye. "I do want that."

"Then what's the problem?"

"I'm..." She held her roller suspended, her expression less confident than I'd ever seen it, even during our counseling sessions in the weeks preceding her entry into my personal life.

"You're what?" I asked, but I was worried about the answer. I wasn't making it as a mom. I knew that.

"I'm... I don't understand... I'm nothing, Dr. Chapman. A poor kid whose mother's in prison."

"You are *everything,* Maggie," I said, the words easily finding life. "You're a living, breathing human being as worthy as the president of the United States of everything this world has to offer. You aren't defined by your mother's choices. You're a product of her environment, but only inasmuch as you let it control you."

Maggie was listening. But I wasn't reaching her. And I slowed down. Struggled to be what she needed me to be. A parent. Not a counselor. The biggest challenge of my life—one I cared about more than any other I'd ever faced—and I couldn't seem to find my way.

"What is it you don't understand?" I finally asked, feeling about as desperate as she looked.

"Why you're doing this. You're busy. You have a whole

life, which I'm disrupting, and now, the paint and the furniture and all the stuff we're doing in here… It costs money…and…why?"

Camy joined us, standing in the doorway, as if she, too, was judging my response. The words of wisdom I'd been about to spew forth wouldn't come.

Holding my paintbrush with both hands, I faced the young woman who was, I feared, far wiser than I'd ever be. The young woman who was showing me things about myself that I'd been blissfully and foolishly ignoring.

"Two reasons," I said. And then scrambled for some innocuous way to express them and retreat without leaving my comfort zone.

Maggie waited. I had her full attention.

"First, because…the truth is, Maggie…I grew up in the same trailer park where you lived with your mom."

The girl's mouth dropped open. "You did?"

"I did." There was more. "It was just me and my mom. Any money she managed to earn went to her drugs first. Our rent and food and clothes second."

"But—"

"My father was…is…" I almost choked on the word. "A dealer. He was her dealer." Needless to say, they'd never married.

"He's still alive?"

"I think so."

"Do you ever hear from him?"

"Not if I can help it."

"When was the last time?"

"Nine months ago." And no one knew. No one. As far as anyone in Chandler, anyone in my life, was concerned, my father had been dead since I was a little girl.

That's the story my mother told me. I planned to stick to it. Except with Maggie.

"Does he know what you do? Who you are?"

Camy lay down in the doorway, but she didn't put her head on her paws. She just kept watching me.

"Yes."

"Does he ask for money?"

The child was perceptive. But then I already knew that.

"Yes."

"And you give it to him?"

God help me. "Yes."

"I guess I'm lucky, then."

"Why?"

"My dad and I, whoever he is, neither of us knows he's my dad."

I should have something to say to that. But I agreed with her.

"What about your mom?" Maggie asked.

"She's been dead for years."

Nodding, Maggie switched the roller to her left hand, but otherwise, didn't move. "So you want to help me because you know what's it like to be where I am...."

"Right."

"You said there were two reasons."

Being a parent didn't get easier.

"The second one is less clear-cut. It's harder to put into words," I began.

Maggie dipped her roller and turned back to the wall.

"It's because I love you, Maggie. As if you were my own child."

The girl froze, arm extended to the wall.

And my phone rang again. I grabbed it off the dresser, looked at caller ID.

Erin.

"Hello?" I caught it on the third ring. Maggie went back to painting. I thought about leaving the room, but didn't.

"I'm pretty sure Rick Thomas is lying to me."

Without even saying hello, Erin told me about the conversation she'd had with her client the day before, about the way he seemed to know about classified investigations. "He said he'd heard things in the army about classified cases," Erin said. "And maybe I'm overreacting, but I still get the sense that he's hiding something."

"Are you taking yourself off the case?" Erin had been adamant about not representing anyone who lied to her.

"I should. I know I should. I can't do it again. I can't defend someone who's guilty and using me to circumvent the system."

"And you think he *is* guilty?" This was Erin's journey. Not mine. My job was to facilitate.

Maggie looked at me over her shoulder.

Facilitating I could do.

"What I think is that this guy has some kind of hold on me." She sighed. "I don't want to turn my back on him."

"Why not?"

"I don't think he did it, Kelly. He's keeping secrets. But I don't think he killed Charles Cook." She told me about the visit to Lakeside that morning. "Watching him with Steve today… I just don't believe he could murder someone…."

Familiar instincts were suddenly in place. "Every good person has bad qualities," I felt compelled to remind her. "And the reverse of that is also true. Most people have good qualities, too."

"So you think he's guilty?"

"I have no idea!" I told her. "All I'm saying is that I

wouldn't judge a person based solely on one set of circumstances, based on how he or she acts in just one situation."

"I know that." Erin sighed again, a sigh that seemed filled with frustration as much as anything else.

I studied my new charge. And remembered the way David Abrams had looked at her the weekend before. David. A man everyone, people who'd known him his whole life, thought incapable of doing harm. We'd all seen his compassion and generosity on so many occasions, in so many different situations.

And yet this was the man who'd taken the virginity of a vulnerable, at-risk, fourteen-year-old girl. After he'd purchased the right from her mother to use the girl to deliver methamphetamine.

"How about if I interview him?" I suggested. The idea had come to me fully formed. I had a light schedule and could rearrange appointments. "It would be good to get away for a few days."

"What about Maggie?" That was part of the point.

"I'll bring her along." Neither of us had ever been on a family vacation. Right now, with David Abrams's influence still so strongly felt, running away felt damned good. Missing a few of school shouldn't be a problem.

And if our time away provided Maggie and me with a chance to bond…

"I was actually going to ask if you'd talk to him for me," Erin said with a small chuckle. "But I have two conditions."

"What are they?"

"The first is that I be allowed to pay you."

"And the second?"

"That you stay here, at my house."

Maggie was staring at me.

A house on the lake might be wonderful for the girl. Help her relax. See life from a completely different perspective. And if we were lucky, Erin and I might just be able to give her the start of a new support system. Something that would lessen her need to believe in the love of a man who'd used her in the worst possible way.

"I accept."

Caylee's car was parked at the top of Erin's long, tree-lined drive when Erin got back from Ludington. She'd tried to call the girl, left several messages since leaving Lakeside, but hadn't heard back from her.

Pulling around Caylee's car, she parked in the garage and was just exiting when she saw the slender figure come around from the back of the house. The teenager's eyes were swollen, as though she'd been crying.

Erin should never have stood her up that morning.

"What's going on?" she called as she approached the girl, reaching out to give her a hug.

"I think someone was up here," Caylee said, frowning.

Not the answer Erin had expected. "What do you mean?"

"A car was parked at the bottom of the hill when I came up your driveway. I had to go around it to make the turn. And I'm sure I saw movement in the woods as I drove up. Someone wearing blue or black. I called out and I was just looking around, but didn't find anyone. Nothing seems to be disturbed."

Erin glanced down her hill. "There's no car down there now."

"I know. I checked, too," Caylee told her. "But I'm positive someone was here."

"Probably just looking for lake access." It wouldn't

have been the first time, though usually she only dealt with that kind of visitor during the summer months, when tourists swarmed Michigan's eastern coast.

Erin led the way through the garage, to the house door, typing her code into the alarm system. Once inside, she grabbed a couple of sodas, handed one to Caylee and dropped her purse on the counter, all the while looking around, just to be certain everything was as she'd left it.

Boots twisted himself around her ankles, mewing at her. And Erin knew all was well. The cat hid under the bed for hours anytime there was anyone he didn't know in the house.

"You've been crying," she said as soon as she and Caylee were situated on the couch. Caylee tucked her legs underneath her. Her sweater was unbuttoned, revealing the V-neck of the long white top underneath.

Caylee ran her fingers up and down the cold can of soda. "Mom and Dad told me they wanted to speak with me this morning," she said. "That's why I wanted to see you so early, because I knew what was coming. They'd already talked to some of the others last night and I had a feeling they were preparing everyone, telling them about the scholarship and why I shouldn't accept it. You know, to form that united front that keeps all of us in line."

Erin didn't recognize the bitterness coming from the girl. Nor would she have recognized it from any other member of the Fitzgerald family.

"Or at the very least, to find out who'd be on their side, and who they had to keep from influencing me to go."

Or to tell you that your mother has an incurable liver disease. And to talk about a possible liver transplant in her future.

Erin now figured she understood the tears. Caylee had

just found out about her mother's illness. Since she knew that the Fitzgeralds always started with the oldest and worked their way down when they had meetings with their kids, she'd guessed it would be a few days before the news reached Caylee. She'd thought they had time.

That she'd be able to work out what to tell the girl about Yale in light of what she'd learned about her mother.

"So I went in armed," Caylee was saying. "I knew what they were going to do and that I'd never be strong enough to stand up to them. I could feel my chances of going to Yale slipping away and something inside me just kind of snapped. I knew I was letting a dream come true pass through my fingers and, if I let it go, I might not ever be given another.

"So before they could say a word to me, I told Mom about the scholarship. Dad tried to interrupt, but I wouldn't even look at him. I couldn't. I told Mom that Dad knew. That he wanted me to turn down the opportunity. And I showed them the letter of acceptance I'd typed this morning and put in the mail before I could chicken out, or before they could convince me otherwise."

Oh, boy. "So what happened?"

"Dad asked me if I'd talked to you." Her glance at Erin was furtive. "I told him I had." And then she rushed on. "I'm sorry, but I knew we were going to talk today and I just couldn't go in there all alone. Noah would've wanted me to take his strength in there with me because I was so sure I was doing the right thing."

"So they think I told you to do what you did this morning."

"I guess. Yeah. Or at least that you knew about it. They think I had your support."

"What did they say?" She was afraid to ask. Based on

the evidence of Caylee's recent tears, the reaction couldn't have been good.

"Mom didn't get a chance to say anything. Dad stood, told me that he and Mom didn't deserve my disrespect. He said I should never have sent that letter without all of us discussing it. That that's what we Fitzgeralds do, he said, we face life as a family.

"But I knew I'd never be able to stand up to him, Erin. Letting my father and then my mom get to me was going to be the same as turning Yale down. I just couldn't do that."

Maybe there'd been a better way to approach things. Maybe Erin could have helped Noah's little sister, could have lived up to the responsibility she'd been given, if she'd taken the time to meet with her as planned.

"My dad said that if being part of the family was so abhorrent to me, that if I was so eager to live on my own, then I should pack up my things and go."

"He didn't mean that."

"Yes, he did." Tears fell from Caylee's eyes.

"Maybe at the moment. But not really."

"He carried my stuff to the car."

Erin couldn't believe what she was hearing. "What about your mother? What did she say, or do, through all of this?"

"I'm not sure. She started to cry and Dad called Margaret and I didn't see Mom again."

Margaret, the eldest living Fitzgerald sibling. The only one Erin had never been able to warm up to.

"Have you talked to Daniel?"

"Not yet. He'd just agree with my dad. He'd say, 'I told you so.'"

With her stomach in knots, Erin scrambled for logic while she wrestled a confusing barrage of emotions.

"You'll stay here," she said. That was the first and most obvious decision.

Kelly and Maggie would be there the next evening, too, but she had four bedrooms.

And three bathrooms. Plenty of linens.

Caylee had a car to get herself to and from school.

They'd have to grocery shop.

And surely Patricia knew that Caylee would be protected, well supervised and loved while under Erin's care. Erin hoped that would relieve her mind at least a little.

And that Caylee would only be with her for a few hours.

"Your parents weren't going to speak to you about Yale this morning," she said next. Right or wrong. She had to start trusting herself again.

"How do you know? Did they call you?"

"Not today. No." Reaching over, Erin brushed the hair from Caylee's face. The amber strands were soft, easily breakable. Just like Caylee. "Your mom's sick, Caylee. They found out the details on Thursday and were going to tell your brothers and sisters and you, starting last night. They wanted to give each of you private time with them to ask questions and—"

"Mom's sick?" Caylee's expression went from horrified to terrified. "How sick? Does she have cancer or something? Oh, my God. How could I be so selfish? Like school even matters if—"

"Hey, slow down," Erin said, taking the girl's hand. "First, no, it's not cancer." Erin told Caylee everything Patricia had told her about the disease, minus the part about needing a family donor.

"So she's going to be fine," Caylee said, still crying.

"The disease is incurable, but the damage to her liver

isn't too great yet, and it's very possible that medication can prevent any further deterioration."

Caylee still looked lost. Scared. And Erin did the only thing she could. She called the girl's mom.

As Erin had expected, Patricia Fitzgerald was relieved to hear from her. She'd hoped that Caylee was with her. She knew Erin would never have told Caylee to act without their counsel, but also understood that Caylee didn't trust herself to stand up to her father. She was proud of Caylee and adamantly wanted the girl to pursue her dreams, and Erin thought they were home-free until Ron Fitzgerald came into the room. Patricia asked for a few minutes alone with her husband. She said she'd call them back. She told Erin to give Caylee her love.

Patricia didn't call back. Ron did.

He needed to make one thing quite clear, he said. He was going to protect his wife and her health at all costs. And to his mind, the stress that would result from Patricia's knowing that Caylee would be leaving them to live alone out east could mean the coming months of medication would not work to put Patricia in remission.

"Don't you think that kicking Caylee out of the house is going to worry Patricia more than knowing she'll be going to Yale next fall?" Erin could feel Caylee's gaze boring into her back as she talked on the phone to her father.

She'd told the teenager about her mother's reaction. Gotten her hopes up.

"The girl is not going to Yale and that's final." Ron used a tone she'd never heard before. One that hurt. A lot.

"Please let her come home, Ron." She tried again, anyway. "Don't rob Patricia of even a week of Caylee's senior year," Erin continued, finally believing she could make things right. "She's got homecoming coming up. And Thanksgiving and—"

"How many children do you have Erin?"

"None."

"I have eight. And so far all of them have grown up to be successful, happy contributors to society."

Erin couldn't argue with that.

"Caylee will come home when she's ready to be part of this family," he said. "When she knows she has to put family first. The lesson might seem tough to you, but once learned, it will serve my daughter for the rest of her life. Because in the end, nothing else matters. Not money. Not degrees. Not jobs. Just family."

"Does her mother agree with that?"

"Yes, she does." Erin heard a muffled, "Talk to her, Patricia," and then Patricia was on the phone again. "As hard as this is, I think he's right, Erin," the other woman said. She still sounded strong. In control. But sad, too.

"I've always had a tendency to baby Caylee, to go easier on her than we did with the other kids. We did right by the rest. I can't sell Caylee short with my inability to be tough on her. If Caylee wants a college education, there are colleges here in Michigan, and we'll help her pay for it. But she had to learn to put family first."

Was the whole world going crazy? Since when was a child's desire to pursue an educational gift some kind of betrayal? The girl had a fully paid scholarship to one of the most prestigious colleges in the nation. A degree from Yale would open so many more doors for Caylee.

"Patricia tells me you've said Caylee can stay with you." Ron was back on the line.

"That's right."

"I appreciate that. Patricia won't worry so much with

her there. I'll drop off money for her support at your office on Monday."

This couldn't be happening.

"Please, Ron…"

"When Caylee writes a retraction to Yale and is ready to be here for her mother, she can come home."

Erin couldn't believe the man had hung up on her. Not even when she was left standing with a cell screen that read call disconnected.

23

Steve wanted to fly a kite. After Rick reminded him that his kite was broken, he wanted to make a new kite. And then fly it. Rick didn't want Steve outside. Not until he'd done more investigation to verify the information he'd gleaned from his beautiful attorney that morning.

Steve still wanted to fly a kite. When an hour's worth of crying, stomping his feet and, eventually, hitting his head on the floor didn't get him a kite, he wanted to go fishing.

Another outdoor adventure. One that was riskier than flying a kite in a private gated area with security alarms and guards in place.

Rick tried to interest him in video games. In movies. In board games and puzzles. In the Erector set. And a balsa wood airplane they could fly in the hallway outside Steve's room.

He finally resorted to bringing out Steve's swimsuit, telling him to put it on and taking him to the whirl-pool sauna room. Steve thought the pool was for fun. Rick knew it was a way of calming down heightened emotions.

At dinnertime, with a word of warning to the private

guard on duty and an apology to Jill, Rick left a pouting and cantankerous, though much calmer, Steve in Jill's care at the door of the dining room. He suggested Steve be offered brownies for dessert if he cleaned his plate, then headed for his truck.

The blocks around Lakeside were quiet. No suspicious traffic or parked vehicles. No people sitting in cars. Rick turned south toward Grand Rapids, made the two-hour trip in an hour and a half and pulled off into a secluded area near the Thornapple River.

A place he'd never been.

There, still armed, he left the truck, locked it and moved into the trees to walk along the river. The trees were camouflage. The water, an escape route.

He probably wouldn't need either.

He hadn't been followed.

Rick walked for a while, listening—to the water flowing a couple of feet to his right and to the world around him.

Someone was spreading a rumor in the drug underworld that Tom Watkins was washed up, whatever that meant. Tom hadn't been much of a presence in that world. And yet Segura, the arms dealer whose family he'd infiltrated, was willing to do business with him.

Though it was still light, the early-evening hour was bringing in a chill. It was supposed to drop down to the forties overnight.

Segura wasn't worried about the rumors. Because he was the one who'd started them? He had connections to the drug world, so he could've spread word among the movers there. At the very least, depending on how widespread the rumors were, he could have heard them.

But if Segura *was* behind this, why? Unless he knew that Rick—Tom—had brought about the end of his lucrative illegal arms business several years before. The business had been stopped. But the man had walked. Because he had a government contact? Someone who smoothed things over for him? Because he'd called in favors?

Or because he had so much cash stashed in various other interests that he'd been able to hire a lawyer good enough to protect him from the fall?

Was there a mole somewhere in the government?

As he walked along the peacefully flowing river, Rick processed what he knew, what he suspected and what he'd heard until he found the confidence that had been guiding life-and-death decisions for the past twenty years.

He took out the scrambled phone and called Sarge.

"I've been waiting for your call," Sarge said quietly.

"Are you alone?"

"Yes."

Rick didn't bother asking where.

"I got bad news, son," Sarge continued. "Someone's passing word among our low-life contacts that you've let your addiction to the bottle get the better of you."

So Eddie was right.

"I heard something about that, but don't know who or why."

"I'm still checking."

"Is someone just pissed at Tom, or is the cover blown?"

"Couldn't confirm that, either, but I think it's Tom they're after. I still get intel on a need-to-know basis and no one sent word that Tom had been cut loose."

No one had challenged the government about Tom's identity or tracked either that identity or the job's he'd done to the United States government. If they had, the government would have cut Tom loose. The government wouldn't protect him. They'd deny ever having heard of him.

And Sarge would immediately be notified and Rick would be told. So Rick had a chance to do whatever he could to protect himself.

"But with someone framing Rick, it seems pretty obvious that someone somewhere has put your two identities together," Sarge went on. "There was always that possibility. Always the danger that someone could run into Rick and recognize Tom."

Rick stepped on a twig. And stopped walking so he could concentrate on his surroundings.

"If my cover's intact, then it's not the government behind this."

"I'd know if it was. But we can't forget about the missing Homeland Security emails."

"A mole, maybe." Rick told Sarge what he suspected. "We're probably looking at one of Tom's contacts who had business with Homeland Security. Someone who's figured out that Tom Watkins and Rick Thomas are the same man, but who doesn't know yet that Tom Watkins was a government agent."

"It's the only theory that makes sense at this point."

"And Brady and Saul—whoever this is was after them, too. Or rather, after Jack and Kit. Both men were killed while living as their aliases. Whoever this is knows we're out there—that we're connected. They just don't know we were agents."

"Right."

"Which would most likely mean we're looking for someone in drugs, ammunitions or human trafficking. Those were the three activities we focused on."

"Agreed."

Rick's mind raced. His ability to rev up, to come alive,

in the face of extreme danger had kept him alive for fifteen years of working against unbelievable odds in the most cutthroat societies.

"And I'm not dead yet, like Brady and Saul are," he said. "Because I'm of greater value to them alive than dead for some reason. But they need to limit my power, which explains the rumors. They're ensuring that no one will associate with me, but not making it so bad that anyone's going to kill me before whoever's behind this gets what he wants."

He'd worked out a lot of it.

"Which means they have a job they want you to do—a job requiring Tom's unique skills…"

"Or one involving something I handled in the past, something I have intelligence on, maybe a contact I made…"

The river was deep, flowing swiftly. Rick couldn't see the bottom lost beneath the swirling mass of brown water.

"Or you have something they want."

It was the validation Rick needed for the conclusions he'd already drawn. "And if I go to work for someone else, I might pass it on, whatever it is. Certainly explains the bad rap being spread around. But that doesn't explain Cook's death. Even if he was on to some emails, had stumbled on some intelligence, why frame me for his murder?"

"So they could keep an eye on you. If you're a murder suspect, they have the law helping them. The very system they want to destroy is helping them keep tabs on you."

Made perfect, twisted sense. In a twisted world.

"Until they either find what I have or come up with a way to make me give it to them," Rick said slowly.

"If they don't find what they want, they'll need you as

backup to lead them to it. Or, like we said, they have a job they want you to do, but the timing's not right. We can't ignore the fact that whoever we're up against is smart. We have to assume he knows what he's doing." Sarge paused. "A name was mentioned," he said, his voice still low, as though he was trying not to be overheard. "I suspect this has to do with the mess in Arizona."

Rick had been caught with his hands in the safe of a government official.

"Then why kill Brady?" he asked. "And Saul?"

"Word is that after you went to prison, Brady did some checking."

"He thought I'd been set up."

"Could be someone thinks Brady passed something incriminating on to you. A computer chip, maybe."

Or a matchbook.

"So why kill Kit?"

"He must have known something."

"Or the deaths could be unrelated."

"It's safest to assume they're related."

Rick agreed. "But Cook's murder might not be," he said.

"Could be you were in the wrong place at the wrong time and an easy scapegoat."

Rick. The itinerant construction worker with seemingly no ties. No one to look too closely if he took a fall.

"Cook had a married lover. They got an APB out on the husband, but so far, he hasn't been found." A good sign. A guy who'd committed murder would be on the run. But it wasn't enough of a good sign to make Rick comfortable. The murder weapon had shown up in his house too soon after the incident to have been a spur-of-the-moment decision.

Even if Charles Cook's lover's husband was letting

Rick take the fall, how would he have known where Rick lived and been able to get the weapon planted in his bedroom within hours of the murder with no evidence of breaking and entering?

Rick's theory was that Cook's murder had been carefully planned.

By someone who knew exactly what he was doing.

"Did you learn any more about the missing Homeland Security emails?"

"Still waiting to hear back from my contact."

The content of those posts could tell them so much. What Cook had found out. If he'd found anything out. Who they'd been sent to. And from. Who was out to get Rick…

And they might tell them nothing.

"If they involve information on drugs, ammunitions or human trafficking, we'd know where to focus," Rick said. "Cook could've been on to something. Maybe there's someone dirty in Homeland Security. And he or they are letting the team—our former team—take the heat for whatever they're doing. It could be someone who knows about the team, but is working both sides. And maybe I'm still alive because he thinks I know what Charles uncovered. Maybe he thinks Charles passed on evidence to me. Maybe Charles's death and my being framed is a warning."

"Maybe. I'll see what I can learn. You don't need me to tell you we don't have much time, son."

"Which is why I'm calling you. I want permission for Tom Watkins to take a job."

"No. It's too dangerous."

"It's the quickest way to find out who's after him. Tom has to get back on the streets, talk to people. We have to know who's spreading rumors about him. Let me do this, Sarge. It's the only way."

The only way to ensure Steve's safety, at any rate.

"I'm not comfortable with it. It's *not* the only way."

"What else is there?'

"We have to figure out what you have that they want."

He'd been over all of that. Many times since the day he'd come home to discover that someone had been in his house, touching his things. "As you said, we don't have a lot of time."

"You went to see Brady's landlady. Did she say anything at all that could help us?"

"No."

"When was your last contact with him?"

"Before Arizona. After I was caught we couldn't communicate or we'd risk blowing the team's cover. You know that."

"He died for a reason. So did Saul. It's connected to Tom. It has to be. Which means you. Maybe what they're looking for doesn't have to do with Cook at all. Or maybe Cook's role is after the fact. I still think this ties back to Brady. He was nosing around the Arizona deal. Maybe they think he gave you something. Some clue."

"It's possible. But I'd have come up with it by now if he had."

"So maybe he gave it to you and you didn't know it."

Not Brady. Not without a trail Rick would recognize, be able to follow. They knew each other too well. That was why he couldn't let go of the matchbook.

The matchbook. Brady *had* given him something. Something Rick needed to keep to himself until he could figure out why his comrade had singled him out.

Whatever was going on had already gotten Saul and

Brady killed. Whatever it was, Brady had determined it to be a danger to Sarge. Otherwise, he would've had Janet Meadows give the matchbook to Sarge, who'd be the one to pick up his things if anything happened to him.

Brady's saving the book for Rick was a clear message to protect Sarge. That was protocol. Period. Rick was going to do everything he could to keep Sarge alive.

"Tom has to go back to work," he insisted.

"No."

"It's the only way," he said again. "We don't know exactly how much time we have. And we don't know when they'll be coming after you."

"Give me a few more days to see what I can find. A couple of key contacts have been out of the country. I'll be in Michigan on Tuesday. Meet me at rendezvous five. At midnight."

That gave him three days with Steve. Three days to put their affairs in order.

Three days to fight off sexy images of his beautiful attorney.

And three days to find the connection between the covert ops team, Brady's matchbook, the Arizona setup, the destroyed yacht and four deaths. Saul, Brady, Maria and Charles Cook.

For the first time since Noah's death, Erin didn't sit in the Fitzgerald family pew at church on Sunday. Caylee went. Daniel, with whom she'd been on the phone for most of Saturday evening, had begged her to. While the young man didn't want Caylee to go to Yale, didn't understand the need, he was being wonderfully supportive where Caylee's father was concerned.

According to Caylee, Daniel thought Ron Fitzgerald's behavior was overbearing and dictatorial.

With Caylee gone, Erin took an hour to clean on Sunday morning, vacuuming the carpets, running a disposable dust cloth over the furniture and shining the bathrooms. She also put extra sheets on the beds. Kelly and Maggie were due to arrive sometime that evening.

And when the house was in order she took pity on Boots—who detested the vacuum cleaner and the smell of household cleansers—and left. With a house full of people, she wasn't going to have her usual evening time for work. She had a couple of briefs to prepare and some paperwork to fill out to inform the court and Christa Hart that psychologist Kelly Chapman was going to be an expert witness in the Thomas case.

She parked in the vacant lot behind her office building just after eleven Sunday morning.

The front door of the building wasn't locked. Odd, but not unheard of. It opened into a vestibule and a lobby with a single long counter used by the couple of receptionists they all shared. Hallways lined with office suites shot off from both sides. They kept the door unlocked during business hours. And their receptionist locked it up each night.

Obviously one of the other tenants—attorneys, an accountant, an investment broker and a family counselor—had been in over the weekend and forgotten to lock the main door. She'd done it herself. Because she'd only had her own private practice for five years, she still worked alone. No researchers or assistants who would've had access to her office.

The doors in the silent hallway were all shut. Erin found the quiet a bit unsettling as the tennis shoes she'd put on with her jeans and sweater whispered against the carpet.

And she remembered watching Rick Thomas walk

down this same hallway. Remembered the unusual energy, the sense of life, he seemed to exude.

There was a break in the straight line of closed doors. One was slightly off.

Heart pounding, Erin recognized the door. It was hers. And she was positive she'd locked it on Friday when she left because she'd dropped her keys and when she bent down to retrieve them, she'd spilled the contents of her purse.

Moving slowly forward Erin stopped just short of her door. Listened. And then peeked around the corner. She didn't hear anything.

But what she saw when she pushed on the door sent a shaft of fear straight through her. The only thing about her office that looked normal was the position of the desk, which was set out from the middle of the back wall, facing the door. The high-backed maroon leather chair lay upside down by the entry to the private bathroom, the wheels hanging in midair. Where carpet should be, she saw only papers. And file folders. Envelopes. And unused computer discs. The once-locked black four-drawer filing cabinet had been shoved over, with a big hole cut in the side.

Desk drawers were scattered around the desk, all of them emptied. Her plants were uprooted, soil everywhere, pots thrown haphazardly about. Her Juris Doctor degree and professional awards, along with a couple of framed pictures, had all been removed from the walls.

Books were pulled out of bookcases and left open, many with pages bent, on the floor. Some looked as though they'd been flung across the room. Her plastic in-box was broken into jagged pieces. An angel water globe had been shattered, the glittery water soaking a pile of papers on the desk.

Even her Kleenex box had been emptied, crumpled on the floor, the tissues lying around it.

She should go. Run. As fast as she could. Call Sheriff Johnson. Get help.

Stepping into the room, she closed and locked the door behind her. Then she checked the closet and bathroom to make sure she had no trespassers lurking there. She probably should've checked *before* locking the door, but right now it felt more dangerous outside than in. Whoever was after her, and it could've been more than one person, had already done their damage here.

Were they out there? Perhaps watching her?

Her chest tightened, making it hard to breathe, and Erin pulled her phone out of the purse still hanging on her shoulder.

And she dialed the number she did because she knew it was the right thing to do.

"Thomas." He picked up on the first ring.

"Where are you?"

"Home."

"How's Steve?"

"Fine."

"You've talked to him this morning?"

"I spoke with Jill. Why?" His tone sharpened. "Do you know something?"

"No." She glanced around the room, trying not to cry. "At least, nothing to do with Steve."

"You sound…odd. What's wrong?"

Erin started to chuckle and choked. "I don't know why I called you," she said, feeling cold. And confused. "I…" She had to call 9-1-1. Someone had to see the place. It was a crime scene.

"Where are you?"

"My office."

"Erin, what's going on?"

"I… It… The place is a shambles."

"Someone's been there?" The urgency she heard was new.

"You could say that."

"Is anything missing?"

"I have no idea. I'll have to sift through the piles of everything I own on the floor before I could tell you that."

"Have you touched anything?"

"No. Just closed and locked the door."

"You're sure you're alone in there?"

"Yes."

"Don't touch anything. Call Sheriff Johnson directly. Don't speak with anyone else. And don't leave. Not until we're sure the area's secured. I'll be there in fifteen minutes. Do I need a special code to get in the front door?" There was that authority again. And she didn't think to question him. It was why she'd called him.

"It's locked," she told him. "Call me back when you're outside and I'll come and open it for you."

"Call the sheriff, Erin."

"I will."

24

Rick considered all the possibilities as he sped the few miles across town to Erin's office. The perpetrator could've been Paul Wagner, the recently enlightened husband of Cook's lover. Maybe he wanted to find out if they knew about him, if he was a suspect in Cook's murder. Or anyone connected to any of the other cases Erin had defended or was currently defending could have broken into her office. Looking for something. Maybe even revenge.

That was precisely why Rick wanted Sheriff Johnson there. And only the sheriff. He didn't trust anyone else in this town.

Not after deputies had "found" a murder weapon in his bedroom.

He didn't wholly trust Johnson, either, but of the law enforcement choices available to them, Johnson was the best.

Rick had to beat the sheriff to the scene, though. Because if this had to do with him, with Tom Watkins, gun runners' muscle, he had to get to the evidence first. And to make certain no one else saw it.

If this *did* have to do with him, with Tom, Erin was in

more danger than anyone could know. Real danger. And Rick was responsible.

If the violation of Erin's space was because of him, he owed her his protection. Until he could figure out how to separate her from his mess.

Dressed in jeans and a light blue sweater, Erin pulled open the heavy outer door of her office building with more force than finesse.

"Thank you for coming," she said. "I don't know why I called you. I mean, I didn't call any of my other clients. But I'm glad I did…."

She was rambling, her stride fast, as she led him back to her office.

"Sheriff Johnson is on his way and I haven't really touched anything, except my files. These were in the cleaning closet…." She held up her hands, which were covered with thin latex gloves. "I couldn't leave confidential papers strewn all over. I haven't looked through everything, not by a long shot, but I searched specifically for my current case files."

She stopped just before her office door, turned and pinned him with a look he couldn't quite decipher. She was afraid. Which was understandable. She'd just been vandalized. What he *didn't* understand was the apology he read in her expression.

"Sheriff Johnson told me I could secure my files. From what I can see without touching, my miniclock collection is missing. And the clock on the wall. The MP3 player and stereo I had set up over there on the bookshelf. My computer's been disassembled. I found papers from all my current case files except yours."

"Mine." He finally got a word in. The clocks sent a clear message. Time was of the essence.

She nodded. "I don't get it, Rick. Some of my other

files are missing. I color-code old files according to type, and the orange ones are my divorce cases. They're all gone. They mean nothing, but yours… Why would anyone want my notes on your case? Or copies of papers they could get at the courthouse? *Who* would want them?"

He could name a few possibilities.

Not waiting to hear any more, Rick stepped past her and entered the office. Entered—and stared. The destruction was acute, far more than would've been caused by someone merely looking for something.

A tornado ripping through the room would have been kinder.

Even her desk chair had been cut, stuffing and springs spilling out.

And his seemed to be the only current case file missing.

Their warnings were getting closer. They'd attacked his attorney. Who would be next?

No matter what Sarge thought, come Monday, Tom Watkins was going back to work. One way or another, this had to end.

It hadn't taken Erin long to figure out that she'd had no business calling Rick Thomas because her office had been vandalized. About two seconds after she'd hung up the phone she'd been filled with mortification, which was further enhanced when the sheriff, having been paged out of church to take her call, arrived. He'd immediately frowned when he saw the murder suspect looking over every detail of the damage done to her office—without touching or moving a thing.

"What are you doing here?" His question was abrupt. Accusatory.

"I called him," Erin said, feeling a need to protect Rick

as she placed herself between the sheriff and his view of Rick. "His file appears to be missing...."

She couldn't look at Rick when she heard the words come out of her mouth. Because he knew she'd called him *before* she'd known about the files. She quickly told the sheriff about the other things that she'd discovered were missing.

The sheriff nodded, took notes then stepped up to Rick. "Where were you this morning?"

"At home."

"Can anyone verify that?"

"No."

And Erin went cold. It should've occurred to her that...

"You think he has anything to do with this?" she asked the man she'd always respected and trusted.

"I wouldn't be doing my job if I just assumed he doesn't."

What was wrong with her? Why hadn't she realized that Rick Thomas, like any of her other clients, could be a suspect?

Even when she'd noticed that his file was the only current one missing, she hadn't thought for one second that...

"I'm not even sure it happened this morning," Erin said as the two men, facing each other, surveyed the damage. "I haven't been here since Friday night."

"Have you called anyone else in the building?"

"Yes. Everyone," Erin said. There were only a handful. She'd called them while waiting for Sheriff Johnson to answer his page. "No one was here yesterday. And I don't think any of the other offices were touched. The doors are all locked."

Sheriff Johnson looked back at Rick. "Where were you yesterday?"

"He was in Ludington," Erin said. "All day. I...saw him there."

"Right. At Lakeside. With Steve Miller." The sheriff studied Rick. "I'm sorry about the Halloway mistake. It won't happen again."

"No harm done." Rick's tone was even, as was his expression. Giving away absolutely nothing.

She'd had the urge to hug him when she'd seen him standing outside the office door half an hour before.

"As for this—" Rick motioned to the room "—I have no need to steal my own file from my attorney. I have complete access to everything in there, unless you want to build a theory around the supposition that I don't trust my attorney to be open with me about my business. In which case, I'd simply fire her and request my records. And I have no need for a new stereo, either."

Sheriff Johnson sighed. "You're right, of course. But since your file is missing, I'd like to speak with you. I'll need a listing of everyone you know who might have any interest in your information. Could you bring it to me by noon tomorrow?"

"I'll get that list for you, Sheriff," Erin said, glancing at Rick. There was no real reason not to let the two men have the private meeting the sheriff suggested, but Erin wasn't going to let it happen, anyway. She was Rick's counsel. He talked to no one without her.

Erin's heart jumped as the outer door banged and it took a couple of seconds for her panic to subside. The forensic team, such as it was—two deputies with bags and a fingerprinting kit—had arrived.

"We'll need the room for an hour," Sheriff Johnson

told her. "Maybe more." She and her client were being dismissed. "I'll call you when we're through."

Erin nodded, grabbed her purse and followed Rick Thomas out the door.

"I'm sorry about that," she said as soon as their silent walk down the hall and out the main door had ended.

"Why? Are you responsible for his thoughts?"

"No, but I should've seen it coming. I mean, in his eyes you're a…"

Rick had been planning to get in the truck, put the pedal to the metal and speed his way to Steve. Erin's words stopped him.

"A murderer?" he finished for her.

"I'm sorry." Her chin lowered and then she looked back up at him, squinting in the sun. "I guess I don't believe you are one."

He said nothing.

"I can't see you as a murderer."

He suppressed the pleasure her words brought him. He couldn't afford pleasure. Not now. And his alter ego, Tom, *had* committed murder.

There hadn't been one damn thing identifying anyone in the devastation he'd just left. No "signature" that he recognized. No familiar mark, cut of a blade or operating method. Destruction without order. No clear motive.

Unless that was the motive. Destruction as a distraction. Because if just Rick's file was missing, the theft would be too obvious.

"How sure are you that mine is the only current file that's gone?" He'd asked already. He asked again.

"As sure as I can be with that mess in there. I found at least some of the papers from every other current file. But none from yours." Erin's shrug was an expression of vulnerability, not nonchalance. She'd been vandalized. He knew how that felt.

He should offer to help her clean up the place. In fact, he felt compelled to do so since he was probably the cause of the crime.

But a whiff of her scent caught him. The same scent that had lingered in Steve's room the afternoon before. Making Rick feel restless.

Filling him with wants he couldn't have, needs he had to ignore.

"I'll need that list the sheriff asked for. Anyone you know of who might have an interest in your information."

He and Sarge were way ahead of them.

He nodded. He'd give her a list. Just not the real one. "Call me if Sheriff Johnson finds anything. Or if you discover that anything else is missing," he said, turning toward his truck.

"I will."

Arms crossed over her stomach, she hadn't moved.

"I can help clean up." The truck key dug into his palm. She shouldn't be there by herself. In case the break-in had been a warning that more damage was on the way. An attempt at intimidation before demand.

She shook her head. "I've got friends coming to visit. And someone staying with me right now. And Noah's brothers…"

She didn't need him.

Good.

"Do me a favor?" he said.

"What?"

"Don't go back to your office alone. Not when the building's empty."

Her chuckle was strength and fear all in one. "No worries there," she said. "You couldn't pay me to do that."

She was a smart woman. An independent woman. She'd be fine.

As long as Rick figured out who was after him and took care of business before any more of it spilled over onto her.

Or Steve.

The sheriff's department couldn't lift any fingerprints from Erin's office. Or from the building. Not from the outer door or the rail leading up the steps. There appeared to be no point of entry. Or exit, either. Her lock hadn't been broken.

No one in the area had seen anything unusual or noticed anyone they didn't know hanging around.

Her unease over the incident drove Erin to Ludington without hesitation when she got a call from Ben Pope late Sunday afternoon. Caylee was with Daniel and his family at their home. Erin hadn't told the Fitzgeralds about the break-in yet. Or Kelly.

Kelly and her young charge were on the road, on their way to Temple. Now more than ever, Erin needed Kelly in a professional sense—to speak with Rick Thomas.

But until she knew whether or not she was a target of the attack or merely a conduit to Rick Thomas's information, she wasn't so sure her guests should be staying at her home. Before she went to Ludington she called a woman she knew from church who ran a lovely bed-and-breakfast down the road from Erin's home. And because it was off-season and the end of a weekend, the place was empty. Putting the bill on her credit card, Erin booked a two-room suite there for Kelly and Maggie. And another room for Caylee. She wanted them someplace else until she could be sure her home was safe.

Ben's office was sandwiched between a deli and a cellular store in a strip mall that also housed a hugely popular Mexican restaurant, a large card and gift shop and a shoe outlet. While some of the stores were closed on Sunday, there was enough traffic around for Erin to feel comfortable leaving her car unattended, but she palmed her keys and watched her back as she approached the investigator's glassed door.

He was waiting for her. Ushered her to his office and, as always, got straight to business. Ben, an average-size dark-haired man, had never once asked her how she was. She didn't ask how he was, either.

"I got your DNA information," he said, opening the top folder on his desk. Withdrawing a sheet of paper, he slid it across to her.

She glanced at the paper. And then back at the man she'd been doing business with since she'd first moved to Temple.

Ben was an organized man. A thorough man. A calm man.

Paperwork was stacked in labeled bins on his desk. His phone was within easy reach. A holder with pens within even easier reach.

The photographs on his walls were nondescript. Trees. A bridge. A country home. They reminded Erin of the sample pictures that came with new computers.

Her heart still pounded, but she was breathing more normally.

Sitting back in the single leather chair opposite Pope's desk, she picked up the sheet. Ben was waiting for her comments.

Or, more likely, her questions.

"I don't understand."

"I can't speak for the man you know to be Rick Thomas," Pope said, "but the DNA sample you gave me came from a man named Tom Watkins."

Yes. She saw that. The words, anyway. She didn't get the connection.

"Tom Watkins was convicted of illegal entry and trespass."

"In a secure government facility." Ben added what wasn't written in front of her. "That's the official scoop."

"And unofficially?"

"I did some checking with some people who you don't want to know about. Something about that Arizona deal sparked a memory. It's not every day a man's caught trying to steal drugs from a government safe. Anyway, based on what I've heard, and this is strictly rumor from people who can't be trusted as far as you can throw them…"

Erin nodded, understanding, feeling nothing.

"My contact has some ties to the drug world. I'm talking big-time stuff, not street-peddling."

"And?"

"Tom Watkins was a name associated with some of the biggest gunrunners. He could have ties to a couple of drug cartels as well and probably has contacts in Mexico, Costa Rica, Miami and Arizona, to name a few."

She continued to listen. To consider. She just didn't believe. Not yet. "It says here that before the Arizona incident, he had no priors."

"That's right. I heard that for a while there his name on the street was 'magician.'"

Erin didn't want to know where Pope got that information. She didn't want to know who he associated with. She didn't want any of this information.

"Magicians are masters of deception," she said.

"He survived tent city." The infamous jail in the middle of the Arizona desert, where three meals a day weren't guaranteed and air-conditioning wasn't provided.

But pink underwear for male inmates had been.

"What about in the past year? What's Tom Watkins been up to?"

"Nothing," Ben said, his brow creased as he met her gaze. "The man left prison on an early release, cleared out the room he'd been renting before his arrest and disappeared off the face of the earth."

No, he hadn't. He'd moved to Temple, Michigan. Changed his name to Rick Thomas. And gotten work as a handyman.

Erin had questions. A lot of them. But she had answers, too.

Like the fact that she was removing herself from Rick Thomas's case.

As soon as possible.

25

Rick was sitting with Steve, watching football, when his phone vibrated, signaling a call. Because it was from Erin—and he'd been sitting there thinking about her, about the attack on her office, about Tom Watkins and Eddie Nogales being scared enough to sell Tom up the river—he took the call.

Eddie Nogales didn't scare easily. And after having worked with the man, having watched Eddie torture a guy for being disloyal to him, he didn't believe for one second that marriage and a kid had made him soft.

"I have to see you. Tonight."

"I'm with Steve."

"Not there. I can't see you there."

Having heard his name, Steve was watching him, and Rick got up, went into the bathroom and turned on the fan.

He and Steve had a long-standing joke about bathroom smells. Steve wouldn't follow him there.

"Are you in trouble?"

"No."

"You're safe?"

"Perfectly."

"Did Sheriff Johnson find something?"

"No."

"What's this about, then?"

"I'll tell you when I see you." She sounded angry. Not scared.

"Dinner's in half an hour," he said quietly. "I can leave then."

Her impatient sigh got his adrenaline pumping. Something was up. Hopefully just delayed reaction to the break-in at her office.

"Fine. Come to my place."

"Your office?"

"No. My house." She gave him the address. He knew the street.

No way in hell was he going there. He refused to be alone with her in her home. Too intimate.

Too tempting. Especially to a man who was going to be leaving the next day, perhaps for good.

And then he remembered her guests. They wouldn't be alone.

"I'd like to know what this is about."

"Then you'll have to come here to find out."

"Why there?"

"You'll see when you get here."

Was she setting him up? "Are you alone?"

"Yes. I'm in my car. Driving."

"Is someone putting you up to this?"

"Of course not." His question seemed to disgust her.

"Look, Mr. Thomas…" He thought he detected an emphasis on his last name. "If you don't want to meet with me, that's your choice. But please understand that if you do not, you will receive my final bill in the morning. Along with another visit from Sheriff Johnson who'll be carrying another arrest warrant."

Shit. "I'll be there."

On the road
Sunday, October 24, 2010

"Do we have to tell my mom about this trip?" Maggie had packed her bag the second I'd told her about our impromptu business trip to Michigan. She hadn't argued or asked questions. Hadn't used school as an excuse to stay in Chandler without me. Didn't seem to mind leaving her Mac....

I'd been sitting in the car feeling good about all of that.

"Why wouldn't you want to tell her?" I asked, glancing over at the girl. With her hair up in a ponytail and no makeup and the sweats she'd put on for the seven-hour drive, Maggie looked about twelve.

Not the experienced woman of fourteen that she was.

I cared about Maggie. I really, really wanted to make this work. To be her family. I was confident I could help her.

Until it came to the hold David Abrams—Mac—had on her. Clinically I understood. She was in a trauma-induced state of denial. Lying to herself. She believed that her Mac and David Abrams were two different men. Professionally I knew how to handle the other man's manipulation and abuse where his victim was concerned.

As a parent, loving a girl who'd given a precious gift to a man who'd deceived her, whose heart had been broken, I felt like a fraud.

"You know how she gets," Maggie said, staring out her side window. "Afraid that I'm going to think I'm better than her. This trip... She might not like it...."

"Because she couldn't afford to take you on vacations?"

"Yeah."

"And what else?" I knew there was something. I could hear it in her tone.

"Your job. You're someone important. Educated. People listen to you. They pay you to help them. I think it makes her feel...stupid."

"There's a difference between uneducated and stupid," I said. "Your mother isn't stupid. At all."

"I know that. But she doesn't."

"It's your choice, sweetie," I finally said. "I don't believe it's a good idea to lie to anyone, let alone your mother. But if you'd rather not tell her we've been out of town, I'm not going to force you to do so."

I didn't see Lori Winston personally. I just transported Maggie to and from her biweekly visits.

Maggie nodded. "Thanks, Kelly. And..." The girl paused. I waited. "And thank you for bringing me."

I was still smiling when the phone rang. It was our hostess.

"You aren't going to believe what's happened," Erin said as soon as I picked up. "The timing of your visit is no coincidence. How far out are you?"

"Three hours."

"Damn. I figured it was something like that, but I was hoping you were closer. I just... So much has happened today and my head's reeling and I guess I should have something to eat. You know. I'm so furious. I should probably be scared, but I'm not. I'm angry. *Really* angry."

I recognized a rant when I heard one. And because the exercise was healthy, I didn't interrupt, no matter how badly I wanted to know what was going on. I gave Erin time to vent.

And then, when my friend's voice slowed, I asked, "What's this about?"

I almost drove off the road when she told me about the break-in at her office. But the sheriff had things under control. He didn't think Erin was in any personal danger. He figured it was professional.

I wasn't so sure.

"What if they didn't find what they were looking for at your office?" I asked. "Wouldn't your home be the next place to look?"

"I thought that, too. Sheriff Johnson thinks Rick Thomas's file was the target. One of his deputies sat with me while I cleaned up the papers strewn all over my office this afternoon. Rick's file was definitely the only current case file missing. The sheriff has a deputy watching my place, but I'm not worried."

She didn't sound worried. She sounded…annoyed.

"He lied to me, Kel. He's a fraud. I'm confronting him tonight, but I still want you to speak with him in the morning, because I want your opinion on record. Then I'm taking myself off his case. The man has serious enemies."

Her agitation was contagious.

"Anyway, I made reservations for you to stay at a nice B and B down the road from me, until I get this cleared up. Just in case. I'll text you the address and phone number. Agnes is expecting you. Caylee's staying there tonight, too. And hopefully tomorrow you all can move over to my place."

"I don't like the idea of you being there alone."

"I'm not the least bit scared of him," Erin said.

In my professional opinion, based on her tone and on what she *hadn't* said, she wasn't being completely honest with herself. I believed she was somewhat afraid of her client. I also understood that she was doing what she had to. Taking control of a situation that had been controlling her.

"You're sure you've got someone watching the place at all times?"

"Positive. I have a deputy on the premises. I can see him now. A few yards down the hill. And I have a two-way radio, too."

"A two-way radio?"

"Yeah."

"You're helping them, aren't you?"

"I'm not wired or anything. I haven't told them Rick lied to me. I'm still his attorney. I can't tell them what I know. They're watching me because of the break-in."

"If anyone wants to get you, you're providing a target, inviting him in—but with surveillance."

Maggie was staring at me. I didn't mind that she was getting a hint of my job.

"Sheriff Johnson and Ron Fitzgerald said it's the only way, although neither of them are happy about the idea. Still, they don't want me out and about with the perpetrator on the loose—whether it's…Rick or someone connected to him. They'd rather have him come after me on their terms."

I didn't like it. But the plan made sense.

"What did Rick Thomas lie to you about?"

"I'd rather wait until you've talked to him tomorrow. I want your opinion to be as unbiased as possible."

"Fair enough." We arranged to be back in touch to make meeting plans early in the morning. She was going to arrange a space for Rick Thomas and me to meet.

"Be careful," I said, wishing I could do more.

"Of course."

With my foot resting a little heavier on the pedal I crossed my fingers for my friend and concentrated on Maggie.

If the deputy hiding in the trees thought Rick didn't see him, he was a fool. But then, he already knew Bruce Halloway was less than stellar on the job. Rick considered walking out there and giving the guy a few tips on surveillance, but figured the effort would be a waste of time.

Time he didn't have.

If he was still free, he was leaving town in the morning. At least long enough to seek out a couple of Tom's contacts in the hellholes where they lived.

And his attorney was angry with him.

He got to the top of the drive, parking by the side door of her impressive, glass-walled home.

Lake Michigan's waves beat against the shore below and Rick remembered Erin telling him how the sound of the waves gave her peace. And kept her company.

"What's up?" he asked her as she met him at the side door.

"I have to speak with you."

"Obviously. You threatened me with a call to the sheriff if I didn't agree to meet. It would appear that you called him, anyway. Is Halloway out there to bring me in when we're through?"

"No, of course not."

"To protect you from me, then?"

"No." She stepped back, still wearing the jeans and sweater she'd had on that morning. But she was barefoot. "Come in."

Her toenails were bright red.

Rick came inside just far enough to let her close the
door behind him. He was in a laundry room. An impressively clean and organized laundry room. The washer and
dryer were computerized, relatively new. A white metal
matching cart on wheels rested between them, bearing
detergents and bleach and dryer sheets. A hand-painted
garden mural adorned the yellow walls.

And to his right a single blouse hung on a garment
rack. A cream-colored silk blouse. Probably hand-washed.
Hanging there to dry.

His sudden urge to touch the damned thing had Rick
needing to leave.

"Sheriff Johnson wants to make certain that I'm not
the target of this morning's break-in," she said. "At least,
not personally. He doesn't want me coming and going
on my own, and I refuse to become a prisoner. The compromise was that I will stay here tonight in the hope of
luring anyone who…needs something from me to come
and get me. The sheriff's assigning deputies to watch the
house. If I'm going to be at risk, he wants me at risk on
his terms."

"I'd do the same."

"You would." Her glance was piercing. Not in a kind
way.

"Yes," he said, not liking this at all. It wasn't often
that Rick was on the vulnerable side of a conversation.
He made it a rule whenever he could not to enter into any
dialogue that mattered unless he knew more about the
situation than his opponent.

"Tell me, Rick. How does a construction worker speak
with such authority on matters pertaining to crime? You
did the same thing this morning when I called about the
break-in at the office. You barked out orders like you were
used to taking control of crime scenes. And yesterday,

too, when we were talking about Charles Cook being involved with something classified."

"Most men view themselves as the guy in charge. Comes with the testosterone."

She nodded, but her shoulders remained taut, her expression rigid. She turned and left the room.

Rick hadn't intended to go any farther into her home. He didn't need to see the lush-looking cream-colored sectional, would rather not be able to picture her there, alone with her waves at night.

He didn't need the scent of lavender in his nostrils, or to see the magnificent view of the water.

"Have a seat."

"I'll stand."

"Uh-uh." Shaking her head, Erin sat on one end of the sectional, leaving the rest of the monstrosity, which was big enough to be a bed, to him. "This is my show, Mr. Thomas. You do as I ask, or I make good on my threat."

"To call the sheriff."

"That's right."

"And have me arrested."

"Yes."

"And to take yourself off my case."

"Right again."

"How do I know you aren't going to do all of that, anyway?"

"You don't. But at least you have a chance to stop me."

He chose the autumn leave upholstered wing chair across from her. It was old. Didn't match the rest of the room.

It meant something to her.

A radio crackled, and Rick tensed but didn't move. If

he was going down, he was going to do it his way. Protecting Steve.

"Ms. Morgan?"

"Yes, Bruce?"

"You okay?"

"Yes."

"That Rick Thomas in there with you?"

"Yes. He's my client. Since we can't meet at my office, I asked him to come here."

"Okay, ma'am. Just checking."

"Thank you, Bruce."

Rick shook his head. "What if you'd been in trouble?" he couldn't help asking, butting in where he didn't belong.

"Then I either wouldn't have answered, or I would've said, 'Of course' when he asked if I was okay and he'd know I wasn't."

Okay, so they had a plan. An elementary one, but it could work.

"We have light signals, too," she said. "And if the front curtains close he knows to call for help and get in here."

Using so many precautions your victim needed a playbook wasn't wise. Too much for them to remember, or confuse, during times of stress. Too much potential for mistakes. Or she could just be giving him fake signals to string him along.

"I take it he doesn't know about whatever it is you think you have on me. Since you're still my attorney. For the moment."

"That's right."

Okay. Good. Now they were getting somewhere. First and foremost, she was being loyal to him.

For the moment.

Energy coursed through Rick, making it difficult to stay in his seat. He had too much to do. People to confront. Information to get. One way or another.

"Have you told anyone else about whatever it is you're going to lay on me?"

"Not yet." As though she was planning to.

"What are you waiting for?"

"You're currently my client. That gives you privilege."

"Only in terms of what I've told you. And you can take yourself off my case at any time." He'd lose his inside informant with the local police, but right now, the murder charge was the least of his worries.

More important to him was whether or not he could trust her. Her choice to come to him first, before she went to the sheriff, was big. He had to know if it was big enough.

He'd introduced her to Steve. Which meant that Steve would be more likely to speak to her again if she showed up asking questions when Rick wasn't there.

He'd done what he thought best on Saturday when he'd called her. But he'd been sloppy. For a second time. The first had been in using Steve's money to get his own ass out of jail. And sloppiness could mean death.

His own or someone else's.

She was staring at him. Watching him. Assessing him?

He stared right back.

"Thank you for coming over, Rick…or should I say Tom?"

26

Rick could play dumb. Pretend not to recognize the name she'd just uttered. But he didn't have time for games. His cover was blown. He had to know how. Where. And at the moment, she was the source of that information.

Rick grabbed the gun holstered inside his shirt, holding it so she—but only she—could see it.

"Who are you working for?"

The two-way radio was off. He'd seen her turn it off when she disconnected from Halloway. But her house could be bugged.

"Until you just drew your gun, I worked for you." She hadn't flinched. Her voice was steady. But she hadn't taken her eyes off his military-issue, small and very lethal automatic.

"I don't have time for games, Erin. If you know who I am, you know that I'll get what I want. Now tell me who hired you."

"You did." Her voice broke. She was rattled. But didn't even hesitate as she answered. She could be telling him the truth.

"I hired you to defend me against an unwarranted murder charge."

"And as part of that defense, I had to find out everything I could about you. In order to be prepared for whatever the prosecution might use against you."

She expected him to believe that a small-town attorney with limited investigative resources had managed to break through a chain of government protocols and expose an alias that no longer existed?

More likely, whoever was after him had contacted her today. After the break-in. Or maybe they'd contacted the sheriff. She could be wired. This could all be a setup.

She was in far more danger than he'd guessed. Than she knew. He had to get her out of there.

His thoughts lining up in clear and concise order, Rick planned their escape. He had to lure Halloway to the house where he had the best chance of taking him down without a fight. He and Erin would have ten minutes or so before the officer regained consciousness to make their getaway.

He'd seen her purse in the laundry room when he'd first come in. She could grab it on the way out. Anything else they'd pick up on the road.

"I took a sample of your DNA, Rick."

Her words, which seemed to come from out of nowhere, interrupted his mental field plan.

"That night at George's Place," she added as he switched gears enough to follow her conversation. "When you went to the restroom, I took your empty beer cup—"

"Take off your sweater."

"What?"

Moving the gun only enough to remind her he had it trained on her, he said, "You have a blouse on underneath."

"Yes, but I will not—"

"It's hot in here," Rick interrupted, moving the

gun again. "Take off your sweater. Toss it over on the couch."

With shaking hands she did as he asked. And when she looked back at him, there was stark fear in her eyes.

He had to leave it there, that fear, until he knew whether or not he dared to speak more freely.

"Unbutton your blouse."

Erin didn't argue again. And Rick vowed that if he made it through the next few days he'd spend whatever time he had left doing what he could to make up for the indignity he was causing her. The terror.

He detested himself. What the job had made of him.

He watched as her fingers moved slowly from the button at her throat to the one beneath it. And the one below that. Watched like a guard insuring that his captive followed orders—not as a man who...

Her bra was silk. White with muted florals. Its sweetness dried the inside of his mouth.

The tops of her breasts fell over the sexy silk contours. And her cleavage... He could almost feel her skin caressing his as he sunk his face between the—

Erin's hand dropped to her lap. And Rick's gaze met hers. She didn't look away, but faced him boldly. Bravely.

And he saw she wasn't wearing a wire.

"Button yourself back up," he said gruffly. Ashamed of what he'd had to do.

She was curled up on her legs so she wouldn't be wearing a calf wire. She was clean.

"Could you show me the restroom?" Rick asked as soon as she'd put herself back together. She glanced at the gun. Stood.

And he wanted to tell her she had nothing to fear from

him. But he couldn't. Until he knew what was going on, he needed her afraid of him.

Banking on the likelihood that the bathroom would be off a windowless hallway, or at least positioned so that Halloway wouldn't be able to see them, Rick followed Erin and pulled her into the room with him. And with his gun more visible, checked the room for bugs.

When he was convinced it was clean, he stood between Erin and the door and reholstered his gun.

The room was fairly large. Double sinks. A garden tub with faux windows whose sills were covered with plants. And a separate room at the back for the john. Decorated in beige and rose, the bathroom could've been out of a women's magazine.

But then, so could its owner. The classiest fashion magazine around.

"I'm sorry," he began. The words didn't feel comfortable on his tongue. "I needed to know that you weren't wired or being coerced in what you were saying to me."

"Of course I wasn't. This isn't television. It's Temple, Michigan, Rick. Or Tom. Or whoever you are."

"One man's already been murdered," Rick reminded her. "Apparently by a professional."

"And that's what you are, isn't it?" Her tone resigned, she stared up at him.

"What I am isn't important right now. Knowing what's going on and getting you out of it is."

"You think I'm in danger?"

"Yes."

"*You're* the only one who's held a gun on me."

"Because I needed to see if you were wearing a wire. I told you that."

"You could have asked."

"If you were hot, you would've lied. You'd have been expected to lie."

"And if I was hot, they would've known you'd realize it as soon as I undid my blouse."

"I was prepared."

"How?"

"They'd have moved in. I was ready."

"Ready how?"

"Just ready."

She glanced at the side of his chest. And didn't press the issue.

"I need the truth, Erin. How did you find out about Tom?"

"Exactly like I told you. I had Ben Pope run your DNA."

"This Pope guy. How long have you known him?"

"Five years. He's not working for anyone, Rick. I'm certain of that. Your DNA gave you away. Why can't you just accept that?"

"Because Tom Watkins doesn't have DNA." Rick had withstood professional questioning from authorities who'd been given the go-ahead to treat him as a hostile and he hadn't said a word. Even after they'd hooked him up to electric shock waves.

He'd been trained not to speak, and in fifteen years had never done so. Not even when, during the shakedown in which he'd saved Eddie's life, he'd had a gun to his head.

"Of course he does. Everyone has DNA."

Rick shook his head. Thought quickly. And knew he had no choice but to trust her. He was living in her world now, not the underbelly he'd inhabited for so long.

The rules were different here.

He stood, hands on the waist of his jeans, facing her. "Tom Watkins doesn't exist."

"He's a convicted felon. I saw his record. He was serving prison time in Arizona until a year ago. Amazingly, that was about the same time you showed up here. Without a past. *Rick Thomas* is the man who doesn't exist."

"You've got it backward."

"What's that mean?"

"I exist." He fought the urge to reach for her. To touch her face. To feel the skin that haunted his dreams. "This past year, for the first time in fifteen years, I've lived my own life."

"Then who is Tom Watkins?"

Making up the rules as he went along was a major part of Rick's life. Changing rules in midstream, the norm. But no matter how many life-and-death situations he'd lied himself into or out of, he'd never once broken the code of silence. Never.

Telling her could put her in danger.

Not telling her might already have done so.

"I need to know you'll never repeat what I'm going to say."

Her mouth was pinched with tension, her brows drawn as she stared at him.

"You are my attorney. I'm speaking as your client," he said. "You cannot take this information anywhere."

She inhaled a deep breath. And released it.

"It has to be that way," he said.

"Okay." Erin relaxed against the marble counter, looking down at her feet and then back at him as she crossed her arms over her chest. "Fine. You have my word. But I can't guarantee that I'm going to keep you on as a client."

"Understood."

"Who's Tom Watkins?"

"He's an alias, created for me by the government of the United States."

Her eyes widened. "You're a government agent?"

"I was."

When Erin's shoulders dropped with relief and her features softened, he had to add, "Sort of."

She frowned. "Don't play games with me, Rick. It's been a hard day and—"

"I worked for a covert operation," he said. "We were formed under the Department of Defense, but not officially. We were there to do all the jobs the government couldn't, but that, for the protection of the American people, had to be done."

"Illegal jobs."

"Yes."

"Who knew about you?"

"No one but our sergeant knew our real identities. But certain people were aware of our group. The president knew, at least initially. I assume, as new presidents came on board, they were informed about our status. The secretary of defense always knew. One or two others. We were funded under a committee assigned to terrorist prevention research, but we were under very deep cover."

"You say you've been doing this for fifteen years?"

"Yes."

"How does a kid of twenty-two get a job like that?"

"I was recruited by my army sergeant."

"You and how many others?"

"There were four us, including the sergeant."

He'd tell her what he had to in order to ensure her co-operation, which he had to have to get her and Sarge out of danger.

He was going to need her support when he skipped town in the morning.

He had to keep her safe while he was gone; he needed her help to do that.

And to keep an eye on Steve for him, too.

Erin told herself not to believe a word he said. The man was holding her hostage in her own bathroom.

And she wanted to hold him.

"You were in prison in Arizona," she reminded him. Reminded herself. Government agents didn't go to jail. Unless they'd turned traitor.

"Tom was. And his DNA was supposed to disappear from the system upon his release."

"So Tom was in prison for some kind of undercover operation? You were there on purpose? Working?" Could she actually be buying this? It sounded like a badly written guy flick.

"No. He was in prison because the job he'd been working on went sour."

"Went sour how?"

"I have my suspicions, but I'm not sure."

The garden tub beckoned Erin. Whether to drown her sorrows or to soak away her pain, she didn't know. She just wanted to escape for a while. To shut off her mind, her doubts, and simply rest.

"I need more, Rick. This is your chance to convince me of your innocence and so far you aren't doing it." Not completely enough to calm her fears, anyway.

"Intelligence said that a highly respected, high-ranking government official in Arizona was on the take. He was in with some Mexican cartel and had been facilitating some pretty major drug trafficking. A stash had been diverted and he'd intercepted it. It was in a private safe underneath the bar in his office at the state capital. I was sent in to retrieve the drugs."

He didn't name names. Erin didn't ask. "So what happened?"

"I got in. Found the safe. Got it open. But as soon as I did, a special agent with the Department of Defense burst into the room and I was arrested."

Her stomach hurt. "Wait a minute," Erin said. "If you were an agent, then…"

"Our team was covert," Rick said, his voice as strong, his gaze as clear, as always.

As clear as it had been when he'd lied to her.

"We operated with the understanding that if we ever got caught, we were on our own. It had to be that way to preserve the anonymity of what we did—to protect the government from ever being held accountable for the jobs we did."

The story was too fantastic. And yet…she was starting to believe him. *Really* believe him.

"But wouldn't whoever had sent you in there have access to other operations? Shouldn't someone have made sure no agents were working against you?"

"Of course they should have."

She was beginning to understand.

"You were set up."

"That's what I believe."

"What did your sergeant say?"

"That the special ops agent had been acting outside protocol. He'd heard about the politician, knew the drugs were going to be moved. He didn't know who to trust so he went in to make sure he could implicate the man before the evidence could disappear. He went into the room under his own cognizance."

"I suppose that's possible."

"The timing was too perfect. Either I'd been given the wrong window of time or he'd known I was going to be there."

"Or that the drugs were."

The way Rick was studying her was different. She wasn't sure how. The air in the room closed in. Became… intimate.

But Erin no longer felt like escaping.

27

No one had been told about the drugs. That was how their jobs worked. When intelligence pointed to the most sensitive issues, Rick and his peers were called in and intelligence went dark. The four of them were the only agents who knew the details of their jobs so that if something went bad, they were the ones left twisting in the wind.

Most times only Sarge and whichever of the three of them was on a particular job knew anything about its existence. And once Sarge had handed off a job to one of them, even he didn't know the details. It stopped with the person doing the job.

But what if Erin was right? What if someone *had* known about the drugs? Had the guy, the other agent, been after the drugs? And not sent after him?

Had he been given the same window of time and just happened upon the room seconds before Rick had gotten out?

He didn't buy it.

"There has to be a tie-in between what's going on here and the Arizona deal," he said aloud. "And whoever's behind this has been planning it long enough that Tom's

DNA didn't disappear from the national registry of convicted criminals like it should have."

"Tie-in to what?" Erin asked. "To the break-in at my office today? Because they were looking for information on you?"

Rick had another choice to make. "To that," he said, then added, "And to Charles Cook's death."

"Cook? What's that got to do with a drug deal in Arizona?"

"I think it's pretty clear I've been framed," he said. "Maybe just to cover up a mistake someone else made. But maybe not."

"You're saying you think the only reason Charles was killed was so someone could frame you for murder?"

The missing Homeland Security emails had not been explained. Or recovered.

"I'm saying it's a possibility. Or that Charles found out something to do with my past, just because I happened to take a construction job at the local EMA office where he worked. And once he knew something, he had to be disposed of."

"I think the killer was Paul Wagner and you were a convenient fall guy."

"That would be fine with me."

"But that still doesn't explain your compromised cover." She was frowning at him. "Or the break-in at my office."

"I know."

"This is serious, isn't it?"

Reading the fear in her eyes, Rick nodded.

She sat on the edge of the tub, hands on either side of her. And after several minutes, she glanced back up at him. "What are we going to do?"

Oh, God. He liked that *we* far too much. This woman

was going to be his downfall. He just knew it. He'd introduced her to Steve. Broken a fifteen-year code of silence.

And got a soft feeling inside because she'd included herself in his battle.

He was thirty-seven years old and he'd lived too long.

"We should call Sheriff Johnson."

"No." He hadn't meant to sound so harsh. But she had to understand. "First and foremost, I am the front man on this," he told her. "There's no discussion, debate, compromise or question on that."

She nodded. "The sheriff's a good man, Rick. We can trust him. And we need him."

He understood her fear. He understood his life.

"Someone planted that knife in my home within minutes of the sheriff's search of my place," he reminded her. "We don't know who we can trust."

"I trust Sheriff Johnson with my life."

"What about the people he works with? The people he'd call in to help?"

"I trust them."

"With your life?"

Her silence satisfied him.

"There's another reason we can't call him."

"What?" She was wary. And he didn't blame her.

"Because I'm going to be leaving town."

"That contradicts the terms of your bail."

He acknowledged the comment with a slight nod.

And Erin stood. "Rick, you can't—"

"I have to," he interrupted. She came closer and he grabbed her arms, holding her gently, maybe imploringly, if he had it in him to beg. "I have to put Tom back out on the streets," he said, weighing his words carefully. Asking her to understand a covert government position had been hard enough. He couldn't push his luck by disclosing the underworld life Tom Watkins had lived to do his job. "It's the only way to find out who's after him. Or me."

She didn't pull back. She probably should have. Erin's eyes as she peered up at him made him soft. Weak. "You're setting yourself up as bait," she said.

"Yes."

"How do you know that whoever's behind this will realize you're out there?"

"If they've framed me for murder, if they've broken into your office to get my files, they know every move I'm making. Or close enough. They'll find me."

"You're going back out there to the people Tom knew, aren't you?"

"It's best if you don't know that," he said. And when she started to pull away, to argue, Rick guided her back to him and said, "I'm serious, Erin. I'm putting you in too much jeopardy as it is, just telling you I'll be gone. You could be charged with aiding and abetting...."

"That's my choice to make."

"It's pretty obvious you've already been a target because of me. I can't tell you any more. I don't want anyone else to have a reason to come after you."

"They'll come after me if they even think I know anything," she said. And she had a point.

"If something happens, if I'm not back by Tuesday night, I want you to go straight to the sheriff. Tell him everything I've told you. And insist on taking a lie detector test. I want it understood that you know nothing about where I'm going or who I'm meeting."

"These people—do they know you're coming?"

"No."

"But they'll find you."

"Yes."

Erin didn't like it. Not any of it. She didn't like being in danger. Having her office trashed. She didn't like being privy to potentially illegal activity. She could lose her career if it was ever discovered that she'd knowingly covered for a client who was breaking the terms of his bail.

Not that Rick had asked her to cover for him.

But she would. She knew that was the choice she'd just made.

"Do you think we should go sit in the living room?" she asked. "Bruce Halloway has to be wondering what we're doing...."

"We could be in your study reading law books."

She stopped as she was reaching for the door, turned and looked at him over her shoulder. "How do you know I have a study filled with law books?"

"I saw it on the way in from the living room."

The door had only been slightly open. And the light was dim.

"You have two bedrooms between here and there, too. One with a white eyelet spread and the other done up in pale green. One has a rocking chair. The other an antique phone table with a seat."

Erin stared.

"Being observant's kept me alive for years," Rick said. "It's a hard habit to break."

She had a feeling she was only beginning to crack the surface of what there was to know about this man.

She opened the bathroom door. "If you knew about the study, why choose the bathroom?" she asked.

"The study's an obvious place to hide a bug. And I had a feeling you weren't going to give me much time."

"You had a gun on me."

"Yeah."

Erin decided he'd just confirmed that he would never have used that gun, although she'd pretty much figured that when he'd pulled it out.

So why had she complied with his wishes? To remove her sweater, her blouse…

"I should be going," he said when they reached the living room.

She agreed. He should.

Her phone rang. Grabbing the cell off the coffee table, Erin recognized Sheriff Johnson's number.

"I have to take this," she said. And remembered Kelly. "But there's something else I need to talk to you about. Can you wait a second?"

"This is Erin," she was saying as Rick nodded.

"Erin? Sheriff Johnson here. You okay?"

"Fine, why?"

"No reason. Halloway called in fifteen minutes ago and said everything was quiet."

"It is." Ron Fitzgerald had probably urged the older man to call. Rick really didn't need to worry about her safety. Not with the Fitzgerald family at her back.

"I've got some news, Erin. They found Paul Wagner."

Thank God. If they could clear Rick of Charles's murder tonight, he'd be free to travel legally in the morning.

If Paul Wagner had killed Charles Cook as part of a lovers' triangle, then the man's death wasn't a part of some bigger plot. "Is he in custody?" she asked. "Did you get a confession?"

"He's dead, Erin."

"Dead?"

"Yeah. His throat was slit. Sometime within the past hour. Blood didn't even have time to clot."

Before Erin even looked at Rick, she picked up the two-way radio. "Halloway, you there?"

"Yeah."

"I feel like a sitting duck. I'm closing the back curtains." The ones facing the road. She never covered the windows overlooking the lake. The house was on the edge of a cliff with a seventy-degree drop-off. Not much traffic out that way.

"You okay, ma'am?"

"Yes."

"Fine. All other plans remain in place."

She pulled the drapes. "Okay."

"Have a good evening, ma'am."

Turning off the radio, Erin dropped it on the coffee table and curled up in a corner of the sectional, facing the lake.

"It helps," she said, breathing in deeply, craving the peace the lake brought her even in darkness.

"What helps?" Rick stood, hands in the pockets of his jeans, between the living room and the kitchen.

"Knowing the lake's right there. With me."

"Who's dead?"

"Paul Wagner."

She'd expected Rick to swear. Or at least express frustration. He didn't even nod.

"Guess he had more enemies than just Charles," she murmured.

"Do they know what happened? Did anyone see anything?"

Erin shook her head. "He was found upstate. Dead inside his truck on the side of the road."

"He'd pulled over, then."

"Apparently."

"Why would someone stop on the side of a road in upstate Michigan at night?"

"Who knows?" Erin was staring out into the darkness.

The sound of the waves bothered him. Set him on edge. He was listening. But he couldn't hear.

The smallest crack of a twig. The faint creak of a floorboard. A tap. A breath.

"Could be he stopped to make a call," she said. "The sheriff said they'd found an open cell phone on the seat beside him, but no call had been made."

"What, someone got to him in his truck before he had time to punch in the numbers?"

"They think whoever killed him was already in the truck. Maybe they were arguing. Maybe it was a woman and they'd pulled over to make out."

More likely, it was someone who lived in Tom's world, someone who, like Rick, could do despicable things and leave no evidence behind. Just like he'd done with the break-in at Erin's office.

Someone who wanted Rick under the eye of the law. Someone who wanted to make sure Paul Wagner couldn't free Rick to travel, to leave the state or the country. Someone who wanted to make sure the court didn't return Rick's passport to him.

"Sit." Erin patted the couch. "Please?"

He wanted to, more than she could possibly realize. "I have to go."

"Just for a minute," she said. "I need to ask you something."

Erin didn't play games. And she had his back.

Rick sat. Not too close. Not close enough to touch her. But not on the other end of the couch nor in the chair across the room, as he should have.

He was leaving in the morning. Going back to the world he knew. Walking face-first into danger.

The complete antithesis of Erin's softly muted living room.

"I need you to do something for me," she said.

"If I can."

"Tomorrow morning, before you get on with your day, I need you to talk to a friend of mine."

He'd checked the room for bugs while she was on the phone, found it clean, but he didn't want to take unnecessary risks. The less he and Erin spoke, the better.

"I thought we'd been through this," he said. What he'd told her that night had to stay between him and her.

"I know." She held up a hand as she answered. "I'm not asking you to confide in anyone."

"What, then?"

"Kelly's an expert witness."

So this was only about the murder charge?

"What kind of expert witness is going to help us prove I've been framed?"

"She's a psychologist."

"You think I'm delusional." He didn't blame her. But he was disappointed. And he was going to bring Tom back to life, anyway, even if she called the sheriff the second he left her house or called Halloway to stop him.

They just didn't get it. These small-town lawmen posed no real threat to Rick. If he'd wanted to disappear forever, he knew how to do it. He was there because he wanted his life back. At the very least, he had to protect Steve. And now Erin.

He had to do what was right. Because he chose to. Not because he was afraid of anything Sheriff Johnson could do.

"No, I don't think you're delusional. I'm afraid I might be." He had to strain to hear her.

"What does that mean?"

"Do you mind if I pour a glass of wine?"

Didn't sound like something she'd do if she didn't trust the company in her home. And she'd closed the curtains. Turned off the radio.

"No."

"Would you like one?"

"You got a beer?"

"No."

He wasn't a wine drinker. Didn't see the sense in sipping fruit from a fine glass. A shot of whiskey was much more efficient.

"Then, yes, I'll have wine, thank you."

Yes. Thank you? Who did he think he was? Some kind of parlor date? A guy with enough class to look at a woman like Erin Morgan and actually think about kissing her?

He'd never climb that high.

Which was fine with him, he reminded himself as his hostess went to pour their drinks. If he got himself up to the pretty lawyer's level, he'd risk falling back down.

And he had a long way to fall.

28

He'd been honest with her. Or at least she thought he had. And if she was right, Rick Thomas had just given Erin something he'd given almost no one else. His trust.

He'd confided in her.

Aside from his sergeant, he didn't—*couldn't*—trust anyone. And now he trusted her. If she could believe him…

With the fancy opener she'd received from one of Noah's brothers for Christmas the year before, Erin opened a bottle from the case of Riesling she'd ordered from her favorite winery in Napa, and poured the sweet wine into crystal glasses.

This might be a huge mistake—the biggest of her life—but something was compelling her to make a choice she didn't fully understand. To trust deeply. A life that had been comfortably the same for four peaceful years was changing faster than she could grasp. *She* was changing.

"If you don't like it, I've got a merlot," she said, joining her guest in her living room. He commanded the room with his presence, his back to her as he gazed out into the darkness of the lake. His blue jeans and black boots, the black corduroy shirt, seemed fittingly somber for the setting, the situation, the time of night.

Turning slowly, Rick took the glass. Downed a quarter of it. And set it on the coffee table before taking a seat in the chair he'd originally chosen.

He was regretting his earlier openness with her. She could read the signs—and she didn't want him to take back what he'd given her. What she hoped he'd given her.

In the corner of the couch closest to him, Erin took a deep breath. "You asked me why I wanted you to speak with Kelly Chapman."

His fingers steepled in front of him, he appeared relaxed.

As relaxed as a jaguar might be just before slipping away into the forest.

"You said you were afraid you were delusional," he said. "Which makes me wonder why I'm the one you're referring to your psychologist friend."

She wanted to trust him. Plain and simple. There it was. She needed this…something…with him.

Erin sipped. Focused on the sweet, distinctive and comfortingly familiar flavor on her tongue.

"I need you to speak with her for two reasons," she said, looking at her client, seeking the lawyer she was used to being while she she wrestled with the woman who was trying to emerge. "First, because if Christa Hart finds Tom Watkins, and we don't have evidence that Paul Wagner killed Charles, we're going to end up going to trial. We're going to need Kelly's testimony regarding your state of mind, your demeanor, your capabilities. You're agreeing to a psychological evaluation. I'm going to ask you to take a lie detector test, too. I want it as an offensive move, not a defensive one after the prosecution attacks your character."

"And the second reason?"

Kelly had told her to listen to herself. But she hadn't explained how to decipher the message. "I want another opinion regarding *my* opinion of you."

When she said nothing more, he picked up his glass. Downed another beer-size swallow, assessing her all the while. "I assume you're going to explain yourself."

She thought she just had.

"From everything I've seen, including yesterday's break-in, you're a strong, confident woman, Erin. You don't seem the type to second-guess yourself. Or to need validation from others."

Exactly. Which was why her current self-doubt was so completely unacceptable to her.

"Everyone has a weak point."

"Implying that I'm yours?"

No. She hadn't been implying that. But…God help her if it was true.

"Believe it or not, I'm struggling with trusting myself as much as I am with trusting you."

He frowned and Erin sat forward, setting her glass on the table and folding her hands together. She'd started this. Was she going to continue exactly as she had been for the rest of her life? Mostly numb? Or was she going to open herself up to all the emotional risks inherent in really living?

"I didn't choose law by chance," she said, as if from a distance. "I knew going in that I'd practice defense law. And I also knew I would never defend someone I believed to be guilty, which is why I'm in private practice instead of working for the defender's office."

Rick took another drink. She thought about retrieving the bottle.

"A month ago, I defended a young man who'd been charged with three counts of vehicular homicide. He was not only guilty, but felt no remorse whatsoever for having taken three lives. He only cared about his driver's license."

"But you defended him, anyway."

"Because I believed he was innocent. I believed his parents. And…I knew that the cop on duty had prejudged the kid based on his age and expensive car and that he hadn't preserved the kids' rights. I knew I could win."

"And winning's important."

There it was again. "Yeah, I guess."

"More important than innocence and guilt?"

"No." She shook her head. "Of course not. But with that case, I saw the win, and missed the signs of guilt."

"You're questioning yourself because of one case?" He sounded doubtful.

Erin wasn't really surprised. The man was astute. Perceptive.

Rick Thomas was not a man to try and fool.

"No, not really. I think the case was my wake-up call." Clarity came in the most unexpected moments.

"Waking you up to what?"

"To why I entered law in the first place."

"And your friend, Kelly—this psychologist you want me to meet—she knows why you got into law?"

"No." Erin finished off her wine. And looked him straight in the eye. "No one knows. No one has ever known." Not even Noah.

He didn't ask. But his stillness spoke to her. As had his honesty that evening. He'd told her secrets he'd kept for fifteen years. Told her and no one else.

"Like you, I was raised by my father," she said, struggling with every word, every breath. That much he already knew. But how did one begin the telling of a secret so deeply held?

"He worked in a factory. In Detroit…"

She was obviously having a hard time with this. Confiding didn't seem to come easily to her, either.

Rick could have stopped Erin's confession. Should have. He had preparations to make. Plans to devise.

His old man had been in manufacturing, too. At a distillation plant that turned a blind eye when assembly workers helped themselves to company product— beer—on break. And didn't realize or care that some of them, Rick's dad, at least, had gone right on helping themselves when their shift was over.

He'd brought the stuff home to keep him company. All night long…

"My mother died when I was born," Erin said. And that was where their stories differed. His had run off.

"Dad and I didn't have a traditional life, by any means. I'm sure if Child Services had visited they'd have gotten involved, but we did okay," she said, her smile distant— and filled with a warmth Rick had never felt himself. Not toward his father.

"You loved him."

"Yes. I did. He and my mom were too young to get married, barely out of high school. But I was on the way and they were in love and…"

She stopped. Rick had no idea why he was still there. He'd talk to her friend. If for no other reason than to buy Erin's continued trust.

"And suddenly, there he was, eighteen, disowned by his parents for going against his parents' wishes and getting married and with a newborn girl to raise. My mom's parents helped that first year but they were older and retired to Florida and we didn't see them much after that. They died within a year of each other when I was in junior high. I might not have had pretty little cards to pass around at school on Valentine's Day, or bows in my hair, or clothes that matched, but I was clean and healthy and I never doubted for one second that I was loved."

Lucky girl.

Lucky dad. In another life, Rick would've been curious to meet the guy who'd single-handedly pulled off something like Erin.

"When I was sixteen, Dad was accused of killing a man for the two thousand dollars the guy had on him. Unbeknownst to me, we'd been about to lose our home and the prosecutor dug up enough other debt to give Dad plenty of motive. Dad was the last person to see the guy alive. A witness had seen them arguing. Dad said the guy had been trying to get him to look the other way on a union vote. Dad swore he didn't touch the guy. I was the only one who believed him. And the only time I ever saw him again after that was when I visited him in prison."

Shit. Rick hadn't seen that one coming.

"Somehow I passed under Child Services' radar. I quit school. Got a couple of jobs. Made enough to save the house until I turned eighteen and was able to sell it. I'd earned my GED by then and used the money from the house, along with government loans, to go to college. And then law school."

"Your father must have been proud as hell."

"He didn't know," she said, the lack of emotion in her voice grabbing his attention. "He was killed by a fellow inmate over a pack of cigarettes when I was twenty. He was thirty-eight. Had a whole life yet to live.

"Two years after he died, the year I graduated from college, new DNA evidence came forth that proved my father wasn't the one who'd robbed and killed the victim in his case. He'd died in prison, an innocent man."

She'd heard before that once you spoke about something that had been buried inside you, you felt better. Erin didn't feel better.

She felt like she was going to cry.

Which was ridiculous. She'd cried any tears she had for her father long ago. And had moved on to live a life that honored him. That prevented other innocents from having their lives stolen from them. From dying behind bars.

But the pressure in her chest grew. As though, once she'd released the ties that bound her secrets, she'd released the ones that bound her heart as well. To inexplicably intense levels. Her vision blurred. And before she could stop them, tears filled her eyes.

There was nothing dramatic about her breakdown. It was just a quiet, exhausted inability to stop crying. She cried for the lost life of the person she'd loved so completely. For the injustice. For all those years of being alone.

The pain she'd hidden was in hiding no longer. She cried for Noah. And his family. For the family of the little boy who'd died in the fire that had taken Noah from her. For Rick—a good man on the run. And for Steve—a boy who would never grow up. And mixed in with the heartache was shame for the fact that while she'd honored her father, she'd betrayed him, too, in her refusal to admit to anyone, once she'd started college and her new life, that her father had been a convict who'd died in prison.

She cried with a pain so consuming she wasn't sure it could ever be assuaged.

She cried because she was scared.

And just like when she was a child and life had defeated her, strong male arms wrapped themselves awkwardly around her, offering a gruff but completely enveloping comfort that she couldn't afford to reject.

Rick was not a nurturer. Of anything. Or anyone. Not even Steve.

He didn't break codes of silence, either.

And the government had always protected his cover.

How could a life that had been predictably the same forever suddenly veer so far out of control? Was he in his own skin? Or had the years of living a lie finally taken their toll on him? After living two separate lives for so long, did he even know who he was?

He couldn't explain to himself what he was doing with his arms around his beautiful attorney.

Or why he was anywhere near a woman's tears, which he always avoided at all costs.

At other times, he would've walked out by now, regardless of how insensitive that made him, but on Sunday night, Rick stayed put. With his arms wrapped around another human being in a way they'd never been before.

Was this comfort, then?

And if so, what did one do next? When did comfort end? How did he extricate himself?

After an unfathomable length of time, the intensity of Erin's emotions lessened, and he said, "I have to go."

He meant the words with everything in him. But he continued to hold the woman in his arms, as though waiting for *her* to end this. To free him...

She nodded, her sigh accompanied by a hiccup, an aftershock of the storm. The nod, the weighted movement of her head against his chest, struck Rick.

Changed him yet again.

The past year had made him soft.

Or maybe Steve had.

Drop your arms, he ordered himself. *Let her fall to the couch. You're in too deep, man.*

Rick acknowledged the accuracy of his thoughts at the same time he ran a hand along the slender strength of Erin's back. One stroke was all he intended.

One stroke was all he could give. A farewell.

She shuddered, relaxing against him for a second. A second he could allow her. A second that turned into two. And then three.

He kissed the top of her head. She answered by pressing her cheek to his chest. And something changed again.

She wasn't crying. And he hadn't left.

Tension took root inside him as dangerous air pervaded the room, spread through the space between them.

And so did a sexual desire that wouldn't let go.

29

Temple, Michigan
Sunday, October 25, 2010

I was having an interesting night. Caylee Fitzgerald, Maggie and I were the only guests at Agnes's renovated castle on the hill down the cliff from Erin's smaller but equally impressive home.

We didn't see Erin, but Caylee pointed out her place to us. We could see it from the balcony of our suite. The teenager was clearly worried about the woman she considered a sister-in-law. Family.

Caylee, balancing on the brim of a new life, had her own trauma to contend with and spent a good part of the evening with us in our suite of rooms, next door to her room. Maggie had been reticent at first, hanging back, not rude, but not friendly, either.

Until Caylee told us about the scholarship she'd won to Yale and started to cry. That was when Maggie moved from a chair at the edge of the room to the other end of the couch Caylee was perched on.

I knew something momentous was happening when I heard Maggie tell Caylee about Glenna, Maggie's friend and mentor, who, like Caylee, had begun her senior year the month before. And, like Caylee, Glenna had just been awarded a full-ride university scholarship.

"You're a senior?" Caylee asked my foster daughter as I sat quietly in a corner of the powder-blue love seat and watched the two of them.

"No," Maggie looked straight at Caylee, instead of affecting the introverted demeanor she used most often, either looking down or away, when she was faced with one-on-one conversation with someone she didn't know well. "I'm just a freshman."

They were two lovely girls, Caylee with her amber hair and green eyes, and Maggie with the dark hair and dark eyes that turned too many heads for my comfort. Both girls were long-legged. Slim.

But it wasn't outside appearances that struck me as I sat there listening to them. It was the sweetness. The innocence. The softheartedness that came through in their perceptions of the worlds they occupied.

"So what happened to your friend?"

I held my breath. Try as I might, I couldn't get Maggie to talk about Glenna anymore. About any of it. In her mind, I'd switched to the other side the night Maggie's mother was arrested and I'd joined forces with Deputy Samantha Jones in an attempt to get Maggie to identify David Abrams as the man who'd had sex with her, taken her virginity, in a tent on the outskirts of town.

Unless Maggie testified against the well-known local attorney, the man would go unpunished, to walk freely among Chandler's citizens. To walk freely around Maggie.

"She was killed," Maggie said. I didn't move.

"Oh, my God! Killed? How? In a car accident?"

"No." Maggie didn't look at me. "She was murdered,"

the girl continued, her voice low but curiously lacking in bitterness. "In jail. By a cop."

"Oh, my God." Caylee turned, leaning toward Maggie, her face slack with horror. "Oh, my God," she said again.

"Her mom's sick." The need I saw in Maggie's eyes tore at my heart. "She's dying of cancer. It was just the two of them and there wasn't much money and this cop offered to help Glenna earn some extra cash getting drugs to kids at school. She got caught. He was afraid she was going to rat him out and…"

Maggie's voice stilled. Her entire body stilled. Almost as though it was no longer occupied.

Frowning, obviously concerned, Caylee watched her, glanced at me, then back at Maggie.

"He strangled her and hung her in her cell to make it look like suicide," I said quietly, knowing Maggie could hear me. Praying that my sweet child could find the strength, the will, to come back to us. To stay with us.

I heard Caylee's gasp in the thick silence. And I noticed a tear sliding down Maggie's cheek.

"She was only sixteen," she said to the room at large, her gaze lost. And I wanted so badly to scoop her into my arms and carry her away to a place where there was no pain. No ugliness. No wrong.

The fourteen-year-old's life had never been easy. Born to a single teenage mother, living in poverty, had been struggle enough. But then her best friend had died of leukemia the year before, and this year, her only remaining close friend, Glenna, had been murdered. Her mother had sold her into drug trafficking. And she'd been manipulated out of her virginity by a pedophile.

It was astonishing to me that Maggie still cared at all. That she had heart enough to cry. The girl was a testament to the strength of the human spirit, an example of a love for life that could withstand all adversity.

I didn't kid myself as I sat there, listening to the teenagers' soft voices as they shared heartaches. Maggie wasn't out of the woods by a long shot. Although Caylee talked about the pain of being in love in the wrong place at the wrong time, Maggie never mentioned her own heartache where the opposite sex was concerned. She never mentioned "Mac," David Abram's alter ego. Or the day she'd spent with the man in the woods.

She didn't mention men, or boys, at all.

Still, I knew a miracle had just happened. Maggie and I had some rough months ahead of us. But Caylee Fitzgerald, with her own sense of compassion and caring, had given me all the hope I needed. She'd shown me that Maggie was still in there fighting.

And I knew then and there that I was going to dedicate my life to seeing that Maggie Winston had a loving, secure home environment where she could heal. And thrive. No matter what.

Because if anyone deserved it, Maggie did.

No man had touched her since Noah. In Temple, no man would dare to try—unless Erin specifically invited the intimacy.

Which she never had. Never would.

And yet she moved into the warm strong fingers rubbing slowly up her back, welcomed the heat emanating from the large hand gently planted at the base of her spine.

She'd lost her father. And then Noah. Enough was enough.

So much pain. Too much aloneness.

Way too much aloneness.

"Oh, God, Rick, I'm sorry." She had to break away from…she didn't know what this was.

That made it all so much more confusing. So much more difficult to escape.

She was in his arms. Lying against him. Leaning on him. He didn't say anything—hadn't since he'd told her he had to go. That had been a while ago.

He continued to hold her. To offer her something she'd been needing for a long time. Something she hadn't known she needed.

Maybe something he needed, too?

Just to connect with another human being. To have a few quiet moments where you didn't have to be strong, didn't have to go it alone, didn't have to shoulder the world by yourself.

Just to be touched.

Her fingers lay on his shoulders, lay there limply, absorbing his heat. Touching him. But not giving to him as he was giving to her. Slowly, aware of every second as though time had stopped, she cupped his shoulders, held on and then explored the muscles behind them. Moved up to his neck, his hair tickling her hands.

Rick's hold changed. Tightened. Pulling her more fully against him, their bodies touching thigh to thigh, stomach to side, chest to chest. She wanted to lift her head. To look into his eyes, his soul, to complete the connection, but she didn't. Her head on his chest, she listened to his heartbeat, letting it take her into its rhythm, become part of the steadiness, the life, the vitality, that emanated from this man.

His hand strayed lower, spreading out, as though laying claim. Not really touching her intimately. Not going low enough to do that. But the tips of his fingers rested beneath the elastic of her bikini underwear.

And she liked it. A lot.

Reaching farther, she linked her hands at the middle of his back, flattening her breasts against his chest. Her nipples hardened. Needing more.

How she'd ever thought she was content, satisfied, fulfilled without touch she had no idea.

Rick's head lowered, his mouth descending to her neck. He didn't kiss her. That would be wrong. He just touched her. With his lips.

And in slow motion, very slow motion, her mouth found the musky warmth of his neck. Felt. And lingered. Not quite tasting.

She could feel the beat of his heart, pounding harder. Energy coursed through her, and yet her body was heavy, forcing her to lean into him. Her hands, her mouth, couldn't be still.

Caressing his back, Erin knew a rightness that couldn't be denied. Couldn't be stopped. The moment was hers. For the moment, *he* was hers. A soul to connect to. To comfort. To know.

He'd trusted her with his most profound confidences. And she'd given him hers.

As her hands moved lower, meeting the denim of his jeans, he shifted back into the corner of the couch, bringing her more fully on top of him. And her thigh brushed against his pelvis.

And encountered his hardness.

Body enflaming, Erin lay still. On a precipice. Everything about her, around her, was changing.

Had changed.

She lifted her head, meeting Rick's gaze. He was staring at her, and his eyes seemed to seethe. With desire and independence. With determination and doubt.

And he continued to hold his gaze steady on hers as he moved the few inches it took to join his lips to hers.

The first touch was tentative, and then nothing was. As Rick's lips absorbed hers, he became, in the kiss, everything he pretended not to be outside it. His mouth opened, demanding, taking. Giving. His tongue wouldn't let her retreat, wouldn't let her be tentative or timid or virginal. He expected all of her.

And so she gave it. Gave him more than she knew she had. A passion, a fire, a life she'd never experienced. His hunger made her hungry. His intensity made her intense. The wildness riding through her was foreign, frightening. And exhilarating.

She'd be his slave. Do anything he wanted her to do. Take off whatever clothes he wanted her to take off. Allow him access. Control. Complete penetration.

He was leaving in the morning. To face danger without protection, on a mission from which he might not return. He was doing it for her. And for his mentally handicapped friend. He was going to try to take back the small portion that was all he believed was left of him.

His fingers, roaming along her side, grazed her breast. Erin moaned.

He needed her. She would fight to the death for him. And…

"No…"

Her throat ached from the force she'd had to use to get the word out. "We…can't," she said, and wasn't surprised when Rick immediately released her. For all his crimes, real or imagined, Rick was not a violent man. Or a mean one.

"I… You're my client," she said, sitting upright, facing the lake that she couldn't see but knew was out there, just beyond her window. "It's unethical." She was breathing hard, having difficulty speaking, but these things had to be said. "We shouldn't make this any more challenging than it already is."

Rick stood, facing the lake, his back to her. "I'd like to apologize," he said, and before she could tell him there was no need, he went on. "But I can't." He glanced over his shoulder at her, then reached for his keys. "I'm not sorry. Except for the fact that we had to stop."

"You need me to be able to fight for you. You need Sheriff Johnson and everyone else to trust me. I'm your only hope with the law at this point."

"I know."

"If we— It's not illegal, but it could cause ethical questions, give the prosecution an edge if they knew...."

Nodding, he said, "Keep on eye on Steve for me."

"Of course." She told herself not to ask the next question, but she had to. "Are you angry with me?"

He spun around then. "Hell, no!" His eyes were blazing, but not with anger. "How could I possibly be angry? But I will be if you don't play it safe. You're in danger, Erin. Because of me. If anyone asks, you don't know where I am. You know nothing. If they find out about Tom, sell me up the river. I can take care of myself. Just stay safe. Insist on the guard out there. Don't go anywhere alone. Do everything the sheriff tells you. Understand?"

She couldn't promise to do as he asked, but this much she could give him. "I understand."

"Good."

It was the last thing he said to her. Without even a farewell, he was gone.

30

After Rick's early-morning meeting with Kelly Chapman, Tom Watkins boarded the southbound flight without incident. His government ID was still valid. Just before the plane took off, he holed himself up in the airline's lounge facility and, using the scrambled phone, put in a call to Sophie Segura.

"Hey, baby, it's me."

"Tom?"

"Yeah, I can't talk, but I have a favor."

"Sure."

"Meet me in Miami this afternoon." She had her own boat. Regularly traveled from her home, which was on a small island off the southeast coast of Florida.

A boat that always had guns. Ammunitions were the family business. No Segura was ever without merchandise. At least for personal use. Rick needed a gun.

And he had to have her put him in touch with her husband. He had to know why Segura was willing to do business with a rumored traitor.

Sophie named an out-of-the-way spot, more of a dock than a marina, and agreed to be there by two.

"I'm already wet, just thinking about it…." Her voice dropped to a needy whisper.

"Save it for me, lover."

Rick rang off, wondering if he'd be able to get hard long enough to obtain everything he needed from the woman.

Or rather, if he could do so without thinking of Erin Morgan. Without bringing Erin into the depths with him.

Temple, Michigan
Monday, October 25, 2010

As soon as Rick Thomas had left the small holding room at the sheriff's office that Erin had set up for our interview, I'd written some notes for my report and then walked the short distance to my friend's office, where she and Maggie were supposed to be at work turning chaos into order. I'd packed my black pantsuit that went with the low-heeled pumps and was glad I had.

I enjoyed the walk. Temple was a bit older than Chandler. And unique with its vantage point above the lake. Still, I was anxious to join Maggie and Erin. Not because I worried about their safety; many of the building's other occupants were in residence and the sheriff had men assigned to Erin around the clock until further notice. But because I'd barely had time to introduce my young charge to Erin before I had to leave her in Erin's care. I didn't want Maggie feeling deserted.

Caylee was in school. But from what I understood, she'd be with us that afternoon. I'd offered to speak with her parents or, better yet, to speak with all three Fitzgeralds together. It's what I would've done at home in Chandler—made that offer, I mean. Caylee had called her folks, left a message, but so far I'd had no response to my proposal.

The receptionist who sat in the small lobby of Erin's office building smiled at me without missing a beat in the phone call she was engaged in.

I heard muted conversations from various offices along the hall as I walked toward Erin's. The carpet looked freshly vacuumed. Lights were ablaze. I could smell coffee.

I sure couldn't tell the place had been broken into the day before.

A uniformed deputy stood a few feet down the hall from Erin's open door.

"I might be a lawyer when I grow up." Maggie's voice stopped me in my tracks. My foster daughter sounded healthy. Strong. At ease with herself and the situation.

I stood there a second, blinking away tears, and realized again how deeply I was committed to this child I'd only known a matter of months. I hoped to God that Maggie's sudden penchant for lawyering didn't have anything to do with David Abrams. Plastering a quick smile on my face, I spun into the room before Maggie could say more. I didn't want to eavesdrop.

I could tell the second I saw Erin's face that something was wrong. Her lips were pinched and her smile didn't seem natural at all.

"Maggie, would you mind running to the supply room for more folders?" Erin asked as soon as I'd said hello. She looked every bit the professional in her gray skirt and jacket with the matching mauve and gray pumps. Her short dark hair, her makeup, were close to perfect.

But I had a feeling she was on the verge of falling apart.

"You want me to grab a soda and hang out in the break

room for a few minutes?" Maggie asked, her expression serious as always. "You guys need to talk, right?"

Shoulders relaxing visibly, Erin nodded. "Sorry," she said.

"No problem." Maggie turned to go, but glanced my way. I smiled at her. She actually smiled back. A real smile, not the valiant attempts that had become our norm.

I handed her a couple of dollars for the vending machine and, pocketing the money in her dark blue hoodie, she left us alone.

Stepping over piles of papers still on the floor, Erin crossed to the door. Closing it. And then, hands behind her back, leaned against it.

"He showed up," I said. "For our meeting."

She nodded. "And?"

"Nothing." I told her what I'd already compiled for the report I would write. "The man was in complete control. He was neither happy to be there, nor put out by the visit. Regardless of what exercise I used, he answered all my questions in the same calm, unemotional tone."

"Which means what? That he's lying to me?"

"In my opinion it means he's capable of shutting down all emotion. Completely. In a way most of us can't. So, yes, he could be lying to you. He could just as easily be telling the truth."

The attorney seemed to sink into the door. "You said most people aren't capable of behaving that way. Do you mean Rick's not normal?"

I shook my head. "No one's really normal," I told her, standing in the middle of her mess, wishing I could help her find the answers she needed as effortlessly as I could help pick up office debris. "Normal is an average we arrive at when we put together all the measurements on the spectrum. What Rick's behavior and his responses say to me is that he was hurt beyond his ability to cope, probably at a very young age, which caused an emotional freeze. When something like that happens to a young child, and no one's there to tend to him, to nurture him, the deep freeze becomes a way of life."

Erin's dismay seemed more than professional and I started to worry. "Is this…this freeze…permanent?" she asked.

"It can be."

Pushing away from the door, she nodded. And I had to add, "In most cases, though, if the individual is willing, he or she can learn to open up. Sometimes that happens even when the person isn't willing. There are rare cases when a person lacks the proper wiring to feel or process emotion, but I don't think that's Rick. In most cases, probably in Rick's, an entire range of emotions does exist."

"In other words, he's not a psychopath."

"Not in my considered opinion, no."

Standing behind her desk, she fiddled with some folders and then glanced up at me. "You're saying the feelings are there. It's just a matter of whether or not he can access them."

"Right."

"Do you believe Rick can?"

"I do."

"Why?"

Rick Thomas knew I'd been hired by Erin specifically to give her my impressions of him. He knew I'd be reporting to her.

"First, because of Steve," I said. "His loyalty to this friend of his, his patience, his desire to spend so much time with him—it all stems from an emotional base."

"He loves him, you mean?"

"Maybe. Or maybe some other emotion drives him. I'd need a lot more time with him to be able to give you my opinion on that one."

"And the second reason?"

"Because he was genuinely worried about you."

"About me?"

Making a decision, I sank down in the high-backed leather chair in front of Erin's desk borrowed from a vacant suite, and crossed my hands over my stomach. "Yes. There's something going on between the two of you, isn't there?" I asked bluntly.

"No! Of course not. He's my client and—" She met my gaze. And dropped into a chair. "I almost slept with him last night. If it hadn't been for the fact that he's my client, I would have."

Once again Erin Morgan proved what an honest person she was. Once again, she impressed the hell out of me.

"Wanting the man isn't a sin," I said.

"I haven't so much as looked at another man…in that way…since Noah died."

"Then I'd say it's long past time you did."

The pinched look didn't leave her face. But she nodded.

"So he was worried about me?" Erin's voice was weak, reminding me a little of Maggie. And I commiserated. Didn't seem to matter how old women got, they were still, somewhere deep inside, high school girls who worried whether or not they'd get, catch, keep the guy.

"He asked me what I thought the chances were that you'd do as he asked."

"What'd you tell him?"

"The truth."

"Which was?"

"That I couldn't say for sure."

"I'm guessing that went over well."

"The same as everything else. Whatever he was thinking, or possibly feeling, took place behind a steel wall."

Erin looked down at the folder corner she was bending back and forth. And I relented.

"He made me promise that I'd urge you to continue accepting around-the-clock protection until they figure out who did this." I motioned to the mess surrounding us.

"He needn't worry there," Erin said. "I've got it whether I want it or not, thanks to Ron Fitzgerald, I'm sure. But don't get me wrong. I'm not complaining."

I knew she wasn't. Erin was scared.

I was afraid she had reason to be.

Rick landed in Miami with three hours to spare. As planned. As soon as he got into the airport, he picked up a prepaid cell phone, registered the serial number with a carrier to activate it and caught a bus down to the beach. He had ninety minutes of talk time that was virtually untraceable to him. Only to a number in Miami.

He had until tomorrow before Sarge expected to hear from him. That gave him a day to do what he had to do without raising his former leader's attention.

What he was doing was right. The only choice. Especially now that he knew Tom's cover had been blown. Contact with Sarge at this point would do nothing but endanger the man—if he wasn't already compromised. In any case, the rule had always been that if a cover was compromised the agent went dark.

That was Rick. Dark.

Truth be told, he couldn't remember a time he hadn't lived in darkness.

Phone in hand as he blended with throngs of locals

and tourists, Rick thought about calling Erin. Just to make sure that she was following orders. Keeping herself safe.

And knew he couldn't. Now that he was on the lam, no contact was the only way.

Instead, he found a corner wall outside a public restroom where he could see if anyone was coming toward him.

And then he dialed the number he'd looked up on a public computer at the airport. When the man answered, identifying himself, Rick hung up, hopped on another bus and walked several blocks until he found the office building he was seeking. He went straight to suite 204.

He opened the glass door with its gold printed letters. Calling the room a suite was a stretch. With the piles of folders and papers lining the walls around the scarred wooden desk that held court against the back wall, the room looked more like a private investigator's office from an old movie than it did a lawyer's place of business.

"Can I help you?" The bald man behind the desk glanced at Rick over the top of a pair of wire-framed reading glasses. The suit and tie he wore seemed incongruous with the stale-smelling room.

"Ralph Guardano?"

"Yes." Papers in both hands, the man waited.

"I need to speak with you about Maria Valdez."

Lowering the pages slowly, Ralph didn't stand. Didn't break eye contact with Rick. He didn't do much of anything. And yet Rick was in no doubt that the man had just gone on full alert.

"I don't know any Maria Valdez."

"Yes, sir, you do. She was a client of yours until she died in prison. Maria was a friend of mine."

The man said nothing.

"I'm prepared to do whatever it takes to find out what you know about her death."

"All I know is what you just told me. She died in prison."

He didn't want to hurt the man. Didn't even have a gun yet. But there were other ways to get information. Based on Guardano's clientele—including a dead prostitute who'd been arrested for drug trafficking—and his surroundings, the man probably had dealings he didn't want exposed. If Rick had the time to investigate he could—

"Who are you?" Guardano crossed his arms in front of his chest.

"Name's Tom."

The lawyer dropped his arms. "Tom who?"

He should have acquired a weapon before paying this call. Chances were Guardano was armed. There was a six-drawer locked file cabinet to his right. Judging by the thickness of the sides and the size of the locks, it was steel. Bulletproof. And heavy. As soon as the other man appeared to reach for his gun, Rick would be behind that cabinet. And then he'd make a dive for the attorney.

He stepped forward closer to the cabinet. "I'm Tom Watkins," he said. That was the point of this trip down south. To out Tom. To track down whoever was after him.

To get answers.

"So you do exist." The man's words were the last thing Rick expected.

"Pardon me?"

"Please." Guardano gestured to the threadbare upholstered and wooden chair by his desk. "Have a seat."

Rick studied the man. And then he sat.

"I knew Maria." Guardano settled back in his chair.

"She was a…friend…before she was a client," he said, adding, "You knew her, too."

As Tom Watkins, yes.

"You and your friend, Jack Dunner enjoyed her…company," Guardano continued, his expression serious. "On a boat."

The yacht again. The week with Brady. The matchbook. Why would Maria have found those days important enough to tell her lawyer about them? About him?

And why had everything to do with that weekend— except for him and a matchbook—been destroyed?

"Jack. Nice guy," Guardano murmured.

"What do you know about Jack?"

"He saw Maria again, did he tell you that?"

A slight turn of his head was Rick's only reaction. But it seemed to be enough.

"Dunner was different from the rest of her associates. Maria was more than a convenience to him, although she was that, too. But he treated her well."

Ah, Brady, what did you do? Get yourself into? Relationships were out. Too dangerous. You knew that.

"Not like some of the others. One in particular. A regular. Guy liked to play it rough. Lots of bruises. Surface blade cuts. Dunner saw the results and got pissed off."

All of this was because of a woman? A whore? Because Brady couldn't keep his dick in his pants?

"He gets Maria to tell him who did it to her. Like I said, the guy was a regular and so were the games he played. But Dunner goes after him. Turns out the guy's got connections. Money. And Maria ends up in jail."

And Brady ended up dead. Because he was going to expose some rich pig.

But what did that have to do with Tom?

Unless the guy was the owner of the yacht and Tom

was guilty by association. A politician into sexual sadism? Someone who'd hide his secrets at any cost?

If the guy was the yacht owner, he might have had access to top-secret information. He'd been a higher-up. He could've known about the special ops. About Tom Watkins. Would have the means to expose Tom. And could believe he had to obliterate the whole team to get rid of all the evidence.

Which meant Sarge was in danger, too. Just as Rick had thought.

Working over the information, mind spinning toward his next move, Rick stood.

"I think you want to hear the rest." Guardano's gaze was direct.

Rick sat back down. Brady's liaison with Maria, his run-in with their mystery benefactor, didn't explain Arizona.

"Dunner didn't give up. He visited Maria in prison a few times over the next year. She says he told her he was on to the guy. Said he'd stumbled on something big."

"Big?" Rick's eyes narrowed. "Where? How?"

"She didn't know. Said he wouldn't tell her. But he'd just returned from a trip to Arizona. She thought maybe it had to do with that."

"When was this?"

"I'm not sure. She asked to speak with me six months ago. She hadn't heard from Dunner in a long time—eight months or more, she said. But she'd just had a visit from the other guy. The abusive client. She was scared. And angry. I arranged a call and she told me what I'm telling you. When I realized what we were dealing with I told her it would be best if we spoke in person. I made an appointment with her for the following day. She was dead before I got there."

"You think someone knew she was speaking to you?"

The man steepled his fingers on top of his desk. "Seems likely."

"This client of hers who roughed her up, you think he had use of the same yacht we were on?"

"I'm sure of it. That's where he usually took her."

So they were dealing with a man who had connections to the Department of Defense. But Rick was still no closer to knowing if it was someone like Segura—a criminal with connections—or someone on the inside.

"Anything else?"

"Yes. Maria told me one other thing. When she begged Dunner to be careful, he said not to worry, that he had backup. He said he'd left something with a person he trusted to give to Tom Watkins, in the event that anything happened to him. That's when she told me about the days she'd spent with the two of you."

Brady had left him a fucking matchbook. Was it supposed to have led him to Maria? Who was now dead?

"Did Maria mention any details about the guy who roughed her up? The one Jack was after?"

"No."

"And you have no idea who any of her clients were? Anything that could lead us to the man who beat her up?"

"Maria called him Pop, but she knew it wasn't his real name. She had a picture. Said Dunner gave it to her. He'd brought it to her for confirmation that the man he was on to was the same one who beat her up. She said it was. She was going to turn the picture over to me the next day."

"What happened to it?"

"According to the warden, no such picture existed."

"Do you believe him?"

"I believe that it wasn't among the things they found in her cell."

"So this picture could've been what they were after. Could've been what got her killed."

"Maybe. I know she was scared. And talking to me got her killed. That, or the picture had. Or both."

And whoever had killed Maria and Brady, whoever had destroyed that yacht, was now after him. Because he had something of value to them. Or they thought he did.

"Who else did she tell that Jack had left something for me?"

Sarge had been right. Rick had something they wanted.

"I have no idea."

"Is there any way this man knew?"

"If he realized she'd spoken to me, realized Dunner had given her a picture, I'd say there's every possibility he knew the rest."

Rick stood again. He had to meet Sophie. Get armed. "Thank you," he said.

The man nodded, but didn't rise.

"And get the hell out of town," Rick said as he pulled open the door. He hoped to God no one had followed him, but either way, Ralph Guardano was a candidate for the casualty list.

31

Kelly took Maggie to explore Temple's quaint downtown shops while Erin worked on a couple of cases. She was going to join them for a late lunch and was just getting ready to lock up her office—which now bore some resemblance to the space she'd left on Friday evening—when there was a knock at the door.

Knowing that a deputy was on the other side—and that the building was filled with occupants—didn't completely quell the nervousness in her stomach as she turned the knob.

"Sheriff!" The older man was in uniform, as he generally was on business days. She certainly hadn't expected to see him again so soon.

Her first thought—that he'd found out that Rick was gone and that she knew about his plans to leave town—was quickly followed by another. Something had happened to Caylee. Or Kelly or Maggie.

The lawman came into the room, his face grim, and shut the door. "I've got some bad news," he said without preamble.

Watching him, she waited.

"We know who broke in here."

And that was bad news…why?

"Who?"

"Bruce Halloway."

The man who'd been guarding her house for most of the night.

The man who'd been at Lakeside with Steve.

What the hell was going on?

"I don't understand."

"Ron Fitzgerald spread the word yesterday that we were looking for anyone seen near this building on Saturday night or Sunday morning. Several people reported seeing Bruce. No one thought anything of it, of course, and neither did I, really. Until this morning when I had a meeting with my deputies and announced, among other things, that we'd found a few strands of hair that had been sent out for DNA testing. Bruce came to me after the meeting."

Feet apart, hands at his sides, Sheriff stood at military ease as he continued. "Bruce admitted breaking into your office."

"Bruce! But why?"

"Halloway claims he was acting under orders. Someone from the Department of Defense had contacted him—gave him a chance to 'serve his country,' as he put it, and earn extra money at the same time. Halloway saw the job as a chance to be a hero…and win his wife back. What he was supposed to do was get Rick's file. And to search your office for anything that might be connected to a Tom Watkins, Jack Dunner, Maria Valdez or a yacht named *The One That Got Away*. He was also told to steal any clocks in the room and ransack the place to make it look like a random break-in. Which is why the other things were missing."

"Steal my clocks? What on earth for?"

"Halloway doesn't know, and neither do I."

"Did he tell you who hired him? Give you a name?" Erin asked, hoping they'd finally have something they could verify. That she could get Rick the information he needed.

"He won't say."

Erin's heart started to pound. "What do you mean he won't say? You're the sheriff. His boss. He comes to you and confesses and then won't give you a name? How can we be sure the whole thing isn't a lie to protect himself because he knows his DNA is going to show up?"

But Erin knew it wasn't a cover-up. Rick had mentioned the Department of Defense, too. Halloway coming up with the same department was no coincidence.

She was more frightened than she'd ever been in her life.

"He claims it's a top-secret matter and he can't say anything else. When the DNA results come in, he wants me to keep them quiet—just until whatever's going to happen happens. He's agreed to stay in jail for the duration, but won't say any more. He's terrified that his mistake, his sloppiness yesterday, is going to put a long-term government operation in danger."

"Did he say what the government wanted with Rick's files? What they're looking for that they thought I might have?"

"No. He didn't seem to know much. Other than the names he gave me."

Names that were not in Rick's formal file. Erin kept separate files locked in a vault under the closet floor of her office when she launched private investigations of her own. She couldn't risk any incriminating information getting into the wrong hands.

"Did he say how much longer the operation, whatever it is, was supposed to take?"

"No. Just that his orders came through a contact in Washington and he was only told what he had to know."

"Is this connected to the Cook murder?"

"That's one of many questions I asked, but he wasn't budging. Not on anything. I suspect there's a tie-in, though. Wagner's fingerprints were clean, and he had an alibi for the time of Cook's murder. Seems he had a woman on the side, too. And when she heard he'd been killed, she came forward. They'd been together upstate the morning Cook was murdered. Had breakfast at a diner that confirms Wagner's presence. We heard from a shift manager at his work, as well. Seems Wagner called in but the shift manager forgot to log the call. The guy in charge this morning didn't know about it."

"So who killed Wagner?"

Wiping a hand down his face, Sheriff sighed. "I have no idea. I'd like to speak with Rick Thomas again. See if he can shed some light on what Halloway had to say. See if there's anything he'd like to tell me."

"I'm going to advise him not to do that, Sheriff."

"I know," Sheriff Johnson said. "Just talk to him, Erin. See if there's anything he'll tell *you*. I haven't got a clue what's going on, but if Rick Thomas has a hope of seeing the light of day once this is over, he needs to come clean."

Sick to her stomach, Erin nodded. She saw the sheriff out. One thing was certain: duplicity was not her strong suit.

With her long chocolate hair, burnished gold skin and round dark eyes, Sophie was a looker. Feminine.

Gorgeous. She stood on the deck of her cabin cruiser, exuding sex. The pull-in she'd chosen had a self-pay gas pump, which she would've avoided, and little else. Rick jumped on board and with a hungry glance over her shoulder at him, Sophie, dressed in white jeans and a navy linen jacket, stepped down to the drive shaft and sped off.

He had a job to do, a part to play, and without looking back, Rick went to work. Joining Sophie, he stood behind her, pressing up against her bottom, and took over the wheel. With his free hand, he cupped one of her breasts, squeezing harder than he might have—hard because she liked it that way.

And when she reached back one beautifully manicured hand, he moved his feet, spreading his legs to give her access.

Everything in life came at a cost. And if one more roll in the hay with Sophie was what it took to put Tom on the market and, most importantly, get enough ammunition to deal with whoever came slinking out of the sewer, then so be it.

Temple, Michigan
Monday, October 25, 2010

I'd interviewed Rick Thomas. Written my report. If there was a trial, and my testimony was needed, I'd come back to town. For now, my work was done.

"I've decided to leave this afternoon," I told Erin as we sat with Maggie at the Roselane Inn having a late lunch. In light of the break-in at Erin's office I figured this wasn't a good time for the visit we'd planned. The place was a renovated mansion on the main street of Temple with a grand, four-foot-wide wooden staircase, linen tablecloths, chairs upholstered in velvet, china dishes, patterned silverware and authentic antiques tastefully arranged.

Chewing a bite of walnut chicken salad, Erin nodded and glanced at Maggie. "Probably a good idea, considering, but I'm sorry. I would've liked us to have more time together."

"Kelly says we can come back next summer," Maggie said, then lowered her gaze. "If that's okay, I mean."

"Of course it's okay." Erin smiled at Maggie, and I was glad I'd made the trip to Temple. And that I'd brought Maggie with me. We felt like family sitting there.

"I was going to mention a return trip," I said. "Caylee and Maggie exchanged email addresses and IM screen names. I told them we'd try to get back to town before Caylee leaves for Yale next year. If she goes, that is."

Ron Fitzgerald had phoned Erin a few minutes before, telling her that, because of everything that had happened, he'd called Caylee at lunch and asked her to come home. Caylee had agreed, though she hadn't backed down on her desire to go to Yale.

"Anyway, I just thought, you've got so much going on, it'd be best if we left."

"They arrested the man who broke into my office," Erin said, looking at Maggie and then back at me, as though asking if it was okay to speak in front of her. I nodded. I was trying to include Maggie in as much of my life, my career, as I could. As was appropriate. I trusted Erin to make that call.

Maggie had helped Erin clean up the mess after the break-in. She was bound to have questions and would be thinking about the incident whether we discussed it or not.

"Who was it?" Maggie got right to the point.

"Deputy Halloway."

"Isn't that the man who was on guard duty at your house last night?" I asked, frowning.

"Yep."

"Oh, no."

"Yeah."

"Why? How do they know it was him?" Just like Maggie, I had questions. A lot of them. And wasn't sure, all of a sudden, that I wanted her in on this conversation. The girl might start to think all cops were dirty.

"He confessed," Erin said, and explained the man had said he was working for someone else, but wouldn't say who. I had a feeling there was more to the story—and that Erin was using the discretion I'd trusted her to use where Maggie was concerned.

But I had to know… "Did it have anything to do with Rick Thomas?"

"Yes." There was more there, too. I could tell. But Thomas's case was an ongoing investigation. Not something we could chat about.

"Does this mean you're out of danger?" Maggie's grilled cheese sandwich was half-eaten.

"I think so," Erin told us both. "Presumably they got what they wanted from me. It's Rick they're after."

"What did he say when you told him about Halloway?" I asked. The man had been on my mind all day. I wasn't altogether sure I trusted him to tell me the truth—but I'd trust him with my life.

Erin's sudden interest in what was going on outside the window made my stomach drop. Especially when she said, "I haven't told him yet. He's fishing today."

Uh-huh. I was pretty sure my friend had just deliberately lied to me.

"We had a crooked deputy in Chandler, too." Maggie's sweet voice got my attention. I couldn't detect any emotion; she could've been talking about the amount of rainfall.

"Kelly told me a little bit about him," Erin said. "He was running a drug ring, right?"

"Yeah." Maggie looked over at me.

And, feeling guilty, I blurted, "I told her about your mom."

Maggie shrugged. "I figured you did," she said. "It's okay. I mean, it's not like people aren't going to wonder why I'm living with you. And everyone at home knows."

I loved the kid.

"Just to be clear," I said, "I don't tell anyone personal things about you. I don't break your confidences."

"I know." She looked at Erin and the grin on her face melted my heart. "Kelly worries a lot," she said, as though imparting news of great importance. "I think it's 'cause she knows too much about how people's minds work."

Erin grinned. "Well, I, for one, feel lucky to have all that knowledge in my life."

"Yeah, me, too," Maggie said. And I just about choked. Being cared about felt so damned good.

And scary, too. I didn't want to let either of them down.

"Hey, I'm sitting right here. Talking about people in front of them makes them uncomfortable. Didn't you girls get that memo?"

Maggie chuckled, and I concentrated on my broccoli soup for a second. And then said, "Not all deputies are bad, you know."

"I know," the girl replied.

"Still it's kind of shocking to trust one and then find out he's a creep." Erin knew I was struggling to get Maggie to talk about the things that had happened to her.

"I guess," Maggie said, pushing aside the rest of her lunch. "I wasn't shocked, though. Chuck Sewell was a creep from the beginning."

Erin, sitting across the table from Maggie, leaned forward. "A creep how?"

I held my breath.

"He…tried to kiss me."

Turning cold, I didn't move.

"Did he succeed?" Erin's soft voice was a godsend.

"No. My mom and I never gave him a chance. She slept with him instead so he'd leave me alone."

I wanted to take the girl in my arms and never let go. "Did your mom tell you that?" I asked instead, hoping I sounded calm enough to reassure Maggie.

"Yeah, but she didn't have to. I heard him giving her the choice. And then she started getting home late. And coming home drunk. I didn't blame her. I'd have gotten drunk, too, if I had to let that man touch me."

"She should have reported him." Erin wasn't hiding her anger.

"Right." Maggie snorted. "It'd be her word against his. Who do you think they would've believed?"

Probably not Lori Winston. But I said, "She should have tried, Maggie. Even if she wasn't believed at first. They'd have to at least investigate. And she could've had help trying to catch him. To prove the allegations."

"He knew she used drugs," Maggie said. "He threatened to have her put in jail."

"She ended up there, anyway." I couldn't let this go. Couldn't let her think… "No matter how evil someone is, no matter how powerful he seems, there's always a way to get him," I said, my voice shaking. "You have to believe that, Mags."

The girl shrugged. "Maybe," she said. And looked out the window. We were done.

For now.

But I wasn't giving up.

32

Rick spent the better part of Monday night at various establishments—some legal, some not—nursing glasses of whiskey he purchased but didn't drink, and watching his back. He stayed mostly along the Miami coastline. Word would travel from there just fine. Renewing old acquaintances in Tom's business was an interesting experience. Those guys could kill someone and eat a hamburger at the same time.

And they'd defend their loyalties to the grave.

He talked to a lot of people. Some he knew. Some he didn't. And hadn't learned a damned thing he didn't already know.

He finally crashed for a couple of hours in a rent-by-the-hour fleabag motel that had the two amenities he needed—double locks on steel doors and bars on the windows. The bed and running water were a bonus.

And after an early-morning breakfast meeting with Hernandez Segura on Tuesday, he used the scrambled phone to call Sarge. They'd scheduled a rendezvous for that evening.

"I'm not going to make tonight," he informed his one-time superior at the outset.

"Where are you?"

"Can't say."

"Dammit, Rick," the man swore. "You put Tom on the street."

"Yes. It was the only way." He stood in a deserted cove along the ocean's edge, a mile down from where he'd had Segura's man let him out of the boat. He wanted his enemies to come after Tom, but he didn't intend to get caught.

Sarge's deep sigh seemed like a sign of age. Of being worn out. They'd all been at it too long. "I'm afraid you might be right," the older man said, his deep voice low, Almost beaten. Nothing like the forceful voice booming orders that sent twenty-two-year-olds scrambling. "I finally had a call back from one of my contacts," Sarge continued. "Intelligence says there's a mole in the Department of Defense. They don't know who, but they've connected him to Hernandez Segura."

It was the information he'd counted on Sarge to find. This was how it had always worked with their crew. Their instincts were honed. To the job and to one another. Sarge's team was the best of the best, which was why they'd been so highly paid. So highly sought after. Why they'd been trusted with the toughest jobs.

For a second there, hearing that validation from Sarge, Rick felt like part of a team again, that sense of belonging to something bigger than himself. And as a familiar surge of adrenaline surged through him, he wondered, just for a second, if he'd made a mistake in getting out.

"How recent is the Segura connection?" he asked.

"Deep enough that it's been going on for years."

"It's someone who had the power to let him walk after our six-month sting." They'd moved a lot of illegal arms out of circulation. Kept them out of the hands of terrorists.

But in the end, in spite of the evidence Rick had risked his life to collect, the man in charge had walked away without punishment. He'd been tempted to quit when Sarge told him the final results of the operation.

"It's the only thing that makes sense. The Segura mission was sabotaged from the beginning."

Sabotaged from inside. By someone with access to personnel records, someone who had the wherewithal to ensure that Tom Watkins's DNA was in CODIS, the national DNA database set up by the FBI to record the DNA of all convicted American criminals.

"Segura's setting me up."

"You've been in contact with him?"

"With him and dozens of others Tom worked for. He's the only one still willing to give me work."

"You're working for him?"

"I've got a job to do tomorrow night. More after that if I want them. Or so he says."

"Be careful, Rick. We don't know how much he knows. Until we learn who the mole is, we have no idea what they were doing that Brady found out about. No idea what they want from you. But it's obviously worth killing for."

"Maybe Brady found out there was a mole. Maybe got the man's identity."

To some, that would be enough to kill for. "If the guy's using government intel to get Segura hooked up, I'm sure he was being very well compensated."

"Or it could be that he was using Segura to get the government hooked up," Rick said slowly.

"How so?"

"The wars we're fighting today are very different from the previous ones. With new technologies, greater communication, with chemical warfare a fact, weaponry has to be different. The rules of engagement are largely a thing of the past."

"And Segura could be feeding the government information about the weapons being developed under the radar. The weapons we could be up against."

"Maybe."

"So whatever Brady found out could have limited our ability to fight back if it ever got into the wrong hands. It could have endangered the lives of American soldiers. But then, why not just call us in? This kind of thing, getting intel from shady sources, is what we do." Did.

"I don't know. More likely you were on the right track. The mole's probably selling American intelligence to Segura, and Brady's exposure would have seen him charged with treason."

Good motivation for murder.

"If that's the case, then American security is at risk," Rick said quietly, watching a whitecap out on the ocean. He was reminded again of breakfast on Segura's boat. And the collection of shot glasses the man had behind his bar. There'd been a hundred of them. At least.

One of them had stood out.

It had the same logo as the half-used book of matches Brady had left for him. It was from The Resting Place.

Brady wanted Rick to find something.

He was getting close.

And stakes had never been higher.

"Still doesn't explain Cook's murder," Rick said now. "Unless, like we've said, he stumbled on some information about me. Or about someone looking for me."

The other alternative was that Paul Wagner had killed him. Seemed like years, instead of two days, since he'd spoken with his attorney. Erin might know by now that Wagner murdered Charles Cook. Or that he didn't.

"We're agreed that I'm the operative on this one, then," Rick said, forcing his mind away from anything that didn't serve the job at hand.

"Yes."

"Fine. But I need a favor."

"You name it, I'll make it happen."

"You were planning to be in Michigan tonight to meet me. I still need you to go there. There's a woman who I want you to protect. Name's Erin Morgan. She's an attorney. My attorney. In Temple. Her office was broken into and my file was stolen."

"I'll find her."

"And there's Steve."

Sarge was the only one who knew the complete truth about Steve. He was the one who'd arranged it all. "Someone was watching him. If they found Rick, they probably know about Steve. He's at Lakeside Family Care in Ludington. Don't let anything happen to him. Or to Erin. No matter what."

"You have my word."

"Thank you."

"Of course. And, Rick?"

"Yeah?"

"Be careful, son. It's just you and me now."

"I won't let you down, sir."

Despite everything that had been going on—Caylee's troubles, Patricia's illness, the break-in, Kelly's visit, meeting Maggie, feeling desire for the first time in years, falling for a man with secrets, living under guard—Erin came home Tuesday evening to a quiet house with only Boots there to greet her. She put food in the cat bowl, scratched the tabby's chin until, purring, he rolled over for her to rub his belly, too.

With Halloway in jail, having confessed to the break-in at Erin's office, the sheriff felt assured that Rick Thomas and not Erin had been the target. So Sheriff Johnson had decided to call off his watch patrol.

And Erin couldn't very well tell him that simply by her association with Rick Thomas—a covert government agent, alias Tom Watkins, who was a friend to the cartels and gunrunners and an ex-con—she was in danger. Halloway knew more about what was going on than she and Rick did. Or the sheriff, for that matter. He'd know if she was in danger.

Was she going to trust a dirty cop?

Unless, as Halloway claimed, he was working for Washington.

But then, what did that make Rick?

Still, if whoever was after Rick had wanted Erin, or wanted her silenced, she'd already be captured. Or dead. Considering that their man, Halloway, had been her watchdog.

"Be careful what you ask for, Boots, my boy," she said, feeling the cat's purr rumble against her fingers. "I question my professional ethics and end up harboring a criminal, lying to the sheriff and letting my client feel my…yes, well, I guess you don't need to hear that part, do you?"

Boots gave her a hard stare, as though she'd annoyed him, and Erin realized she'd quit scratching. She moved her fingers slowly along his spine and he closed his eyes. At least there was one man in her life who was straightforward.

Fixing a cup of tea, Erin made some toast, slathered on peanut butter and settled into a corner of the living room couch, gazing out into the darkness over the lake. There were no lights bobbing on the water tonight. Nothing signaling the presence of humanity.

She hoped the darkness didn't have any particular significance, other than that the weather was turning colder and fewer boats were out. She wondered where Rick was. What he was doing. If he was okay. Alive.

And when she couldn't find peace sitting there, she moved into her library, curled up in a chair and tried to lose herself in a book. Then she switched on the television she rarely watched. She ran water for a soak in the tub, but couldn't make herself sit there. She thought about putting on pajamas, but changed into jeans instead. Maybe she'd sleep in them. On the couch. With a kitchen knife close by.

In her bedroom, she dug in her nightstand for the can of mace one of the Fitzgeralds had given her last Christmas. It was probably still good. She could test it.

But didn't want to chance blinding herself. She'd had a run-in with pepper spray during law school—a carefully controlled run-in so that she'd know what it felt like and what to do if anyone ever sprayed her.

Had Rick found the people he'd been going after? Or had they found him?

Was he ever coming back?

She'd called Lakeside that afternoon. Talked to Jill. Steve was fine. He had a new kite. Erin was going to see him the next afternoon.

And then it hit her. She could make Steve some cookies. Chocolate chip. All boys loved chocolate chip cookies, didn't they? Steve liked chocolate. That much she knew. Especially brownies. But she didn't have any mix to make those.

In the kitchen Erin dropped an egg. And cleaned it up. She overfilled the cup with flour. And when the stick of butter plopped onto the kitchen floor she slid down to the tile, and had to admit she was scared to death.

Scared for Rick. For Steve. Scared to be alone in her own house. She couldn't do this. Couldn't live this way. She couldn't let her mind play with her and—

What was that?

Stiffening, Erin turned her head, listening. Something had…what? She couldn't be sure. But there'd been a sound. The wind blowing a branch against the house?

Boots jumping up on his cat tree?

No. He was right in front of her. Snoozing on his chair at the dining room table.

She was losing it. Erin stood, butter in hand, then bent with a paper towel to wipe up the greasy mess she'd made. Dropping the bundle in the trash, she walked into the living room. She would not be held hostage by her own mind. Period.

There was no one in her house. No one out to get her. She checked the living room and then marched down the hall, just to prove her point. She made it past the library, the spare bedroom and then stopped. There. That was it. The bathroom fan was on.

To camouflage the sound of…what? A burglar peeing?

She was taking ridiculous to a new level. Shaking her head, Erin reached in to turn off the fan she'd obviously left on when she'd run her bath.

Not that she remembered turning it on. She generally only used the fan when she showered.

But…

The switch was just beyond the tip of her finger. She leaned in.

Someone grabbed Erin's wrist. A big male hand.

She screamed. Went weak. Couldn't breathe.

And then it hit her.

Rick was back.

He didn't want to be seen. Or heard.

She…

Her thoughts flew and then swam as she was pulled into the dark, windowless room.

"Don't say a word."

The rough whisper told her one thing.

Her captor was not Rick.

33

Rick wasn't due to work for Segura until Wednesday night. That gave him twenty-four hours to find a government mole and put an end to the nightmare his life had become.

The gunrunner had plans for Rick. Just not the ones he'd talked about. They'd be far more painful than the risky job he'd outlined. And more final, too, once Segura realized there was nothing he was going to get from Rick.

Once he realized Rick was of no use to him.

So Rick either beat Segura and the mole at his own game, or he died. That pretty much summed things up.

He might be shot at close range, like Brady. Or sent off a cliff like Saul. If he was lucky. Chances were, his death would be more painful. Involving torture.

Whatever.

Didn't really matter. If he didn't figure this out, he was going to be dead, anyway.

All he knew was that a mole in the government had ties to an illegal arms dealer. And thought Rick could somehow prove it. But who was the mole? And what proof did he think Rick had?

Standing in a dark corner of a hangar at a private

airstrip, Rick waited for the pilot he'd hired to finish his preflight check. He was right back where he'd started. Alone with a matchbook.

Brady, help me out here, man. What do you need me to see? What am I missing?

There was no answer. The team had gone dark. He had nowhere to go but back to that weekend. The boat was gone. Maria was gone. Brady was gone. All that was left was a little island bar with a friendly bartender, a few outdoor stools and a wall of liquor bottles.

A bar from which Segura had a souvenir.

Rick kept seeing that shot glass, one among many. It spoke to him. And he knew better than to ignore the message.

There was something at the bar that Brady wanted him to find. What, he had no idea. But he had to go there.

The pilot signaled to Rick that he was ready to leave and Rick boarded the plane.

A thousand bucks cash, a three-hour flight—each way. Would he find any answers when he got there?

Her shoulders ached. Erin sat as still as she could, as upright as she could with her hands tied behind her back, in the front seat of the black SUV and still every bump jolted her, wrenching her arms. There had to be a moment when she'd be able to do something. To get the attention of anyone out there on the dark road, watching them drive by.

They'd left Temple over an hour ago and were heading into the wilderness of upper Michigan, where a body could lie undetected forever and fade quietly away to dust.

"Where are you taking me?"

She was used to the silence, which was his response to anything she said. He'd only gagged her long enough to get her into his truck. But her ability to speak didn't seem to concern him.

Houghton Lake. Grayling. The towns continued to pass by.

"Who are you?" she tried again. If she kept talking, she could keep panic at bay. She could breathe. Because breathing was a natural part of talking.

She was going to die. That seemed quite certain at this point. She prayed it would be quick.

That she wouldn't be raped.

She should have slept with Rick. She was going to die without having shared the ultimate intimacy with him.

A minor thing like professional ethics hardly seemed to matter as she sped away in the dark.

She glanced at the man beside her, looking for any weakness, any chance that she could escape. Dressed in beige slacks and a black jacket, he seemed more rock than man.

He reminded her of someone. She just couldn't figure out who. It wasn't so much the military haircut; it was more the way he held his head. Straight. Unbending. His face expressionless.

Above all, it was the silence.

The man sat there completely rigid. Uncompromising. Silent.

Just like Rick had been that first night she'd crawled out of bed at his behest. The night she'd decided to represent him.

Oh, my God, Rick. What have you gotten me into?

Rick had expected traffic at The Resting Place, the Bahamian bar, to be minimal, considering the cool October weather, but all the beach stools were occupied when he showed up a little after nine.

He'd changed into a pair of khakis, a light blue and beige striped, long-sleeved button-down shirt and sandals, rolling up the sleeves of the shirt. He'd left his bag in a locker at the private airstrip where he'd landed and bummed a ride out to the beach with the pilot, who was going to amuse himself until morning.

Ordering a gin and tonic, Rick leaned against the outside wall of the bar, sipped his drink and watched.

A woman who might've been a hooker chatted up an obviously out-of-his-element older businessman. He was most likely a salesman. Trying for a stab at freedom.

A stab he was going to regret. Probably before morning. And for the rest of his life.

Rick had seen the scenario a hundred times. Different man. Same story. Same sorry ending.

Guys who could handle the traveler's life didn't drink so much. Didn't have that nervous grin or the wild-eyed look.

There were more bottles behind the bar. Expensive brands that hadn't been there before. Business was good.

Stools were new. Different bartender.

Damn.

Nothing was coming easy.

Not easy for Rick, anyway.

The older man got up, half leaning on the woman who clutched his arm. She was gushing all over him.

He slid on to the vacated seat, prepared to nurse the second half of his drink. Rick could handle many more of them without feeling a thing, but he was in for a long night. He had to pace himself.

An hour later, on his second drink, Rick was no closer to finding anything out. He'd had flashes of his time there with Brady.

A vision of his buddy's smiling face as he offered a

toast. A dark and somber look on the other man's face as he'd gazed out at the ocean a hundred yards away.

Rick had taken the expression as a result of the life they lived. Now he wondered how much of that week Brady had spent reliving the death of the little girl. While they'd been lounging around on the boat, soaking up rays and alcohol, had Brady been besieged with images of the child's face? Had he laughed extra hard, talked louder and more to cover the sound of the young girl's cries or, worse, screams, raging through his head?

Rick knew how it worked. He had hells of his own that were never going to leave.

"You up for another?" The thirtyish bartender, a tall clean-shaven man with dark hair and an easy manner, stood in front of him.

Nodding, Rick pushed his glass forward.

The place had cleared out except for a couple sharing a chair—and kisses—on the other side of the bar.

"You here for business or pleasure?" the man asked when he set the glass back down. *Ron,* the tag on his flowered shirt read.

"Pleasure," Rick said.

The man chatted with Rick in between serving drinks to various patrons who came and went and doing the other things that bartenders do. Stocking. Loading the glass-washer. Emptying it.

"This your first time to the island?" Ron asked as he polished a highball glass.

"No, been here once before." Rick sipped. "A few years back." He'd dissected every crack in the floor behind the bar. Studied the walls. *What was Brady telling him?* "The bartender, his name was Shots, he still work here?"

"No, man. He passed."

Rick's entire system went on alert as the man moved to wait on a new arrival.

The bartender who'd been friendly with him and Brady was dead. Everyone who was associated with that trip was gone. Or going soon?

"Did you know him?" he asked Ron on the man's next stop.

"Shots?"

"Yeah."

"Yeah, I knew him. He was a fun guy."

"Was he into more than fun?"

"What's that mean?"

"Guns, maybe. Judging by his name. Booze and guns…"

"Hell, no, man. Shots was a preacher in his other life. He took this job because he said this was where the people who needed him most hung out. He was here to save souls. Not corrupt them."

"His name was Shots and he poured drinks."

"I know. I'm not sayin' he was a conventional guy. But he was pretty solid."

"So what happened? How'd he die?" He sounded half bored, half curious. And he sipped.

"The owner of this place, he sometimes got the use of a yacht."

Rick tensed. Another yacht.

"So this one day he couldn't go, and offered it to Shots. He was only out about an hour when the thing exploded, man. Bad shit. Body parts…well, you don't need me going any further with that." He shook his head. "Ironic, too. The name of the yacht—*The One That Got Away*. Only Shots didn't."

Not *another* yacht. The *same* yacht.

A regular user of that yacht owned the bar Brady's

matchbook had come from. Segura had a shot glass from the same bar.

"He's actually the reason I'm working here."

"Who? The owner?"

Ron leaned his forearm on the bar. "No, man, Shots. I did a tour in the Middle East. It messed me up. After I got out, I came down here and tried to forget everything except sun, sex, booze and drugs." ·

It was a choice Rick could understand all too well. He'd been tempted to make it himself. More than once.

"Shots started talking to me. Not preaching. Hell, I never knew he was a minister until after he was killed. He just poured drinks and invited me back. Night after night. He gave me a place where I felt like I belonged. Helped me reconnect with humanity. You ever hear of Maslow's hierarchy of needs? Once you get past food and a bed to sleep in, you get to the next level. Love and belonging."

"Shots told you all this?"

"Eventually. Anyway, I started hanging around more. I'd tended bar before my tour and when the summer season hit, I helped out a time or two. Another guy quit, and Shots put in a word for me with the owner."

"He live around here?" Rick asked casually. *Give him to me, man. I'm running out of time.*

"No, Pop doesn't live anywhere, near as I can tell. He's some head honcho military guy into classified stuff. But he's been good to me. Career military. He completely gets what combat does to a guy. Didn't blink an eye at having me running his place, even though I have occasional bouts of PTSD—you know, post-traumatic stress."

Rick barely heard the man's words. He was hot. And cold. Stone-cold. Every muscle, every nerve, stiffened to the point of pain. Pop. Maria's abusive client—the man Brady had been after—she'd called him Pop.

Pop was career military. Not Department of Defense. Not a politician.

"Career military? Into classified stuff?" It didn't mean anything. Couldn't mean anything. He stared straight ahead. Saw red in his peripheral vision. The pieces were flying together—but the picture they formed was incomprehensible.

"Yeah. Great guy, like I said, but kinda weird."

"Weird how?" He was speaking normally because he knew nothing. Was having crazy thoughts.

Rick was suspended in time. In space. Could hardly hear his own thoughts as something pounded at the edge of consciousness.

"His dress, man. The only thing the guy ever wears is khakis and a black jacket. This is an island. Sea. Sand. But don't matter how hot it is, or how close to the water he is, I've never seen him without that jacket."

The glass Rick was gripping broke. Cutting into his hand. He welcomed the pain. It was real. Something he could concentrate on.

"What the…" Ron grabbed a towel. And reached for Rick's hand. "You okay, man?"

Standing, Rick pulled out his wallet. Threw a bloody fifty-dollar bill on the bar and left.

Just like that, it all came together. *The One That Got Away*. The Resting Place. The owner of the bar being career military… Black and beige.

The pieces fit.

But nothing made sense. Except for one horrible realization.

Rick had orchestrated his worst nightmare.

He'd sent a cold-blooded killer to Erin and Steve.

34

The road they turned onto was bumpy at best. Every inch jarred the muscles in Erin's shoulders. After having them held in the same position behind her back for a couple of hours, the pain was excruciating. So much so that she was actually relieved when the truck came to a sudden stop.

Lurching forward, she almost lost the toast she'd struggled to swallow earlier that evening.

Had it only been that evening?

Seemed like she'd been driving through darkness for days. Or a lifetime.

There were moments she didn't care what happened to her. She just wanted it over.

And other times, panic raced through her until she could hardly breathe.

Her thoughts were all over the place.

Caylee and Maggie. Kelly. She thought about seeing her dad and Noah again.

And almost constantly, she thought about Rick. Obviously her abduction had to do with him. She just didn't understand how. Did he know she'd been taken? Was he behind this?

As hard as she tried to tell herself that he'd ordered her

captivity, she couldn't believe it. And knew that if Rick was still alive, he'd do everything he could to find her.

"Wait here." Until then all she'd heard out of the man was the rough whisper he'd used for his two brief orders at her home. *Don't say a word.* And *Move.* That was after he'd used a nylon rope to tie her hands behind her back.

With a sweater draped over her shoulders and his body supporting hers, he'd walked her out the front door. She had no idea how he'd gotten into her house to begin with.

He'd had a gun on her beneath the sweater. That she'd known.

On her last glimpse back at the living room before her captor had shut the door behind them, she'd seen Boots make a beeline for her bedroom.

How long would it be before someone realized he was alone and go in to feed him?

At least she didn't have to worry about his finding a good home. Noah had given him to her. Any of the Fitzgeralds would be glad to have him.

The man had exited the truck. Slammed his door. She could hear him doing something in the back of the vehicle. Sounded like he was unlocking something. She heard chains. And thought about running.

If she could get her hand around the door handle.

She tried, ignoring the tears that sprang to her eyes. She'd break her damn shoulder if she had to. A shoulder could heal.

Or she could live without it. She didn't care if she never moved her arm again—if she could avoid whatever hell was awaiting her.

She managed to grab the edge of the handle. Pulled. Nothing happened. Because her door was locked. Erin twisted again. Got her finger up to the armrest. Another few inches and she'd have the automatic lock button within reach.

How far would she get before his bullet hit her in the back? Or worse, until he caught her. He was only a few feet away.

But it was dark. He might miss.

Her door opened suddenly, and she tumbled halfway to the ground.

"Get out."

She didn't have much choice. If she didn't comply, he was going to yank her out. She didn't want him touching her. She scrambled to her feet.

"Move." He pushed her shoulder and Erin braced against the pain, blinking back tears.

Somehow that seemed important. Not letting him see her cry. This was not a man who'd have patience with weakness. Of any sort.

A grunt sounded. An animalistic growl. And yet unmistakably human. Not from her. Or her captor. Hearing it, Erin stumbled. And received another push for her blunder.

There was someone up ahead of them. Somewhere. All she could see was blackness.

Smearing the keys of his new phone with blood, Rick dialed Lakeside as he cased the beach at a trot. His pilot had to be nearby.

"Lakeside."

"Angela." He recognized the caregiver's voice. "Check Steve's room. Now."

"Mr. Thomas? Rick? I was just down his hall five minutes ago. The guard's outside his door."

"Check. Now." He gritted his teeth to keep from shouting. He had to stay calm. Think. Get his ass off the island and back to Michigan faster than planes could fly.

"Fine," Angela said.

How could he have been so stupid? So trusting?

"The guard's sitting there," she said. Rick didn't need to hear her, "Oh, my God!" He'd known.

"He's…oh, my God!" Angela's voice was a panicked screech. "Oh, my God! Security!" The woman was hollering.

Someone came running. Angela was trying to be coherent. "Call the police," a muffled voice said.

"Angela," Rick yelled into the phone, earning him dirty looks from tourists on the beach. "Angela," he called again, uncaring of the response around him.

"He's dead! The guard's dead." Angela's words came in spurts. "I have no idea how long he's been sitting there dead! And Steve…he's gone. I don't know when. Oh, my God, Rick, he's gone!"

Blood dripped from Rick's hand and he tore off the bottom of his shirt, wrapping the cuts without missing a beat. He had glass in his flesh. Something he'd deal with later. If he got the chance.

An excruciating half hour later, he found his pilot. About one drink short of too drunk to fly. Buying a drink-holder filled with coffee cups, he corralled the man back to the road, plying him with coffee. He could fly the damn plane, but he needed the pilot to clear them through at the airport.

Twenty minutes later, they were in the air.

He wasn't sure it mattered.

He'd tried Erin twice.

She hadn't picked up.

They'd come to a cliff.

He was going to push her over. Into the lake she could hear sloshing against the rocks below. She wanted to think that it was her lake down there. The same waters that were, right then, gently caressing the rocks under her living room window. But she knew that wasn't possible. They'd driven northeast. It was Lake Huron's frigid waters crashing beneath them.

"Move." The voice again. Directly behind her. "Go."

He expected her to jump? Just like that?

Would she die on the way down? Or feel her body ripped apart by the force of the water?

Fifty degrees felt like thirty below. And a hundred above. This was it. She was going to die. All her worries about ethics and losing herself, her fears of forfeiting her place in the Fitzgerald family, her pleasure in finding a friend in Kelly—it was all for nothing.

And Rick.

Now she'd never—

"Go! Don't piss me off." The hand at her shoulder shoved again, and Erin almost threw up. She stumbled. And was still alive, her foot on solid ground.

There was a path. A steep one. But a path. He wanted her to take it.

Thankful to be alive, Erin took a step. And then another. The animal sounds were louder now. A combination of deep howls and childlike whining. Erin moved toward it. Thinking of helping this person in pain, of offering comfort, gave her strength. As though even in the face of her own mortality, being needed was something that mattered.

The way was steep. Erin slipped and fell, her chin colliding with the ground. A rock cut her cheek. And then her captor's fingers were digging into her arm as he hauled her back to her feet.

She didn't fall again. Erin had taken two steps on flat

ground before she saw the boat. A small, obviously old cabin cruiser.

"Get on."

She'd have to walk through a couple of feet of icy water to get there.

And then she'd be on a boat.

Erin loved the water. Loved listening to it. Respected its merciless power.

But she never, ever went in it.

She couldn't swim.

The gun jammed into her spine, breaking the skin.

Erin fell to her knees in the water. It was cold. Half submerged, she gasped. She had to get out. Had to breathe.

And the only dry place ahead was the boat.

She heard a sob and moved toward it. She wanted to call out that everything was going to be okay, but she didn't have enough air.

And it wasn't going to be okay.

She just wanted to believe it could be. *Had* to believe it could be.

Slipping on the ladder, partially because she didn't have the use of her hands, Erin cried out. Her captor's hands were splayed across her butt, shoving her up and onto the boat.

And that was when she saw the huddled body chained to a captain's chair across from the driver's seat.

"Steve!" Erin moved to the man instinctively. He reeked of urine. "It's okay, Steve. It's Erin. Remember me?"

The man didn't look up. Burying his head farther into his arms, he shuddered. "I'm going to take care of you now, okay?" She kept talking somehow. Just kept talking.

The boat's engine roared to life. She could feel the water's resistance against the boat as they sped away from shore.

"I'm not going to let anything happen to you," she said. "I promise."

Steve moaned, and she wondered if he was in pain. Wondered if the fiend who'd kidnapped a handicapped man had done more than just terrify him. If he'd wounded the man. And she wondered if Steve even knew she was there.

Sitting down next to him, she pushed her body close to his. "You aren't alone anymore," she told him. "I'm right here beside you."

And she was going to stay there until Rick found them. She was going to protect Steve for him. She had a purpose. Something she had to do.

And she would.

Because Rick was coming for them.

She needed to believe that.

The boat stopped and Erin glanced around them, seeing nothing. The man who'd taken them prisoner got up and pocketed the boat's key. Throwing an anchor over the side, he came toward them. Erin sat up straighter, sheltering Steve's huddled form. The black-jacketed man grabbed her ankle, locking a thick metal cuff around it. Their kidnapper attached a chain to the cuff and the other end to the boat's steering column. A second chain was already locked there. Steve's. The man opened a door that led below and walked over to where they'd boarded the boat.

"There's a bathroom and some food down below. Your chains will reach that far. There's a bomb fastened to the hull. I have the detonator. If Thomas manages to live through the next twenty-four hours, which he won't, and then gets lucky enough to find you, you might survive. If not, by this time tomorrow night, you'll both be dead."

"Wait…" He didn't even hesitate as he dropped over the side of the cabin cruiser. A couple of minutes later she heard rowing sounds in the water. He was leaving them out in the middle of a lake in the middle of the night. With a bomb attached to their boat.

It was sometime after midnight, by her best guess. She'd taken off her watch for her bath. She wasn't going to be able to figure out where they were, or hope to see anything that would help them, until morning.

The temperature was dropping by the minute.

"Steve? We have to get downstairs." Could the man even walk? As big as he was, Erin didn't have much chance of bearing his weight with her arms free, let alone with them tied behind her back. Her hands had gone numb.

"Steve," she said again, a mix of panic and authority in her voice. "We have to go downstairs. Now."

The man raised his head. Stared at her. And she smiled.

"Hi," she said. "Remember me?"

Steve nodded, shuddered and lowered his head again.

Nudging him with her elbow, Erin said, "No, Steve, don't do that. Look at me. Please."

The man looked, his eyes swollen. He'd been crying. Had he also been hit? She had no idea how long Steve had been held in captivity. Hours. Or longer? Rick had been gone for two days.

"You're safe," she said, keeping her tone even. "The bad man's gone. Rick is on his way to get us. He wants us to go downstairs where it's warmer and wait for him. Do you understand?"

With a hiccup, Steve nodded.

"Can you stand up?"

He moved his legs. And started to cry, shaking his head.

"Yes, you can, Steve. Rick wants you to be strong," she said. If ever she'd needed the ability to convince someone to believe her, it was now. "Come on. I'm going to stand first, and then you have to stand, too. It'll be a game. Like Simon Says. I do it and then you do it."

"Do I get to be Simon, too?" The question was asked with childlike innocence in that deep male voice.

"Yes. As soon as we get downstairs."

It took him two tries, but Steve made it to his feet. He pushed up against her and every time she moved, he did as well.

Holding her elbow against Steve's arm, and with their chains clanking behind them, Erin led the way down the four stairs to the area below. A small light was on over the tiniest sink she'd ever seen. The space measured maybe six by six with a kitchenette on one side and a blue padded bench on the other. A table was folded against the wall. Feeling claustrophobic, she left it where it was. A door on the far end opened to a two-by-two square with a toilet. Their chains stretched the length of the room, but there wasn't space for them to pass each other on the way.

"I gotta pee."

Judging by the stains on his pants and the smell that was sickeningly stronger now that they were in the confined space, he'd already done so repeatedly.

"Okay, hold on," Erin said. This wasn't a time for modesty. Or delicate sensibilities. Turning her back so she could reach his fly, she winced at the pain in her fingers as she struggled to unhook the button on his jeans and then unzip them. With his arms strapped behind him,

Steve couldn't help. He stood completely still while she worked his pants and then his briefs down his body.

"Okay, go ahead," she said, pointing at the toilet room. "You'll have to sit down."

He didn't close the door.

Erin busied herself backing up to the cupboards and drawers she could reach, searching for a change of clothes.

She found a pair of drawstring sailor pants. They were probably too short, but they'd have to do. Steve's pants and underwear had to go. Thank God her clothes were mostly dry.

She had to use the toilet, too, but was planning to hold it as long as she could. At least until after they'd had time to work on each other's knots. That was their next activity. Whether Simon said so or not.

She was absolutely not going to die with her hands tied behind her back.

35

Rick had lost a precious five hours by the time he was belted into his seat on the flight from Miami International to Grand Rapids.

And he was facing dawn when he drove his truck out of the Grand Rapids airport garage. He made it to Erin's house before eight. She didn't answer his knock. And when he pulled a tool from the kit he'd removed from the storage bin in his truck and unlocked her back door, he found exactly what he'd known he would—an empty house.

Nothing was disturbed. No sign of forced entry. But then there wouldn't be. Sarge was the best of the best. A real pro.

Rick ought to know. The older man had taught him everything. Sarge understood how Rick thought because he'd taught him to think.

He'd know what Rick would do next. And the move after that. He could predict every reaction. Every option Rick would come up with.

And he'd have a plan to thwart them all.

Rick had to focus. To think. But that meant he'd be walking into sure death. Every instinct he had, every nerve that had kept him alive for fifteen years of covert operations, was all a detriment to him now.

How did he outthink his own thoughts? Outmaneuver a man who'd controlled his mind for almost two decades?

He didn't even stop to wonder why Sarge was doing this. Didn't matter. Saving Erin and Steve mattered.

Nothing else did.

He tried to decide what to do. His internal radar pushed him toward the water. Water left no trace. Sarge knew Rick would expect him to go to the water, that it was the first place he'd look.

So did Sarge take them somewhere else? To thwart him yet again? Or was he sitting on the water with them, waiting for Rick?

Did Sarge even know that Rick was on to him?

He'd thought about calling from the island. And again from Miami. But he didn't want Sarge to know he was on his trail just yet. He had to find Erin and Steve first.

Steve had to be scared to death. Pissing himself.

Oh, God. Stevie. What have I done to you?

The scrambled phone rang. Rick had ditched his disposable in the Miami airport.

Sarge's number flashed on the screen.

"Yeah," he said, putting himself in another time and place. A mental state in which he'd trusted his sergeant with his life.

With Steve's life.

What had the bastard done to Steve?

"Do you have something?" Rick asked as though they were still working together and Sarge had been calling with another update. In their old life, Sarge wouldn't be calling for any other reason.

"Yes, as a matter of fact, I do."

"You found the mole."

"No. He found me."

Brady had wanted him to know that Sarge owned the bar. When he'd first found out about Sarge's connection to the bar, to Brady's Maria, Rick had been so sure his friend was telling him that Sarge was dirty. But why? Because he'd owned a bar he hadn't told them about?

"Is he there now?"

"Yes."

"Forcing you to make the call."

"Yes."

Brady had found the mole. He'd provided Maria with a picture of the man behind it all. Pop. Sarge. A picture to turn over to her lawyer.

And Brady had left Rick with the information, too. In the form of a matchbook.

"Is he listening?" Rick asked the questions he knew were important. Information he'd be expected to look for.

"Yes. He has Erin and Steve, Rick." Sarge's voice contained just the right amount of calm. And intensity. Was he acting? Or was he victim, not mole?

"What does he want?" That was what Rick needed to know. Didn't so much matter who "he" was at the moment. Sarge or someone else.

"You have something he wants."

"He can have it." It was in his pants pocket. The matchbook was no longer useful to anyone. Rick knew the truth and had no further reason to hide the clue that had eventually revealed it.

"Hold on," Sarge said.

The phone rustled. Rick heard voices. Could be Sarge talking to himself. Or not.

"You know what he wants," Sarge said.

"The proof Brady left for me."

"And you have it."

"Yes."

"Hold on…"

Air crackled as the phone was moved—roughly.

"Bring the proof to the bridge off Route 23 near Rogers City," a man's voice barked. "Seven o'clock tonight. Come alone and don't be late or all three of them will die."

Seven o'clock. After dark. Giving him time to make his way back to Michigan from Miami, where he was still supposed to be.

Sarge didn't know he'd returned. It was all the edge Rick was going to get.

The weight against her chest was too heavy. Boots wasn't that heavy. But it wasn't Boots.

And then consciousness came slowly back. With the bitter onslaught of memory. It wasn't Boots sleeping against her. It was Steve. They were downstairs in the cabin cruiser. She'd made a game out of getting their hands untied during the night.

That had helped a lot. Steve was much calmer when he was playing games. And almost happy once his hands were free. He didn't like the chain on his foot, but the fact that Erin had one, too, that she was playing the same game he was, satisfied him. For now.

She'd searched the boat and found pitifully little. No tools. No silverware in the kitchen. The fridge didn't work. There was no running water.

Their captor had said there was food. She'd found saltine crackers and peanut butter. And bottled water.

She recalled from their lunch at Lakeside that Steve liked peanut butter.

He liked her, too. He had to be touching her at all

times, either holding her hand or leaning on her, and oddly, that was more comfort than irritant. When she'd decided there was no more she could do until daylight, when she'd run out of the energy to play games, she settled with Steve on the padded bench in the cabin, took him in her arms and ran her fingers through his hair until he fell asleep.

Her father had done that for her once. She'd had strep throat and been afraid she'd suffocate if she slept.

Steve had been asleep within minutes. She hadn't expected to sleep. She'd figured she'd sit there quietly and make a plan. But the boat's gentle rhythm, coupled with her emotional and physical exhaustion, had lulled her into slumber.

How long had she been asleep? Minutes? Or hours. The cabin was still dark, but she could see a sliver of dim light beneath the door she'd closed and locked.

Dawn had arrived.

And chain or no chain, Erin had to find that bomb. And hope to God she could get it away from them without detonating it.

The first thing she was going to do was pull up the anchor. With Steve's help they'd be able to do that, at least. And if she could figure out a way to get to the bomb, to remove it without setting it off and drop it in the bottom of the lake… And if they drifted far enough…

Maybe they could get to shore or pass another boat, attract someone's attention.

One way or another, she had to save their lives.

Or this would be the last dawn either of them would ever see.

Rick drove too fast, ran a red light, double-parked in the sheriff's office lot and stormed inside the building he'd hoped never to visit again. Sheriff Johnson was sitting behind his desk, a cup of coffee in hand. Rick pushed past the people who tried to stop him, and into the glass-walled space that set the sheriff apart from the rest of the room. He shut the door.

"I need help."

Sheriff Johnson came around the desk. The fact that he didn't immediately reach for his gun was a good sign. "You're in trouble?"

"Not the kind you mean, and more than you can imagine. Look, Sheriff, we don't have time for long explanations. I was a government agent, part of a covert ops team. I retired a year ago. Since then, the other two men on my team have been murdered. A girlfriend's been murdered. And a bartender we knew. I believe Charles Cook's murder is part of this, too. I've just found out that the man behind all this was our superior officer, my sergeant—or at least he's involved. I don't know why. And I don't know who else is working with him or for him. They've got Erin Morgan. And Steve Miller."

The older man's face was a rock, his gaze intense. "Got them. How? For what?"

"I got a call. My sergeant said he's being held, too, and that they made him call me. I don't believe him. But he wasn't alone. They're convinced that one of my peers left me some evidence that will point to their involvement with an illegal arms dealer. They want that evidence. If I don't deliver by seven o'clock tonight, they're going to kill Erin and Steve."

Sheriff Johnson took Rick's arm, leading him out of the room. If the man thought he was going to lock Rick up now, he was—

"Roberts," he shouted as he charged through the office. "Get every available deputy in here and wait for my orders. And call Fitzgerald, too."

"Yes, sir."

Rick barely heard the answer as he raced beside Sheriff Johnson outside into the bright morning sun.

"We'll take your truck," Johnson said, heading toward the trunk of his car. He pulled out a duffel bag. "My car would be a dead giveaway."

So would the man's uniform. But Rick had a feeling Johnson already knew that. Hence, the duffel.

Instead of approaching Rick's truck, Johnson turned to the back of the building. "Come on," he said.

Rick followed as the sheriff led him through a private door into a special holding area. Not where Rick had been jailed. This space held one cell.

He was shocked to see Halloway sitting inside.

"Sheriff." Halloway, wearing standard dark blue jail garb, stood immediately. And then, noticing Rick, stepped back. "What's going on?"

"Tell him what you just told me," Sheriff Johnson demanded, looking at Rick.

Not sure what was going on, but knowing he was out of time—and options—Rick did as Johnson ordered.

Once silence had fallen, Johnson faced Halloway. "And now you're going to tell me who you were working for," he said, steely determination in his tone.

What the hell?

"Halloway broke into Erin's office," Johnson explained, staring the deputy down. "He claims that he was working on a top-secret assignment through Washington. For someone with high government clearance."

After one more glance at Sheriff Johnson and then at Rick, Halloway straightened his shoulders. "I'm not just claiming," he insisted. "I know this man was legitimate.

His name's Sergeant Randall Wyatt. I saw his identification."

Randall Wyatt. Sarge's given name. His official army name. Goddammit. Rick knew he'd been right.

Keeping all emotion in check, Rick stepped forward. "Who was he working for?"

"He wouldn't say."

"Did he mention any other names? Or speak to anyone in your presence?"

"No. I only saw him once. He just showed up here. He was waiting outside for me one night when I got off shift. He showed me his ID. Told me the Department of Defense needed a local man and I was their guy because I'd been in the army reserves. That was about two months ago. All our other communication was over scrambled phones."

"Before Cook's death."

"Yeah." Rick's instincts clicked into high gear.

"Wyatt killed Cook."

"He said Cook was a traitor, part of an arms conspiracy in the Department of Defense. He said that when he confronted him, Cook came after him and in the ensuing scuffle was stabbed."

Cook was no more a traitor than Rick was. "If Wyatt had been on official business, he'd have identified himself as an agent and when Cook came after him, he'd have shot him." Rick's voice was low.

Time was running out. A lifetime of work and he was down to hours.

"You planted the knife at my place." Rick was only guessing, but he made sure he didn't sound like it.

"Wyatt called me. Said they knew you were involved with Cook but that they didn't have enough on you yet to get an indictment. They were going to hold you on

Cook's murder until they could gather the rest of their intelligence, build a strong enough case to put you away for good this time. That's why he had me search your place again, later, when he had you out on a boat. I was looking for evidence."

"*This* time?" Johnson asked, peering at Rick. "Put you away for good *this* time?"

"I'll explain in the truck." They had to get going. Seconds were ticking away. Seconds that could make a difference between life and more death.

"This Wyatt—just to be sure we're not dealing with a stolen identity—he wouldn't have been wearing a black jacket with khaki slacks, would he?"

"Yes, he was."

Rick took out his wallet, retrieved a bent-up old photo he'd kept in the storage compartment in his truck. A photo left from regular army days. He held it out to Halloway. "This him?"

Rick and the rest of his platoon were in the photo. But there was no mistaking who their leader was.

"Yeah, that's him."

Erin didn't know a lot about bombs. But she knew enough to realize that if a light was blinking, she had a greater chance of staying alive if she didn't disturb anything.

Leaning over the boat as far as her chain would allow, she stared at the blinking red beacon and tried not to cry. Her tears would unhinge Steve. The man-child was not at his best this morning. He wanted to fish.

"If Rick really knew I was here, there'd be a fishing pole," Steve said petulantly from just behind Erin. He was leaning against her back.

Steve was the smartest five-year-old she'd ever met.

And if she wasn't careful, he was going to be a very frightened and panicked five-year-old in a six-foot-two male body.

They had another problem. The bomb wasn't directly attached to the hull, but to a chain that was attached to it. And just below that, the chain continued down into the water.

It was attached to the anchor.

Bottom line, if she pulled the anchor, they'd explode.

36

Sheriff Johnson dispensed jobs to every person on his payroll. All the shifts. And he called in private contractors, as well, at the insistence of Ron Fitzgerald, who would foot the bill. A forensics team to cover Erin's place. Investigators to cover every inch of Temple and the surrounding areas.

Deputies went door to door. A picture of Sarge was sent by cell phone to every single law enforcement official on the search.

APBs were launched.

The FBI was on alert.

Johnson called law personnel in Ludington, who were already conducting a full investigation at Lakeside. With one man dead and a patient missing, the FBI was also on the scene. Private investigators were covering the area with pictures of Steve and Sarge, trying to find a trail from Lakeside, from Ludington, to know what direction Sarge had taken.

They had to find out where he was holding Steve and Erin before Rick was due to meet with him.

In between phone calls, Rick had filled Sheriff Johnson in on a few things. His jailtime in Arizona, his alias and everything he knew about the way Sarge's mind worked. They needed that information.

And Rick needed help. He couldn't do this alone. He had to trust someone and that someone was Huey Johnson. Rick had made his decision. He didn't second-guess himself. He focused on the job.

"I'm assuming you've got the evidence on you," Johnson said as Rick drove north. With others scouring the state in various directions from Temple and Ludington, he and Johnson were heading toward the rendezvous point. Their thought was that Sarge would keep his hostages close enough to get to them.

Rick couldn't think about Steve and Erin. He wouldn't be able to rescue them if he weakened his focus.

"What evidence?" Rick asked. Both hands on the wheel, he kept his gaze firmly on the road.

"You don't have anything to give them?"

"Not really." He reached into his pocket. Pulled out the memento Brady had left. "Just this."

"A used matchbook?" It wasn't much. But it had done what Brady had intended it to do. Eventually.

"That's all I've got."

"Then why do they think you have something they want? Something that can incriminate them?"

"Two reasons."

"I'm listening."

"First, because I told them I do."

"Understandable, considering the fact that they were making a ransom call. You couldn't very well tell them you didn't have the ransom."

Johnson, now in jeans, a flannel shirt and boots, attire similar to Rick's, with a gun at his waist and another, smaller pistol and a knife strapped to his ankles, was a good man. And a smart one. "Right," Rick said.

"What about the second reason?"

In as few words as possible, he told Johnson about the week on the yacht with Brady. About his friendship with the other agent. About Maria. And Guardano. And…the matchbook.

Ending with his trip to The Resting Place the night before.

"And then I figured it out," he said. "Brady knew what was going on. He knew the players. He just didn't have the proof. And he couldn't go to anyone without it. Sarge would cover his tracks and hang Brady out to dry. We were covert, remember. Sarge was the only official agent among us."

"A dangerously vulnerable position for you young men to be in."

"Which is why it paid so well," Rick said dryly. He'd been in it for the money. For Steve.

And for his country. His life hadn't seemed worth much, but doing such dangerous work, something few could or would do, had given him a sense of value.

"Sarge obviously worked out that Brady was on to him. He had Maria arrested. And had someone on the inside keeping track of her."

Rick was silent a moment until Huey nudged him. "Go on."

"He also knew that Brady had left something for me. He expected to find it when he cleaned out Brady's room. He would've been looking for anything that would implicate him."

"But we still don't know exactly what he's guilty of. And while I agree he's likely responsible for several murders, and now we suspect he's behind the kidnappings, we still don't have anything solid. He could be a hostage himself right now, just like he said."

"We know he killed Charles Cook. We have Hallo-way's testimony."

"I assume you have a plan."

"I trust Brady implicitly," Rick said. "He knew that if he left me that matchbook I wouldn't let it go. He knew I'd keep searching until I found out what it meant. Sarge owned the bar. Maria was his woman. Segura has an inside contact who lets him walk away from everything he's ever done, even though we know without a doubt that he's dealing illegal arms on a worldwide scale. And…he has a souvenir from Wyatt's bar, The Resting Place."

"I'm not disagreeing that Wyatt's involvement is obvi-ous, or that his guilt is pretty clear. Only that everything's circumstantial and we don't have time to do anything about it."

"There's something Brady knew that we don't. Some-thing Sarge thinks we can prove," Rick said. "Brady couldn't come to see me in prison. It would've compro-mised both our covers. So it makes sense that he left me whatever proof he had. I plan to let Sarge think I can hang him—but that I'd rather die, and would rather let Steve and Erin die, than give it to him."

"You figure I'm going to let you walk in there alone? With nothing?"

"I know you are," Rick said. "Even if I had the evi-dence he wants, especially if I had it, the man's going to kill Erin and Steve. Why wouldn't he? As long as they're alive to testify, he's a kidnapper. And if I give him what he wants, he has no further use for me, either."

"But holding out on him is also going to get them killed."

"Not if we beat him at his own game."

"And how do we do that?"

"I'm going to tell him I've left the evidence in an FBI

safe to be found in the morning. That I knew he'd kill Erin and Steve, anyway, so I did the right thing. The only thing I could. I protected my country by exposing him."

"What if he asks for specifics?"

"I know he's in with Segura. I believe the things Sarge told me about Segura were true. He knows I'd try to verify what he said. Not because I didn't trust him but because we always had our own backs. Check and double check. He knew me." Rick was glad he'd had no breakfast. It would've come back up on him. "He played me. But he played me with the truth. That's all that would've worked. He just gave his own motivations to some unknown fictional DOD mole."

"Unless there really is another player. Someone from inside the government. Have you considered that?"

"Yeah. Doesn't really matter. It's us against the bad guy. Bad guy has government connections—whether it's just Sarge or Sarge and someone else. Our job is to get him, or them, to implicate themselves so we have the proof we need to take them down."

"How are you planning to do that?"

"This is where you come in."

"I rather thought it might be."

"I can't go in with a wire. They'll look for one first thing."

"Agreed."

"You go in early, on foot, from some other direction and get close enough for a transmitter feed."

"Not much good without a wire."

"The node will be in the butt of my gun. They're going to confiscate the gun the second I get near them, but they'll keep it close. It's ammunition. Sarge's number one rule—ammo is sacred. He'd never expect me to tamper with it. Or be without it. And he's going to keep it on him because he knows my M.O. will be to try to get it back as quickly as I can. He taught me many methods for doing that. All of which he'll be watching for. And be prepared for."

"And in the meantime I'm sitting in a tree listening."

"Right. And if he asks me for specifics, I start spitting stuff about Segura, engage him in conversation—and we've got him. At least on that score."

"And if he doesn't ask for specifics about whatever you supposedly turned over to the FBI?"

"I offer him a deal. He gives me sixty percent of his cut, and I get the info back from the FBI. Breaking and entering, retrieving irretrievable items, was my specialty."

"And he'd believe you'd do this?"

"He knows all I have of any value in my life is Steve, and the only thing Steve needs is money."

"What about Erin?"

Rick glanced away from the road for just a moment, taking in the fatherly expression on the other man's face.

"What about her?"

"I thought I picked up on something in her office the other day," Johnson said. "And Halloway reported that you were at her place for several hours Sunday night. At her place and out of sight in the back of the house long enough to have…"

"I didn't have sex with her. She's my attorney. And not the kind of woman you take to bed and walk away from."

"I'm glad you realize that."

"I realize far more than you know, Sheriff."

Johnson gazed out the windshield as miles and miles of desolate woodland sped by.

"So you offer Wyatt a deal. He takes it. You get him to implicate himself. Then what?"

"Then I tell him the whole thing is contingent on Steve and Erin's release. As soon as I have confirmation they're safe, I retrieve the evidence. I'll let him know if that doesn't happen, or if anything happens to me, the FBI will have time to move on what I've left for them."

"And if he balks?"

"Then you have your man."

"And you, Erin and Steve end up dead."

Rick's hands tightened on the wheel. "You got a better plan, Sheriff?"

"No, I don't. But that doesn't make me any fonder of this one."

"Then let's hope someone finds those two before our meeting with Randall Wyatt." He couldn't think of the man as Sarge anymore. Rick had loved Sarge like family.

He should have known better.

As the sun rose, so did Steve's irritability and Erin's panic. She and Steve were about three hundred yards away from the closest shore. But they weren't in plain view. They were on the back side of an island cove, not likely to be seen by any passing boaters. And if anyone was looking for them and decided to search Lake Huron, their chances of finding the small cabin cruiser were slim to none.

Whoever had taken them meant business.

And he wasn't an amateur.

She kept reminding herself that Rick wasn't, either. That he'd had fifteen years of covert ops success. That he knew tricks she wouldn't even be able to imagine.

And still, she vacillated between needing to throw up and trying to stay calm.

"I want to fly a kite." Steve's whine was getting harder to take. She wanted so badly to please him. Needed to help him.

And didn't have any idea what to do.

The man-child sat next to her on the deck of the cabin cruiser, his long legs stretched out alongside hers, as they played another game of tic-tac-toe with saltine crackers and water bottle caps. It wasn't like they were going to be around long enough to finish the two boxes of saltines, or drink the entire case of water.

They'd been at it for almost an hour. She'd lost track of the number of games, but Steve was certain he'd won twenty and she'd won nineteen.

As far as Erin could tell, he couldn't count past twenty.

And as long as she stayed one game behind, he continued to tell her he'd give her a chance to catch up.

"We don't have a kite," she said as she moved her square cracker next to one of Steve's round bottle caps.

"Are we going to die?"

"No, we are not."

"My dad died. When the truck hit the tree."

"Well, we're not going to die."

Steve's face fell. "'Cept Ricky didn't come save us."

"He will, Steve. You know Rick. He goes away but he always comes back." It was something Steve had said to her the previous night just before he'd gone to sleep.

"I can make a kite."

"But we don't have the things we'd need."

"Yeah, we do. We can use that metal stuff that came off the counter around the sink."

Aluminum trim. She could bend it enough to break it in half. And then twist the pieces together to form a base.

"And the paper bag the food was in."

Steve's eyes were wide-open, shining with excitement.

"And we've got the string that was around our hands. And some from the buoy on the side of the boat, too."

If building a kite was all it took to make Steve happy, she'd willingly spend the last hours of her life doing so.

Because it was becoming more and more clear that these *were* the last hours of their lives.

37

They'd been on the road for a couple of hours. Johnson had taken multiple calls from multiple sources. No one had a single lead on either Erin's or Steve's whereabouts. No one even knew for sure when they'd been snatched.

Erin had been seen Tuesday afternoon, leaving the office around three.

And Steve…he'd had dinner and then everyone had assumed he was in his room with his guard right there, keeping him safe.

No one recognized Randall Wyatt from the picture they were passing around.

Ron Fitzgerald had put in a call to the governor, who'd called someone he knew in Washington. The secretary of defense was aware of the situation. After some checking, he verified Wyatt's status within the department. Verified that he'd had a covert ops team. But all three men were still alive.

And still working for the government, though no longer for Randall Wyatt, who'd retired two years before.

What the hell?

"All three are still alive? That doesn't make sense."

He'd been to Brady's grave. Or rather, Jack's grave. What the fuck was going on?

"Did you say he retired two years ago?"

Johnson glanced over at him. "Yeah." And his phone rang again.

Two years.

After Rick went to prison. But before Brady was killed. Wyatt had no longer been working when Rick got out. When he'd made all the arrangements for Rick's retirement…

"We have zero clues and less than six hours to find them," Johnson said when he hung up from yet another call. "You said Wyatt trained you. So where would you take them if you had them?"

"They're on the water someplace." He was sure of it now. "Water leaves no trail. No tracks to follow. No physical evidence of someone having been there."

Johnson nodded.

"They have to be on a boat," he added.

"You sound sure about that."

"I am…" Rick glanced at the man at his side, and had a moment of sheer panic. He'd just discovered he'd been a fool for trusting one man, and here he was, doing it again.

But he trusted Erin. And she'd trusted him, enough to keep his secret. She was probably trusting him to find her. And she trusted the man sitting beside him.

"Steve…my friend…he's lived in institutions for the past fifteen years. At Lakeside for the past ten. Any change, any situation or surroundings that are unfamiliar to him, and he flips out. He can become virtually uncontrollable very quickly. Picture a five-year-old having a tantrum in the body of a grown man."

"He'd certainly attract attention."

"Right. But Sarge knows that Steve loves to fish. He loves boats. He must've told him he was there to pick up Steve for me. And that he was taking him fishing. That I was meeting them there. There's no other way he could've gotten Steve out of there without a very noisy fight. He couldn't have carried him. Or dragged him out unnoticed. A gun to Steve's back or any hint of danger would only have intensified any tantrum."

"So they're on a boat somewhere. Or at least they were. I think it's safe to assume he's keeping them both in the same place."

"Yes. Less effort. Less chance of discovery. Only one place to guard…" And one place to burn down. Or sink.

"He could dispose of the bodies easily in Lake Michigan," Rick said aloud.

"Or Lake Huron," Johnson suggested. "The area he's chosen for your meeting isn't far from Lake Huron."

"So he'd have them close enough to monitor them."

Or kill them.

Before they'd gone another mile, Johnson had the coast guard on full search for any kind of boat out on Lake Huron bearing a five-foot-three-inch female and a mentally handicapped six-foot male. By the next mile, private boaters had been added to the mix.

"I want to color it!" Steve jumped up and down as he watched Erin bend pieces of aluminum counter trim around the brown paper bag.

"Steve! Don't jump!" Her voice was sharp with tension as she thought of the bomb. Steve's lower lip protruded and he started to cry.

"Hey, buddy, I'm sorry," she said, immediately reaching for him. He came to her readily, resting his head against her shoulder. "Don't cry. It's okay. I'm just... I can't swim," she said. "I'm afraid of the water."

"You can't swim?" The man giggled. "Ricky taught me how to swim a gazillion years ago. Why didn't he teach you?"

"Because, goofy—" she poked at his nose "—I didn't tell him I don't know how. And I don't want you to tell him, either, 'kay? Let's keep it our little secret."

"'Kay, but don't be mad at me, Erin. I don't like it when you're mad at me."

"I wasn't mad, buddy. I was scared."

"Yeah, Ricky says girls get kinda silly about some things."

She'd just bet he did.

"When did he say that?"

"Oh, one time when I kicked sand in my friend's face and she didn't think it was funny. She got all hurt feelings and stuff like I was being mean when I wasn't. I just wanted to make her laugh. She's really pretty when she laughs."

Steve's expression, as he tried to show Erin how his friend looked, made *her* laugh. And she felt closer to Rick than ever before as she sat there with his childhood friend.

He had to find them.

And he had to do it fast.

As the afternoon wore on, she knew every minute was critical. Their captor had said they'd die sometime that evening.

Their time was running out.

Randall Wyatt was alone. At least as far as he was letting Rick know. Rick's gun was tucked in the waistband of the older man's khakis. When he'd first informed his ex-whatever-he'd-been that he'd planted his "evidence in an FBI safe" Rick had thought Wyatt was going to pull that gun and use it on him.

Out of sheer, uncontrollable anger.

The one who lost control first lost the game. Sarge's words from long ago came back to him.

"Steve and Erin are dead, Thomas."

Maybe. He couldn't think about that right now.

"A shame, too. She was tight. Sweet. Probably the sweetest bitch I ever fucked."

Maybe. He couldn't think about that right now.

"Then I guess we're done here," Rick said tonelessly.

They were playing with each other. They both knew it. What they were saying might be true. Could just as easily not be.

Could be some truth and some fiction.

The words didn't matter except as a way to get his opponent to lose control.

Rick turned to leave, knowing that although he had a chance of feeling one of his own bullets, Sarge had a thing about shooting a man in the back. Saw it as a sign of weakness.

"Wait."

He didn't turn around to face him.

"You didn't come here just to tell me you'd squealed on me."

Rick waited.

"You said you were going to offer me something."

There might be information in an FBI safe. And there might not. Sarge knew Rick would have a backup plan. Rick was counting on the fact that the man wouldn't be willing to take the risk that he was bluffing.

"For something in return," Rick said. "If Erin and Steve are dead, you have nothing I want."

"Maybe I do."

Rick turned. "Like what? You know me, Wyatt. Other than money for Steve, which isn't necessary if he's no longer alive, there's nothing you could possibly give me that I'd want."

"What deal were *you* going to offer?" Wyatt countered. Why had Rick never noticed how beady his eyes got when he was closing in on his prey?

Or maybe he had. Maybe he just hadn't cared because he hadn't been the target.

"I'll retrieve every piece of incriminating information from that safe before morning. But only after I've got verification from someone of my choice that Erin and Steve are alive."

"Would you settle for one out of two?"

Taking a chance, Rick said, "No."

"Doesn't matter," Wyatt said, grinning at him as if they were buddies sharing a beer.

In the past, maybe. Not now. And never again.

"Because they're dead," Rick said. And he thought of Johnson. And the tape. He had a job to do. "Because you killed them."

"If you don't retrieve that information, you're going to rot in prison right alongside me. So I guess there *is* something you want." Wyatt was still grinning and Rick swore that before he died, he was going to wipe that grin off the man's face with his bare hands.

"You want your freedom." His old mentor practically spat the words at him.

"I have my freedom."

"Not if you turn me in you don't."

"How do you figure?"

"Because you aren't who you think you are, that's how I figure."

Rick knew, without a doubt, that Randall Wyatt spoke the complete truth.

And he thought of Johnson. And the tape. He had a job to do.

"Then why don't you tell me who *you* think I am?"

"You, son, are a murderer. And a thief. You *are* the underbelly. The best of the best. Which makes you the worst of the worst."

Rick turned to go. "I don't have time for riddles."

"You have the time, Richard." The coldness in Wyatt's voice stopped him. "I was the head of a special ops team, just like I told you and your buddies," Wyatt said. "But it wasn't made up of you three."

Johnson's words, *All three are still alive,* repeated themselves calmly in Rick's mind.

"What were we, then?"

"All that evidence you have on me, the corruption, the illegal arms deals, the millions in drug money you now know I pocketed, it all rests on your shoulders, man. Where do you think I got the ammunition? The drugs?"

Rick didn't move.

"You stole them for me."

Swinging around, Rick said, "I stole guns to keep them from terrorists. I did it to protect my country."

"No, Rick, that was my *legitimate* ops team. You guys, you stole for me."

"The drugs? And the guns? That was all to line your pocket?" He'd been a pawn? A goon man? He was nothing more than a low-life criminal? Worse than any of the dregs he'd been with in prison?

He'd enriched the fucking bastards he'd been risking his life to put away? He'd put his own country at risk by helping to arm those fiends?

"Of course. That Arizona deal? I knew from my real special ops team that those drugs were there. We were set to implicate the officials later that day and get the drugs. I sent you in to get 'em before our legitimate operation went down. But then one of my guys, the one assigned to do the real job later that day, heard that the dirty official had changed his plans, was moving the drugs earlier than expected. He didn't have time to inform anyone. He went into action earlier than planned. He was set to make an arrest—but it wasn't supposed to be yours."

"And that's what Brady found in Arizona. He came face-to-face with your legitimate team and discovered that we were an illegitimate band of criminals. You sold out your own men, your country, for money."

"Don't get self-righteous on me now, son. You were happy enough to do the jobs as long as I was lining your pockets, as well."

"I thought I was serving my country!"

"And that makes it all right?"

"For me it did." Mostly. At least it made him feel okay about taking the money.

That seemed to give Randall Wyatt pause. And for a second, Rick was reminded of the man who'd seen him through four years of combat as a kid barely out of high school. The man who'd been there for him when his old man died.

When there'd been no one else to watch out for Steve…

"Why?" he asked. Because for that brief moment, it mattered.

"Think about it, Rick," Wyatt said with a smirk. "You were there. In the army. We risked our lives every day— and for what? For the guys in Washington to get more powerful. For the rich to get richer. For moms to dress their girls in pretty dresses and give them away to rich businessmen. And what do we get except a pat on the back, the promise of a bed in the VA hospital and enough money to keep us in an apartment for life. Sometimes, if we were lucky, we got a little bit of appreciation. Most times, not even that. But, hey, we were heroes, while we sat home alone in rented rooms with demons in our heads for company."

Maybe. Some of them ended up that way. Not most.

Rick thought of Huey Johnson out there, hearing all this, recording it. And knew he wasn't done yet. He had a job to do. One last assignment.

And with Erin and Steve most likely dead, with his own life worthless, he had nothing left to lose.

"What did Charles Cook do to earn your wrath?" he asked.

"The fool saw me poking around in your truck one morning, but only because he'd come out to help himself to a roll of electrical wire that he took from your supplies and dumped in his trunk."

"So you murdered him because he saw you outside the office?"

"No, I killed him because after I showed him my ID he reported me to Homeland Security. Luckily I still have friends in high places and I was able to explain that the man was on the attack because I caught him stealing. The emails were destroyed."

The truth behind the stolen Homeland Security emails.

That was how it was with Sarge. That was how things worked. There had to be an element of truth behind every lie.

"And Saul?"

"Brady told him what he knew."

"Which was?"

"That you three weren't a legitimate ops team."

"If Brady knew that, then why didn't he tell someone official?"

"For the same reason you aren't going to say anything. The same reason you're going to get that evidence back tonight. Because if he reported me, he was going down with me. You guys have too many crimes on your heads to ever see the light of day again."

"And that was the plan, wasn't it? To get us so far under that we'd never have a chance of coming out."

Wyatt shrugged. "Didn't occur to me at the time."

"So what *were* your plans at the time?" He was just curious. His life was over. Might as well know the details.

"You'd stay employed as long as it worked."

"And then?"

"I think you know the answer to that."

Sarge had planned to kill them all along. Kill them when he was done with them.

"You trashed Tom's reputation on the street, didn't you?"

"Of course. Who else would have done it?"

Rick thought of Brady. Of Saul. Of three lives purposely wasted. "Why us? How'd you choose us for your gutter trash and the others for the legitimate operation?"

"You three had no family to speak of. No money. No connections."

Only Wyatt. He was their one connection. Because they were covert ops he'd been the only person who reported back to them. There were no checks and balances.

"We were expendable."

Wyatt shrugged again and Rick could have killed him right then and there with his bare hands. Except that…he couldn't.

Whatever else anyone might think about him, he knew he would never, ever have taken one assignment for any amount of money if he hadn't thought he was serving his country.

He'd thought all those years of hell, those months in prison, that he'd been serving the president of the United States.

And instead he'd been sewer slime.

"I'm not stealing for you again," Rick said, facing Wyatt, completely unarmed and uncaring. "I don't give a shit if I rot in prison. Apparently that's where I belong." He'd never meant anything more in his life. And Randall Wyatt clearly got the message.

Wyatt's shoulders stiffened, his eyes glazed. The man had no idea which FBI office Rick had supposedly visited. And even if he guessed correctly, he wouldn't know which safe. Nor was he skilled enough to get in and out of a building, or a safe, in the hours before morning. Which was when the fictional evidence would be exposed.

"Then we both lose," Wyatt said. Reaching into the back of his SUV he pulled out a device. At first Rick thought he was going to blow them both up with a grenade.

And then he saw what it was. A remote used to detonate bombs.

And he knew.

"Steve and that woman, that lovely woman…did I tell you how beautifully she screams when her legs are spread and she's in pain—"

"No!" Rick yelled, an animal sound he didn't recognize as he lunged. "You bastard!"

Wyatt jumped back, holding the detonator up and away from Rick. "They're still alive, Thomas, out on

Lake Huron, on a little boat. I kept them safe for you.
I liked you. Out of all my soldiers, over all those years,
you were my favorite. But now, right this minute, they
are going to die." His fingers moved over the detonator
and Rick flew through the air.

"No!" he cried again. But he was too late.

Randall Wyatt had exploded the bomb.

38

It was Huey Johnson who pulled the trigger and killed Randall Wyatt. But only after Wyatt had shot Rick Thomas.

Luckily, at Johnson's insistence, Thomas had been wearing a vest. And Wyatt didn't get the chance to take a second shot.

Rick didn't really care one way or the other. Life was over whether he was breathing or not.

Johnson called in his backup patrol and the coroner. Then he led Rick back to his truck. Johnson took the wheel.

Before he drove away, he handed Rick the tape. "It ends here," he said.

"It doesn't matter," Rick said. "Steve and Erin are gone. I have no right to live."

"Bullshit."

Startled, Rick glanced at the other man.

"Any court in this country would exonerate you for what you did," Johnson said. "That tape makes it very clear that you were an American soldier following direct orders from your commander. You thought you were serving your country."

"I killed innocent men."

"I doubt it," Johnson said. "The circles Wyatt was traveling in were the furthest thing from innocent."

"I stole defense secrets. He sold them."

"We're going to write a report delineating Wyatt's crimes. The man's dead, with no next of kin. We aren't putting him on trial. We're just making a record of what we know. We'll include all information regarding any national security issues. Because there will be no charges against him—no trial—there's no need to produce the hard evidence that didn't exist before tonight."

He *could* turn in the tape. And drag Brady's and Saul's memories into disrepute. Or he could go quietly away.

Either one was fine with him.

"You're a hero to this country, son."

Don't call me that. The words rang out in Rick's mind with a vehemence. He kept them there.

"If not for you, Randall Wyatt wouldn't have been exposed. He would've gone on for another twenty or thirty years raping, robbing, murdering—and putting national security at risk. You knew him. Were closest to him. You're the only man who could have done what you did."

"What? Face him down?"

"You beat him at his own game, Rick."

Maybe. It might have mattered. Yesterday. Or earlier today.

"Erin and Steve are dead," he said, no inflection in his voice. Or in his heart.

Johnson, who'd been driving, pulled off to the side of the deserted, wooded road and turned. Rick had no idea what he'd been about to say because Johnson's phone rang.

"It's the coast guard," he said, his expression pained. "I'm sorry, Rick. I have to take it."

With a wave of the hand, Rick told him to go ahead, staring out the windshield as though there was anything there that could possibly interest him.

Anything he could really even see.

Instead, all he saw, all he heard, was a black asphalt roof beneath his feet, a piece of cardboard clutched in his hand, the ground too far below him and the sound of two little-boy voices. One, the older of the two, ordering the younger to get on that ladder and climb down, or else.

Rick should've been the one to fall off the roof that day. He was the one who'd climbed the ladder to retrieve his Frisbee. He was the one who'd refused to climb down. Steve had only gone up that ladder to rescue Rick.

If only he could go back. Just live that day over again...

"Rick? Did you hear me?"

Rick turned, facing the man behind the wheel of his truck. "I'm sorry," he said. "Did you say something?"

"I said they're alive."

"What? Who?" Those two boys? Rick already knew their fate.

"Erin and Steve. They'd been anchored in a cove, behind an island, hidden from view so the search boats missed them. Wyatt had attached a bomb to the anchor. They were chained to the boat. But they made a kite...." Rick wasn't really listening to the older man's words, but the tears in Johnson's eyes, the catch in his voice, reached him.

"They were flying a kite," Johnson said again, and Rick understood that he was talking about Erin and Steve.

Steve and his kites...

"About an hour ago, a coast guard boat saw the kite and followed it to the cruiser. They got Erin off first—"

"Erin's alive?"

"Yes, she's alive."

Chills swept through him. Over him. He stared. And then burned.

"And Steve?"

"Apparently he fought them…."

No. Oh, no, God. Stevie…

"They finally got him loose with Erin calling to him from their boat."

"So he's okay?"

"The bomb exploded just as they were getting him off the cruiser, Rick. He's alive, but he's hurt."

"How badly?"

"They aren't sure. Emergency crews are with him now."

"Where?"

"A couple of miles from here. I told them we'd meet them there."

Erin stood beside the stretcher, holding Steve's hand, shivering.

He was unconscious, but he clutched her hand. The medical personnel working on him insisted that was a good sign.

She trusted them.

She and Steve were alive.

But she was cold. So cold. She glanced around, looking for someone, anyone, who could tell her what was going on.

Did they get the guy who'd kidnapped them?

Where was Rick?

She needed to know what had happened to a man she'd

known only a few weeks, a man who'd lied to her, who'd put her life at risk, a man she loved with every single part of her.

Loved like she'd never loved before.

She could try to deny her feelings, but she no longer wanted to hide from the truth.

And the truth was, she'd been unhappy with her life for several years. Not so much because of the cases she was taking or not taking, but because she hadn't been true to herself. She'd lost her father and then Noah, and had run scared. Unable to take the risk of losing someone she loved again, of feeling that anguish, she'd let herself fall into the safety and security of hiding out in the Fitzgerald family. She'd loved and been loved—but only on the periphery of their world.

She'd only been partially alive.

That was why winning had seemed so important. Her cases were the one thing she'd put any life into. Any real emotion.

And…maybe because she wasn't living honestly, she'd felt she had to earn the Fitzgeralds' love, their respect. By being the best attorney in town, she could maintain her value and in turn maintain a place in their family.

She'd almost died out there on that boat. And realized just how much being alive meant to her. She wasn't going to waste another second of her time on earth.

Whether she ever saw Rick again or not, she would live up to loving him. She would take care of his friend. If Rick didn't make it back, she was going to get custody of Steve. She'd spend the rest of her life visiting him. And watching out for him.

And she would open her world and her heart to whatever else life had to bring. Losing those you loved hurt. But it was worse still to die not having loved.

She thought she was imagining things when she saw Rick's truck pull up. Felt sure she was hallucinating when she saw Sheriff Johnson jump down from the driver's seat.

Sheriff Johnson in Rick's truck? That was almost ludicrous enough to be funny. If Steve had been awake, she would've shared the joke with him.

And then the passenger door opened and there he was.

Rick. Dressed in jeans and a flannel shirt, looking exactly as he had in her living room that Sunday night eons ago when he'd held her. And kissed her.

The night she should have slept with him when she had the chance.

He walked straight toward her.

She felt Steve squeeze her hand at the same time that one of the medics beside her said, "He's coming around."

"Erin?"

"Yeah, buddy, I'm here."

"Is Ricky here, too?"

"Yeah, I'm here now, sport."

Rick's voice, coming from behind her sent shivers through Erin.

And those achingly familiar arms closed around her. Erin couldn't have stemmed the rush of overwhelming relief and sheer joy, even if she'd wanted to.

"Rick?" she asked, although she didn't turn around.

His hold wasn't gentle. It was urgent. And frantic. "Yeah, it's me, sweetie."

Sweetie. Her father used to call her that. She started to cry.

"Ricky? Erin's crying."

"I know, Steve. But it's okay. She's just happy."

"We 'bout died, Ricky," Steve said, still clutching Erin's hand as he lay on the stretcher. He had an IV in his arm and someone taking his blood pressure and didn't even seem to notice. He was glaring at Rick.

"I know, sport. I'm so sorry."

Steve frowned, obviously confused. "Why, Ricky? You're sorry that we only *almost* died? Didn't you want us to live?"

"Of course I did. You're all the family I have, sport. I'm just sorry you were in danger at all. Not sorry that you almost died."

"You said family." Steve's voice was deadpan.

"I know."

"We can't say that, Ricky, 'member?"

"We don't have to keep the secret anymore, sport."

"You mean we can tell them?"

Erin turned then, and intercepted the look of intense love in Rick's eyes as he gazed at the man on the stretcher.

"You have a secret?" she asked Steve. "One you didn't tell me last night?"

He'd run through the gamut, from Rick's brownie gluttony to the time he'd touched his friend's breast by mistake and couldn't look at her for a long time.

Steve nodded. And winced. He had a large bump on the back of his head. And a gash.

But otherwise seemed okay.

They'd said if he woke up, he probably had only surface wounds.

"What's your secret?"

Steve glanced at Rick, who said, "It's okay, sport. You

can tell anyone you want. It doesn't have to be a secret anymore."

Steve's expression grave, he looked up at Erin. "He's my little brother."

"First, you're an agent. Secret number one. Then you're not because your sergeant did you dirty. Secret number two. And now you have a brother. That's three strikes, Rick. What else is there?"

Sitting in Erin's living room much later that night, cuddled with her under a blanket to ward off the chill from the window she'd insisted on opening so she could hear *her* waves, Rick smiled at the petulant tone in Erin's voice.

She deserved to be a little petulant. A lot, actually. For that matter, he was willing to sign on to a lifetime of petulance.

"Steve's my third and final secret, Erin. Forever. You're right. It's three strikes and I'm out of the secret-keeping business forever. I give you my word."

She nodded, her head moving up and down against his chest. Her legs were tangled around his, too, and if she didn't quit moving them, he was going to have to excuse himself.

She'd had a horrendous night and day, very little sleep—though, thank God, Randall Wyatt's claims of abuse had been a complete fabrication aimed at breaking Rick down. She was emotionally exhausted. He couldn't ask her to make love to him. Not yet.

But God, he needed her. Like he'd never needed anything before in his life.

Mind control, man, he told himself. He could do it. Had spent a lifetime doing it. He just didn't want to anymore.

He'd been given a miraculous second chance at life. A chance to be part of a real family. To claim Steve. Maybe even bring him home.

"Sarge told me that, in my line of work, I couldn't have a family. Said it made men too vulnerable." Rick didn't really know how to share, but he figured he'd better learn. So he started saying aloud the thoughts running through his mind. "The night my father died, I was home on leave. He'd been drinking, as usual, and getting impatient with Steve. I told him to get out. He grabbed Steve by the hair and dragged him along. I ran after them. They didn't make it ten feet down the road before he slammed into a tree. I thought I'd lost them both."

His throat tightened, and Rick held on to her. "Steve was alive. My father wasn't. I called Sarge to tell him about Dad's death. He arranged for the press to have the information he wanted them to have. I was due back on base in two days and I had no idea what to do with Steve. Sarge had already offered me a position on his special ops team." He grimaced as he said that. "I'd already accepted because I knew I had to make a lot of money fast to get Steve away from my father. And when I called Sarge to tell him about the accident, he came up with a plan to take away any vulnerability I might have. And to give Steve protection from anyone who could come after me."

"Oh, Rick," Erin whispered.

He went on as if she hadn't spoken, as if he had to get it all out.

"Sarge told me to report that both my father and Steve died that night. He arranged to have the crash site deemed military jurisdiction and to have the 'bodies' picked up and taken to the nearest military base, where a coroner pronounced them both dead."

"And he gave Steve a new identity." Erin filled in the rest.

"Yeah. Steve Miller. I told Steve it was our secret."

"And he's kept it all these years."

"Yeah."

"Because he loves you that much."

Rick hoped so. Because his big brother certainly owned his heart. He always had.

"Ron Fitzgerald called while you were in with Steve's doctor," Erin said, moving her body more fully onto his. The doctor was at Lakeside, watching over him for the night, although they didn't expect any serious repercussions. Everyone thought it best for Steve to be in his own space. In his own bed. At least for the next few weeks, until the horror of the kidnapping and explosion faded.

"We owe him," Rick said now, thinking of Fitzgerald's immediate generosity that day, arranging for private investigators at his own expense.

"He's a good man," Erin said. "A very wise man. He told me that when he heard I was in danger, he realized Caylee could have been here with me last night. She could've been at risk, too. And that although he'd spent all these years trying to protect his wife and me and Caylee and the others from the pain of Noah's death, it isn't possible. He believed he was trying to make life easier for us, when, in reality, he was the one with the unresolved issues regarding his son's death. He was holding on to us all so tightly, suffocating us, because he was afraid to admit that ultimately he can't hold on at all. But his possessiveness gave him back the sense of control Noah's death stole from him. He told me that today he realized there are no guarantees. But that if he truly loved us, he had to let us all be free to live our lives as we need to live them. Caylee's going to Yale. She and Daniel plan to get married once she graduates."

"I think Johnson knows I'm in love with you."

The words were a mistake. An aberration. They hung in the room like a dark cloud that threatened rain.

So much for sharing. For speaking aloud the thoughts in his head.

Erin didn't say a word. She didn't move. And Rick had absolutely no idea how to extricate himself.

"Johnson told me that Paul Wagner was killed for the fifty dollars he had in his wallet," he said. "He'd picked up a hitchhiker. Some kid high on drugs. They picked up the kid this afternoon. He was wearing Wagner's watch…."

He wasn't even sure Erin would remember that Wagner was the husband of Charles Cook's married lover.

He hadn't remembered it when Johnson passed along the news as they drove back to Temple earlier that night. Erin and Steve had been taken by ambulance to the hospital in Ludington—the same ambulance, at Steve's insistence—and Rick and Huey Johnson had followed in Rick's truck.

Rick had spent the trip in a daze, partially brought on by the odd concept that he wasn't the only person in the world who cared about Steve anymore. Or the only one Steve cared about.

Johnson had also destroyed the tape after Rick gave it back to him. And with it any questions about the money Rick had earned over the past fifteen years. Money that would insure Steve's care for life.

"Did you just say you're in love with me?" She still hadn't moved.

He'd promised her no more secrets. "Yes, but…"

"No." His beautiful attorney turned, placing her finger against his lips. "No *buts*. Just *yes* is fine for now."

He felt he owed her more, anyway. The statement had been so random. The feeling so…out of place. He hardly knew her.

"Truth is, I don't know how to love a woman," he said. "I've never said those words, or anything even close, to a woman in my life."

"I find that hard to believe." Erin's grin told a different story. His guess was that she believed him. And was glad she'd been the first. "You're one of those men who wears his experience all over him," she said.

"I've slept with a lot of women," he told her. No more secrets. "But I've never loved one."

"Then I have to warn you, Thomas, loving a woman can be a challenge. We have needs and desires and emotional breakdowns and sometimes we just plain get bitchy."

"That's all the good stuff. What about the bad?"

She burst out laughing. And then she wasn't laughing anymore. With her body along the length of his, she turned over, her stomach against his, and looked him in the eye. "I love you, Rick Thomas. With all my heart and soul and everything in between. I can't promise the future will be easy. I can only tell you that as long as you are in my life, I will be there for you. I will believe in you. I will have your back."

"And I, Erin Morgan, have yours."

"I'd kinda prefer it if you had another part of my anatomy right now."

She wiggled against him and he realized she'd known what she was doing to him all along.

She'd known and had been doing it on purpose.

And Rick was lost.

That night, for the first time in his life, Rick Thomas made love.

Chandler, Ohio
Thursday, October 28, 2010

It was late. I should've been in bed but was too restless, so I sat at the kitchen table and sipped half a glass of wine. I'd just gotten off the phone with Erin Morgan. I could hardly believe everything that had happened since Maggie and I had left her three days before. And I had to admit, it warmed me that she'd called to tell me about it.

I'd helped Maggie with some homework earlier. Sitting at the table poring over geometry problems. I couldn't believe how much I enjoyed the experience.

And wanted more of it.

Camy was tired. She scratched at my arm as I lifted my glass, her little paw curling around my wrist, pulling my hand to her.

She was right, of course. I had to get some sleep. I had a full day of appointments starting at eight in the morning. Turning off the lights as I made my way to the back of the house, I stopped outside Maggie's door. She left it open every night.

And every night I stood there for a moment on my way to bed to listen to her breathe and watch her sleep.

And offer up a whisper of thanks along with a request for guidance.

We had some tough times ahead of us. I knew that. Maggie believed herself in love with a man who should be in jail for what he'd done to her.

But there could be lots of joy in store for us, too.

"Kelly?" The girl's sleepy voice startled me.

"Yes?"

"Thank you."

"For helping with your homework? No problem, sweetie. I was happy to do it."

"For that, yeah, but no."

"What, then?"

I could barely see the girl's face in the glow from the hallway night-light, couldn't really make out her expression.

"For caring about me."

Oh. "Of course I care, Maggie, how could I not? You're a very special young woman."

"You're special, too, and…"

"What?"

"You know that stuff about keeping me?"

The conversation we'd had while painting Maggie's room.

"Yeah?"

"Well, you're going to, right?"

"Keep you?"

"Yeah."

"You bet I am. I have custody of you, which means you're stuck with me until you're eighteen."

"Or unless you get married and have kids of your own."

"No, Maggie. You're my child now. If I get married someday, whoever marries me will be getting a package deal. And if I have babies, you'll be their older sister." These were all pretty outlandish *ifs,* considering my non-dating status, but I understood Maggie's fears.

And needed to put them to rest.

Maggie had to feel loved, secure, if she was ever going to be free of David Abrams's insidious hold on her.

"You say that now, but—"

"No, Maggie." I went in and sat on the side of her bed. "I haven't just taken you into my home," I said, feeling the tears welling up. "I haven't just taken on legal responsibility for you." The teenager's eyes were wide and staring intently at me. "I've taken you into the deepest parts of my heart. If you were to go, I'd be heartbroken."

I willed the tears away, but my will wasn't strong enough. They pooled in my eyes and I sat there, helpless, as they slid down my face.

"I've got a double bed," Maggie said. "You want to stay for a little while?"

And I had my first parental insight. Maggie didn't want to sleep alone that night.

"How about if you come into my room?" I said. "My bed's bigger and we can watch TV until we fall asleep."

The girl was out of her bed and in my room before I was. She pulled down the covers and slid beneath them and I tossed her the TV control as I went into the adjoining bathroom to brush my teeth and put on my pajamas.

By the time I returned Maggie was sound asleep, with Camy snuggled next to her.

Turning off the lights, I slipped carefully onto my side of the bed so I wouldn't disturb either of my princesses. They were right. We didn't need TV. We just needed to know we had one another.

* * * * *

Look for the ultimate Chapman File next!
In The Fourth Victim, *Kelly goes missing—*
and the FBI is brought in to search for her.
The kidnapper could be anyone she's ever
testified against, someone she's dealt
with in a professional capacity.
Or even in a personal one…

Could she be the fourth victim of a man
who's already responsible for three deaths?
That's what Agent Clay Thatcher and
Detective Samantha Jones believe.
But there are *other possibilities.…*

Test your instincts and investigative skills
against theirs!

Watch for The Fourth Victim
from MIRA Books next month.

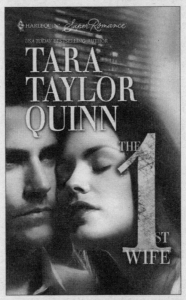

REQUEST YOUR
FREE BOOKS!

2 FREE NOVELS
FROM THE SUSPENSE COLLECTION
PLUS 2 FREE GIFTS!

YES! Please send me 2 FREE novels from the Suspense Collection and my 2 FREE gifts (gifts are worth about $10). After receiving them, if I don't wish to receive any more books, I can return the shipping statement marked "cancel." If I don't cancel, I will receive 3 brand-new novels every month and be billed just $5.74 per book in the U.S. or $6.24 per book in Canada. That's a saving of at least 28% off the cover price. It's quite a bargain! Shipping and handling is just 50¢ per book.* I understand that accepting the 2 free books and gifts places me under no obligation to buy anything. I can always return a shipment and cancel at any time. Even if I never buy another book, the two free books and gifts are mine to keep forever.

192/392 MDN E7PD

Name _____ (PLEASE PRINT) _____

Address _____ Apt. #

City _____ State/Prov. _____ Zip/Postal Code

Signature (if under 18, a parent or guardian must sign)

Mail to **The Reader Service:**
IN U.S.A.: P.O. Box 1867, Buffalo, NY 14240-1867
IN CANADA: P.O. Box 609, Fort Erie, Ontario L2A 5X3

Not valid for current subscribers to the Suspense Collection
or the Romance/Suspense Collection.

Want to try two free books from another line?
Call 1-800-873-8635 or visit www.morefreebooks.com.

* Terms and prices subject to change without notice. Prices do not include applicable taxes. N.Y. residents add applicable sales tax. Canadian residents will be charged applicable provincial taxes and GST. Offer not valid in Quebec. This offer is limited to one order per household. All orders subject to approval. Credit or debit balances in a customer's account(s) may be offset by any other outstanding balance owed by or to the customer. Please allow 4 to 6 weeks for delivery. Offer available while quantities last.

Your Privacy: Harlequin Books is committed to protecting your privacy. Our Privacy Policy is available online at www.eHarlequin.com or upon request from the Reader Service. From time to time we make our lists of customers available to reputable third parties who may have a product or service of interest to you. If you would prefer we not share your name and address, please check here. ☐

Help us get it right—We strive for accurate, respectful and relevant communications. To clarify or modify your communication preferences, visit us at www.ReaderService.com/consumerschoice.

MSUS10R